Jean .... pre-eminent authors of historical fiction for m... of the twentieth century, is the pen name of the prolific English author Eleanor Hibbert, also known as Victoria Holt. Jean Plaidy's novels had sold more than 14 million copies worldwide by the time of her death in 1993.

For further information about Arrow's Jean Plaidy reissues and mailing list, please visit

www.randomhouse.co.uk/minisites/jeanplaidy

Praise for Jean Plaidy

'A vivid impression of life at the Tudor Court'
Daily Telegraph

'One of the country's most widely read novelists'
Sunday Times

'Plaidy excels at blending history with romance and drama'
New York Times

'It is hard to better Jean Plaidy ... both elegant and exciting'

'Jean Plaidy c.. the past wi...

'Plaidy has brought the past to life' *Times Literary Supplement*

'One of our best historical novelists' *News Chronicle*

'An excellent story' *Irish Press*

'Spirited . . . Plaidy paints the truth as she sees it'
Birmingham Post

'Sketched vividly and sympathetically . . . rewarding'
Scotsman

'Among the foremost of current historical novelists'
Birmingham Mail

'An accomplished novelist' *Glasgow Evening News*

'There can be no doubt of the author's gift for storytelling'
Illustrated London News

'Jean Plaidy has once again brought characters and
background vividly to life' *Everywoman*

'Well up to standard . . . fascinating'
Manchester Evening News

'Exciting and intelligent' *Truth Magazine*

'No frills and plenty of excitement' *Yorkshire Post*

'Meticulous attention to historical detail' *South Wales Argus*

'Colourful . . . imaginative and exciting'
Northern Daily Telegraph

'Effective and readable' *Sphere*

'A vivid picture of the crude and vigorous London of those
days' Laurence Meynell

Flaunting, Extravagant Queen

JEAN PLAIDY

arrow books

Published by Arrow Books in 2007

3 5 7 9 10 8 6 4

Copyright © Jean Plaidy, 1957

Initial lettering copyright © Stephen Raw, 2007

The Estate of Eleanor Hibbert has asserted its right
to have Jean Plaidy identified as the author of this work.

First published in the United Kingdom in 1957 by Robert Hale and Company
Published in paperback in 1972 by Pan Books Ltd

Arrow Books
The Random House Group Limited
20 Vauxhall Bridge Road, London SW1V 2SA

www.rbooks.co.uk

Addresses for companies within The Random House Group Limited can be found at:
www.randomhouse.co.uk/offices.htm

The Random House Group Limited Reg. No. 954009

A CIP catalogue record for this book is available from the British Library

ISBN 9780099493389

The Random House Group Limited supports The Forest Stewardship
Council (FSC), the leading international forest certification organisation.
All our titles that are printed on Greenpeace approved FSC certified paper
carry the FSC logo. Our paper procurement policy can be found at:
www.rbooks.co.uk/environment

Typeset by SX Composing DTP, Rayleigh, Essex
Printed and bound in Great Britain by
CPI Antony Rowe, Chippenham, Wiltshire

❖ Contents ❖

✤ Chapter I ✤

THE ARCHDUCHESS AT SCHÖNBRUNN

'It would seem, Madame,' said Prince von Kaunitz gleefully, 'that at last we have what may be termed a firm offer from His Most Christian Majesty.'

Maria Theresa, Empress of Austria, suppressed the smile of triumph which she felt rising to her lips. If Kaunitz were right, this should be one of the happiest moments of her life. But she feared there was little happiness left to her. She was in her fifties and she could not believe that she had long to live. The ruling of an Empire and the glorification of the House of Habsburg had made great demands on her natural shrewdness; and her deep-rooted sense of duty had insisted she fulfil them; but she was beginning to realise that she was a weary woman. It was being brought home to her that a woman who gives all her thoughts to state duties misses much of the pleasures of family life; and Maria Theresa, shrewd ruler of an Empire, felt the sudden desire for softer emotions.

The mood was ephemeral. If Kaunitz were right, and old Louis really serious about the marriage of his grandson to Maria Theresa's youngest daughter, then there should be no room for any emotion but joy.

'There have been many promises which have not yet been fulfilled,' she said.

Kaunitz nodded in agreement. 'But not because of Your Excellency's servants at the Court of France. They have worked assiduously to bring about your wishes. Scarcely a day passes when some allusion is not made, in the King's hearing, to the Archduchess. His Majesty has been made aware of the many enchanting qualities of your daughter, Madame.'

Maria Theresa smiled tenderly. 'She grows in beauty every day,' she said. 'I am sure that if the King could see her he would be enchanted.'

'And His Most Christian Majesty is, even at his age, most susceptible to feminine beauty, Madame,' added Kaunitz with a smile.

The Empress frowned. It was undignified to discuss royal scandals with servants, but at the same time it was necessary to know all that went on in rival courts; and she was enough of a woman of the world to realise that the bedchambers of monarchs were often the hot-houses in which great events were planted, forced and nourished. This applied particularly to the Court of France, for French monarchs, it seemed, had through the ages been more susceptible to feminine charm than other kings; and in France it was almost a tradition that the King's mistress should be the most important person at the Court.

It therefore made her faintly uneasy to ponder that the ageing voluptuary had replaced Madame de Pompadour by Madame du Barry who was, so it had been reported from many sources, a woman of the people, a low upstart who at one stage of her career had been nothing more than a low-class prostitute. And it was to this Court, the most brilliant doubtless but certainly the most cynical in the world, reigned over by a prostitute and an ageing sensualist continually on the look-out for new sensations, to which she would be utterly delighted to send her enchantingly lovely, high-spirited and somewhat wilful fourteen-year-old Marie Antoinette.

She spoke her thoughts aloud. Kaunitz was of course a trusted servant. 'His Majesty of France would show nothing but respectful admiration to his grandson's wife.'

'Assuredly so, Madame.'

'And the Dauphin?'

Maria Theresa was conscious of the shadow which passed over Kaunitz's face. The Dauphin, the grandson of Louis Quinze of France, was a quiet boy, fond of hiding himself from his fellows, not exactly stupid yet nervous to such a degree that he seemed so. The fact that he must one day – and that day soon, for Louis Quinze was sixty years of age and had no son to succeed him – ascend the throne of France seemed, instead of inspiring him, to have filled him with horror of the future. In fact, for all his rank, for all that he was heir to one of the most coveted thrones in Europe, young Dauphin Louis, Duc de Berry, was a poor creature, and the glowing reports of those eager to promote the marriage could not completely hide this.

'He is young,' said Kaunitz now. 'Scarcely more than a boy.'

He was not yet sixteen and Maria Theresa told herself that she should be pleased because he was not in the least like his grandfather. There was one thing of which Maria Theresa could be certain: her daughter would not allow her husband's mistresses to dominate *her*, as so many Queens of France had been compelled to do.

'He will grow up,' she said firmly, and refused to worry about him.

The marriage was what she desired more than anything in the world. It was necessary to Austria. There must be peace between her country and its old enemy. Habsburg and Bourbon must join hands and stand together in this changing world. The little island off the coast of Europe was growing far too powerful. It was clear that that Protestant community of islanders was already contemplating the acquisition of an Empire which was to exceed in might all other empires. In a changing world friendships must be formed with old enemies.

'And,' went on Kaunitz, 'His Majesty has appointed the date. He suggests that Easter would be a good time for the wedding.'

'I agree wholeheartedly. Easter-tide when the year is young. It will give us plenty of time to make our arrangements.'

She was smiling, determined to forget her misgivings regarding this marriage. She was also going to forget her anxieties about her son Joseph whom she had made co-regent a few years before, and whose head seemed full of the wildest plans which she feared could bring nothing but disaster; she would forget Maria Amalia, her daughter, whom she had married to the Duke of Parma and who was already, by her levity, attracting scandalous gossip; she would forget all her children who had disappointed her and think of her youngest, her little pet, her enchanting Antoinette who would make the most brilliant marriage of all, would sit on the throne of France and make firm that friendship between Habsburg and Bourbon which was so necessary to Austria.

She dismissed Kaunitz, for she wished to be alone with her thoughts.

When Kaunitz had left her she went to the window and looked out on the gardens.

She was thinking that she must go ahead with her preparations, that old Louis must not be given an opportunity to retreat from his promise, that she must watch for mischief from her old enemy, Frederick of Prussia, who would naturally do all he could to prevent the match. She hoped Joseph would not be indiscreet. She feared that indiscretion was one of the most persistent characteristics of her family. From whom had they inherited it? Not from their mother. From their father, François of Lorraine, perhaps. In any case, she must guard against it.

She must be continually on her guard. How she longed to pass over the reins of government to young Joseph! But how could she trust Joseph? Was she going to let him throw away all that she had built up with shrewdness and careful planning? No, she must remain in command until she was sure that her son had come to wisdom and understanding.

She could smile at herself; she was a woman who had wished to be an Empress and also a mother. She asked too much of life.

As she stood looking down on the garden she heard the sudden barking of a dog which was running across the lawns, past the fountain, its lead trailing on the grass.

'Catch him,' cried a voice. 'Catch him . . . quickly, I say. Mops! *Mopsee* . . . Come here, I say.'

Now she came into sight – a small flying figure – and the Empress' throat became constricted with her sudden emotion. She was so lovely, that child; so young, so innocent. Of them all, thought Maria Theresa, I love my little Antoinette the best.

Oh, what daintiness, thought the mother. She is small for her age, but doubtless she will grow. She is like a fairy creature

5

with those dainty limbs and those wide blue eyes, that flowing golden hair and skin like rarest porcelain. Surely she is the loveliest child in the world. She will do well at the Court of France, where beauty is admired.

'Come here, Mops! Did you not hear?' The voice was high-pitched and imperious, yet clearly it was telling the young pug-dog that this was a game; he was to try to elude her while she was trying to catch him. A childish game for an archduchess to play when she was fourteen years of age and shortly to become Dauphine of France.

Now another figure had come into view. This was one of the serving girls. Young Antoinette, so Maria Theresa had heard, chose her friends where she would, without consideration of rank. Maria Theresa had not curbed this trait in her daughter. 'Nay,' she had said, 'it is well for her to form her own judgements.' But was she right? Had she, so obsessed with matters of state, neglected her duties as mother? Was that why Maria Amalia was taking her lovers in Parma; was that why Joseph seemed determined to go his own way?

In any case it was time that Antoinette ceased to romp in the gardens with dogs and serving girls.

The dog had turned and was running towards the girls, barking joyously. The servant girl succeeded in grasping the strap attached to the dog's collar. Antoinette closely followed; the dog darted away but both girls had their hands on the leash and so they collided and fell sprawling on the grass.

A strange sight, thought Maria Theresa; a serving girl, a pug-dog, and an Archduchess rolling on the grass together in the garden of the Imperial Palace.

What would the ladies and gentlemen of Versailles say to one another if such a scene were reported to them? And who knew that it might not be, for there were spies everywhere, she was convinced. Her own spies assured her that the etiquette at Versailles was so rigid that it was more important than any other matter. A man would rather lose his mistress than commit a breach of etiquette. His future at Court depended on the most trivial acts, the most lightly spoken words.

Maria Theresa called to one of her pages. 'Have the Archduchess Antoinette brought to me at once,' she commanded.

✦ ✦ ✦

The little girl stood before her mother. Maria Theresa noticed the green stain on her dress, and she tried to make her voice sound stern as she said: 'It is scarcely fitting for the Archduchess of Austria to roll on the grass.'

Antoinette began to laugh at the memory. 'Mother, it was so *funny*. You see, Mops is always running away. He does not really run away, but he wants to be chased, so . . .'

Maria Theresa held up a hand. 'I have no doubt it is amusing, my daughter; but you are of an age now to have more serious pursuits than playing with dogs.'

'I shall always love dogs,' declared the girl. 'And I shall always play with my dogs because, do you know, Mother, dogs love to be played with. They grow unhappy if you do not play with them. They are like children, Mother. And you must make them happy. If you do not, *you* are unhappy . . . then you are all unhappy, so you see it is senseless not to play with dogs.'

'My child, my child! How old are you?'

'I am fourteen; but you know, Mother, surely.'

'A girl of fourteen is no longer a child, 'Toinette.'

Antoinette smiled charmingly at the shortened form of her name. The Empress used it indulgently, so she was not really scolding. Not that Antoinette assumed that she was – seriously. Few people scolded her. Why should they? She never hurt anyone if she could help it. It never occurred to her to do so. She was the darling of them all. The servants adored her. When she remembered that she was the Archduchess and was just a little haughty, they were ready to fall in with her mood and give her all the respect she demanded. When she wanted to be on equal terms with all, play games with them, they did exactly as she wished. It was the same with her tutors; she had quickly learned how to coax them away from tiresome lessons. 'Let us talk about you,' she would say, smiling. 'Tell me about your journey into Russia . . . England . . . France – or wherever it might be. Tell me about the days when *you* were my age.' They would protest, she would wheedle, and invariably the lesson time would pass most pleasantly and they were happy to feel her wondering blue eyes upon them, to listen to her sympathetic comments, to be warmly embraced by those slim white arms and told that she loved them; as for herself, she was happy, for she had had an enjoyable half-hour instead of a tedious lesson. In any case, who wanted to learn French? Such a tiresome language! Who wanted to learn English which was almost worse? As for mathematics that was intolerable. No, it was far more pleasant to coax and wheedle and to feel triumphant because she had skilfully eluded tiresome verbs and loathsome figures.

Now she did not doubt that she would overcome her mother's disapproval as she had her teachers'.

'That is so, Mother,' she said. 'There are times when I feel quite old.'

'My dearest child, you must know that you will soon be leaving us.'

8

'Soon, Mother?' Alarm showed in the blue eyes. 'Oh – not *soon*!'

'The King of France has decided that you shall marry his grandson the Dauphin next year.'

'Next year!' The voice was blithe again, the smile serene. In the reckoning of the young Antoinette, next year was an age away.

'Ah, my child, the time soon passes. I should not want you to disgrace us when you go to France.'

Antoinette's eyes were wide with amazement. Disgrace them! She, the darling of them all, the little beauty, the petted one, to disgrace them? She did not want to go to France, but it did not occur to her for a moment that she would not instantly win loving admiration in France as she had here in the Schönbrunn Palace.

'You will find Versailles a little different from your home, my dearest. There is much ceremony, and you will be expected to conform with their customs. I think from now on you and I must spend more time together. There will be a great deal for you to learn. From now on we will often speak French, for since you will one day be the Queen of the French you must speak their language as they do.' Maria Theresa had spoken the last sentence in French, and her daughter was smiling vaguely. 'You understand that, do you not?' asked the Empress.

'But, Mother, you go much too fast. We do not speak as fast as that in French. And do not let us speak French. I confess I do not greatly like it. It is much more fun speaking our own language when we have so much to say. To speak in a foreign tongue one must pause so often to think . . . and I do not like that.'

Maria Theresa's expression was a little grim. She said: 'It is only one of the lessons we have failed to teach you. In the next few months, my child, you must learn many things. First you shall have a new French tutor – a Frenchman whose accent is impeccable. You will share my apartment so that I may keep an eye upon you.'

The girl threw herself into her mother's arms, laughing happily.

'Mother, it will be wonderful to be with you often – so wonderful.'

What could Maria Theresa do but bend her head and kiss the lovely laughing girl?

Suddenly she held her daughter to her in an embrace which was fierce and protective.

'Holy Mother of God,' she prayed silently, 'protect my little one. Make the whole world love her . . . even as her mother does.'

✻ ✢ ✻

During the weeks which followed, Antoinette tried to forget, in the excitement of the preparations for her marriage, the fact that to achieve that marriage she would have to leave her home and her mother. Each day messages arrived in Vienna from Paris. Maria Theresa had heard of the strict etiquette of Versailles; now she was experiencing it. It seemed to be of the utmost importance whose name should first appear on the marriage contract, her own or that of the King of France; how many attendants should accompany the bride into France; how many should part company with her at the border. That the dowry should be discussed at length was comprehensible, but it seemed a little unnecessary that importance should be attached to matters such as who should take a certain place in a procession, and as to what presents should be given by whom to whom; but in the estimation of the French the entire negotiations could break down if one of these small details did not receive its due attention.

Maria Theresa was in financial difficulties, but she was determined that her little daughter should go to her new country richly apparelled and with a dignified escort. The Court dressmakers were busy and young Antoinette was forced to stand impatiently while fine linen, silks, velvets and the finest lace were fitted to her slender form. She tried on precious jewels. This was quite enjoyable; she delighted in the glittering stones, and most of all she admired diamonds.

The beautiful garments, the sparkling gems, the excitement of preparation, made her forget the sorrow of parting, of which they were really the heralds.

I won't think of it, she would tell herself. Perhaps Mother will come with me after all. Why should she not? We could leave Joseph behind in Vienna.

Thinking thus she could enjoy her preparations, for she realised that if her mother were with her she would have nothing to fear from the French.

Louis, now that he had signified his agreement to the marriage, was determined to show the world that very little had changed in France since the days of le Roi Soleil. He was going to dazzle these Austrians with his magnificence. He gave orders that the Embassy in Vienna should be almost rebuilt, for in its present state it was by no means worthy to house all the guests who would attend the marriage by proxy of his grandson.

While the French Embassy was being rebuilt Maria Theresa was spending a great deal of time with her daughter; she was alternately affectionate and scolding; but the scolding was not without its tenderness. Maria Theresa was not a sentimental woman, but how could she help being utterly charmed by her youngest child? Antoinette was so eager to please that even her wilfulness was charming. It was not that she deliberately refused to concentrate on her lessons but that it was so difficult for her to do so. There were after all so many exciting things to do. There was one tutor with whom she did work hard; he was Noverre, the dancing master.

Noverre was very pleased with his pupil. 'The Archduchess is the best pupil I ever had,' he declared. 'She is so light on her feet, so dainty in her movements, so quick to learn the new steps. Her dancing will excite the admiration of all France.'

But then of course she enjoyed dancing. She would cry when the lesson was over: 'No, no! I want to try that again.' And flushed and so pretty, looking like an exquisite doll, she would twirl on her toes, or hold herself with stately majesty, as the dance demanded, and Noverre would applaud and compliment her and declare that the perfection of her movements brought tears to his eyes.

It was quite another matter when a language must be learned, when literature was discussed, or when it was necessary to grapple with mathematics.

Abbé de Vermond, whom Louis had sent to Vienna to be her tutor when he had heard that her mother had appointed two French actors to teach her French, despaired of making great headway with her.

It was not, he wrote to his master, that she was by any means stupid – far from it. Her mind was lively, but it was an impatient mind; it would not allow itself the careful study which was necessary if certain subjects were to be mastered.

The Archduchess was somewhat frivolous, and quite lazy where something she was not interested in was concerned. She was far from lazy when it was a matter of dancing or running about the house and garden playing with her friends or the servants. His Majesty must not think that his granddaughter-to-be was not a delightful creature. Indeed it was this very charm of hers which had caused her to be a little spoilt. Not that the spoiling had harmed her character more than to make her lazy-minded and incapable of concentration. She was sweet-natured, generous, graceful of figure and beautiful of face. Indeed, were she a little taller (and it was possible that she yet had time to grow) and were she studious, she would present such an excess of virtue that she would frighten all from her presence.

It was quite clear that, although the Abbé de Vermond despaired of making his charge a scholar, he was completely enchanted with her.

Louis wrote that he was very desirous of greeting his grandson's wife and that he was having an opera house built at Versailles so that the celebrations might take place there. He was having two carriages specially made by the royal coach-maker in Paris, and these should be sent to Austria to convey his grandson's bride to her new home; and the Empress might expect any day the arrival of his envoy, Durfort, whom he was sending to Vienna to escort the bride to France.

Now Antoinette must think about her departure. Durfort had arrived. He had ridden to Vienna with forty-eight six-in-hands, in the centre of which procession were the two magnificent carriages which had been specially built in Paris for the use of the future Dauphine.

The Viennese had rarely seen such magnificence, for the

coaches were lined with satin inside, while the outsides were painted in brilliant colours, decorated with paintings of golden crowns and covered with a coat of glass. Never before had such beautifully made carriages been seen in the streets of Vienna; and there was great rejoicing in the city and throughout all Austria on account of the French marriage which was calculated to bring such glory and long years of peace to the country.

Maria Theresa took her daughter to her apartments and talked to her long and seriously.

'My darling,' she began, 'it will not be long now before you leave your home.'

Antoinette, seeing herself suddenly face to face with all that this parting would mean, threw herself into her mother's arms. 'Mother, need I go?' she asked childishly.

'Need you go! Now that is folly, is it not? How could you not go when the King of France has sent his envoy here to take you back with him, when he has had those two magnificent coaches built especially for you, when in a few days' time your marriage by proxy will take place? No, do not let us waste the precious time left to us in foolish talk. My child, you are so young. Fourteen is not very old, but you will soon be fifteen and heirs to great crowns must not linger in their childhood. Sometimes I blame myself. I have been too indulgent towards you.'

'Mother, you have been the dearest mother in the world. Whatever happens to me I shall remember that. It is better to have such a memory than all the learning in the world.'

'Perhaps you are right, my child. But you have been inattentive with your tutors, and your French is not good. Your handwriting is unformed and excessively untidy, for you have done far from well at your lessons. But do not look so downcast. It may be that you have other qualities.'

'What qualities?' asked Antoinette eagerly.

'You are gay, and the French like gaiety. You are pleasant to the eye and they like that too. When you dance you can look very graceful and very stately. We must make do with what you *have* learned, but dearest, apply yourself more. Do not be so impatient when there are lessons to learn. Never forget that you are the Archduchess of Austria and Dauphine of France. My darling, it may not be long before you are Queen of France. You must make the Court both love and respect you, and that is not always an easy thing to do.'

'I will do it, Mother,' said the girl with confidence.

'I believe you will. But do not be careless of the feelings of those about you. Carelessness makes many enemies. You must make sure that you never offend the King and your new relations.'

'Most of all my husband,' said Antoinette with an air of wisdom.

'I think you will find him forbearing and tolerant. He is young and he will love you, but his grandfather is the King and he may have friends to whom he wishes you to show respect. You must do this, but in such a way that it will bring no disrespect to yourself. You will understand what I mean. You must study their customs and make them your own. When you make your formal renunciation of your Austrian rights before the crucifix, you become a Frenchwoman, and you must never offend French etiquette. Always remember that I shall be here to help you. We may not meet, but there will be letters passing between us. If there is any matter however small which worries you, you must write to me of it. And you must take my advice.'

'Oh, Mother, it won't be like a real parting, will it? I can always write, and you can tell me what to do.'

'Yes, my child, and I shall give you a list of rules which I want you to promise me that you will read once a month. Will you do this, 'Toinette?'

'Indeed I will.'

'Read as much as you can, and finish what you start to read. Do not idly begin a book and then put it aside because you wish to dance and play – as you have done so often, my darling. I fear that you will forget to say your prayers, that you will become neglectful of your duties, and lazy. Suppress these faults, my dearest child. Remember that I am thinking of you constantly, that I am praying for you, and that any appeal from you will never fail to touch my heart, and that I would give my life to see you happy.'

There were tears in Antoinette's eyes now. She looked at her mother with alarm, and realised in that moment how very much she was going to miss her.

The climax of the ceremonies had been reached; the balls and banquets, the reviews and theatrical performances were over, and at them all the young girl had appeared in the rich garments which had been made especially for these occasions. The people of Vienna had cheered their Archduchess whenever she had appeared: they had delighted in her beauty, sighed over her youth. 'She is so young to leave her home and go far away to another Court,' they murmured. But they rejoiced in the ceremonies; and the splendour of the emissaries of Louis was such as to make them gasp with wonder.

There came the great day – the day of the marriage.

Antoinette stood at the altar in the Augustinian Church and, with Archduke Ferdinand proxy for the Dauphin of France, Marie Antoinette became the Dauphine.

It was bewildering but not yet alarming, for she still had her mother constantly at her side and her friends about her. She still felt herself to be their little darling, their little pet.

But that state of affairs could not last long. Her mother had often explained the importance of etiquette in the Court of France. She was reminded again and again that the King of France, whom she must now think of as her grandfather, was insisting that she must completely forget her Austrian nationality. When she journeyed into France her clothes must be French; even her shift must be a French shift; and because the French were very formal in their Court ceremonies, the young Dauphine was to be handed over to her new country at a certain ceremony, and this was to take place in a building which had been erected for the purpose on a sandbank in the Rhine.

'Why could it not be here,' asked the bride, 'if it has to be done?'

'Because,' explained her mother, 'the French would wish it to be carried out on French soil, and we on our own soil. This is a compromise. It is to be in neutral territory, and that satisfies both sides.'

'Mother, sometimes I think it is like a war rather than a marriage between two countries.'

'We must constantly bear in mind French etiquette.'

'I cannot but bear it constantly in mind, for I hear of nothing else. I shall no longer call my new country the land of the French; I shall call it the land of the Etiquette.'

''Toinette, my dearest, curb your levity. You laugh too readily.'

'Mother, I am afraid that when I leave you I shall cry too readily.'

Her mother could not refrain from embracing her daughter, remembering that there was not much time left for embraces.

And the next day their final farewells were said, and the procession made its way through North Austria to the frontier.

Sitting in her coach, magnificently dressed, sat the lonely little Dauphine, and as the procession passed slowly through the land the people crowded to the roadside to look at the child who so recently had been their Archduchess and now had a grander title.

'Good luck,' they cried. 'Long life and happiness!'

Temporarily she forgot her grief as she bowed and smiled and waved to them.

'She is a little enchantress,' the people said to each other. 'The French will love her. How could they do otherwise?'

They were strange days for Antoinette. She was bewilderingly unhappy at times, feverishly gay at others. Such fêtes and banquets were arranged for her in the various towns in which they spent the night, and during the long delays at the posting stations where the three hundred and forty horses in the procession had to be changed before they could go on; her friends and maids of honour from her mother's Court grew sadder as the journey proceeded; for they knew that when they reached that sandy stretch of neutral territory they would be forced to say good-bye to their little mistress.

And at length they came to that hastily constructed building which consisted of two small rooms facing the left bank of the Rhine, a hall in the centre of the building and two similar rooms facing the right bank.

It was in this building that Marie Antoinette was to realise how the French could be almost farcical in their love of formality.

When they arrived she was led into one of the rooms on the right-hand side of the great hall. Several of her Austrian attendants were with her and, waiting for her in this room, was the Comtesse de Noailles.

When Marie Antoinette entered, the Comtesse fell to her knees, took the girl's hand and kissed it.

'I am at your service, Madame la Dauphine,' she said. 'I am honoured to be your lady-in-waiting-in-chief.'

Antoinette smiled and cried in her halting French: 'Oh, pray do not kneel. We shall be great friends, I am sure.'

The Comtesse looked surprised and rose to her feet; she stood back as though waiting.

Two of the Austrian women unbuckled the Dauphine's girdle, and began stripping her of her clothes.

'But I am cold,' cried Antoinette petulantly.

'We will be quick, dearest . . .' began one of the women and, catching the Comtesse's eyes upon her, added quickly: 'Madame.'

'I know I am to wear a French dress,' said Antoinette, 'but pray be quick.'

The Comtesse had come forward and was giving instructions to the Austrians. 'Everything must be removed . . . every single thing,' she said.

'You shall not take my shift,' protested Antoinette.

'Madame, you cannot enter French territory wearing anything but French garments,' insisted the Comtesse.

Antoinette was now completely naked, shivering before them all, angry, feeling herself shorn of her dignity; but she felt too frightened to protest, because she suddenly realised that she was shedding more than her clothes.

Madame de Noailles slipped the French silk shift over her head and, taking pity on the shivering child, said: 'These petticoats were made in Paris, and you know, do you not, Madame, that the best petticoats are made in Paris?'

Antoinette could never control her tongue. 'We make good petticoats in Vienna,' she said shortly.

Madame de Noailles ignored that. 'These are *French* lace,' she said. 'And these shoes were made by the royal shoemaker.' When they had dressed her in her French garments she seemed to be an entirely different person but, as she smoothed the folds of her dress, she knew that the clothes she was now wearing were more becoming than those she had discarded; and miserable as she was the thought gave her some small pleasure.

Madame de Noailles cried out in dismay, for she had discovered a ring on the girl's finger.

'My mother gave it to me,' said Antoinette.

'It is Austrian, Madame, and His Majesty has given orders that you must not step onto French territory wearing *anything* which is not French.'

'I shall not give up my mother's ring,' said the girl defiantly.

'Madame, those are the King's orders.'

'But we are not in France yet.'

'You are the King's subject, Madame.'

'I . . . I . . . I am Dauphine.'

'Yes, Madame, and therefore a subject of the King of France.' Madame de Noailles firmly removed the ring.

'What will you do with it?' asked the little bride.

'It shall be returned to your mother.'

'Then I shall ask her to give it back to me, and when I am at the Court I shall tell the King I will not be deprived of my mother's gifts.'

Madame de Noailles appeared not to be listening. It was as though she implied that what the Dauphine was saying was no concern of hers. She had been commanded to remove all that was Austrian from the Dauphin's bride, and this she had done.

And as soon as the ring was off her finger, Antoinette felt desolation touch her. Now she was indeed far from home.

Her eyes brilliant with rebellious tears which she was holding in check with all the restraint of which she was capable, she turned to the door where Count Starhemberg was waiting to conduct her into the great hall.

She laid her hand on his arm, and in that moment the small slender girl looked like a queen. The rich skirts of her French dress, so becoming to her youth and beauty, rustled as she walked, and the French, who stood on the west side of the great table, which had been placed in the centre of the hall like a barrier between two countries, were touched by her youthful charm although their faces, stiff with formality, did not show this.

The furniture in the hall had been lent by the citizens of Strasbourg for this occasion, and the rich tapestries which adorned the walls helped to disguise the rough workmanship of the hastily constructed building. But the young girl did not notice the furnishings; she was only conscious of the solemn men on the west side of the table and her own countrymen and women who stayed so significantly on the east side.

The Count was leading her towards the table. Her legs were trembling and she wondered how she could have laughed so gaily and enjoyed all the festivities which had really been leading up to this moment.

The Count was ceremoniously drawing her round the table,

and there was a deep silence in the room as all eyes were turned on her. She felt this was the most solemn moment of her life, far more solemn than the marriage ceremony had been. To her that had been like a piece of elaborate play-acting, for the man who had stood beside her had not been her husband.

Now that she had passed round the table and was on the west side, it was almost as though there was a sigh of relief from the watchers, as though they had expected her to refuse to take the necessary steps, or to lie on the floor and kick and scream her refusal to become a subject of King Louis and demand to be taken home to her mother, as she would have done when she was four years old.

Now they were ready to receive her – their Dauphine who would one day be their Queen.

One by one they approached her; they bowed; they kissed her hand. And when it was the turn of Madame de Noailles to curtsy, Antoinette could not hold back her tears. They began to fall silently.

Madame Noailles rose in alarm, and turned to one of the men in attendance.

He said: 'The carriages are here. We should leave at once.'

Thus the ceremony was cut short that the quiet tears of the new Dauphine should not become noisy sobbing. Etiquette must be preserved at all costs.

So Marie Antoinette left the neutral territory of the Rhine and, as the bells of Strasbourg pealed forth, said her last goodbye to her old home and journeyed on to France.

In the apartment of the King of France Madame du Barry dismissed all attendants as she wished to be alone with the King, and the word of Madame du Barry was law at the Court of France.

Poor France! she was thinking. He is looking old to-day.

She liked to refer to him familiarly as 'France'; it reminded her that he was the King and that because she wielded great power over him, she was, in a measure, ruler of the land. That was a pleasant thought for the daughter of a Vancouleurs dressmaker and, apart from a few uneasy moments, she was a contented woman. Nothing delighted her more than to receive her guests in her salon and to realise that they counted themselves highly favoured to be received thus by her, for it was understood that if they wished for honours at Court, it was to Madame du Barry they must look for them.

'France' had been good to her; he had provided her with a useful husband – none other than the Comte du Barry – who was, at the King's command, ready to marry her and then remove himself from Court so that he never embarrassed any by his presence there, thus giving her the title of a great lady while the riches and honours were supplied by Louis. They were good to each other – she and Louis. It was true that he was sixty years old and looked it; not even Kings could live lives such as Louis Quinze had led and remain unmarked by their vices; she was twenty-seven and, if she were beginning to look a little raddled, she knew how to repair such ravages at her mirror; and those jewels and costly garments which were not supplied by Louis were bestowed upon her by those wishing for the King's favour.

Since the death of Madame de Pompadour, some six years before, the Comtesse du Barry had been the most powerful woman at the Court of France.

She was a happy woman. It comes, she would tell herself, of

23

having known less fortunate days. She had no patience with fine ladies who were dissatisfied with their lives of leisure. She would like to take them to Vancouleurs and show them the attic in which she had been born. She would like to make them work with their needle by the light of tallow candles. She would like to turn them adrift in Paris without a sou, with nothing but their bodies to sell. Then, said Madame du Barry, would these fine ladies appreciate their good fortune – even as Madame du Barry appreciated hers.

She made little attempt to ape their manners. She was herself – bold, brazen, handsome, vulgar and very much in love with life.

There was an anxiety however which was ever present. Louis was ageing and, if he should die, what would become of Madame du Barry? It was so natural that a woman in her delicate and yet so greatly influential position should have made many enemies. Of all the tasks which she must accomplish, that of keeping the King alive was of paramount importance. Moreover she was fond of him. Vulgar and acquisitive she might be, but she was good-hearted and, when one had known poverty such as she had, gratitude towards those who had made life easy could never be forgotten.

So now she was studying her lover with tender solicitude.

'You are tired to-day,' she said. 'Your little visitor was too much for you last night.'

Louis smiled at the recollection of last night's little visitor.

'Nay, 'twas not so,' he said.

'And you found her charming, eh?' murmured du Barry, smiling with pleasure, for the King's enjoyment of the charming little girls whom she brought to him from time to time was a compliment to herself. She was too wise to expect

24

him to remain faithful to her. Louis had so long practised promiscuity that it would have been unnatural for him to do otherwise. Therefore his whims must be gratified and, although he must take pleasure in other women, the shrewd du Barry was determined to see that she shared in that pleasure. Accordingly she had made it one of her tasks – when she imagined his passion for herself was declining – to bring him young girls to stimulate his erotic desires. She was not only indulgent mistress and shrewd adviser; she was procuress as well.

'All the same,' she went on tenderly, 'you must have a quiet night to follow – with only your loving du Barry for company.'

He smiled at her again; she was amusing; she was clever; and he was fond of her. He often laughed to think of her in her sumptuous apartments in the great Palace of Versailles, with the little staircase he had built to connect her apartments with his, and the apartments of his three prudish daughters separated from hers only by a few rooms. He was content that she should be the reigning star of his Court. He was too old for ambitions; he had never been like the preceding monarch, his great-grandfather Louis Quatorze, Grand Monarque, le Roi Soleil, with his ambitions to build a great Empire the centre of which was flamboyant, brilliant, autocratic Versailles, and in truth the King himself. *'L'état c'est moi,'* had said that ambitious Louis; and it was true that much glory had been brought to France in his name, yet it was the predominance of literature and art which would make that reign for ever memorable. Racine, Molière, Corneille, La Fontaine, Boileau! What bright stars to illuminate a glorious reign of more than seventy years! Le Roi Soleil was one of the fortunate Kings of France. He had been as handsome as a god, adored, and doubly blessed, for although he had come to the throne when he was a boy of four, the affairs of the country had been in the capable hands of Cardinal Mazarin. The Court had sparkled with genius. La Rochefoucauld, La Bruyère, Pascal, Poussin – one could go on indefinitely recalling such great names. More fortunate still, Louis Quatorze had lived in an age when men were more ready to accept the divine rights of Kings to rule. Although he himself had been called *Bien-Aimé*, there was not the same tolerance shown to Louis Quinze as there had been for Louis Quatorze, and for all his preoccupation with pleasure he was fully aware of this.

The position of France in the world had deteriorated rapidly in the years of his reign. England was in command of the seas, and England was the perennial enemy of France. France was losing control of her colonies, and Louis was indifferent. He was too old for anything but indifference. He had given himself up to pleasure; he had been ruled by women and he could not break the habit. Now that he was getting older there were periods of alarm when he surveyed his past life and, during these periods, he would be overcome by the urgent need for repentance. Then he would shut himself away from his pleasures and try to live like a monk. But as soon as his health improved he would send for Madame du Barry, and she would continue her task of pandering to his pleasure and helping him to forget the need for repentance.

There they lived – he and du Barry – in the utmost splendour; yet he was aware of impending doom. They might shrug it aside, but ever in the background of their minds was his fear of being called upon to expiate his sins in hell, and her fear of the loss of power which his death would mean to her.

Du Barry was not worried about her soul. She was young

still and fear of the future life was a malaise which did not attack until middle-age.

She said to him now: 'When are you going to dismiss Choiseul? Has not the man governed you long enough?'

'There is time . . . there is time . . .' murmured the King wearily.

Du Barry could be tenacious where her enemies were concerned. The great politician, Choiseul, caused her some anxiety. For twelve years he had held undisputed power; he was not, however, the man to bow to the will of one such as du Barry, and she knew that she dared not allow a man who did not do so to remain in such a position. It was in her circle that the plot against him had been launched. With the Duc d'Aiguillon and the Abbé Terray she had assured the King that Choiseul must go, and that he could be replaced by another more able than himself.

'Think of what harm this man can do to you,' said du Barry. 'Have you forgotten the Guiana settlement? What a fiasco! Think of all those settlers who died because they had been sent out to the new country lacking all that they would need. *Equinoctial France* did not remain French long, Louis. Everywhere the English triumph over us. And why? Bad management at home! And who manages affairs at home? It is Choiseul. It is always Choiseul! You know you would have rid yourself of the fellow long ago but for his pretty wife who cleverly remains virtuous and rejects the royal advances. And what impudence is this! To reject France!'

'My dear, you grow too vehement.'

'And so I shall when any woman thinks herself too good for the bed of France. But she'll come fast enough, Louis, my *bien-aimé* . . . once Choiseul is in disgrace.'

27

'There may be something in what you say,' said Louis indolently. 'But do not forget that he arranged this marriage with Austria.'

'Marriages as good could have been arranged, and think you not that Aiguillon could not have arranged the marriage had you wished him to ?'

Louis was silent. He was thinking of his grandson the Dauphin, Duc de Berry. He was often sad when he thought of the boy.

'How will he fare as a husband, think you, my dear?'

'Berry?' Du Barry laughed, rather loudly, raucously, the laugh of the market places of Paris. 'He'll grow up.'

'He'll be King of France one day . . . .'

'That day is far distant,' said du Barry fiercely.

The King smiled at her, half tenderly, half compassionately. He was very fond of her; he relied on her. What will become of her when I'm gone? he often wondered. But he did not want to think of when he was gone. When he did so he found himself veering towards one of those periods of repentance. He hated them; and in any case he always left them to plunge more violently than ever into debauchery.

'The Kings of France,' went on du Barry lightly, 'have given a good account of themselves with women.'

'So good,' said Louis, 'that mayhap for that reason there must be the occasional exception.'

'Nay, he'll grow up.'

'He's quite different from his brothers, Provence and Artois. Sometimes I think it is a pity that one of them was not the eldest.'

'It is often seen that there is depth in these quiet ones,' soothed du Barry. 'I have heard that the little Austrian is quite

28

charming; in fact, a regular little beauty. Put them to bed together and, mark my words, France, there'll be no need to complain of the Dauphin's lack of virility.'

'The boy gives me great cause for alarm,' said Louis.

Du Barry was uneasy. She must continually guard the King from unpleasant thoughts, and she knew from experience that thinking of his young grandson could often lead him to repentance. She was afraid of these fits of repentance which resulted in her banishment from his presence, and could so easily bring about her banishment from his life.

'It is long since I saw him,' said the King. 'Send for him, my dear, and I will have a word with him about this marriage.'

'*Bien-Aimé*, you are feeling tired after last night's little gallantry.'

Louis, still smiling, said firmly: 'Send for the boy, my dear.'

Du Barry, frowning lightly, went to the door. She called to a waiting page. 'Go at once to the Dauphin's apartment and bring him here. It is His Majesty's command.'

Louis was staring at his ringed hands, not seeing them but thinking of the past. An old man's habit, he mused, thinking of the past and wishing it had been different. If he had been more like his great-grandfather, Louis Quatorze, would France have been in its present state of unrest? Six years ago, when there had been great agitation against the Jesuits, he had tried to stand aloof. He had felt that his parliament was striking at him through the Jesuits. He had then begun to wonder whether the monarchy, which had seemed to stand so firm in the reign of his predecessor, had not begun to shake a little. He would never forget a letter – an anonymous one – which had been addressed to him and Madame Pompadour, and which declared: 'There is no longer any hope of government. A time

will come when the people's eyes will be opened, and perad-
venture that time is approaching.' Jean Jacques Rousseau was
writing perniciously against the monarchy. François Marie
Arouet de Voltaire was another of those philosophers who
made uneasy reading. The memory of that anonymous letter,
like the thoughts of hell-fire, often crept up on the Well-
Beloved like assassins in dark and lonely places.

That was why, when he thought of his young grandson, he
was remorseful. Had the boy been different – say a young
Louis Quatorze, or better still a young Henri Quatre – he
could have forgotten his fears. But young Berry was indeed a
problem.

What bad luck that the Dauphin had died. Who would have
believed that could happen? It was only five years ago when he
was in camp at Compiègne, and there had over-taxed his
strength, it was said. Only thirty-six! It was young to die; and
France needed him.

He had been unlike his father – pious, perhaps too devoted
to the clergy, but would that have been a bad thing for France?
He had been an ideal Dauphin; he had even produced three
sons, and it had seemed that he would fulfil his duty to France
when France needed a strong hand. Then he had disappointed
the sober members of the community by dying. There had
been so many deaths at that time. Louis' Queen, the Polish
woman Marie Leckzinska, had died three years after her son,
and a year before that the pleasant little Dauphine, Marie-
Josèphe of Saxony, had followed her husband to the grave.
These two women, quiet, modest and shrewd, were lost to the
little boy who would so sadly need advisers.

Louis would never forget the day he had heard of his son's
death. He had sent for his grandson. Little Berry had stood

before him, tall for his age, yet so lacking in charm, so slow – though they said he was not stupid at his books. He was merely lethargic and seemed unable to think quickly. His tutors assured his grandfather that the boy was conscientious, even clever, but lacked the gift of fluency, the ability to come to a quick decision.

And looking at that big heavy boy with his lustreless eyes, Louis had murmured: 'Poor France! A King of fifty-five, and a Dauphin of eleven!'

It was then that he had begun to feel uneasy.

Now the boy was being ushered into the apartment. A pity that it must be done with such ceremony, because the Dauphin was always at his worst on ceremonious occasions. He shuffled rather than walked to where his grandfather was sitting; he almost stumbled as he fell on his knees. The King's hand was seized in a grip that hurt; he winced in an annoyance which did not smother the tenderness he felt for his grandson.

'You may get up, Berry,' he said.

The Dauphin rose. He said nothing; he merely stood expectantly; a somewhat strained expression in the short-sighted eyes.

The King waved his hands to the pages.

'Leave us,' he said; and they bowed and retired. He studied his grandson with pitying eyes while the Dauphin looked from his grandfather to his grandfather's mistress as though apologising for his clumsiness, his ungainly appearance, and the fact that he could think of nothing to say.

'Berry,' said Louis, 'we have called you here to speak of your marriage and to show you the newest portrait of your little Dauphine. We are charmed. She is quite enchanting. Show Berry the portrait, my dear.'

31

Madame du Barry went to the Dauphin and laid a motherly hand on his shoulder. 'Here, Berry. You will see that she is in truth the loveliest of Dauphines.'

She led him to a table on which lay the picture.

The Dauphin looked at the charming oval-shaped face which was piquant rather than classically beautiful. The lips – a Habsburg heritage – were a little thick; the forehead was high and the colouring was so exquisite and the whole appearance one of such dainty charm that it occurred to Berry that, had they searched for a woman who was less like himself than any other in the world, they must have chosen Marie Antoinette.

He tried to say this, but hesitated. It might not please his grandfather. The Dauphin was cautious by nature; he never rushed into anything. He always considered so long and so carefully that by the time he had formed an opinion it was usually too late to express it.

'Is she not charming?' prompted du Barry.

'Why . . . yes . . . yes . . . indeed so.'

'You are the luckiest bridegroom in France, Berry.' The woman had thrust her painted face close to his, and he suppressed a shudder. He hated the suggestions in her eyes; they brought with them a renewal of his fears. He was dreading the marriage, for he was not like other boys of his age. He had listened to their talk of conquests; even his brothers, young as they were – Provence fourteen and Artois thirteen – had made their amatory experiments. Not so the Dauphin. He had no wish to, although there were pretty girls who were prepared to be more than charming to one who would one day be the King of France. He avoided them; they alarmed him; they made him certain that he was different. He did not care for those erotic excitements which seemed so attractive to others of his age. He

32

only wanted to be alone, or with the blacksmith, Gamin, who was teaching him his trade. He found great pleasure in forging and filing and using his strength, as did his friend the blacksmith. When he was tired from his physical labours he liked to read or study the geographical charts which he treasured. It seemed to him that there was a deeper satisfaction to be gleaned from books than from the society of young and frivolous people; in the books of great writers he could preserve his solitude, think his thoughts slowly, and sink into that peace which he so loved.

Therefore the sight of the portrait, far from delighting him, filled him with apprehension.

'Think,' said Madame du Barry, 'the delightful creature is already your wife. She is already on her way to you.'

The King said cynically: 'I see, my dear, that the Dauphin can scarcely wait for the consummation of his marriage.'

A burst of laughter escaped from Madame du Barry. The Dauphin turned his slow gaze upon her. Some might have hated her for the implied ridicule, but the Dauphin neither hated nor loved readily. His feelings were so slow to be roused that by the time he had realised them they were robbed of either venom or affection. He merely felt uncomfortable – not so much because he felt his grandfather's eyes upon him, but because he was wondering how he was going to greet his wife.

'Well, he is young, and the young are ardent,' said du Barry almost tenderly.

'Bring the portrait to me, my dear,' said the King; and du Barry obeyed. 'Ah,' went on Louis, 'you are indeed fortunate. Would I were sixteen years of age, and a Dauphin waiting to greet such a charming bride.'

He looked down at the picture; he was reminded of those

young girls whom he had so much enjoyed in the Parc aux Cerfs, whither they had been brought for his pleasure in his more virile days. Oh, to be young always, to be far away from the terrors of remorse! He believed he was getting dangerously near one of those periods of repentance.

'Grandson,' he said, 'you have learned the new dances, I trust?'

'Well, sir . . . I . . . I . . . I do not excel at the dance.'

The King nodded grimly. 'A wife will make a difference to you, Monsieur le Dauphin,' he said. 'You will discover through her much that makes life pleasant.'

'Yes, Grandfather.'

'What preparations are you making for her?'

'I . . . I . . . Should I make preparations?' There was a helpless look in the shortsighted eyes.

'You will have to stop thinking of other charming girls now you have a Dauphine,' said du Barry falsely, knowing full well that he had no interest whatsoever in charming girls. He met her gaze stolidly. He did not blush. When he stammered it was due to his slowness of thought.

'Indeed yes,' said the King. 'And Berry, we want heirs for France. Do not forget it.'

The Dauphin said: 'There is time. We are both young.'

'There is never too much time for kings, my boy. The sooner the children appear, the better pleased shall we all be – myself, and the people of France. Your marriage will take place here at Versailles, in the chapel of your ancestor Louis Quatorze; as soon as that ceremony is over, the Dauphine will be in very truth your wife. I think we should delay the consummation until after that ceremony.'

'Indeed yes,' said the Dauphin thankfully.

'Go now, my boy. Take the portrait with you. You will want to treasure it, I doubt not.'

He took the portrait, made his clumsy bow and went from the apartment.

'I could not bear to go on looking at him,' said the King when he had gone. 'He fills me with misgivings.'

'He will grow up,' soothed du Barry.

'He'll never make an ardent lover. He is unlike a King of France.'

'I tell you, when he sees this lovely girl he will grow up suddenly. He is just slow in coming to maturity. He is hardly sixteen, remember.'

'When I was sixteen . . .'

'You, my *bien-aimé* . . . you were a god.'

'My dear, I am uneasy. I was but five years old when the death of my great-grandfather made me King of France. My great-grandfather, the Grand Monarque, was of much the same age when he came to the throne; and it is not a good thing for minors to be kings.'

'Then you should not be uneasy, for the Dauphin is now sixteen and almost a man; and you have many years before you yet.'

'Times change. It may be that I have many years ahead of me. Who shall say? France is not the country I inherited from my great-grandfather, nor that country which the Grand Monarque inherited from his father. I am often uneasy. I remember a day thirteen years ago, when I was descending one of the staircases at Versailles, a man rushed at me and stabbed me with a penknife. The wound was not deep and I soon recovered, but I first began to think then that countries change, and the people who love us one year may hate us the next.'

'That man with his penknife was a fanatic, a madman. His criminal act did not mean the people's love had turned to hate. Why, Henri Quatre was stabbed to death, yet he was dearly loved and there are many who mourn him still.'

'That is so; but I saw death close then . . . and I pondered many things. Times have changed since Damiens sought to take my life and died a hideous death as punishment. Now it would seem to me that we are less safe. We have our troubles here and abroad. There would seem at times to be friction between me and my ministers, and when that happens . . .'

'Come, France, you grow morbid. Are you not known as Louis *Bien-Aimé?*'

'Rarely now, my dear. That was a title bestowed on me long ago. The sight of that boy has upset me. I begin to think that now I am sixty life here in France is different from what it was when I was twenty. Sometimes I think of Cardinal Fleury and that the troubles of France have increased since his death. He was a good minister – another Richelieu, another Mazarin. He was my good tutor, and I fear my licentious ways distressed him greatly. No, my dear, France is not the happy country she was. I have been careless. I see that now, in my old age. And now I am too tired to be different. Sometimes I have dreams. The sight of that boy reminds me . . .'

'He is a good boy, the Dauphin,' soothed du Barry. 'It is not a bad thing that he is serious.'

'He would seem to lack the kingly qualities – that is what I fear. He shuffles; he lacks dignity. Can such a one uphold the honour of France?'

'He is but the Dauphin. He has many years to learn to be a King. You have nothing to fear.'

The King grasped her arm suddenly. His eyes were glazed slightly as he looked into space.

'I have nothing to fear,' he said. 'I shall die and France will go on. *Le roi est mort. Vive le roi.* It has always been thus, has it not, my dear? But there are times when I say to myself: The kingdom will last my lifetime and . . . *après moi – le déluge.*'

⚜ ⚜ ⚜

The bridal procession had reached Alsace. Bells were ringing, streets were strewn with flowers, and there was wine to take the place of water in the public fountains. The boats which sailed along the Rhine were bright with torches, and sweet music came from their decks.

The people were enchanted by the lovely young girl in the glass chariot – a true fairy princess, they told each other. It was indeed a happy state of affairs when a marriage could unite two countries. And the bride who was to come to France and to her Dauphin was young, even as he was young. This was a happy augury for France.

In the Cathedral, to which she was conducted to hear Mass, Marie Antoinette was received by the Prince de Rohan. He was young and handsome and his eyes gleamed with admiration as they rested upon her.

She was artlessly surprised that one so young should greet her; she had expected the Bishop, whom she knew to be by no means as young or handsome as the man who did not seem to be able to take his eyes from her face.

He had taken her hand; his lips lingered on it. He did not release it but kept it in his while he said, in a voice which seemed over-charged with emotion: 'You will be for us all the living image of the beloved Empress, your noble mother, whom all Europe has so long admired and who posterity will never cease to venerate. It is as though the spirit of Maria Theresa is about to unite with the spirit of the Bourbons.'

She smiled her thanks and withdrew her hand; but as he led her to the altar she was conscious of him – of his handsome looks, of his ardent eyes. She knew that, although he talked of the spirits of two countries, he was thinking of two people – herself and himself.

It was a strange feeling to experience in a church, a strange beginning to her life in her new country; he was telling her so clearly that she was the most enchanting creature he had ever set eyes on; and in that moment she began to feel less misery, less longing for her mother and her home.

In a few days she would have forgotten his name, but in that moment she warmed towards him. He had brought home to her the fact that she was young and lovely and that wherever she went she must excite admiration.

So, because of the ardent glances of the Bishop's nephew, Louis, Prince de Rohan, apprehension was replaced in the facile mind of the young girl by excited anticipation.

In the forest of Compiègne the procession was halted. Here branches had been decorated with garlands, and banners of silk and velvet were draped across the trees. The ladies and gentlemen of the Court, exquisitely clad, waited under those trees for the ceremonial meeting between the Austrian Dauphine and the King and Dauphin of France.

The King's guard, in brilliant uniforms, was drawn up in a glade while heralds and buglers played a fanfare of greeting.

In the glass carriage Antoinette knew that the great moment had at last arrived.

The King alighted from his carriage. Antoinette saw him and, with charming grace, left her own, and with a childish abandon ran towards the King of France and curtsied in the manner which she had practised again and again before she had left Vienna.

Louis looked down at the dainty creature. So small, so exquisitely formed, he thought her like a china doll, and her charm moved him, for he had a deep-rooted tenderness for young girls.

He lifted her in his arms and could not take his eyes from the flushed oval face with the exquisite colouring, the artless expression of an innocent desire to please and a certainty that she could not fail to do so.

The King embraced her with slightly more fervour than was necessary; then he held her at arm's length; and kissed her cheeks.

'Welcome! Welcome to France, my little one,' he greeted her. And he let his hand linger on her shoulder. Such firm plump flesh, he thought; and he envied his grandson.

He was aware of all those who looked on. They would be smiling, understanding; they would be murmuring: 'Here is one the old voluptuary must relinquish!'

It was true. A pity . . . a pity. But where was the Dauphin?

The King looked over his shoulder. It was the signal. The Dauphin shuffled forward – at his worst on such an occasion – and looked at the lovely girl as though she were a wild animal of which he was truly scared. Can he be a future King of France? wondered the King. A pity it was not Provence, or Artois. It would not have been such a tragedy to have a boor like this for a second or third grandson – but the eldest, the Dauphin, the heir to the throne! It was the Polish blood in him. His grandmother Marie Leckzinska had been the daughter of the dispossessed King Stanislaus of Poland. His mother was Marie-Josèphe, the daughter of the Elector of Saxony; and the Dauphin had inherited many qualities from the distaff side. He was heavy, clumsy, beside the polished grace of Frenchmen.

'My dear,' said the King, reluctantly taking his hands from her, 'here is the Dauphin, your bridegroom.'

Antoinette was now face to face with the Dauphin. My husband, she thought, and looked anxiously into his face. She saw a tall boy not much older than herself, with sleepy sheepish eyes which did not seem to want to look at her, and which reminded her, by very contrast, of the eager good looks of the young and handsome Prince de Rohan. His forehead receded rather abruptly from his brows; his nose was big – the Bourbon nose; his chin was rounded and fleshy. He was tall and not altogether unprepossessing; she did not know why it was that he looked so unlike a royal Dauphin. Was it because his clothes, though elaborate, did not seem to fit; was it because his hands were not as shapely as those which had lifted the monstrance for the benediction such a short while ago?

The priest had looked at her as though she were a bride; her bridegroom looked at her as though he had little desire to make her further acquaintance and was wondering how soon he could escape from her.

She saw that his neck was short, a flaw which robbed him of dignity, and that although he was tall he was somewhat fat. Still, there was nothing cruel in his expression.

Now he had laid his hands on her shoulders as his father had done. Everyone was watching while he kissed her cheeks in the formal way of greeting.

The King's kisses had been warm and lingering – kisses of admiration and affection, but the Dauphin's lips scarcely touched her skin, and he released her as though she were a burning ember which scorched him.

'Now come,' said the King, 'join us in our chariot, and away to Versailles.'

She sat in the royal coach between the King and the Dauphin. The Dauphin had moved as far into the corner as he could; the King pressed against her.

'My dear,' whispered the King, 'this is indeed one of the happiest days of my life.'

'Your Majesty is gracious,' murmured Antoinette.

'And it shall be our great desire to make you our happy granddaughter.'

'You are so kind,' she answered.

'You are as happy as I am . . . as the Dauphin is?'

'I miss my mother,' she admitted.

'Ah! There is sadness in parting. But that is life, my dear. The Dauphin will not let you be long unhappy. Is that not so, Berry?'

The Dauphin started as though he had not heard.

'I was saying it is our greatest wish to make this dear child forget she has left her mother; we shall do all in our power to make her love us and France.'

'Y . . . yes,' agreed the Dauphin uncertainly.

The King laughed; he brought his face near to that of his new granddaughter. 'Forgive him, my dear,' he said. 'He is overcome by your beauty . . . as I am.'

And riding through France, sitting beside the King, Antoinette was so intoxicated by the admiring glances of the people and many of the men about her – including the King – that it seemed to her that the Antoinette she had become was a charming, irresistible woman who bore little relationship to the young girl who had so recently left Austria.

✢ ✢ ✢

The true and second ceremony of marriage was performed in the Chapel of Louis Quatorze at Versailles. May sunshine penetrated the stained-glass windows and shone on the young bride and her groom. Never yet had Antoinette looked so beautiful as she did in her wedding garments; she was a fairy-like being in the midst of all those splendidly apparelled men and women who attended the ceremony. None but the most noble was allowed to be present. Beside her the bridegroom, breathing heavily, sweated uneasily. He was glad that his bride did not share his fear. He himself was terrified, not of the ceremony – there had been many ceremonies in his life – but of that moment when they would be left together in the nuptial bed. He feared that he would be unable to accomplish what was expected of him.

During the ceremony, while he put the ring on that slender finger and gave her the gold pieces which had been blessed by the Archbishop of Rheims who was officiating, he was wondering what he would say to her, how he could attempt to explain his inadequacy. What explanation was there? Would she understand? His grandfather would be ashamed of him; everybody would be ashamed of him; and he would be ashamed of himself.

He fervently wished that he need not marry. He much preferred the company of Gamin to that of this pretty young creature. He would much rather file a piece of iron than dance, rather listen to the ring of the anvil than the inane conversation of frivolous young people.

The Archbishop was giving them his blessing, and two pages were holding a silver canopy over the heads of himself and his bride.

He could not pay proper attention to the religious ceremony. She must be aware of his damp and clammy hands; she who was as dainty as a spring flower must find him gross.

His spirits lifted a little. Perhaps he could say to her: 'Do not expect anything of me . . . *anything* . . . and I will expect nothing of you. Is it our fault that they have married us?'

But no. They had their duty. He had been brought up on a diet of etiquette and he knew that he could not evade his duty. If he had been anyone but the heir to the throne, he might have been able to do so. But he was the Dauphin; he must beget sons for France. The thought horrified him.

Always he was conscious of this difference in him. He envied the light-hearted Artois, who had no such disabilities.

I can but try, he promised himself.

✦ ✦ ✦

The ceremony was over and the King was signing the marriage contract.

Now it was the bride's turn to sign.

She took the pen in her hand and wrote laboriously, as a child. There were amused glances among the lookers-on. The girl was enchanting, full of grace; but her education must have been rather neglected since she seemed to find the wielding of a pen something of an ordeal.

Her tongue protruded slightly at the corner of her mouth as she proceeded with the effort. 'Marie Antoinette Josepha Jeanne', she wrote. A blot of ink gushed from the pen, and the bride gave a half-apologetic smile at the King.

She had spoilt the neat page, but the King's fond glance told her that he would be ready to forgive far greater sins of one so charming.

So she smiled at him and thought how pleasant it was to be reassured that she was so attractive. Only her husband seemed not to be impressed by her charm; and that was odd.

❖ ❖ ❖

The people of Paris had come to Versailles to see the Dauphin and his bride. They thronged the gardens, crowded the avenues and dabbled their fingers in the fountains.

The King was determined that the people should long remember the wedding of his grandson, and had arranged pleasures for them to rival those provided by his grandfather Louis Quatorze.

The wedding feast was spread out in the great salon, and to this the common people could not be admitted, for even the nobility could not join in the feast, although they would be allowed to look on from the galleries. The people could only look through the windows at all this splendour, but for their especial enjoyment the King had arranged that all the fountains should play and that as soon as darkness fell there should be a firework display to outrival any that had as yet been seen.

So crowded were the gardens that it seemed as though all Paris had come to Versailles.

The people were delighted; they told each other that in the day of le Roi Soleil there had been many such pleasures. Those were the good old days. It might well be that when the old King died and the new King was on the throne with that perfectly enchanting young bride of his, there would be gaiety as there had been in the past.

That afternoon they began to long for the day when the Dauphin became King. Instead of 'Dauphin Louis' they began to call him 'Louis le Désire'.

The early afternoon was warm and sunny; the scent of flowers filled the air and the fountains and waterfalls sparkled in the fresh May sunshine; but very soon the sky was overcast, and by three o'clock the first rain had fallen.

There were anxious looks at the sky.

'It will soon clear,' people told each other as they sheltered under the trees. But this was optimism, for soon the rain was falling in torrents and the trees could offer little shelter. Lightning flashed and thunder rolled.

A bad end to the wedding day, the people grumbled.

And it was soon obvious that there would be no firework display in the gardens of Versailles on that day.

Wet to the skin, sick with disappointment, the people began to leave the gardens. In the early evening the rain was still falling and the gardens of Versailles were deserted; the road back to Paris was crowded with carriages and people on foot.

But in the great salon the candles were lighted, the musicians were playing, and the royal family sat down to the banquet, watched in the galleries by the noblest in the land.

On the right-hand side of the King sat Antoinette, young enough to delight in the rich strange foods, young enough to be dazzled by splendour such as she had never seen before.

The King clearly showed his affection for her; the rest of

the family seated round the table were eager to follow his example and let her know how welcome she was. Only her bridegroom seemed aloof, sitting silent on the other side of his grandfather.

She was very interested in the members of her new family. There were two brothers-in-law and two young sisters-in-law; there were her husband's three aunts – Madame Adelaide, Madame Victoire and Madame Sophie.

Her brothers-in-law seemed to be watching her all the time. The elder of the two was fourteen years old; he was Louis Stanislas Xavier, Comte de Provence, a proud boy, who seemed a little resentful of his elder brother; the other brother was a boy of thirteen, Charles Philippe, Comte d'Artois; he was more artless than Provence and too delighted by the ceremony to show any envy. Clothilde, the elder of her sisters-in-law, was plump and rather plain; Elisabeth the younger was very quiet and prettier than her sister. As for the three aunts, they were terrifying, partly because they looked so prim, partly because they were so watchful. Antoinette felt that nothing she did could escape their sharp eyes.

There was one present whom Antoinette could not believe to be a member of the royal family. She was a boldly handsome woman with a loud and raucous laugh and an air of easy familiarity when she addressed the King. She was the Comtesse du Barry, and Antoinette could not understand why she – the only person not a member of the royal family – should be allowed to sit with them.

She found it difficult to hold back the question which rose to her lips, and once was on the point of asking the King in what way Madame du Barry was connected with the family.

It was only when she caught the eye of Madame Adelaide

and the expression in that lady's face showed such alarm that she stopped short; she realised then that the Dauphin was shifting uncomfortably in his chair, and that young Artois seemed to be smothering a fit of choking.

The King had tactfully turned to her and laid his hand over hers.

'You must try this dish of quails, my dear . . . a French delicacy. We must teach you to understand our French . . . concoctions, must we not?'

So she tried the quails and declared them delicious.

Calm was restored to the table.

❖ ❖ ❖

The banquet was over and night had fallen on the Palace of Versailles. Now had come that moment to which the Dauphin had looked forward with such dread.

The King placed the Dauphine on his right hand and the Dauphin on his left and led them to the bridal chamber.

It was a solemn ceremony – as solemn as that which had taken place in the Chapel of Louis Quatorze. The Archbishop of Rheims was blessing the bed, praying that it might be fruitful, as he sprinkled it with holy water.

The bride was flushed and eager; the bridegroom seemed sullen and indifferent.

Oh, my poor Berry! thought the King, as he handed his grandson his nightshirt, while the Duchesse de Chartres, as a married lady with royal connexions, handed Antoinette her nightgown.

Thus ready for that ordeal of which the bride was quite ignorant and the bridegroom terrified, they approached the bed; and in it they lay side by side – two children, the bride not quite fifteen, the bridegroom not yet sixteen – while the curtains of the bed were drawn about them.

❧ ❧ ❧

The next day the Dauphin wrote in his diary one word: *'Rien.'*

❧ Chapter II ❧

THE DAUPHINE AT VERSAILLES

*I*t was not long before Antoinette realised that life at Versailles was not going to be very different from that in the Schönbrunn Palace, for her mother had sent strict instructions as to how her education was to be conducted; she had even sent the Abbé de Vermond, that her daughter might continue to study under him. She had written to the King of France to the effect that her daughter was very young and that marriage had interrupted her education; she wished her therefore to live as quietly as possible in her new home until she was mature enough to fit her new position with grace.

The King had readily agreed. He was too indolent to concern himself with the upbringing of his new granddaughter and quite prepared to let her mother continue with the responsibility.

What Maria Theresa did not realise was that, although it was a comparatively easy matter to keep her daughter childish in her own Court, in the brilliant one at Versailles – where *amours* were the order of the day and the reflection of all that wit and brilliance which had graced the Court of Le Roi Soleil still lingered – the young girl was bound to find the life planned for her irksome.

There was intrigue all about her.

She quickly discovered this when, on the morning after her wedding night, she was visited by the three aunts, 'Les Mesdames' as they were called throughout the Court.

Madame Adelaide, the eldest of the three unmarried daughters of Louis Quinze, was clearly the most dominant; Madame Victoire was kind but neurotic and apt to panic at the slightest difficulty; Madame Sophie was the ugliest of the three and, being constantly aware of this, was very shy. The two younger sisters were very much under the influence of the eldest, and the three were more often than not in each other's company. The whole Court, following the King's example, was inclined to treat them with ridicule. They were Princesses for whom husbands had not been found; they were middle-aged and far from prepossessing; and they had been foolish enough to band themselves together against the King's mistresses. They should have known better, and suffered accordingly.

They were pious and disapproving, and Adelaide, unable to stop herself meddling in Court intrigue, carried her sisters along with her.

Madame Adelaide had deeply resented the Austrian marriage and was determined to hate Antoinette. But, as she told her sisters, 'This we must hide, for through the child we may discover a great deal.'

So together they visited her as she sat with the Abbé de Vermond, wondering what difference there was after all in being Dauphine of France instead of Archduchess of Austria.

The aunts entered with ceremony: Adelaide first, Victoire next, and Sophie bringing up the rear.

The Abbé rose at the sight of the Princesses. He bowed low, but they ignored him.

Antoinette rose also; she curtsied, and Adelaide patted her cheek.

'We have come to pay our respects to our little Dauphine,' said Adelaide.

'Thank you, Mesdames,' replied Antoinette.

Adelaide bowed her head in acknowledgement of the thanks. Victoire did the same, and a few seconds later so did Sophie. They looked so odd, three middle-aged ladies very much alike, standing there nodding, that Antoinette found it difficult to restrain her laughter.

Adelaide turned to the Abbé; she did not speak; she merely gave him a haughty look. He said: 'You wish to be alone with the Dauphine, Madame?'

Adelaide nodded her head, while the other two imitated their sister's haughty look.

The Abbé bowed and left them. He had been warned to be very careful not to offend French etiquette.

'Now the man has gone,' said Adelaide, 'you may call us *Tantes*. I am Tante Adelaide, dear child.'

'And I am Tante Victoire,' said the second.

'And I am Tante Sophie,' murmured the third.

'My dear Tantes, I welcome you all,' said Antoinette. She stood on tiptoe and kissed them in order of seniority.

'That is charming,' said Tante Adelaide.

'Charming!' 'Charming!' echoed Victoire and Sophie.

'We are going to be friends . . . very dear friends,' said Adelaide.

Antoinette found herself looking at the others for the confirmation she expected. 'That is why we come to you at once . . .' went on Adelaide.

'Before others contaminate you,' put in Victoire.

'Be silent, Victoire!' said Adelaide sharply. 'But your Tante Victoire is not far wrong, my child. There is much evil at the Court of France. You are a good and virtuous girl. I see that.' Again Antoinette looked quickly at the others. They nodded, implying that they too found her a good and virtuous girl. 'And you, my dear, began to uncover a little of that evil during the banquet.'

The others tittered, but Adelaide held up a warning hand. Antoinette was fascinated by the way in which the other two immediately obeyed their leader. They were serious at once.

'You wondered about that coarse creature who had the temerity to sit at table with us.'

'Yes. Who was she?'

'She is known as the Comtesse du Barry.'

'And she is a member of the royal family?'

'A member of the royal family! Indeed she is not. The King, our father – and although he is our father we say this, for, my dear, we will have truth however unpleasant that truth may be – the King has strange habits. He has taken that creature from the gutter, and she shares his life. Do you know what we mean?'

'She . . . lives as one of the family?'

'As its most important member.'

'But why so . . . since she is vulgar, as you say? Why does the King like her so much?'

'Men are weak,' said Adelaide; her sisters nodded in agreement.

Antoinette looked in astonishment from one to another of the three aunts, who continued to nod vigorously.

'The woman shares the King's bed . . . as you do the Dauphin's,' said Victoire, quickly putting her hand to her mouth.

Adelaide's eyebrows shot up, and she looked very angry.

'That is quite different,' she said sternly. 'Our little Dauphine is married to Berry. That woman . . . is not married to our father.'

'Then she is . . .' began Antoinette.

Adelaide put her fingers on her lips. She brought her face close to Antoinette's ear. Antoinette looked at the skin which lay like grey *crêpe* beneath her sly, narrow eyes, and shuddered.

'A harlot!' she whispered; then she drew herself up and went on. 'But we will not speak of it. It is too shocking. I rejoice that we are here to protect you from evil things. Our sister Louise is a Carmelite nun. She often declares that the King will fall on evil times if he does not give up that woman. But we will defeat her yet. She hates us . . . because she is evil and we have always lived virtuous lives. We have come to advise you, my dear.'

'Do not let that woman come near you,' cried Victoire shrilly.

'How can she help that?' enquired Sophie.

'She must ignore her as best she can,' said Adelaide. 'Be cold to her. Do not confide in her. If you wish to confide in any, remember your three aunts who will be most anxious to help you.'

'You are very kind,' said Antoinette.

They nodded in unison.

'Don't forget. If you are in difficulty, come to Tante Adelaide . . . '

'And Tante Victoire. Please do not forget Tante Victoire.'

'And Tante Sophie,' whispered the youngest aunt.

'For,' went on Adelaide, 'we are after all poor Berry's own aunts.'

'Why do you call him poor?' asked Antoinette.

'The King, our father, always calls him Poor Berry,' said Victoire.

'He was always a quiet boy – not like his brothers,' Adelaide whispered. 'He was always timid . . . never wanted to play with other boys.'

'He was born like it,' said Victoire. 'Always quiet, always dull. Poor Berry!'

'Poor Berry!' echoed Sophie.

'His father died when he was eleven,' went on Adelaide. 'His father was wonderful. Had he lived, everything would have been so different.' The aunts with one accord dabbed their eyes. 'But he died of consumption when he was quite young. He said: "I am dying without having enjoyed anything, and without having done any good to anyone." '

'He was thirty-six,' said Sophie.

Adelaide continued: 'It happened quite suddenly, and his wife followed him quickly to the grave. She suffered from the same disease . . . and those poor children were orphans.'

'They had their aunts,' said Victoire with a nervous titter.

'Yes, they had us. We have been mothers . . . *mothers* . . . to those poor orphans.'

'Then they have not been so unfortunate,' said Antoinette. 'In place of one mother they have had three.'

'That is so; Berry's two elder brothers both died.

Bourgogne was nine when he died; Aquitaine but five months old.'

'That made Berry Dauphin,' said Victoire.

'Poor Berry!' chanted Sophie.

'His father supervised his education,' put in Adelaide, determined to dominate the conversation. 'He made him work hard. He was fond of his books. I do not know why he should appear so *dull*. It is perhaps because his brothers talk so much . . . and are so gay . . . particularly Artois. Did you not think Artois handsome? But I know you did. I saw you looking at him.' Adelaide's eyes were wicked suddenly. 'Yes, I saw you looking at Artois. It is true he is younger than his brother, but not much younger than you. Were you wishing that Artois was the Dauphin . . . eh? Were you wishing the Archbishop was sprinkling holy water on a bed you would share with him, eh?'

Antoinette drew back, sensing that the conversation had ceased to be artless. 'I am very happy with the husband I have,' she said firmly. 'I wish for no other.'

The aunts exchanged quick glances, and Adelaide went on hurriedly: 'I knew it. I said that but to tease. It was nothing more than a joke, my dear. You will learn that we French love to joke. I was telling you about poor Berry who has always been so quiet. Why, often when he was but a boy I have called him to my apartment and cried to him: "Come, my poor Berry! Here you can be at your ease. Talk, shout, make a noise. I give you *carte blanche*." But did he? No, no, no!'

The other two shook their heads sadly. 'No, no, no,' said Victoire. And 'Poor Berry!' said Sophie.

'Artois is of course the bright one. He flirts already, the bad boy. Quite unlike Berry.'

'Was Berry so quiet when the curtains were drawn last night?' asked Victoire.

They were all watching the bewildered young Dauphine.

'Poor Berry,' said Adelaide significantly. 'I fear he was.' Victoire began to giggle, but her elder sister silenced her. 'You must come to us when you want advice on anything,' said Adelaide. 'Remember we are your very dear aunts who love you and want to make you very happy in your new home. If you are worried about anything . . . you must come to us. If you find Berry . . . strange . . . tell us, and we will talk to Berry. Remember we have been as mothers to him. There is no one in whom you could so happily confide as in us . . . dear child.'

'I thank you all from the bottom of my heart,' said the Dauphine prettily.

They kissed her in turn and made to depart.

'Do not forget,' said Adelaide, 'have nothing to do with that wicked woman, the du Barry. If you do, everyone at Court will think you are as bad as she is. They will accuse you of loving Artois of Provence better than your husband.'

'But why?' asked Antoinette.

'Because she is wicked, and they say like goes to like,' Adelaide assured her.

Antoinette was thoughtful after they had gone and, when the Abbé de Vermond came to resume the lesson, she was more inattentive than ever.

The young members of the family were very interested in her, and she was received with delight in the royal nursery. She seemed of an age with the children, yet possessed in addition the dignity of being married.

The baby Elisabeth, a quiet little girl of six, was seen to be enchanted with her; she insisted on touching her new sister's wonderful hair.

'It is the colour of gold,' said Elisabeth.

Antoinette blossomed under the admiring gaze of her new relations.

'Have you brothers and sisters?' asked eleven-year-old Clothilde.

'Yes, but I am the youngest. They were not often with me.'

'We shall not be always together,' said Clothilde. 'We shall marry one day.'

Her brother Artois, slender, elegant, who had inherited less than the others from his Polish grandmother and German mother and was far more French than they, strolled over to admire the newcomer.

'You will never find a husband, Clothilde,' he said. 'You grow too fat . . . . Does she not, dear sister?'

His alert bright eyes were smiling into those of Antoinette, and she returned the smile.

'She will grow more slender as she grows older.'

'Mayhap she will grow like the aunts,' said Provence.

'I will not, I will not!' cried Clothilde indignantly. 'I would rather die than be like the aunts.'

'You will never be like them, dear Clothilde,' said Elisabeth, 'and you will have many husbands.'

'Foolish Elisabeth!' said Provence. 'She does not know that one husband is all that a virtuous woman asks.'

'Mayhap I shall not be virtuous,' said Clothilde.

'You will,' said Artois, 'from necessity. You will be too fat to be otherwise.'

'You tease your sister,' said Antoinette.

'But 'tis true,' said Artois, 'that, in the Court, they call Clothilde *Gros Madame*.'

Clothilde shrugged her shoulders and laughed. It was obvious that she was not unduly worried by her plumpness.

'And how like you life here in France, sister?' asked Provence.

'Everyone is kind,' Antoinette told him cautiously.

'But you are disappointed,' insisted Artois. 'Come, you need not stand on ceremony with us. Tell us exactly what you think of us.'

'It is not in you that I am disappointed. But I live here in much the same way as I did at home. I must do lessons.' She grimaced in a manner which made them all laugh. 'I must not do this . . . I must do that. Madame de Noailles tells me continually that a Dauphine should not behave as a hoyden. There are more rules for a Dauphine than for an Archduchess, and I had thought I should be free.'

'You long to be free,' said Artois.

'From etiquette and the need to do as I am told. I should like to do wild things. . . . '

'Such as going to Paris, dressed as a washerwoman?' asked Artois.

Marie Antoinette nodded. 'I long to see Paris. I am here in France and have never seen Paris.'

'Oh, there will be a formal entry,' said Provence. 'You are the Dauphine and there must be music and soldiers and pageants. The people will expect such things.'

'I understand that. But it does not happen. I am here at Versailles, and I learn my lessons and etiquette . . . etiquette . . . etiquette. Continually I am told in France you must do this . . . you must not do that. You must curtsy thus to one person, but another will require a deeper curtsy, being of higher rank. And forgive me, but I think that some of the things which you do for the sake of etiquette are a little silly.'

'We think so too,' agreed Artois. 'But we must do them. Have you told Berry of this?'

'I see little of Berry . . . except when we go to bed.'

The brothers exchanged glances, and their lips curled.

'And your meetings with Berry are . . . pleasant?' asked Artois.

Provence said: 'Be quiet.'

'You see,' went on the daring Artois, 'we also see little of our brother. He shuts himself in with his books, and then he has his dear blacksmith.'

'He is clever, I know,' said Antoinette.

'I don't think it very clever to neglect a wife like you,' said Artois boldly. 'I think it folly – even though he is pleasant behind the bed-curtains.'

'You should not speak thus of the Dauphin,' said Antoinette, remembering her dignity suddenly. Then she smiled to show them she was not displeased.

'Berry is always quiet,' said Clothilde.

'I love poor Berry,' Elisabeth told her.

'Grandfather is sad when he thinks of him,' said Provence. 'Grandfather tries not to think of things that make him sad, and that is why he thinks so little of Berry.'

'Berry is more happy with common people than with his family and the nobles of the Court,' added Artois. 'It has always been so. He will talk to Gamin and be perfectly at ease; but with us . . . or Grandfather . . . he has scarcely a word to say.'

'He is very sad,' said Clothilde thoughtfuly, 'when he sees

59

the poor people in the streets. If he can do it without anyone's knowing, he gives money to the poor.'

'Then he is kind,' stated Antoinette.

'So your husband satisfies you, Madame?' put in Artois. 'What would you say if I told you that at this moment, instead of seeking your company, he is engaged with the workmen in his apartment? He is having a new wall built, and there he is working with the men. When that wall is built he will want to pull it down and build another. It is not that he wishes for a wall. It is building and such labour that he likes so much; he likes the conversation of the men.'

'Let us go and see how the work progresses,' suggested Provence.

'So you think we might?' asked Antoinette.

'Madame de Marsan said we were to entertain the Dauphine in the nursery, and not leave the apartment,' said Elisabeth.

Artois was haughty. 'Then you stay, little sister, since you are afraid of your *gouvernante*.'

'She will be angry if we disobey.'

'I doubt not,' said Antoinette, 'that it is not etiquette to visit the Dauphin's apartment while he is with the workmen. In that case there is nothing I wish to do so much as visit the Dauphin and his workmen.'

Her two brothers-in-law laughed approvingly.

'It is a sin,' said Artois softly, coming close to her and laying his hand on her arm, 'to shut such as you, Madame la Dauphine, in with Etiquette.'

'Madame de Noailles is a good woman, I doubt not,' said Antoinette, 'but she thinks of nothing but the conventions; I call her Madame Etiquette. Come, let us go and see the Dauphin and his men at work.' She took Elisabeth's hand. 'If your *gouvernante* should scold, I will tell her that you came at my command.'

'Let us stay here and dance,' said Artois. 'Do you dance the French dances, dear sister?'

'I was taught to dance them.'

'Let us try a step or two.'

Antoinette always enjoyed dancing, so she allowed Artois to take her hand and lead her into the middle of the apartment. Clothilde held out her hand to Provence who looked at her with scorn; his eyes were sullen as he watched his brother and sister-in-law. They made a graceful pair.

Clothilde clapped her hands and cried: 'Your steps fit perfectly.'

'Do you think I dance the French dances like a French woman?' asked Antoinette of her partner.

'You dance them with more perfection than anyone – French or otherwise – ever did before.'

'You flatter me, brother. You will be telling me next that I speak perfect French.'

'But the French you speak is more enchanting than all other French, because none speaks it quite like you.'

'I have been scolded often because I speak it so badly.'

'Then those who scolded should in turn be scolded. I would rather listen to your French than that spoken by anyone else.'

They were aware of a slight tension among the other children who had become silent.

Antoinette turned and saw that a woman had come into the apartment. She was saying to Provence: 'Pardon, my lord. I thought to find Madame de Marsan.'

'I know not where she is,' said Provence haughtily; and the woman retired.

Artois led Antoinette back to the group. 'She came here to spy, of course,' he said.

'Spy?' cried the Dauphine. 'But why to spy?'

'*Mon Dieu,* I know not,' said Provence.

'She is one of the aunts' women,' added Artois. 'They spy on us continually. And now of course you are here, and you are the wife of the heir to the throne, so you are doubly worth spying upon.'

'You mean they will say that we should not dance . . . that we have offended against mighty Etiquette by dancing?'

'I doubt not they will say that. And you and I danced together – ah, that will make them nod their fusty old heads together, and Loque, Coche and Graille will mutter that it is all very scandalous.'

'Who are these?' asked Antoinette.

'Loque, Coche and Graille? Oh, those are Grandfather's names for them. Is your French not good enough to understand, sister? Loque means rags and tatters, Coche is an old sow, and Graille a crow. There you see what His Majesty the King thinks of his three daughters!'

'It does not seem as though he employs the etiquette when speaking of them,' said Antoinette with a giggle. 'The names suit them. But I should not say that, for they have been kind to me.'

'Kind! They have questioned you doubtless . . . asked many questions about you and Berry. They'll not be kind. Tante Adelaide knows not how to be. As for Victoire, she is a fool, and Sophie is another – they do all Adelaide tells them to.'

'I am no longer in the mood to dance,' said Antoinette. 'Let us go and see the building of the wall.'

Three men were busy working in the Dauphin's apartment, and it was some seconds before Antoinette recognised one of these as her husband. When they entered he had been talking naturally with the men, shouting orders, giving advice. He carried a pail in his hands, and his eyelashes were white with dust which also clung to his clothes. As soon as he saw the members of his family a subtle change came over him.

'So, Berry, you have become a workman,' said Artois.

'Ah . . . yes,' stammered the Dauphin. 'I wanted this work done and I . . . thought I would supervise it myself.'

'It is very clever of you,' said Antoinette.

'Not clever at all. You see, I wished for a partition here, and then I have had the floorboards taken up and replaced. We have much work to do here yet.'

Provence yawned. 'What a mess!' he murmured.

Artois said: 'I feel this atmosphere chokes me. Berry, why do you not give instructions and leave these fellows to carry them out?'

The Dauphin did not answer. Clothilde said: 'We have been dancing. Berry, why do you not come and dance with us?'

'He prefers to stay here,' said Elisabeth. She was smiling with great affection at her eldest brother. 'It is more interesting to make something, is it not, Berry, than to dance.'

'But to dance is to make something also,' insisted Artois. 'Pleasure, shall we say, for oneself and one's partner.'

Clothilde put in: 'Walls last longer than the pleasure of dancing.'

'How can you say how long pleasure lasts?' demanded Artois. 'It could live in the memory. As for the walls built by my brother – they last only until he pulls them down, because he wants to start building them all over again.'

As they talked one of the workmen fell from his ladder; he let out a cry of alarm and then lay silent on the floor.

Antoinette ran to him and knelt beside him while her silk gown trailed in the dust and dirt.

'He is badly hurt,' she cried; 'bring me some hot water, Elisabeth. I will bathe his wound. I think we should send for a doctor.'

Artois said: 'You are spoiling your dress. Come away. We will send someone to deal with this man. You should not do that.'

'So I should let him bleed to death,' cried Antoinette scornfully, 'because it is not etiquette for me to help him! No. I shall do as I wish. Get me bandages and hot water. You, Clothilde. You, Elisabeth.'

The Dauphin was kneeling beside her, and as he did so the man opened his eyes. 'He is not badly hurt,' said the Dauphin to Antoinette. And to the man he went on: 'All is well.' Antoinette noticed how soothing his voice was, and how the man looked at him with affection.

'I am sorry, sir,' he said. 'I do not know how it happened ... I must have slipped.'

'Madame la Dauphine is concerned,' the Dauphin told him. 'She fears you must have done some damage to yourself.'

'Madame,' cried the man, struggling to his feet, 'I am honoured ...'

He was too weak to stand, and the Dauphin caught him in his strong arms. 'You see, you are dizzy still.'

'Let him sit here . . . with his back against this piece of furniture,' suggested Antoinette.

'He fears he should not sit in your presence,' her husband explained.

'What nonsense!' She laughed her gay spontaneous laughter. 'I suppose if a Frenchman is dying he must remember etiquette, for etiquette in France is more important than life and death.'

The Dauphin laughed with her. It was obvious that he was happy to have her with him.

Elisabeth and Clothilde came back with bandages and water. Artois said sulkily: 'This atmosphere chokes me!'

'Come,' said Provence, 'we can do nothing here. Clothilde! Elisabeth! You will return to your apartments.'

The little girls, who both wanted to stay and watch the strange behaviour of the Dauphine, looked appealingly towards their eldest brother; but he did not see them; he was watching his wife's deft fingers as she bathed the wound. There was nothing they could do therefore but obey the orders of Provence.

'There!' said Antoinette. 'It is not such a bad wound after all. Do you feel better?'

'Yes, thank you, Madame.'

The man's eyes were large with wonder that this exquisite creature could have taken so much care over him.

'Now you should rest awhile,' she commanded. 'You should not continue with your work.'

'It is true,' said the Dauphin. 'We will work no more to-day.'

The men bowed and went out, leaving the Dauphin and his wife together.

When they were alone, the Dauphin said: 'You are so quick. You know what to do at once and you do it. I . . . wait too long. When I saw he had fallen I was . . . uncertain what to do.'

'It is wrong, they tell me, to act without thinking. My mother continually scolds me for it.'

'It was right this time.' He was looking at her wonderingly.

65

She gazed down at her hands and the marks on her dress. She grimaced. 'I should change my dress,' she said.

'Not yet,' he begged.

'Not yet?' she echoed. 'Then I must not let any see me, for if I am seen in this condition I shall be reprimanded.'

'Antoinette . . .' he said. 'You . . . you are happy here?'

'That is what they all ask me,' she told him. 'Yes, I am happy. But France is not what I thought it. I thought we should have balls and parties every night. But what happens? I get up at half past nine or ten, dress and say my prayers. Then I have my hair dressed. Then it is time for church, and we go to Mass. We have our dinner while we are watched by the people, but we all eat very quickly and that is soon over. Then I retire to my room, where I do needlework. Then the Abbé comes and I have lessons. In the evening I play cards with the aunts. Then we wait for the King, and spend a little time with him. Then to bed. And that is all. It is dull; it is sober. It is not very different from life in Vienna.'

'You have not seen Paris,' he said. 'There is much gaiety in Paris.'

'Why can I not see Paris? I long to see Paris.'

'It must be arranged one day.'

She stamped her foot impatiently. 'But I want it now . . . now.'

'You could not go without the consent of the King.'

'Then can we not get the King's consent?'

'The aunts are against his giving it.'

'The aunts! But why?'

'They think you are too young.'

'But he does not care for their opinions.'

The Dauphin looked uncomfortable. He was silent for some

seconds, then he said: 'Antoinette . . . did you . . . did your mother . . . talk to you before you came to France?'

'She talked to me continually. She writes to me continually. She tells me all I ought to do. If I wish to know anything, I am to write to her. It is to be as though she is still with me.'

'Did she . . . talk to you about . . . us . . . about our marriage . . . about what you must do . . . what you must expect?'

'Oh, yes. She said I must have children . . . and soon . . . because that is what is expected of the Dauphine of France.'

A look of furtive horror crept slowly across his face. Antoinette went close to him and looking up at him whispered: 'You *do* like me, do you not, Berry?'

'Yes,' said Berry, staring unhappily at the half-finished wall. 'I like you very much.'

She had darted to the door suddenly and opened it.

Standing outside it was a man. He bowed, looking decidedly uncomfortable to be caught thus.

Antoinette said imperiously: 'Who is this, Berry?'

'Why . . .' stammered the Dauphin, 'it is Monsieur de la Vauguyon. Did you wish to see me?'

'I wondered, sir, how the work was progressing.'

'It progresses well, but there has been a little accident and we have decided that it shall be finished for the day.'

'I do not think, Monsieur de la Vauguyon,' said Antoinette, 'that we need your presence here. Though I would rather see you stand before us than outside our closed door.'

The man looked startled, the Dauphin confused; but after a short hesitation Monsieur de la Vauguyon bowed again and went away.

Antoinette turned to her husband. 'He was listening at the door. Did you know that?'

The Dauphin's slow nod told her that he thought this was possible.

'Why did you not show your anger?'

'He is my tutor.'

'That gives him no right to listen at doors. Does it?'

'No . . . it does not.'

'Then we are in agreement that this Monsieur de la Vauguyon is an insolent man.'

'He . . . he is my tutor,' reiterated the Dauphin.

Antoinette looked at him quizzically; and at that moment a tenderness was born within her for the young man she had married.

He was so shy, afraid of many things. It is due to his grandfather's shutting him away from affairs, she decided; it is due to his always referring to him as Poor Berry; and it must also be due in some way to that odious Monsieur de la Vauguyon who listens at doors.

She was fierce in her hates and loves. She was now ready to love the shy Dauphin and hate all those who had been responsible for making him afraid – of what, she was not quite sure.

❖ ❖ ❖

It was two years since the marriage of Marie Antoinette, and still she lived the quiet life in the Palace of Versailles; still she had not visited the Capital.

Her life was set in a certain pattern, governed by Madame de Noailles, her chief lady-in-waiting, whose one great passion in life was the observance of convention. Madame Etiquette infuriated the girl and made her determined to act in an unconventional manner whenever possible.

Letters came regularly from her mother. Maria Theresa was

watching over her daughter's career from afar. The Comte de Mercy-Argenteau, ambassador from Maria Theresa to the French Court, regarded it as one of his most urgent duties to spy upon the girl and report to her mother every trivial detail of her daily life. Antoinette was aware that she was under constant surveillance for often would come a reprimand, a word of advice concerning some little incident which she had not realised had been noticed by anyone.

Each morning she must go to Mass, must visit the aunts in the company of her husband; she must keep up a regular correspondence with her mother. She was embroidering a waistcoat for the King, which she feared would take her years to complete as she hated sitting still very long with her needle; she would have liked to run and romp in the gardens with her dogs, but Madame Etiquette was always at her elbow admonishing her. 'Madame la Dauphine, but it is not for a lady of your position to do this, to do that . . . '

She must not play with the bedchamber woman's children. Antoinette was sorry for that; she loved children and had in fact engaged the woman on account of her children, and it had been such a pleasure to encourage high spirits. She could not bring all her dogs into the apartment, for some were not too clean in their habits. 'Madame la Dauphine, it is not possible for a lady in your position . . . What a weary round it could be! Curtsying as she walked soberly in the gardens – a bright smile for a Duchess because she had royal blood in her veins, a haughty nod for a humbler personage; and of course she must learn to look at some people as though they did not exist.

'You must do this; you must do that.' There were injunctions from every side. She enjoyed riding; but Mercy wrote to her mother regarding the dangers of riding for one so young. It was said that riding spoiled the complexion and added to the weight. The impulsive young Dauphine had appealed to her husband for permission to ride. He had hesitated. It was not, he explained in his laborious way, that he wished to curtail her pleasure; it was merely that he hesitated to go against the wishes of her mother. 'Then,' she said, 'if others agreed to let me ride, would you?' He admitted that he would; and she construed that as his consent.

When she was next with the King she asked him to give his consent to her riding, and as Louis hated to refuse pretty young girls anything, and never did so when what they asked could be given at no cost to himself, he agreed that she might ride when she wished.

But still Maria Theresa protested. She had heard that beauty was of great importance at the Court of France and, through Mercy, she forbade her daughter to ride anything but the quietest donkey.

Such had been the power of Maria Theresa over her daughter's youth that Antoinette could not escape from it after two years' absence.

She rode her donkey and on one occasion, when she fell from it and all those who were with her rushed to her aid, she sat on the grass and declared: 'You must not touch me. You must leave me here on the ground while we wait for Madame de Noailles who will show you the right way in which to pick up a Dauphine who has tumbled off a donkey.'

It was quite clear from the very beginning that the young Dauphine was one who would not take kindly to the enforcement of authority and conventions.

She rebelled against squeezing her slender young body into the *corps de baleine* – so necessary, it was said, to preserve a graceful figure; and it was only after much remonstrance in her mother's letters that she submitted to this mild torture.

News went to Maria Theresa, through Mercy, that her daughter had slighted certain noblemen of German nationality who were visiting the Court. 'I pray you,' wrote Maria Theresa, 'do not be ashamed of being German. You show this shame by your *gaucherie* towards Germans. German blood is in your veins, and you must accept and be proud of it.'

She was a source of great anxiety to her mother and of some amusement to the Court. She was an impulsive wayward girl who acted often in a most unexpected manner. Her goodness of heart was always ready to lead her into trouble. When she had been hunting with the royal party, and a peasant had been wounded by a stag, she had hurried to his rescue and, to the shocked amusement of all, insisted on driving him to his cottage in her coach. One day one of her postilions was hurt, and it was she who sent for the physician and stayed beside the postilion, soothing him until help arrived.

The people heard these stories, and they said: 'She is charming, this little Dauphine. It will be a happy day when she is Queen of France.'

But there arose some matters which were of a more serious nature, and into which she plunged in her impulsive way.

When she arrived at Versailles there were two opposing parties at Court. One was headed by the Duc de Choiseul, who was the King's minister-in-chief, the other by the Duc d'Aiguillon who aspired to that office. Choiseul, although by no means handsome, was a man of great charm, and because he had arranged the Dauphin's marriage he set himself out to be particularly charming to the Dauphin's wife. Choiseul had refused to submit to the dominion of Madame du Barry, and she had long ago decided to end his career. The King was lazy; Choiseul's enemies grew in number. The Abbé Terray, an unscrupulous man, allied himself to the Duc d'Aiguillon, and both these men aided by du Barry set out to bring about the overthrow of Choiseul.

Antoinette, who was without advisers at Court (for the Dauphin never allowed himself to become part of political quarrels), was in the hands of the three malevolent aunts, who, for strange reasons which had grown in the unbalanced mind of Tante Adelaide, were determined to be the enemies of the Dauphine. The three aunts, who hated Madame du Barry, found great pleasure in setting the young wife of the Dauphin against the woman who enjoyed most of the privileges which should have been accorded a Queen.

The aunts dominated Antoinette at this time of her life, for she was forced to spend much time in their company. They were determined – since the King despised them, and Madame du Barry was indifferent to them – to mould the future of the girl who must one day be Queen.

They would talk to her as they sat together playing cards or sewing. They asked question about herself and the Dauphin and made allusions to Madame du Barry concerning the life she led with the King.

Thus they set her on the side of Choiseul, although she knew nothing of the politics of France; and when, under pressure from his mistress, the King at length dismissed Choiseul, she was angry not with the King but with the woman who, so the aunts told her, through her wickedness ruled all France.

So here she was, after such a short time in France, and still an unworldly child, dabbling lightheartedly in the politics of her adopted country.

The other matter which was becoming increasingly clear to her, and which was now beginning to cause her acute embarrassment, was the impotence of the Dauphin.

When she had come to the Court of France she had been both ignorant and innocent. That Court which was ruled over by her mother had been free of scandal, for Maria Theresa had set the tone, and none dared change it.

It was very disturbing for a woman of Maria Theresa's principles to contemplate her daughter at Versailles where the King not only lived openly with his mistress, who was treated as Queen of France, but amused himself with the young girls provided for him by that mistress. There were times, Maria Theresa was constantly reminding herself, when a woman must remember that she was first a great ruler, and only after that a mother.

She knew her daughter well. Marie Antoinette was light of heart and had from early childhood turned away impatiently from anything that threatened to disturb her pleasure; she rarely read a book from beginning to end, for she tired so quickly of any serious thought, and this must necessarily mean that her knowledge of men and women was superficial. She would improve of course, insisted the apprehensive mother, but she must be carefully watched.

It was brought to the ears of Maria Theresa that her frivolous little daughter was not only riding out on her donkey and when she was some distance from the Palace changing her mount to that of a horse which those wicked old aunts had provided for her, but that she was openly slighting Madame du Barry.

This called for a carefully worded reprimand. She must, wrote the Empress, restrain her feelings; she must be gracious towards a lady whose mission, so the Empress had heard, was to please the King and keep him amused.

Antoinette betrayed her complete innocence in her reply. The King was kind to her, she said. She was fond of him. And as it was Madame du Barry's mission to please and amuse him, she hoped to be her rival.

Such letters filled the Empress with the utmost apprehension, and in consternation she wrote to Mercy, who replied that he had heard rumours concerning the Dauphin.

Now sly questions were asked of Antoinette. Sly hints were given her.

In her irresponsible way she asked of her husband: 'Should we not soon have an heir? I think it is expected of us. I am sometimes asked questions . . .'

The Dauphin was alarmed. He tried to explain.

And so gradually Marie Antoinette began to understand and to dread that moment when the curtains were drawn about their bed. She did not dread it any less because she knew the Dauphin hated it as much as she did.

They must do their best, he said.

But their best had never succeeded.

Rumours circulated through the Palace of Versailles. Antoinette did not know it yet, but the relations between the Dauphin and his wife were made the subjects of jokes in the streets of Paris.

The letters from Vienna took on a more urgent note. Antoinette must tell her mother *all*. She must hold nothing back.

Antoinette was faintly unhappy now. Provence and Artois gave her secret, amused and pitying looks. She became obsessed with the desire for a child, and when she saw any child in the Palace she would immediately call it to her and play with it, and try to pretend it was her own.

She was no longer innocent. She knew why these people smiled behind her back and whispered about her and the Dauphin. She knew why she failed to have a child.

And because she saw Madame du Barry in her comfortable relationship with the King, because she had heard stories of the frolics in the Parc aux Cerfs, because she knew with what pleasure the most notorious courtesan of France shared the King's bed, she began to hate the woman with a fierce anger which she did not realise was due to the fact that every time she saw her she was reminded of her own unhappy position.

She was plunging gaily into the pleasures of Versailles and, as she was now sixteen, she refused to obey Madame de Noailles so rigidly. She would do anything to escape those shameful fumblings in the nuptial bed which never achieved their object. She danced each night, for dancing was her favourite pastime, and by dancing she could postpone that moment when she must hear the curtains drawn, shutting her in with the Dauphin. The Dauphin did not dance. He was spending more and more time in his blacksmith's shop. He liked to work the bellows and tire himself out, so that by the time she came to bed he was fast asleep.

In the morning they would look at each other and utter feigned apologies, though both knew that they were con-gratulating each other on that night's respite. But the guilty feeling persisted, for they were both aware that, as future King and Queen of France, it was their duty to beget children, and the begetting of children could not be done in any other way but this, which they so loathed because it was beyond the Dauphin's power to accomplish it.

And so, humiliated, bewildered, half child and half awakened woman, Antoinette came to loathe the sight of the flamboyant painted woman who symbolised the fulfilment of all that she and the Dauphin were vainly trying to attain.

It soon began to be noticed that the Dauphine was putting Madame du Barry in a very unfortunate and unpleasant position; for she refused to address the woman and, according to Court etiquette, a woman of lesser rank must not speak in the company of a lady of higher rank unless she was invited to do so by that lady. Urged by the aunts, Antoinette had decided that she would ignore Madame du Barry and, as the Dauphine was the first lady of the Court since the King's wife was dead, Madame du Barry, who was in all but name the ruler of the Court, must sit mum among the ladies because the impertinent girl of sixteen refused to give that lead which would allow her to join in the conversation.

The Court was enchanted with its little Dauphine. She was providing drama. There were bets as to when the Dauphin would overcome his infirmity; and bets as to how long the little Dauphine would be able to flout the du Barry.

Du Barry stormed into the King's apartments. She was by nature easy-going, but this situation, which had been created by that impertinent child who was determined to humiliate her, was becoming unendurable. People were seen to be laughing behind their fans. How was it possible for her – the most influential woman at Court – to be forced night after night to sit silent because the sixteen-year-old Dauphine refused to address a word to her?

'Something must be done,' she told the King.

'My dear, we cannot alter the rules of the Court.'

'No, my dear France, but we can alter the impertinence of Madame la Dauphine.'

'I hope,' murmured the King, 'that she is not going to prove herself a little trouble-maker.'

'She has already proved herself to be that.'

He looked at his mistress. He was very fond of her. He depended on her. She might have sprung from the people, but she was a clever woman and he took her advice on many matters. He would never forget how, at the time when he had had trouble with his magistrates and he had felt an inclination to govern without a parliament, it was Madame du Barry – no doubt on advice from the more astute of her friends – who had advised him against taking this course. He could visualise her now, standing before the picture she had set up in her apartments – a picture of Charles I of England, painted by Van Dyck. He would never forget how her eyes had flashed as she had cried: 'France, your parliament could cut off *your* head too.' She had so impressed him that he had capitulated; and she had been right. He sometimes wondered what might have happened had he not taken the advice of du Barry at that time.

It was therefore inconceivable and intolerable that she should be perpetually snubbed by the little Dauphine. Moreover, in slighting the King's mistress, the girl was slighting the King.

'My dear,' he said, 'this shall not go on. I myself will speak to her *gouvernante*.'

'That is Madame de Noailles. I will send for the woman, that you may speak to her at once.'

Madame de Noailles stood before the King.

In accordance with custom Louis did not go straight to the point.

'It is a great pleasure for us,' he said, 'to have Madame la Dauphine with us here. She would appear to be a young lady of much distinction and charm.'

Madame de Noailles bowed her head in apparent pleasure, but she was uneasy, for she knew that the King would not have sent for her merely to compliment the Dauphine through her.

'She is young,' went on the King, 'and youth is so charming . . . Who does not love youth? A little impetuous perhaps . . . but who of us in our youth has not been impetuous? However, impetuosity should have its limits.'

Madame de Noailles' expression was one of horror. Her charge had failed to please the King, and she held herself responsible.

'Our little Dauphine,' went on Louis, 'talks a little too freely, and she is perhaps not always as gracious as she might be to certain members of the Court; and such behaviour could have a bad effect on family life.'

The King's meaning was obvious.

Madame de Noailles assured His Majesty that she would do all in her power to correct the faults of the Dauphine.

She went at once to Antoinette.

'Madame,' she cried, for once forgetting the usual routine, 'you must speak to Madame du Barry this very night. Those are the King's orders.'

'Madame du Barry is a courtesan,' retorted the Dauphine. 'I cannot believe that the etiquette of the Court of France demands that the first lady of the Court should chat with such.'

With that she left Madame Noailles and went straight to the aunts.

Madame Adelaide chuckled with glee. 'You are right, my dear,' she told her. 'Be bold in this. All – even the King – will respect you for it.'

Aunts Victoire and Sophie nodded agreement.

But when the Abbé de Vermond passed the news of the King's reprimand on to Mercy, and Mercy in his turn passed it on to the Empress, there was grave concern; for Maria Theresa knew that out of such petty storms could grow big ones.

Maria Theresa was in a quandary. A woman of stern moral principles, she could not insist on her daughter's making friends with a woman as notorious as Madame du Barry; yet since it was the wish of the King of France that the Dauphine should do so, clearly some compromise was needed. Maria Theresa's son Joseph was now the Emperor and co-ruler of Austria, and she and he did not always agree. She was for ever wary of Catherine of Russia and Frederick of Prussia, both of whom she regarded in the light of formidable enemies.

Frederick and Catherine were determined on the partition of Poland; Joseph wished to join these two and support the partition; and Maria Theresa, who had always tried to live as a good woman as well as good ruler, was deeply disturbed. The partition of Poland was a cruel move – yet if she attempted to prevent it there might be war, and Austria was in no position to engage in war against Prussia and Russia. And now her daughter, whom she had brought up to share her principles, was registering her disapproval of a courtesan – which her mother should have applauded if her upbringing meant anything. Now here was the painful task of commanding the girl to accept this woman because it was expedient to do so.

Maria Theresa felt that she could not in person command her daughter to do this, so she ordered Kaunitz to write to Mercy that it might be arranged through the Ambassador.

❖ ❖ ❖

There was long argument. Antoinette declared that she could not be expected, after refusing to speak to Madame du Barry, to be the one to capitulate. Mercy said she must be. This was not an idle quarrel between two women; it was a matter of politics. Did she wish to upset the friendly relations between France and Austria because of a whim?

'My mother would not wish me to speak to a woman like her,' she insisted.

Mercy grew exasperated. The trouble with the Dauphine was that she never seemed to keep her mind on one thing for long. While he was trying to impress upon her the importance of speaking to the du Barry she was wondering what she would wear at the card party that night.

'I must impress upon you,' said Mercy, 'that your mother commands you to speak to Madame du Barry to-night. I have arranged it so that it will not be awkward for you. After the card party you will make your rounds of the room, speaking to every one. I shall be engaged in conversation with Madame du Barry, and when you reach us you will say something to me and then turn naturally to Madame du Barry.'

'And these are my mother's orders?'

'Not only your mother's, Madame, but those of the King of France.'

Antoinette bowed her head.

When she had left Mercy, a messenger came to her and asked her if she would visit the aunts. They clustered about her, their faces flushed, their eyes gleaming with their love of intrigue.

'What are they trying to force you to, my dear?' asked Aunt Adelaide.

She told them.

The aunts exchanged glances, and Victoire and Sophie waited on their sister's next move.

'To-night,' said Antoinette, 'I am to speak to her. Mercy will be with her, and I speak to him first and then naturally to the du Barry. These are my mother's orders and the orders of the King.'

Adelaide made a clucking noise and the others immediately did the same.

'A young and innocent girl,' murmured Adelaide; and her eyes were alight with mischief.

✤ ✤ ✤

Mercy had taken his place beside the Comtesse du Barry. They were talking lightly.

The Dauphine had risen from the card-table and was making the rounds of the room before retiring.

Each lady made the expected curtsy and answered her when she spoke to her. Everyone was tense. Here was the great moment for which they had all been waiting. Madame du Barry had won, as of course everyone had guessed she would. The Dauphine must publicly acknowledge the King's mistress.

Now Antoinette was close to Mercy and Madame du Barry. Antoinette was aware of the du Barry's taut expression – half apprehensive, half triumphant. This incident would proclaim her power more definitely than anything that had happened before.

But as Antoinette was pausing in front of Mercy, and Mercy was preparing to make his deep bow, Madame Adelaide had glided to the Dauphine's side with Victoire and Sophie close behind her.

Adelaide took on the commanding voice of an aunt, and said: 'Come, my dear, it is time we left. The King is waiting to see you in Victoire's room.'

As Antoinette turned away, a slow flush rose to Mercy's face, and Madame du Barry was suddenly scarlet with mortification.

There was a deep silence throughout the salon as Madame Adelaide triumphantly led the Dauphine away, with Victoire and Sophie tripping behind her.

✤ ✤ ✤

The whole of Versailles was talking of this added insult given by the Dauphine to Madame du Barry. The aunts enjoyed their secret satisfaction. Adelaide talked to her sisters at great length, showing them what a clever diplomatist *she* was. Had she not successfully kept the Dauphine from going to Paris? It was two years since she had come to France, and she had not yet visited the Capital. All France knew that the Dauphin's wife was looked upon as a child, and of no importance. And after to-night all France would know that the King's mistress was of no importance either.

'This,' said Madame Adelaide, 'is diplomacy of the first order. Our father will learn that he cannot flout his daughters. Let him laugh at us. Let him call us Loque, Coche and Graille. Let him insult us. We can make him as uncomfortable as does our sister Louise who is constantly warning him that he is destined for hell-fire.'

'And now,' said Victoire, 'Madame du Barry will hate the Dauphine.'

'Trouble, trouble, trouble . . .' murmured Adelaide gaily. 'The Dauphine flouts du Barry, and du Barry hates the Dauphine . . . and that Austrian Mercy consults with Abbé de Vermond, and the treaty of friendship between France and Austria is likely to be broken! Who knows, there may be war, and *we* may have brought it about!'

Victoire and Sophie looked at each other with wonder, but their eyes went almost immediately to Adelaide, their leader and the inspiration of all their venturings.

But Madame du Barry was in a rage, and she had inspired the King to share that rage.

'We have been deliberately flouted and insulted,' she declared. 'The whole Court laughs at us.'

The King sent for Mercy.

'Your efforts with the Dauphine have been futile,' he said. 'And it would seem that her mother ignores my requests. It appears that this supposed friendship between our two countries is an illusion. The Empress must know that France cannot be treated as a vassal state.'

Mercy was shaken. He saw in this a deep political threat. He implored the King's forbearance and hastily sent a despatch to the Empress, warning her that owing to her daughter's childish folly the Austro-French alliance, which had been forged by the marriage, was in danger of cracking.

Maria Theresa knew now that she could not stand aside. Much against her principles she had been forced to agree to the partition of Poland and, as she had always been afraid of French reaction to this, she was terrified now that the anger of the King of France might so be whipped up against her that he would declare war over the Polish problem. She must placate him. She must make her daughter understand that war with France would be disastrous, since Austria was in no position to go to war. Therefore on the pious Maria Theresa's shoulders fell the task of commanding her daughter to make friends with the most notorious courtesan in Europe; and Maria Theresa greatly feared the effect of this on her daughter's young mind.

She wrote Antoinette: 'What a pother about saying Good-day to someone – a kindly word concerning a dress or some such trumpery. After your conversation with Mercy, and after what he told you about the King's wishes, you actually dared fail him! What reason is there for such conduct? None whatever. It does not become you to regard the du Barry in any other light than that of a lady who has the right of entry to the Court and is admitted to the society of the King. You are His Majesty's first subject, and you owe him obedience and submission. If any baseness or intimacy were asked of you, neither I nor any other would advise you to it; but all that is expected is that you should say an indifferent word, should look at her beseemingly – not for the lady's own sake, but for the sake of your grandfather, your master, your benefactor.'

As soon as she read this letter Antoinette knew that her mother was insisting on her obedience.

It was New Year's Day and the Court was assembled to watch the final victory of Madame du Barry over the Dauphine.

Antoinette stood formally while the ladies of the Court passed before her to accept her New Year greetings and to give theirs.

The Duchess of d'Aiguillon, who was the wife of the chief

minister of state and a protégé of du Barry, was with the Comtesse, and the whole assembly was acutely conscious of the fact that the space between the two protagonists in the battle was growing less and less.

Madame du Barry stood before her. Antoinette's whole nature rose in revolt. Her expression hardened for a moment; she was aware that every eye was upon her and du Barry; she was deeply conscious of the silence which had fallen.

She wanted to turn away, but she dared not. She could visualise the stern eyes of her mother.

She looked at du Barry and murmured: 'Il y a bien du monde aujourd'hui à Versailles.'

Du Barry's good nature bubbled to the surface. The wilful girl had spoken the necessary words. All that the Comtesse had fought for was won. She knew what it had cost the girl, and she was not vindictive in victory. All she wanted to do now was to savour her triumph; then she was ready to soothe the Dauphine in her humiliation.

She sparkled with good humour. She declared, Yes, there were a great many people at Versailles to-day.

The Dauphine was already giving her New Year greetings to the next person.

Du Barry's waiting-woman begged to see the Dauphine.

Antoinette received the woman coolly, her blue eyes wide open as though she were wondering what Madame du Barry's woman could possibly have to propose to her.

'I have come to speak to you on behalf of my mistress, Madame,' said the woman. 'It has come to her ears that Boehmer, the jeweller, has a pair of diamond earrings the value of which is seven hundred livres.'

Antoinette nodded gravely. She had seen these earrings. They were the most beautiful that had ever come her way. She had tried them on and they had suited her to perfection. Diamonds were her favourite stones; their cold brilliance accorded well with her warm and youthful beauty.

'What of these earrings?' she asked.

'My mistress thinks that they would become you well, Madame. She thinks that she might prevail upon His Majesty to give them to you.'

Antoinette was torn between her desire for the earrings and her determination not to accept favours from the woman she had for so long fought against acknowledging.

She knew that, if she showed interest, the earrings would be hers; and she longed for them.

But she turned to the woman and said: 'Your mistress's proposal does not interest me. Indeed it seems to me quite sordid. If I wish for earrings I shall not ask a courtesan to sell her favours in order to buy them for me.'

'But, Madame . . .'

'Your presence here is no longer necessary,' said the Dauphine.

And the next time she saw Madame du Barry she looked through her as though she did not exist.

The Court was amused. It was of little consequence now. She had acknowledged the du Barry and the du Barry was satisfied.

The aunts tittered.

'Antoinette is but a girl,' said Adelaide to Victoire and Sophie, 'and when she is Queen we shall know how to manage her.'

❧ Chapter III ❧

THE DAUPHINE IN PARIS

Marie Antoinette had one great desire – to go to Paris. Was it not time she went? she asked Madame de Noailles. When she went to Paris, she was told, it must be done according to tradition; the city must be made ready to welcome her for it would be a state occasion.

And still she remained at Versailles, with the spies about her – her mother's spies, the Abbé de Vermond and Mercy-Argenteau, and the spies of the aunts, headed by the Comtesse de Narbonne who loved drama so much that when it did not occur she invented it.

Then there was Madame de Noailles, always watching lest she should commit some breach which called for immediate reproach and the mending of her ways.

New enemies were introduced to Versailles. The Comtes de Provence and d'Artois had been provided with wives. These were the daughters of Victor Amédée III of Sardinia. Victor Amédée ruled not only over Sardinia but also over a rich part of Northern Italy, and the marriages were considered worthy of his grandsons by Louis Quinze who even tried to marry

Clothilde to Victor Amédée's son; but Clothilde was considered too fat for the alliance. The King of Sardinia declared that he believed fat women were frequently unable to bear children.

The marriages of the two young men were concluded and when their brides arrived at Versailles, Provence and Artois were shocked by their unattractiveness. Having seen the enchanting Austrian Archduchess they had expected their wives to be equally charming. Provence compared his Marie Josèphe and Artois his Marie Thérèse with the dainty Marie Antoinette who was growing more lovely every day.

Was it fair, they demanded of each other, that they should have such ugly brides while Berry, who cared more for his blacksmith's shop than his marriage, and was impotent in any case, should have the lovely Antoinette?

Antoinette was too young to do anything but laugh at them and preen herself a little, taking more pains than ever to look charming in the eyes of the two disgruntled brothers. This made them furious with her, and their wives even more furious.

The three aunts looked on and laughed together.

It was a good thing, said Adelaide, that there were so many in this royal house who were inclined to regard the frivolous young Dauphine with distrust.

We must see, declared Adelaide, that when Berry is King she does not have too much influence with him.

Her sisters as usual nodded. And it became their custom to have Josèphe and Thérèse to play cards with them; and they would all sit together – three old witches talking secrets with two jealous girls, and the subject of their conversations was invariably the many imperfections of Antoinette.

It was so dull at Versailles that Antoinette decided that she would speak to the King about going to Paris, and seized the first opportunity.

Angry as he might be with her when she was not present, Louis could feel no rancour towards her when she was near him. He thought her so pretty. He wished she were not the wife of his grandson, that he might seduce her. He thought of poor Berry who was impotent. It made him angry.

'And how are you, my dear, this day?' he asked her.

She smiled at him, aware of his admiration and liking it – rather disgusting old man that he was – because people noted it and smiled at it; moreover it displeased Madame du Barry.

'Very happy to be near Your Majesty.'

Louis leered. 'Then come nearer still and be happier yet.'

He took her hand and brought his old face near her young and smooth one.

'You are the loveliest Dauphine France ever had,' he declared. 'And you will be her loveliest Queen.'

She drew back in horror. 'That will be a long, long time away.'

'I know not,' said Louis; and he frowned, forgetting her for a moment. He was feeling far from well, and Madame Louise, his Carmelite daughter, had written him a long exhortation to repent. Louis was constantly looking over his shoulder for death, warding off the dread visitor, not so much because he feared the pain death might bring, but the repentance which must precede it. He was afraid that he would have to send du Barry away before he could begin that repentance, and he hated the thought. And now this girl, by her very loveliness and glowing youth, reminded him of death.

'Yes, it is so,' she cried with such conviction that he must believe her. 'Your Majesty looks younger with each day. I tell my mother that I believe you have discovered the secret of living for ever.'

'You not only know how to look pretty but how to say pretty things, Madame la Dauphine. When ladies say such things to me I wonder if they are about to ask for something.'

She looked at him archly. 'There was a request, Your Majesty, but if you refuse it, I will still say that you look younger every day.'

'Then it would indeed be churlish of me to refuse it.'

'It is such a simple little request. I have been here more than two years, and I have never been to Paris.'

'So Paris has been denied the pleasure of seeing you for so long?'

'It is so,' she told him.

'Poor Paris! I'll tell you who is to blame. It is those three old witches: Loque, Coche and Graille.'

Antoinette laughed gaily. 'Your Majesty, may we outwit the witches?'

'There is no other course open to us, if their wishes do not coincide with those of my beautiful Dauphine.'

'So it is to be to Paris! When, Your Majesty?'

'You go too fast. These things must be arranged. But go you shall. Now you may kiss your old grandfather for being so good to you. Nay, not my hand. That's for the witches. Come . . . kiss me as though I am the young man I could wish to be.'

Lightly she kissed his cheek; and he watched her as she moved away. He was regretful for his lost youth, and when he thought of her with his grandson his lips curled.

'Poor Berry!' he murmured.

She insisted that the young members of the family should all come to her apartment. There was Berry, reluctant, the grime of the blacksmith's shop under his nails; there were Provence and Artois with their two jealous wives.

'We are to go to Paris,' she announced. 'I have the King's consent. Berry and I are to make our formal entry.'

The eyes of Josèphe and Thérèse glittered with envy. During the formal entry all eyes would be on the Dauphine, the future Queen of France; *they* would be pointed out merely as the wives of the Dauphin's brothers. Worse than that, those Parisians would compare their lack of beauty with the Dauphine's glowing charms. It was quite unfair.

Now she had a mad plan. Why should they wait for the formal entry? The King had given his consent, so why should they not all go into Paris, disguised – masked, say, in fancy dress ?

'Please come,' she cried. 'It would be so exciting. When we make the formal entry there is one who will ride with us every minute of the day and night – Etiquette.' She grimaced. 'How I hate Etiquette! What fun to *do* exactly what we like. To *say* exactly what we like. To go to the Opéra ball . . .'

She seized Artois and made him dance with her. He smiled with pleasure, for he enjoyed taking her in his arms before them all. Thérèse watched them with smouldering eyes. Let her, thought Artois. Serve her right for being full and heavy, for not being pretty and dainty and gay and eager to do reckless things; serve her right for not being Antoinette.

'Yes,' said Artois, 'let us all go . . . *masked*. It will only take us just over an hour to reach Paris in our carriages. I will have them made ready. No one will guess who we are . . .'

Berry shook his head. 'No . . .' he began.

But Antoinette had run to him and seized his arm. 'But you must come . . . you must. There must be three ladies, three gentlemen . . . Oh, Berry, you must . . . you must indeed. I insist.'

He looked down at the charming eager face. He felt he wanted to please her, he wanted to make up for those shameful and uncomfortable nightly experiences for which he was solely to blame.

'I do not think we should,' he said.

'Nor I,' said Josèphe.

But Artois and Provence decided that they would; and with Antoinette they persuaded the others.

As a result, one bright and starry night, the carriages were brought to a side door, and the excited party made the short joumey between Versailles and the Capital.

During that midnight adventure, Antoinette saw the city in moonlight; saw the gleaming river and the great buildings – the Bastille, the Invalides, the Hôtel de Ville, the cafés along the Quai des Tuileries and Notre Dame.

This, the Dauphin explained, was the route the procession would take when they made their formal entry.

But what excited Antoinette was the fact that the city seemed full of life even at this late hour. There were people in the streets . . . women, men, noisy people, people who, it seemed, would never be disturbed by that grim bogey, Etiquette. How different was Paris from the town of Versailles with its Place d'Armes and the Church of Notre Dame on one side and the Church of St Louis on the other, and the avenues de Sceaux, de Paris and de St Cloud which, apart from the château, seemed to make up the town.

This was a glorious city, a city of wide and narrow streets, of splendour and squalor, of contrasts and a thousand delights, where anything might happen.

She persuaded them to stop the carriages that they might visit the Opéra ball. Berry was very much against this, but Antoinette was firm. They had come so far. Were they going to spoil the adventure because they were afraid to carry it to its conclusion?

Artois agreed with her. Provence was half-hearted; and as Berry rarely expressed any great desire or any great disinclination to do anything, they went to the ball.

The glitter of that ball completely enchanted Antoinette. She was amazed that Versailles had nothing as exciting to offer. Here were glittering jewels and gorgeously attired men and women; but they were exciting people, hiding behind their masks. Here, decided Antoinette, was excitement and adventure.

She danced with Artois. Many eyes were on her; for she was like a dainty Sèvres ornament come to life. She was laughing behind her mask, wondering what these people would think if they knew that the girl dancing so merrily among them was their Dauphine.

Berry was nervous, eager to be gone; and eventually he managed to instil the same anxiety in his brothers.

They left the Opéra ball and drove back to Versailles.

Few people at the Palace knew of their adventure and, as they were up early for the next morning's Mass, it was undiscovered.

But Antoinette felt that nothing in her life could ever be quite the same again. She was in love – in love with Paris.

It was a hot June day when the royal procession entered the Capital.

At the gates of Paris the old Governor of the City, the Duc de Brissac, waited to welcome the Dauphin and his wife and to present them with the keys of the city.

The old man's eyes were appreciative as they rested on the flushed and lovely young Dauphine. She smiled at him as Berry laid his hands on the keys which were being presented to him on a velvet cushion. What would the Duc think, wondered Antoinette, if he knew she had visited his city in secret a few nights before?

But Paris was more enchanting than ever in sunlight. Great triumphal arches had been put up, and flowers decked the streets.

The market women had come from their stalls in the Halles to cheer her. The merchants of St Germain and St Antoine called a greeting; and guns were fired from the Hotel de Ville, the Invalides and the Bastille. The Place du Carrousel was bright with flowers and arches made of cloth of gold and purple velvet, decorated with the golden lilies of France. The bridge over the Seine looked as though it were one seething mass of people, all cheering, all calling *'Vive le Dauphin! Vive la Dauphine!'*

At last they were standing on the balcony of the Tuileries, and again and again the crowds shouted a welcome. Antoinette had never seen so many people, and tears filled her eyes at the expression of such loyalty; for tears, like smiles and sudden anger, came quickly to Antoinette and quickly passed.

'Mon Dieu!' she cried out with emotion. *'Que de monde!'*

The Duc de Brissac came closer to her and whispered: 'Madame, I trust His Highness the Dauphin will not take it amiss, but you have before you two hundred thousand people – the people of Paris – and they have all fallen in love with you.'

She stood there smiling, happy, enchanted. She had fallen in love with Paris, so it was meet and fitting that Paris should have fallen in love with her.

❖ ❖ ❖

Every night she wished now to make the journey from Versailles to Paris. There was so much in the city to delight her; so many reasons why she had no wish to remain in Versailles. She had come to hate the aunts, with their continual backbiting, and she understood at last that they had never been her friends. It was pleasant to escape from the watchful eyes of Madame de Noailles and the ever-intruding ones of de Vermond and Mercy. She liked to dance until the early hours of morning, to attend the card parties, the Comédie Française and the Comédie Italienne; she liked to attend the Opéra; but delightful as she found these occasions, what seemed most important was to avoid returning early to bed.

The Dauphin did not care for these gaieties; he was tolerant and he made no effort to interfere; but after a hard day's work in his blacksmith's shop or in the open air he would want to retire early. Therefore, though they must share the same bed, there were ways of not spending many of the same hours in it, and she would creep in at an early hour of the morning when he was fast asleep.

Often her brothers-in-law would accompany her to Paris. The King rarely went. He was unpopular in Paris, and Paris did not hesitate to declare its dislike. There had been a great deal of trouble throughout the country owing to disaster in foreign affairs, bad harvests, and increased taxation. Louis was afraid that if he passed through the streets of his Capital he might meet not only hostile words, but actions. Some years before he had had a road built from Versailles, so that he could reach Compiègne without passing through Paris.

Antoinette soon discovered that the King's unpopularity did not apply to his family. She herself was greeted warmly wherever she went. She was so charming to the eye, and that appealed to the Parisians; her quick emotions were evident, and they had heard stories of her kindliness to poor people. Wherever she went she was cheered and admired.

This was delightful, but after a while it grew tedious, for a certain restrained behaviour was expected of her as the Dauphine. It was then that she took up the practice of going masked to Paris, and in particular to the Opéra ball.

There she and her brothers-in-law, and occasionally their wives, would dance until after midnight; and in the early morning their carriage wheels would be heard on the road from Paris to Versailles.

There was one ball which lived in her memory.

The great fun of these balls was the fact that she and members of her party roamed freely among the dancers; and it was on one of these occasions when she found herself dancing with a tall young man, masked like herself, whom she judged to be of her own age.

She was delighted with him because he was a foreigner in Paris and in love with the city even as she was.

'You are young,' he said, 'to be at such a ball unchaperoned.'

'I am not unchaperoned,' she told him.

'Then how is it . . . ?'

She laughed and said: 'Ah, Monsieur, it is a great secret.'

He said: 'Your hands are the most delicate I ever saw. And when I first saw you I thought you were a statue . . . until you moved. And when you moved I realised that I knew what true beauty was.'

She laughed. She was beginning to understand the art of flirtation, and it pleased her.

'You may not be French, Monsieur, but in your country they teach you how to pay a good compliment in French.'

'It is easy to pay compliments in your presence, Mademoiselle,' he said. 'One has but to speak the truth.'

'Tell me of yourself.'

'What is there to tell? I am passing through France while making the Grand Tour.'

'You are enjoying this Grand Tour?'

He pressed her hand more firmly. 'Can you doubt it?'

'And you love Paris?'

'To-night,' he said, 'I am in love with Paris.'

'But only to-night! It is your first night in Paris?'

'It is only to-night that I realise that Paris is the only place in the world where I want to be.'

'That is a wonderful discovery to make, Monsieur. To find that where you are is where you want to be!'

'But I am afraid that all this happiness which has suddenly come to me might pass away from me as suddenly.'

'Paris will not pass away, Monsieur.'

'You may.'

She laughed. He said: 'I must know more of you. Your name . . . what you are doing here . . . alone like this . . . so young, so exquisite. Your family should guard you better than this.'

'They guard me so well,' she said, 'that I feel the need to

97

escape on nights like this one.'

'Tell me your name. Please tell me that. What may I call you?'

'You may call me Marie.'

'Marie . . . There are many Maries, but I never heard the name sound so sweet.'

'Will you tell me yours?'

'Axel.'

'A strange name.'

'It is common enough in my country.'

'And your country is?'

'Sweden.'

'I shall remember . . . . Axel from Sweden.'

'May we meet again here to-morrow?'

'I do not think that will be possible.'

'You have another engagement? Break it, I beg of you.'

'I . . . It is with my grandfather.'

'Then you must tell him that you have arranged to meet another.'

'I could not tell my grandfather that.'

'He is despotic?'

'He expects and demands absolute obedience.'

'Odious man!'

She laughed. 'You should not say that,' she said. 'You really should not.'

'I will call any man odious who keeps you from me.'

'One would think you had known me for a long time instead of half an hour.'

'It is sometimes possible to know in the first moments of a meeting that that meeting is like no other which has ever taken place in one's life . . . nor ever will.'

'You speak with fervour, Monsieur.'

'Marie . . . *chère* Marie . . . I mean to make you agree with me that what I said is true.'

'You mean that ours is an important meeting. How can that be? To you I am Marie . . . of the Opéra ball, and you to me are Axel of Sweden.'

'Comte Hans Axel de Fersen at your service always.'

'I . . . I shall remember.'

'I have given you my confidence. You must give me yours.'

He had led her to an alcove where they were hidden from the dancers by the palms and flowers.

With a quick gesture he removed her mask. She flushed scarlet and snatched at the mask in his hand.

He had turned very pale. 'You . . . you are afraid to show your face . . . when it is the most beautiful in all Paris,' he said. 'I understand why, Madame la Dauphine.'

'You . . . you know me then?'

'I have seen the pictures of you in the shop windows.'

With trembling fingers she adjusted her mask.

He bowed stiffly. 'Madame,' he said, 'I will conduct you to your party.'

She took his arm and he led her back to where Artois and Provence were anxiously looking for her.

Fersen bowed curtly and turned away.

'Come,' cried Artois, 'we will dance together; but I do not think, Antoinette, that you should dance with others. It should be one of us.'

Josèphe and Thérèse, who were of the party, were looking at her strangely. She was aware of their looks. They see everything, she thought.

And in that moment her desire to dance left her. The only person she wished to dance with was Comte Hans Axel de Fersen.

'I am tired,' she said. 'It is time we went home.'

'Tired? You?' cried Artois.

'Do you not see,' said Josèphe, 'that something has happened to make her tired?'

'I want to go home,' said the Dauphine imperiously. 'I want to go back at once.'

And in the rumbling carriage all the way back to Versailles she thought of him, remembering each word he had said. If he had not recognised me, she told herself, when he removed my mask, he would have kissed me.

She tried to imagine what that would have been like. Of one thing she was certain; it would be quite unlike the fumbling embrace of the Dauphin.

Josèphe and Thérèse sat with the aunts.

'She insists on going into Paris often. There is scarce a night when she does not go,' Josèphe murmured.

'Paris is a wicked city,' said Victoire.

'Papa hates it,' Sophie declared. 'That is why he never goes there.'

'*She* goes there,' said Adelaide, her eyes narrowed. '*She* flaunts herself about the city, and the people come out and call her their beautiful Dauphine.' She turned to her sisters. 'The people of Paris hate Papa. They blame him for their famines and the taxes,' she continued as though she were teaching backward children their lessons. 'When the price of grain goes up they accuse Papa of hoarding it. They are very angry then.'

'Why?' asked Sophie.

'Because they cannot afford to buy bread when the price of grain is so high.'

'What a pity,' said Victoire, with sympathetic tears in her eyes, 'that they cannot be persuaded to eat pastry crust. I hate it myself, but it would be better than nothing for the people.'

Sophie nodded, but Adelaide said sharply: 'If they could not get bread they could not get pastry either. You are being foolish, Victoire, and your nieces are laughing at you.'

'Oh, dear,' said Victoire unhappily, and Josèphe and Thérèse assured her that they were not laughing; they felt nearer tears, on account of the disgraceful behaviour of their sister-in-law.

'What has she done now?' asked Adelaide eagerly.

'You know, do you not,' said Josèphe, 'that she goes disguised to Paris. Why, do you think? She goes to the ball, and there she dances with strange men. She was there last night and there was one masked man with whom she danced and with whom she disappeared for a while. She seemed most upset when she said goodbye to him.'

'So this is how the Dauphine spends her time!' said Adelaide. 'Come, my dear Josèphe, and you, my dear Thérèse, you should tell your aunts all that you know.'

They sat talking for a long time; and later they called the Sardinian Ambassador that they might tell him of the Dauphine's conduct.

He shook his head sadly and said how much happier it would be for France if the future Queen had the wisdom and prudence of *his* Princesses.

So they sat together, whispering and nodding, pretending to deplore while they delighted in what they called the *légèreté* of the Dauphine.

One April day in the year 1774 the King, who was at that beautiful house, the Petit Trianon, which he had given to Madame du Barry, felt suddenly more ill than usual.

His servant, Laborde, helped him to bed and, when Madame du Barry came to sit by his bedside, she was alarmed by his fever and his shivering fits.

Terrified she called in Lemoine, his physician, and so alarmed was Lemoine that he immediately summoned the surgeon-in-chief, La Martinière, to the King's bedside.

La Martinière examined the royal body and declared that the King must be removed immediately to the château. It was assumed from this that he believed the King to be in imminent danger, for the etiquette of the Court would be seriously hurt if its monarch died anywhere but in the royal apartments in his own Palace.

The King, while submitting to custom, was thoroughly alarmed. His condition was by no means improved by the move; the next day his fever had increased, and bleeding helped him not at all. Before that day was over it was discovered that Louis Quinze was suffering from smallpox.

The château was in a turmoil of excitement. Everyone believed that the King was too old and infirm to survive such an illness. Du Barry came hurrying to his bedside. She would nurse him, she declared. The three aunts came into the sick-room. They too would nurse him, declared Adelaide. They knew they risked infection of this most dreaded disease, but he was their father and it was their duty to remain at his bedside.

The Dauphin and the Dauphine were forbidden the sick-room. There was too much danger there for the heirs to risk death.

The King lay on his bed and knew that his last hour was not

far off, and he was filled with remorse as he had been so many times before. He thought of the country he had inherited from his great-grandfather, and he thought of the country he was leaving to his grandson.

'A not very glorious reign,' he murmured, 'though a long one.'

Then he remembered that during it the finances of the state had deteriorated, that the government was in debt to the extent of seventy-eight million livres. Where had he gone wrong? He had squandered much on his mistresses and the upkeep of such places as the Parc aux Cerfs; he had made heavy demands on the taxpayer.

The Seven Years' War had ended in disaster for France. She had been forced to give up her Canadian possessions to England; the same thing had happened in India. He knew that the French did not take kindly to a King who engaged in wars and did not lead his people in battle. He had heard the whispers about the greatness of Henri Quatre. There had been comparisons, and the great Henri had gleaned even greater honour from these. There had been famine, and certain men – including the King – had been accused of hoarding grain in order to get higher prices for it. During his reign the common people had become more and more wretched. They complained bitterly and continually against the levied taxation. They growled in the streets of Paris about the imposition of the salt tax, that *gabelle*, and the wine tax, the *banvin*. The people declared that those who had the least paid the most in taxes, which was iniquitous. The peasant paid taxes for his King, for his seigneur and for the clergy. 'We will not do this for ever,' growled the hungry people.

Louis had lived during the last years in a state of

indifference. The kingdom will last my lifetime, he had told himself. The old phrase rang in his head now: *Après moi – le déluge*.

He would not be here to see it. That would be for poor Berry and that bright young girl he had married.

Now, with death close, he saw how wrong he had been to shrug aside his responsibility with a 'Poor Berry!'

'I must repent,' he cried, 'for I feel the weight of sin heavy on my conscience.'

❖ ❖ ❖

His priests were at his bedside.

'If you would repent, Sire, you must show first a humble heart, a true desire for forgiveness,' he was told.

'I do desire it. I do,' cried the suffering King.

'Then, Sire, first you must dismiss your courtesan from your bedside.'

'No,' cried du Barry. 'We have been together, France, these many years. I'll not be parted from you now.'

'You must go, my dear,' said the King. 'It is not good for you to be here. This is a vile place – this room. The stench is fearful. I smell it myself. Go, my dear. It is best.'

'I'll not leave you. I myself will nurse you.'

'So you loved me truly,' said the King.

'I will stay with you.' She clung to his hands, and the tears ran down her cheeks. 'I'll never leave you . . . never . . . never . . .'

The priests looked on. 'There can be no hope of saving your soul, Sire, while this woman remains; and time grows short. Will you go to hell for the sake of dying in her arms?'

Du Barry saw his distress and went weeping from the room.

The doors of the sick-room were closed while the priests required the dying man to recount all the sins of his life. This was necessary, the King was told, if he would win absolution.

So he lay on his bed, scarcely able to breathe, scarcely conscious, while he tried to remember all the wickedness of the past. He thought of the carelessness, the indifference, the rule which had touched with decay the very roots of a great kingdom, so that he was leaving a tottering throne to his grandchildren.

But it was not these sins of which he must unburden himself. It was those exploits in the Parc aux Cerfs, the heinous act of living in open sin with such as Madame de Pompadour and Madame du Barry, and thus contaminating the morals of all France.

The confession was made and the Host was carried under a canopy from the chapel to the room in which the King lay dying. Soldiers were stationed on the Palace steps, and the Swiss Guards lined the route through the Palace to the room of death.

Spectators crowded into the ante-room to see the King receiving Holy Communion. The Cardinal who had officiated came to the door of the room and declared in a loud voice:

'Gentlemen, the King instructs me to tell you that he asks God's pardon for the scandalous example he has set his people; and to add that, if God vouchsafes his return to health, he will give himself up to repentance and to relieving the lot of his people.'

A few days later Louis Quinze was dead.

In the streets the people shouted: *'Le Roi est mort. Vive le Roi.'*

The citizens of Paris were wild with joy. They had hated Louis whom they had once called the *Bien-Aimé*. Now they turned to one whom they christened *Louis le Désiré*.

Antoinette, waiting with the Dauphin in a small room, knew that the King was dying. She knew that, at any moment now, crowds would burst upon them; she knew that the life of reckless gaiety was over, and that the careless Dauphine must not be a carefree Queen.

The door opened suddenly. Madame de Noailles was hurrying into the room. She knelt, never forgetting for one moment the correct posture, although she was visibly moved.

'Long life to the King and Queen of France!' she cried.

At that moment others were bursting in upon them. There were many seeking to kiss their hands, to swear to serve them with their hearts and bodies.

Antoinette turned to look at her husband. She saw the fear in his eyes and she understood.

A flash of wisdom came to her then, and she found that she was offering up a silent prayer.

'Lord God, guide us and protect us, for we are too young to rule.'

Chapter IV

THE QUEEN AT VERSAILLES

Madame du Barry was weeping bitterly in her own apartments. She thought of the years when she and Louis had been lovers. They were over and what she had feared for so long had come to pass; this was the end, as she had known it must come to her.

What was there left to her now? Nothing, but to wait on events. And what had she to hope for from Louis' stolid successor, a man who would never have known the pleasures in which she and her lover had indulged with such abandon. What had she to hope for from a young Queen who had openly declared herself her enemy?

She could not stay here at Rueil, on the estate of the Duc d'Aiguillon, where Louis had told her to find a haven while the priests set about saving his soul. D'Aiguillon would soon be out of favour, she doubted not.

She would go to the Petit Trianon, that charming little home which Louis had given her; there she would stay among her treasures, awaiting her doom.

She said farewell to the Duchesse. 'For if I stay here I may bring the royal wrath upon you also,' she explained.

The Duchesse lifted her shoulders; she said she thought that the departure of Madame du Barry could not save them from that.

'Oh, I am not sure,' said du Barry. 'Antoinette is a haughty piece but she is too careless to sit brooding on revenge. As for the new Louis, he is like a bar of iron out of his own workshop. Nothing will dent him. Still I think it would be better if I left you.'

So she came to the Petit Trianon, that house in which she had known such happiness. When she had first seen it she had loved it; even she had recognised it as in exquisite taste, with its windows facing the beautiful lawns, and the gardens making a show of glorious colour. It was not a big house when compared with the palaces of kings, for there were only eight rooms. Versailles could not be seen from it, nor could Versailles see it, and yet it had been so conveniently near. Louis *Bien-Aimé* had called it a little love-nest, and she knew that before her day he had entertained many of his mistresses there.

Now it was hers, her beloved little home; and she had not realised how beloved until she feared she might lose it.

She had been in residence but a few days when the messenger came to her. She saw him approaching through the garden across the green lawn.

'Madame, a message from His Majesty.'

She accepted the scroll and went into the house, taking it into the bedroom where she and Louis had so often spent many interesting and unusual hours. She guessed its contents before she read it.

His Majesty was telling her that her presence would no longer be required at court. He was suggesting that she retire to a convent.

She walked about the house, seeing afresh every small detail.

'Well,' she told herself, as she prepared to leave for her convent, 'I am not the first. It has happened to many before and so often that it should not surprise me.'

So the glittering du Barry, once the most influential woman of the Court, was robbed of her glory and slipped away into retirement.

✤ ✤ ✤

The three aunts were excited. Adelaide was wondering how best she could dominate the new King; her sisters watched her, hanging on her words.

They could not help being relieved that their father was dead. Led by Adelaide they had remained in the sick-room until the end, insisting on performing even the most menial tasks, ostentatiously risking infection. They felt now as though they wore halos about their heads; they were convinced that all their mischief-making and backbiting was righteous behaviour. How could it be otherwise when they had taken such risks in their father's sick-room?

But now the King was dead, the King who had despised his Loque, Coche and Graille; and they, who had risked their lives to nurse him, had had the pleasure of giving him those significant martyred looks as he lay dying, to impress upon him, as they had never been able to during his life, how sinful he was to have laughed at saints such as they were.

'The next task,' said Adelaide, 'is to see that the new King does not make the mistakes of the old.'

Victoire and Sophie looked at each other. 'Poor Berry!' said Sophie.

'He is no longer Berry,' said Adelaide sharply. 'He is Louis Seize. Remember that. You must not call him Berry now; and remember too that you must not treat him like a little nephew. He is the King. What we have to do is prevent that wicked wife of his from influencing him and so ruining the country.'

Victoire and Sophie glanced at each other and nodded.

'I am going to see him,' said Adelaide.

'Shall we go too?' asked Victoire.

'You may not go. You forget we have so recently been in the sick-room of our father.'

Victoire and Sophie looked astonished: they wanted to say that, if they had nursed their father, so had Adelaide; but they never questioned Adelaide's decisions.

'They will need me,' said Adelaide, 'and I must go to them.'

Victoire was ready to fly into one of her panics, for, although she and her sisters had been allowed to accompany the Court to Choisy, they had, on account of their recent proximity to the infection, been installed in a house outside the Palace. She knew that fifty people had already caught the smallpox from the King and that several of them had died: for it was a particularly virulent variety which had brought about the end of the King.

Sophie looked from one sister to the other, not knowing what to make of this situation. Adelaide was clicking her tongue in exasperation.

'Do you not understand that Louis will be completely under the control of that foolish girl? And what will she do? She will bring Choiseul back. She was always a friend of his. At all costs we must stop her.'

Victoire said: 'It is better for our young King to catch the smallpox and die, than that Choiseul should come back. There would still be Provence. He would be King then.'

Adelaide said sharply: 'You talk nonsense. I shall have my carriage made ready at once.'

'The King will be busy with all his new duties,' suggested Victoire.

'Not too busy to see his aunt – the aunt who was a mother to him!'

Sophie nodded. 'We were mothers to poor Berry,' she said.

Victoire looked sly suddenly. She said: 'Adelaide, you are pale. Are you feeling well?'

If Adelaide had not been pale before, she was then. All three sisters had been watching themselves and each other for symptoms ever since the King had died.

'I feel quite well,' said Adelaide obstinately.

'Sit down,' said Victoire.

'Why, Adelaide, you are trembling,' put in Sophie.

'You should rest,' murmured Victoire, 'instead of going to see the King.'

Adelaide was looking at them suspiciously. The memory of the sick-room came back to her. She said faintly: 'I think I *will* rest before going to see the King.'

That night the news went forth that Madame Adelaide had a mild attack of the smallpox.

✣ ✣ ✣

Provence was in his apartment alone with his wife. He had dismissed all their friends and attendants because he felt so excited that he was afraid he might betray himself.

Josèphe watched him. She knew the meaning of his excitement, and she shared it.

He said: 'The death of my grandfather has altered our position considerably. We are only a step away from the throne.'

'Unless, of course, the King and Queen should have a child.'

'It is impossible,' said Provence. He glanced at his wife and looked away quickly. 'It would seem that there is some curse on our family.'

'Which,' said Josèphe, 'does not seem to have affected your brother Artois.'

'That we cannot say yet,' said Provence. 'We cannot be sure.'

Josèphe thought: If I cannot have a child, neither can Antoinette. She may be beautiful but she cannot have the King's child for all her beauty.

'Kings and Queens!' said Provence. 'They are unfortunate when it comes to getting children.'

'Your father had three sons and two daughters.'

Provence turned to her suddenly. 'If aught should befall Louis, then I should take my place on the throne.'

'Yes,' murmured Josèphe; and she saw herself riding into Paris, the people acclaiming her as the Queen, the beautiful Queen – for a little beauty in a Queen went a long way, and she would look handsome enough in royal robes of purple velvet decorated with the golden lilies, a crown on her head.

And it could so easily happen. Only one life stood between Provence and the crown, so how could they help considering the joyful fact that there could never be another life to stand as an obstacle between them, since Louis was impotent?

Provence came close to her and whispered: 'She may try to deceive us.'

'The Queen?'

112

He nodded. 'Have you not noticed her? Have you not seen her eyes follow children in the gardens, in the Palace – any children? She has but to see them to call them, to stroke their hair; she has bonbons ready to give them; her eyes light up as she listens to their absurd prattle. I doubt not that her head is full of plans.'

'What do you mean?' asked his wife.

'There are times when I think she might stop at nothing to get a child.'

'If she adopted a child – and that is the only way she could get one – that child could not harm us.'

Her husband looked at her with contempt. 'Adopt a child! It is not a child she wants – it is an heir. Josèphe, there must not be an heir.'

'There cannot be an heir,' she said.

'With such as she is there might be.'

'You mean . . .'

'There were occasions at the Opéra ball when she disappeared for a while. Do you remember that Swede? She changed after she met him. There might be others. A little manoeuvring . . . you understand me?'

'No! She would never foist a false heir on France.'

'I know not. I know not. But I have seen desperation in her eyes.' He bent his head and his voice sank to a whisper so that Josèphe could hardly hear. "Watch her,' he said. "Watch her as you have never before, so that if there is a child we shall know whom to blame.'

⚜ ⚜ ⚜

When the news came to Antoinette that Madame Adelaide had taken the smallpox, she immediately forgot that the old lady had been far from a friend to her, and was filled with concern.

'But it is so sad,' she cried, 'that she should suffer so quickly for the great sacrifice she made in caring for her father.'

She sent kind messages to her aunt, telling her that she would have come to see her had she been allowed to; but although she had had smallpox already, the King would not hear of her visiting the aunts.

Now she looked at her husband with fear. 'You, Louis, have never had it. What if you should catch it?'

'Then I should either recover or die.'

'You speak of it too lightly. I have heard that there is a new treatment whereby a person is inoculated with serum from a mild case of smallpox. The person has the disease but mildly, soon recovers, and then is immune. Louis, I want you to try this.'

Louis shook his head. 'I have my work. I must not delay carrying on with that.'

'You will delay, and do worse than delay, if you catch this disease. Louis, to please me, to set my mind at rest, try this new treatment.'

He smiled at her slowly. He also had heard of the treatment, and he liked to try new things.

She was so eager, and when she desired something desperately he found that he wanted to give it to her. He could never forget that it was due to him that they had no children. He knew that her mother was continually writing to her of the need to have an heir – as though it were her fault. When he thought of that he felt that nothing he could do for her would compensate for the difficult position in which he had placed her.

He was determined though that he would not allow her to influence him in his new role. His grandfather had never made any great effort to show him how to be a king, but he had read a great deal of history, and it had occurred to him during the course of his reading that the wives and mistresses of many kings had been responsible for ruining their kingdoms.

That should not happen under his kingship.

When he thought of his new position he felt great desires rising within him. He had ridden through the streets of Paris and seen the squalor there. He wanted it to be said that in the reign of Louis Seize France found her greatness again. When he passed the statue of Henri Quatre on the Pont Neuf he felt as much emotion as he was ever capable of feeling. He said to himself then: One day mayhap they will set my statue on a pedestal to be beside yours; and is it possible, my Bourbon ancestor, that they will be able to say: 'There are France's two great Kings'?

But because he had failed to give Antoinette the child for which she longed, and because he had decided that she must not be allowed to interfere too much in politics, he wanted to give way to her on smaller matters.

Now he said: 'Well, I will allow them to inoculate me with their serum, and we shall see what results there are.'

Antoinette clapped her hands. 'And I will be your nurse.'

'I am glad of that, for I will not have any servants to wait upon me who have not already had the disease.'

It was characteristic of Louis that he should be thus careful of the most humble of his servants.

There was a great deal of criticism when it was heard that the King had been inoculated. The people of Paris grumbled; the Court declared the King was mad; but Louis le Désiré was the most popular of Kings, for on the death of his grandfather he had distributed two hundred thousand francs to the poor, and he had declared that it was his intention to restore France to greatness. The people expected miracles; and they saw in this boy, who was not yet twenty, the saviour of their country.

'Soon,' said the poor, 'we shall be driving in our carriages. The rich will not be quite so rich and the poor will be richer. We shall all be of equal richness. *Vive Louis le Désiré!*'

And now the frivolous Queen had persuaded him to submit to a new craze. The King, newly come to the throne, was confined to his apartments with the smallpox. The people saw themselves cheated of their hero.

Provence was excited. If Louis died . . . He and Josèphe were almost delirious at the thought. No need to watch the frivolous Antoinette. She would be of no importance whatever, without Louis.

But Louis did not die. He recovered from his mild attack of smallpox, and having once had the disease, it was said, he would never have it again.

Provence and Artois both submitted to the new treatment. They too suffered mild attacks and quickly recovered.

The people were astonished. This was indeed a revelation – a sign of the good times ahead. Soon the world would be free from that scourge which had visited each country at short intervals and robbed so many of their lives.

The people of Paris, the people of France were in the mood for miracles.

Someone wrote on that pedestal on the Pont Neuf, on which stood the statue of Henri Quatre, *'Resurrexit.'*

The King, hearing of this, looked at Antoinette with worried eyes.

'I mean to devote myself to my people,' he said. 'I mean to do good. I mean to restore morality and justice to France. But if they think that I am Henri Quatre, brought back to serve them, then they are mistaken.'

'Why should you not be?' demanded Antoinette.

'There was never a King of France less like great Henri than myself.'

The depression touched him; it touched her then. Both were thinking of France's greatest King – the libertine who had scattered his seed all over France, so that in villages and towns it was possible to recognise traces of the bold features.

And to this King, who could not even give his wife a child, the people were attributing the qualities of Henri Quatre.

'There are times,' said the King, 'when I feel that the whole universe has fallen upon my shoulders.'

Everywhere were pictures of the new King and Queen. Whenever and wherever they appeared in public cheering crowds followed them.

They had taken up temporary residence in the Château de la Muette in the Bois de Boulogne, and the crowds remained outside the railings from early morning until late at night, chattering excitedly, talking of the end of the bad old days and the beginning of the good ones; demanding of each other whether it was not the pleasantest sight in the world to see this young pair together – she not yet nineteen, he not yet twenty – their new King and Queen. Two loving people to set an example to all married couples. How different from disgusting old Louis with his young girls, his Parc aux Cerfs, his de Pompadours and du Barrys to spend the public money.

Louis, full of ideals, determined to make the lot of his people happier than it had been under his grandfather, began by throwing open the gates of the Bois de Boulogne, so that the citizens of Paris could come and go at their will; and thus they saw the King and Queen constantly. They crowded about them, cheering and applauding.

The people now felt that they were closer to their new sovereigns. How different was young Louis from old Louis who remained at Versailles and never set foot in Paris if he could help it. He knew, the old villain, what his reception would be when he did, for the Parisians had never hidden their feelings.

One day Antoinette was riding in the Bois, and the King came out to meet her. The crowd, looking on, saw the lovely young girl dismount from her horse and, with charming grace, run towards her husband. Whereupon Louis laid his hands on her shoulders and before them all tenderly kissed his Queen. The people cheered; some wiped their eyes. 'This,' they cried, 'is a lesson to us all. Now we shall see a new morality in France.'

Louis, seeing the pleasure his display of affection roused in his dear people, gave his Queen two more hearty kisses; and the people surrounded them as they went towards the Château de la Muette, and stood outside cheering for a long time.

Antoinette was deeply moved. She went straight to her room and wrote to her mother; for how pleasant it was to be able to record happy things, and how happy she was to be Queen. Gone were those misgivings which had come to her when Madame de Noailles had led the retinue which had come to kiss her hand immediately after the death of Louis Quinze. Now Queenship seemed a sunny prospect. The first thing she had done was to remove 'Madame Etiquette' from her place as *gouvernante*, for one of the joys of being a Queen was to dispense with such a familiar. Abbé de Vermond could no longer remind her that it was lesson-time.

She was Queen; she was grown-up; it was for her to give orders to others, not for them to order her life.

So, with the cheers of the people ringing in her ears, she sat down and wrote to her mother – gaily, enthusiastically, the letter of a young girl who was beginning to find life good.

Louis came to her while she was writing.

'I am telling my mother how the people love us,' she said to Louis who stood behind her; he put out a hand to touch her, but he did not do so. It was easier to show affection in the Bois de Boulogne under the admiring eyes of his subjects than when they were alone.

He rejoiced to see her happy; he felt in that moment that his disability as a husband was less of a tragedy than he had thought it, if she could be as happy as this.

'Antoinette,' he said, 'it is the custom of the King of France to give his wife a house when she becomes a Queen.'

'A house! You mean you are going to give me a house . . . a house of my very own?'

She had stood up, her blue eyes sparkling.

'It is not a very big house, but it is a pleasant one. I speak of the Petit Trianon.' Louis lifted his shoulders. 'It is not a Queen's house by any means, but I thought you would like to have it and there retire with a few friends when you feel the need for a little quiet.'

'Louis,' she cried, 'I shall love my Petit Trianon. I want to go at once to see it.'

'We could ride there together,' suggested Louis.

'Now, please, now. This very moment.'

Louis thought how childish she still was, and again he was conscious of the desire to please her.

✢ ✤ ✢

How delighted she was with it – that little house hidden away from the world.

She ran from room to room, exclaiming with delight, seeing it as entirely hers, a dolls' house in which she could shut herself away from the Court. All the furnishings seemed elegant, yet dainty compared with the glories of Versailles; this place had been designed for a love-nest, and so it was. The hangings were in pastel shades rather than deep reds and purples; everything was light and ornamental. The paintings on the walls were those of Jean Antoine Watteau; there was a rustic quietness brooding over the miniature palace so that it seemed impossible to believe that it was not very far from Versailles or Paris.

The gardens were full of delightful flowers, and the colour and perfume were intoxicating.

She stood with Louis at the windows and looked out on the stream which watered the grounds, at the beautiful English garden which Louis' grandfather and du Barry had started to lay out and left unfinished.

'I will finish the English garden,' she cried. 'I shall make of this place a retreat to which we can come when we need to be free from Versailles. Louis . . . Louis . . . I know I am going to be happy here. I will open the gardens to the people for one day each week. On Sundays, shall we say? They shall come in and see the flowers and enjoy it all, even as we shall. Why should they not have the pleasure of my gardens as they do of the Bois?'

Louis smiled his slow satisfied smile.

'It will be such a pleasure to watch them,' she prattled on. 'The poor people of Paris who have only the streets to walk in, and who will never have seen flowers such as I shall grow in my gardens ... The children will play on the grass ... Oh, yes, most of all the children shall enjoy my gardens ...'

Louis had turned abruptly from her, and Antoinette's happy smile faded. She should not have spoken of children. They were reminded of their state duties and the sadness which was theirs.

Into the bright and beautiful little house had crept a shadow, a premonition of impending tragedy.

⚜ ⚜ ⚜

Maria Theresa wrote to her daughter: 'The prospect is great and beautiful. I flatter myself to see the reign so happy and glorious. The whole universe is in ecstasy. There is good cause for it. A King of twenty and a Queen of nineteen and all their actions full of humanity, generosity, prudence and the greatest judgement. Religion and morals which are so necessary in order to draw down the blessing of God and to keep a hold on the people, are not forgotten. In a word my heart is full of joy and I pray God He may preserve you for the good of your people, for the universe, for your family and for your old mother to whom you give new life. How I love the French at this moment. What resources there are in a nation that feels so vividly. One needs only wish them more constancy and less frivolity. By correcting their morals they will change that too.'

Antoinette showed the letter to Louis. He frowned over it. 'So much is expected of us,' he said.

'We shall perform all and more than is expected of us.'

'We shall do our best. I have heard so much of the injustices of my grandfather's reign that I am determined to remedy that.'

'Louis,' said Antoinette, 'the Duc de Choiseul was a great man in the reign of your grandfather."

'My grandfather dismissed him,' said Louis.

'But . . . was he wise to do so?'

Louis was looking at his wife suspiciously. He was thinking of all he had read concerning feminine rule and how the present state of France was doubtless due to the late King's extravagances with his women.

'I would never have him back,' said the King stubbornly.

'He is a good man,' insisted Antoinette. 'He arranged our marriage. I was always very fond of Monsieur de Choiseul.'

'One does not choose ministers for their charm,' admonished the King. 'I will never use a minister who worked against my own father. He suppressed the Jesuits, and my father was their strongest supporter. When my father died there were some to say that Choiseul even had a hand in that.'

'It is quite impossible,' declared Antoinette.

'I am not sure of that; but on one thing I have made up my mind. I will not have Choiseul in my ministry.'

Antoinette was sorrowful. She would have liked to do a good turn to Choiseul.

The King went on: 'I am recalling Maurepas.'

'Maurepas! Is he not the friend of Tante Adelaide?'

'That may be so.'

Antoinette looked at him with surprise. He was allowing Adelaide to influence him.

'It is not for that reason I have recalled him,' said Louis promptly. 'He is my Minister without Portfolio and President of the Council, because I consider him to be an able man. I have decided to dismiss the old Cabinet with the exception of Maurepas' brother-in-law, de la Vrillière. I have decided to dismiss the Chancellor and Terray, because the people dislike both of them so much. I am making Turgot Comptroller of General Finances, and this will delight the people.'

Antoinette's thoughts were wandering. They had come to rest in the gardens of the Petit Trianon. What fun to collect plants from all over the world and replant them in her gardens! She would have all the rarest shrubs – magnolias . . . and trees from India and Africa. It would be gratifying to see the delight of the people who wandered there on Sunday afternoons, and with them would be little children, the dear little children, peeping out from their mothers' skirts to catch a glimpse of the Queen.

Louis had stopped speaking and was thinking of Abbé Robert Jacques Turgot who had already attracted attention by the manner in which he had opposed the Abbé Terray's taxation. The man was already known throughout France as a reformer. He had set up in distressed areas those *ateliers de charité* to aid the starving people; he had built roads and his reforms had made of Limoges, his native town, one of the most advanced areas of France. The King had been drawn to him, not only because their ideas were in accord, but because he was shy, even as Louis was shy, because he walked awkwardly and was generally *gauche*.

'Turgot already has a programme prepared,' stated the King. 'He sees as through my eyes. He is determined to help me make the people happy. He says there shall be no bankruptcy, yet no increase in taxation. I am delighted with his ideas. I am certain that together we can put right much that is wrong.'

'It will surely be so,' said Antoinette dutifully.

'We ourselves,' Louis explained, 'must set an example. It will not do for us to be extravagant while we try to enforce reforms.'

'That is quite true,' murmured Antoinette.

'I have decided to cut down on my personal expenses,' Louis told her. 'I told La Ferté, when he came to me asking for orders because he was the Comptroller of my *Menus Plaisirs*, that I should no longer need him, for my *Menus Plaisirs* are to walk in the park, and that I can control those myself.'

'That is the way to please the people,' cried Antoinette. 'I will tell them that I no longer need that money which is called the *droit de ceinture*. *Ceintures* are no longer worn, therefore I have no need of it.'

'The people shall be told of that *bon mot*,' said the King with a smile. 'It will amuse them, and it will show how eager we are to do what is right.'

'Louis, you are happy, are you not? You are not so much afraid of being King as you thought you might be?'

She had moved closer to him, and she saw that he was startled. He feared, she knew, that she was about to reopen the dread subject.

⚜ ⚜ ⚜

Antoinette knew that she could not persuade Louis to employ Choiseul. She was discovering that her husband was a stubborn man. But at the same time she remembered all the humiliation she had been forced to endure at the hands of Madame du Barry, and she was determined that the Duc d'Aiguillon, the protégé and friend of the du Barry, should not retain his position at Court.

Maurepas, the new Minister without Portfolio and President of the Council, while realising that the King was determined not to be governed by his Queen, sensed also that the Queen was too frivolous to be likely to do this; at the same time he remembered her obstinacy over the du Barry incident, and he was eager not to upset her.

He therefore decided to throw out the Duc d'Aiguillon in order to placate the Queen and show her that he was her friend. All those who had supported d'Aiguillon blamed the Queen and determined to do everything in their power to undermine her growing popularity.

They had the aunts and Antoinette's sisters-in-law to help them in this. They had suspected that Provence's ambition would bring him to their side, although Provence was clever enough to hide his animosity.

It seemed then, to those who wished the Queen ill, that it would not be difficult to work up a strong faction against her.

This became apparent in a very short time.

Since her accession Antoinette's immediate circle had enjoyed a relaxation of the usual strict etiquette in the intimacy of her company. They relished this the more because it was a novelty.

'I suffered from a surfeit of "You must do this . . . you must do that",' she told them. 'Depend upon it, my dears, I shall not impose those rigours on *you*, for if I do you will hate me, and I want you to love me.'

The ladies crowded round her and kissed her cheek, instead of her hand. 'As though anyone could hate Your Majesty!' they cried.

The Marquise de Clermont-Tonnerre, the youngest of all her ladies and something of a tomboy, picked up a coif and put it on her head, pulled a solemn face and cried in accents very like those of the banished Madame de Noailles: 'Your Majesty must not allow your ladies to kiss your cheek. No . . . Your Majesty's hands are for kissing . . . not your cheeks!'

'Be silent! Be silent . . .' warned the more sober ladies.

But Antoinette only laughed. 'You imitate her very well,' she said. 'We shall give you a part in the theatricals, my dear.'

'So we are to have theatricals?'

Antoinette had not thought of them until that moment. Now she decided they would perform a play for the benefit of the Court, and she herself would take the principal part.

'The Court will disapprove heartily,' she was told. 'A Queen to play a part! Versailles will stick its head in the air and declare it does not know what the Court is coming to.'

'Versailles will do what it likes. We shall give our play at Muette . . . or perhaps at my dear Petit Trianon. But play we shall.'

The daring little Marquise took the Queen's hand and, kneeling ceremoniously, held it to her lips.

They all laughed together; and the ladies told each other afterwards that there had never been such an adorable and affectionate Queen of France as Her dearest Majesty.

Then came that day when she must receive certain dowager ladies who had called to condole with her on the loss of her grandfather, and to congratulate her on her accession to the throne.

Her ladies were laughing as usual while they helped her dress in the sombre mourning which the occasion warranted.

'Now we must remember,' she admonished them, 'that this is a very solemn occasion, and these old ladies will doubtless expect me to weep. So do try to compose yourself, my dears.'

'Oh, yes, Your Majesty,' they chorused.

Antoinette tapped the cheek of the little Marquise. 'You especially,' she said. 'Curb your high spirits until the departure of the dowagers.'

The Marquise smiled charmingly; two dimples appeared in her cheeks. She was such a delightful creature that the Queen's smile deepened. It was such a pleasure to choose those she would have about her.

Then began the ritual. It was as formal as any ceremony in the previous reign. Each of the ladies must approach the Queen, fall to her knees, remain there precisely to the required second, must rise and wait for the word from the Queen before she began to speak; and then the Queen must chat with each for a certain time, which must be neither more nor less than the time she chatted with any of the others.

So they came – dreary old ladies in their mourning coifs, looking, thought Antoinette, like a flock of crows, like a procession of gloomy *beguines*.

She was weary of them. Her fingers impatiently fumbled with her fan.

About her her ladies had ranged themselves, the little Marquise de Clermont-Tonnerre immediately behind her so that she was completely hidden by the Queen's dress with its panniers which spread out on either side of her.

Then, as she was talking to one of the elderly ladies, Antoinette heard a giggle behind her.

That bad child, she thought. What is she doing now to make them laugh? It was as much as Antoinette could do to suppress a smile; and to smile, she knew, would cause grave offence on this occasion when she was receiving condolences for the death of the King.

'Madame,' she was saying, 'I thank you from the bottom of my heart. This is indeed a time of deep sorrow for our family. But the King and I pray each day that God will guide us in the way we should go for the glory of France. . . . '

She felt a movement at her feet and, glancing down, she saw the little Marquise hidden from the old dowager by the panniers of her – Antoinette's – dress, sitting on the floor, peeping up at her, pulling her face into such a contortion that, in spite of its round and babyish look, she bore some resemblance to the lady who stood before the Queen.

It was too late to check the sudden smile which came to Antoinette's lips. She hastily lifted her fan; but there were too many people watching her. Josèphe had seen. Thérèse had seen.

Almost immediately she collected herself; she went on with her speech; but for a Queen – and Queen of France – to laugh in the middle of a speech of thanks for the condolences of an honoured subject was so shocking that her enemies would not allow it to be passed over lightly.

Josèphe and Thérèse went as fast as they could to confer with the aunts. The aunts made sure that the story was circulated in those quarters where it would do most harm.

Provence seized on it. If at any time it should be necessary to prove the lightness of Antoinette such incidents as these should be remembered. Moreover they should be stressed at the time they happened; it would make them all the more effective if it should be necessary to resuscitate them.

The Duc d'Aiguillon's party saw that it was repeated and exaggerated not only in the Court but throughout the whole of Paris.

She laughed, this chit from Austria, it was said. She dared to laugh at French customs.

For she had made fun of great and noble French ladies. And in doing that, was she not ridiculing France!

Her enemies wrote a song, for that was always the best way of making the people take up a cause for or against a person or a principle. Soon it was being sung in the streets and taverns.

'My little Queen, not twenty-one,
Maltreat the folks as you've begun,
And o'er the border you shall run . . .'

Antoinette heard it. She was bewildered.

'But the people love me! Monsieur de Brissac said, when I first went into the city, that all Paris was in love with me.'

It was another lesson she had learned. The people could love one day and hate the next, for the people were a fickle mob.

❧ Chapter V ❧

REHEARSAL FOR REVOLUTION

*D*uring that year a new fashion began at Versailles. The King, in his affection for the Queen, was often seen walking with her in the gardens arm-in-arm. Then must the ladies and gentlemen of the Court follow their example, so that husbands and wives who were known to hate each other, even to be notoriously unfaithful to each other, must nevertheless wander through the Galerie des Glaces, through the Cour de Marbre or the Cour Royale, arm-in-arm.

It was pleasant to see the King and Queen so happy together, for it seemed that the longer they were married the stronger grew their affection. It was rare to find such devotion between a King and Queen of France – so rare that many doubted its authenticity.

These doubts were fostered by the Queen's enemies.

Was it possible, they asked, that one so young and beautiful, so fond of gaiety and pleasure, so frivolous, so ready to listen to flattery, could love a man so *gauche*, so heavy, so unattractive to women as their Louis ?

Louis! The strangest King who had ever sat upon the throne of France. There had been a time when some of his friends had sought to make a normal man of him, and talked to him of charming actresses at the Comédie Française. And what said Louis? Oh, he was not interested. If he had time to spare from his duties, he liked to spend it making locks in his forge or hunting the stag.

And it was to this boor, known to be impotent (for had not his grandfather forced him to submit to an examination, and had it not been one of those secrets which leak out and become common knowledge?) that a frivolous and quite lovely young girl was declared to be a faithful wife!

Is it possible? asked her enemies; and eventually the people in the streets began to ask the same question.

She was so careless of etiquette.

They had all heard how it was at her *lever*. The Royal *lever* and *coucher* had been matters of strictest etiquette for generations. The Queen's chemise could only be handed to her in the bedchamber by the person of highest rank. Thus the lowest servant must first pick it up and hand it to the *femme-de-chambre*, who must then give it to one of the ladies-in-waiting and, if that lady-in-waiting was of the highest rank present, she could then hand it to the Queen. But if, while that lady-in-waiting was about to hand it to the Queen, a lady of higher rank such as Madame de Chartres or one of her sisters-in-law entered, it must immediately be taken from the lady-in-waiting and given to the Queen by the lady who had newly arrived on the scene.

The malicious sisters-in-law did all they could to plague Antoinette and show those about her how careless she was of the dignities appertaining to the throne of France.

The Comtesse de Provence would make a point of coming in at the moment when Madame d'Artois was helping

Antoinette into her chemise; then must the ritual begin again with Madame de Provence taking the principal role.

At length Antoinette declared that she found the ceremonies of rising and going to bed too tedious to be borne, and would go to her dressing-room, where she would dress and undress privately.

This was not only flouting tradition, it was depriving certain people of duties which they prized and which gave them special standing at Court.

Mercy's letters to Maria Theresa were full of anxieties. The Queen's *légèreté* was causing consternation, he wrote. Her spirits were too high; she was too fond of riding, too prone to ignore etiquette.

She had started a new fashion, aided by her hairdresser, Monsieur Léonard, who drove to Versailles in some state from Paris every day because she, fearing he might lose his skill if he devoted himself entirely to her, insisted that he continue with his business. He would comb the Queen's hair, stiffen it with pomade until it stood straight up on her head, then with gigantic hairpins he would dress it into a tower – sometimes as much as three feet in height – and adorn it with decorations of flowers or miniature landscapes, gardens, or houses. Monsieur Léonard delighted in being topical, so that it was his pleasure to illustrate little scenes from Court life and display them on the Queen's coiffure. Soon all the ladies were following the fashions set by the Queen, and this fashion was ridiculed by the citizens of Paris who had hoped for impossible blessings from the new reign. Pictures were circulated throughout the cafés – pictures of the Queen, her hair towering ridiculously above her head.

Maria Theresa's letters were reproachful.

'I cannot refrain from touching on a matter which has been brought to my notice. I refer to the way in which you are dressing your hair. They tell me that from the forehead it rises as much as three feet, and it is made higher by the addition of decoration, plumes and ribbons.'

Antoinette read her mother's letters and shrugged aside the criticisms. She was after all a Queen now, not a child to be corrected; and, as all the ladies of the Court were following the hair fashions set by herself, they did not seem ridiculous in Court circles — which was, in her estimation, the only place where opinion on such matters was important.

But she was careless indeed, and she had never been able to differentiate between what was important and what was trivial; nor could she realise how easy it was to step from the trivial to the significant. Thus she began to make enemies among those who might have been her friends.

Her brother, the Archduke Maximilian, paid a visit to the Court of France during the month of February. She was delighted to see her brother again and planned many fêtes and balls that she might entertain him worthily.

The younger branches of the royal family were very jealous of their honour. It was so difficult for any member of a lower branch to forgive those higher up the tree; the King they must accept as the eldest son of an eldest son of the royal house. But this frivolous wife of his, who insisted every day on flouting the recognised etiquette of their noble house, angered them all; and Antoinette's worst enemies became the men and women who were closest to her.

On the visit of Maximilian the three heads of the lower branches of the royal family – the Duc d'Orléans, the Prince de Condé and the Prince de Conti – waited for the Archduke to call on them; but Antoinette laughed with her brother over the formality of her new relations.

'There is nothing I like so much as to say to them: "So! You have always behaved thus – well, now we will behave thus no longer!" Max! It infuriates them.'

Maximilian lacked his sister's frivolity and had in its place a little of their brother Joseph's pomposity.

'Why should I put myself out to visit them?' he demanded. 'I am the guest. Let them come to me.'

'Yes,' agreed Antoinette. 'Let them. Now let us talk about home.'

Her eyes sparkled as she talked of home, but she knew in her heart that she would not wish to go back to Schönbrunn Palace even if she could. She would not want to go back to her mother's watching eyes and continual scoldings. Why, that would be almost as bad as the disapproval she met at her own Court.

But the matter of her husband's relatives did not end there. Orléans, Condé and Conti considered they had been insulted. Did they think this young woman – *l'Autrichienne,* as they called her – could treat them with the lack of respect with which she treated old dowagers in her salon?

She would find it was a very different matter to insult members of the royal house.

Moreover Maximilian complained that he had not been visited by her husband's relatives and that he thought this was a scurvy way to treat their Queen's brother.

'It is indeed!' cried Antoinette, and forthwith sat down to write impulsively to Orléans.

There was no reply to this letter and it was left to the King to command the return of his offended relatives to Court. The most angry of all was Conti, who craved the King's indulgence, but declared that he was suffering from an attack of gout which would keep him away from Court for some time.

Mercy of course reported all this to Maria Theresa, and the Empress, feeling old and often very weary, prayed for her daughter and wondered whither her recklessness would lead her. She wrote reproachfully to Mercy and de Vermond, and beneath her reproaches was a plea: Take care of my little daughter.

There were more letters from her mother.

'There are times,' Antoinette confided in her dear friend the Princesse de Lamballe, 'when I put off opening my mother's letters. They are almost certain to contain some warning against my doing something I want to do, some reproach for something I have done. My mother is the best woman in the world. She loves me as only a mother can, but I fear I give her as many uneasy moments as she gives me; and now it seems that even something which should be as full of pleasure as Max's visit is turned into depressing failure because of those old uncles, who are determined to make trouble.'

And although she could eventually forget her mother's criticisms of her hair-styles and her defiance of conventions, there was one continual complaint coming from Vienna which she could not ignore.

It was very important, wrote the Empress, that there should be a Dauphin. Maria Theresa could only be contented when her daughter announced that happy event.

In the streets they were singing:

> *'Chacun se demande tout bas:*
> *Le Roi peut-il? Ne peut-il pas?'*

It was disconcerting to have one's intimate life discussed and watched.

She knew that the servants of the bedchambers examined the sheets each morning with the utmost care, and she guessed that while they did so they hummed together that song which the people were singing in the streets.

It was more than disconcerting. It was heartbreaking.

She was relieved though when Conti at length returned to Court and treated her with the deference due to her.

'That little trouble is over,' she told the Princesse de Lamballe.

But she had much to learn yet.

Antoinette had tried to forget her longing for a child in the pleasure she derived from possessing her own little house. There she felt she could live like a simple lady who did not have to worry because she was childless. In the small house she would stay with a few of her friends and tell herself that there was a great deal to be enjoyed in a rustic existence. She would spend whole days there, arriving early in the morning and returning to Versailles in the late afternoon. The gardens were beginning to look very beautiful indeed. She was completing the English garden begun by Louis Quinze and Madame du Barry, with the help of Prince de Ligne who had created his own lovely garden at Bel Oeil.

Often he was with her and her ladies; endlessly they discussed the planting of flowers and what shape the flower-beds should be.

On Sunday – that day when the people from Paris came to the Trianon to look at the Queen's gardens – Antoinette, with some of her friends about her, including the Prince de Ligne, sat under the trees talking idly.

The people wandered by, and it was not at the flowers they looked but at the beautiful Queen who seemed more exquisite in her rustic garden than ever before. She was like a dainty shepherdess with her easy manners, her pleasant smile and that dazzlingly fair complexion.

The Queen's eyes followed the children always. She would not have them disturbed even when they romped in the flowerbeds. 'For they are happy,' she said. 'And it does me good to see happy children in my Petit Trianon.'

Now she was saying to the Prince de Ligne that she would like to build a little village about the Trianons – a model village with a few houses wherein would live families whom she would select; poor people who needed looking after because they could not make a living in the town, people who loved the country and sought the peaceful life. She would like to have her little village – *un petit hameau* – where everyone lived the perfect rustic existence.

'Ah,' said the Prince, 'I know what has put this in your mind. You have heard of the plan which once so delighted Madame de Pompadour. She thought of it, talked of it, but never put it into practice.'

'Yes, I have heard of that,' admitted Antoinette. 'She planned to dress as a milkmaid and keep cows in her little farm at Trianon. There must be some magic in this air which suggests such a plan. For, you see, it comes to me too that one could lead an ideal existence thus.'

'The idea grew from a romance which was written by my friend de Boufflers,' the Prince told her. 'I remember it well. It was called *Aline Reine de Golconde*, and Aline was the queen of her village, and charming she was in her white petticoat and corselet. She so impressed Madame de Pompadour that that lady, seeking new experiences, decided she would like to exchange Versailles for a village, and be queen of that.'

'And she never did it?'

'No, the plan was not completed.'

'Then mayhap I shall complete it one day.'

She was smiling, looking into the future. The Prince thought, she would build a world of romance to escape from reality. If she could but have a child she would be content.

And he was sorrowful, contemplating her, for he was secretly in love with her.

A small girl with a tousled curly head was pulling at her skirts.

'Hello, Queen!' she said.

The Prince rose in consternation, frowning as he looked about him for the mother or guardian of the child.

But Antoinette told him not to trouble. She took the child's hand and said: 'Hello, my dear.'

The child laughed and put out a finger to touch the silk of the Queen's gown.

'Pretty,' said the child. She ran a grimy finger about the lace of the pocket.

'Would you care to see what is in the pocket?' asked the Queen.

Busy fingers explored. 'Bonbons!' cried the child.

'Try them. I think you will like them.'

The little girl nodded.

Now her mother had appeared and was standing at some distance. The child had seen her and called: 'Maman, the Queen gave me bonbons.'

'Madame,' cried the woman, advancing in dismay.

'I pray you do not disturb yourself,' said Antoinette. 'I like the children to come and speak to me.'

Now others had heard the magic word, bonbons. They came running up and stood a little way off, wide-eyed, their mouths watering.

'Come,' said the Queen. 'There are more bonbons here.'

And soon a group of children was about her, sucking the sweetmeats, looking at her with wondering and admiring eyes. She asked them questions, and they answered her without embarrassment. Little François had three brothers. He was going straight home to tell them about the pretty Queen who gave away bonbons. Little Marie admitted she had never tasted bonbons before. Susette would like to take some bonbons home to her brother who could not walk.

The Queen was touched, and there were tears in her eyes. And every Sunday after that she made sure that she had a good supply of bonbons for the children.

It was of course unseemly for a Queen to mingle with the people in the gardens; it was unqueenly to allow grubby little fingers to pull at her gown. This was not the way in which a Queen of France should conduct herself. Her enemies, watching her, declared that such behaviour was a further proof of *légèreté*.

Madame d'Artois, being pregnant, regarded her sister-in-law with only slightly veiled triumph, as though to say, See what a better Queen I should have made.

Madame de Provence, who could not flaunt pregnancy for the same reason that Antoinette could not, showed herself to the world as a model of decorum, so that people might say, That is how a Queen should behave. It is a great pity that Provence was not the eldest.

As for the aunts, they lost no opportunity of circulating gossip. If any man was seen talking to the Queen, Adelaide would demand of the others what that meant, in such tones as would express no doubt that she herself had very shrewd suspicions as to the answer to her question. Then the aunts would react in their different ways – Victoire growing excited and saying that such a frivolous Queen would wreck the kingdom, and Sophie shaking her head and murmuring 'Poor Berry!' and hastily correcting herself to 'Poor Louis!'

So her sisters-in-law, her aunts and her enemies, headed by the Duc d'Aiguillon, deliberately misconstrued Antoinette's love of children and her softheartedness into wickedness; and there were several people who never failed to refer to the Queen as *l'Autrichienne*.

❧ ❧ ❧

It was a sunny May morning, but the King looked tired as, with a few of his friends, he descended the Escalier de Marbre and passed into the Cour Royal. He had been talking late into the night with Turgot, his Minister of Finances; and Turgot, with Maurepas, had just set out for Paris.

The King's ministers had advised him to make use of the pleasant weather by riding out into the forest to hunt, for, they assured him, he could do no good by brooding in the château. A little relaxation, they persisted, and he would feel the better to deal with the nation's pressing problems.

Louis was uneasy. He was realising now that all those doubts which had beset him at the beginning of his reign were by no means unfounded. It was one thing to have high ideals; it was quite another to carry them out. It seemed that his people expected him to make bricks without straw.

There was trouble all about him, for how could he repair the evils which had been accumulating over the years merely by his heartfelt wish to do so?

The people were asking for miracles, and he could only give them his word that he cared for them, that he wished to be their little father, that his great desire was to see a happy France.

That was all very well, but the people wanted more. They wanted relief from poverty; they wanted to see bread in the shops which they could afford to buy.

Turgot shared his King's ideals, and the two worked in unison, but Turgot also was an idealist and not a practical man. It was simple, said Turgot, to reduce the price of bread by introducing free trade. He had not taken into consideration the fact that bad harvests could send up the price of corn, and that he needed better roads and a canal system to transport the grain.

The harvest of the preceding year had been unusually bad and, to counteract the growing unrest which this caused, Turgot put corn on the market from the King's granaries at a reduced price.

This placated the people for a time, but when the price of grain necessarily rose, they were more disgruntled than ever. They were more angry with what they considered ineffectual reforms than they had been with no reforms at all. During the winter, when the roads were blocked with snow, it was impossible to convey grain to Paris, and the price of bread rose. Threatened with starvation, the people looked for scape-goats, and they chose Turgot who, they said, was persuading the King to keep up the price of bread.

As a result there had been bread riots in several towns, and these reached alarming proportions in Villers-Cotterets, where men and women had begun to raid the markets.

What was more alarming still was the obvious fact that these riots were organised by agitators, for the grain which was taken from boats on the Oise was not put to any useful purpose, but thrown into the river.

When this news was brought to Versailles the King was deeply distressed. He could not bear to contemplate the sufferings of his people, and it was a hard blow to realise that he and his good minister Turgot were so grossly misunderstood.

So that morning Turgot and Maurepas, fearing that the riots would extend to Paris, and there be more violent than they had been in the provincial towns, had set out for the Capital, advising the King to spend the morning hunting, which would restore his jaded health, and give him new strength to deal with his problems.

Now as he rode out of the château he saw in the distance a crowd of ragged men and women; they carried sticks and they were shouting '*A Versailles*'. They looked very dangerous and, as he pulled up his horse to watch, he saw that they were emerging from the Saint-Germain road and making straight for the market.

The riot was, he guessed, to take the same form as those which had already occurred in Saint-Germain, Poissy, Saint-Denis and other places. The insurgents would break up the bakers' shops, throw the grain and bread into the streets, and steal what they could.

For the first time in his life he realised that he was face to face with a situation which he must manage himself.

His ministers were already on the way to Paris, and he must thank God for that, for he could be sure that if there was trouble at Versailles there would be greater trouble in the Capital.

He immediately sent for the Prince de Beauvau and the Prince de Poix, and bade them call out the bodyguard and close the gates of the château. Then he hurried inside to find the Queen.

Antoinette was in her bed; she had retired late the night before and was still sleeping. She started up when she saw the King, for his face was ashen and his fleshy lips were trembling.

'You must get up immediately,' he told her.

She stared at him. 'Louis . . . what is wrong?'

'The people are marching on Versailles.'

'The *people*!'

'It is the *Guerre des Farines*. Poissy, Saint-Denis, Saint-Germain – now it is Versailles and Paris.'

'Louis . . . the people . . . they are hungry?'

Louis nodded miserably. 'But Turgot says there are those in our kingdom who agitate them to revolt. We are doing all we can. We have our *ateliers de charité* . . . I know not what else can be done.'

'Louis,' said Antoinette, 'there are times when I am afraid of the people of France. They love us so devotedly one day; they hate us so venomously the next. I no longer put my trust in the people of France.'

'You must dress quickly,' said the King. 'Come to me in my apartments when you are ready.'

'Louis, are they going to march on the château and destroy it as they have destroyed the bakers' shops? Are they going to kill us?'

He shook his head. 'But come as soon as you can.'

Her women hurried to her side and she went with them into her dressing-room, thinking of the angry people marching on Versailles; then she wondered whether they would meet with poor Monsieur Léonard on his way from Paris and do him some harm.

Thinking of poor Monsieur Léonard she ceased to worry about herself.

❖ ❖ ❖

The mob had climbed over the gates; they were massed in the courtyard.

'Come out, Louis!' they cried. And added derisively: 'Louis, we would see you. Louis le Désiré, come forth.'

Beyond the balcony Antoinette stood with Louis.

'I must go onto the balcony to talk with them,' said Louis.

'You must not. You do not know what they will do.'

'They are asking for me, and I am their King.'

'You are not to blame for this trouble. Are you responsible for the bad harvest?'

'A King is always responsible.' He muttered almost mechanically: 'I feel as though the whole universe has fallen on my shoulders.'

As he stepped onto the balcony a roar went up from the crowd.

'Louis!' they cried. 'What do you there, Louis? What have you eaten this day, Louis? Bread . . . bread like this?'

Several of them were waving mouldy pieces of bread in their hands. Some of these were thrown at the balcony. One hit Louis on the cheek. He caught it as it fell.

'Try it, Louis,' they cried. 'Eat it, Louis. Did you ever taste the like? That is the filth you ask your subjects to eat.'

He lifted his hand. 'My good people . . .' he began.

There was a derisive roar.

'We want cheap bread. You promised us cheap bread . . .'

The shouts and cat-calls persisted, and it was impossible for him to make himself heard. Several times he raised his voice. They would not listen.

Antoinette called to him: 'Come back, Louis. They will do you an injury. They are lashing themselves to fury against you.'

Wretchedly he stepped back into the room. His plump cheeks were shaking with emotion; his short-sighted eyes filled with tears.

⚜ ⚜ ⚜

The Prince de Beauvau had ridden out into the courtyard at the head of the guards. The crowd began throwing grain at him from the sacks they had pilfered.

'If you will not retire in order,' warned Beauvau, 'I shall be forced to use arms. The King has commanded me not to do so except in self-defence, as he is eager that you should not be harmed.'

The answer was a handful of flour thrown in his face.

The Prince was desperate. He could see that the leaders of the mob were doing their best to rouse their followers to a frenzy.

'If you will not let me speak,' he shouted, 'what can I do to help you?'

'Come down from your horse, Monsieur le Prince!' shouted the leader. 'Come down and eat the mouldy bread you and your kind ask us to eat.'

'Is the mouldy bread the same as that which you carried in Saint-Germain?' shouted the Prince.

'All over France Frenchmen are eating mouldy bread,' he was answered.

'It is not the bread sold in the shops,' he cried. 'That is good bread.'

The leaders of the mob were really angry now. They cried: 'To hell with the Bourbons! To hell with those who live on the fat of the land while good citizens starve!'

Beauvau lost his head. He was terrified. He remembered what he had heard of the damage men like these had inflicted on Villers-Cotterets. In his imagination he saw the château in flames, the King and Queen murdered before his eyes.

He held up his hand. 'One word. If you have justice on your side, listen to me. If you are truly rioting because bread is dear and not because you are enemies of your King, listen to me!'

'Come!' cried the leader. 'Shall we listen to these Princes? Come, my friends. Forward! Into the château!'

'Let's hear him first,' growled a voice in the crowd; and others took up the cry.

Beauvau had one thought in his head – to drive the mob from Versailles and save the King and Queen; and seeing only one way to do this he acted boldly. 'At what price do you want bread to be fixed?' he roared.

'At two sous!' answered the ringleaders, believing this to be impossible.

Beauvau shouted: 'Right! Two sous it shall be.'

There was silence in the courtyard. The mob began to murmur, 'Bread at two sous!' There was no longer any excuse for a riot.

Someone shouted: 'To the bakers! Come! Let us demand our two-sou bread.'

In a few minutes the courtyard was cleared.

The riot at Versailles was over.

But that was not the end of the *Guerre des Farines*.

Turgot came hurrying from Paris. His worst fears had been realised. The rioting there had been more violent than anywhere else.

Beauvau had averted disaster at Versailles, but it was impossible for the bakers to sell their bread at two sous, and that promise would have to be revoked. The price of bread would have to stand, for the time being, at that high price which had given the rioters their reason for rioting.

But Turgot had even more disturbing news. It had been necessary to arrest some of the rioters in Paris, and it had been discovered that many of those dressed as women had been in truth men; they had been by no means the poorer class who had good reason to complain and who could not be expected to understand the difficulties which beset the King and his new ministers. Instead they had been men of some means. Two had been confined in the Châtelet, and they had turned out to be Jean Desportes who was a master wig-maker, and Jean Lesguille who was a gauze-worker. These two had been arrested while they were pillaging one of the raided shops, and they had been proved to be men well fed, with money in their pockets, who could quite easily afford to buy bread. As for Lenoir, the chief of the Paris police, instead of quelling the riots he had helped to stimulate them.

'It would appear,' said Turgot, 'that the rising was by no means a riot of the people, which had come about because the price of bread was so high that they were starving. These riots have been organised with great care.'

The King was not often angry, but now a rage possessed him which was not less fierce because his lethargic nature was so rarely stirred in this way. He was filled with righteous indignation, for he realised that, while he wished to serve his country with all his heart and all the mind of which he was capable, there were enemies in his kingdom who, seeking to destroy him, would make France suffer as she had not suffered for two hundred years.

His righteous anger was so great that it swamped his embarrassment, and in that moment Louis was truly King. He dismissed Lenoir and called the *Parlement* to Versailles.

When it arrived it was to find a banquet awaiting it, and after the members of the *Parlement*, somewhat mellowed by good food and wine, were ready to listen to what the King had to say, Louis told them that he was determined to stop the dangerous brigandage which must soon degenerate into revolution. He wanted tribunals set up so that the real culprits might be discovered.

His speech was fluent, and it was as though a new man had taken the place of the old Louis.

'You have heard my intentions,' he declared. 'I forbid you to make any remonstrances on the orders I have given or do anything to counter them. I rely on your fidelity and your submission at a moment when I have resolved to take measures which shall ensure that during my reign I shall never again be obliged to have recourse to them.'

Afterwards Turgot congratulated him, and there was wonder in this statesman's eyes. Could this be the dull King who always seemed so awkward with his ministers and his courtiers? Could this be Poor Louis, as they had often called him, even as his grandfather had dubbed him Poor Berry?

'The fact is,' Louis confided to Turgot, 'I feel more embarrassed with one man than with fifty. Moreover this I feel so strongly.'

He had need to feel strong when, on the door of his apartment, he found a notice which told him: 'If the price of bread does not go down and the Ministry is not changed, we will set fire to the four corners of the château.'

On the walls of the château was written: 'If the price does not go down we will exterminate the King and the whole race of Bourbons.'

The King was more distressed than ever for he knew that his enemies were within the Palace.

He wanted to talk of this with someone whom he could trust. He turned to the Queen, but could he trust her? She would mean no harm but she was too impulsive; she spoke without thinking. No, he could not speak to the Queen.

And thinking of her, he remembered those men whose blood was his blood, his own relations.

Antoinette could not grasp how deeply she had offended Orléans, Condé and Conti, when her brother had been visiting France. Antoinette could never put herself in the place of another. She saw the world through the eyes of Antoinette – a gay and lovely place where everyone should be kind to others and all should realise that nothing was of any great moment compared with enjoyment of the sunny hours.

And thinking thus, Louis remembered Conti, Conti, the most vindictive of them all, Conti who had held aloof from the Court, blaming his gout. Conti, whose house of L'Isle Adam was in Pontoise, that area in which, so it had been discovered, the riots had started.

Conti, the King knew, had speculated heavily in grain, and Turgot's edict which was calculated to bring down prices – and which would have succeeded but for bad harvest and lack of transport – had been resented by him, Conti, who was hostile to Turgot, hostile to the Queen.

It was alarming. An enemy so close. An enemy in his family. And an enemy who could contemplate the destruction of the monarchy.

Louis trembled. He knew he must act with firmness.

The wig-maker and the gauze-worker were publicly hanged, and the sight of those two men on the gallows brought about a more serious mood among the rioters.

The example had been necessary. Those men who had been paid to begin the *Guerre des Farines,* and who, when arrested, had been found to have money in their purses, were glad to be released, and keep the peace.

The great turning-point of Louis' life had come; but he did not know it, and he hesitated. His moment of firm determination was over.

Because of those hideous suspicions which had been aroused in his mind, he was afraid to continue with the enquiry. He was afraid to discover who might be behind this rehearsal for a revolution.

Louis was not the only one whose suspicions had fallen on his cousin. It was being whispered in knowledgeable circles that Conti was deeply involved in the disturbances. Louis was afraid, and he continued to waver.

To Turgot he wrote: 'The suspicion is dreadful and it is difficult to know what line to take. But unhappily, those who have said this are not the only ones. I hope for the sake of my name that they are only calumniators.'

The riots had subsided with the punishment meted out to the wig-maker and gauze-worker.

Louis' hour of boldness had passed. He took a definite

turning on that day when thankfully he decided to let matters rest because he was afraid whom revelation might expose.

❖ Chapter VI ❖

THE EMPEROR AT VERSAILLES

*I*t was a June day, and the citizens of Rheims were eager to show the loyalty they bore towards their King and Queen. Forgotten were the recent riots. Here was pageantry, all that royalty meant to people whose lives were so drab that they rejoiced in those days when the kings and queens came close to them in their brilliant splendour.

On the previous night the Queen, with her brothers-in-law and sisters-in-law, had ridden through the moonlit streets while the crowds had cried: 'Long live the Queen! Long live the royal family!'

This was the day when Louis Seize was to be crowned King of France.

Antoinette was not with him. Louis was anxious to spare his country the expense of a double coronation; he was even anxious to spare the country the expense of his own traditional crowning.

'I would rather,' he declared, 'hold my crown by my people's love. There is no need for them to swear to serve me. Let them do so only while it is their will that they should.'

Louis in any case hated such ceremonies.

But his desire for privacy and avoidance of expense was overruled. The people wished for the ancient ceremony to be performed.

'Soon,' he had said, 'we shall have further expense with Clothilde's wedding. Then there will be the lying-in of Thérèse.'

But it was no use. The people demanded to see their King in purple velvet. So Louis must submit, although both he and the Queen had agreed that he only should be crowned.

So the ancient ceremony began that morning with the procession arriving at his bedchamber and the Grand Chorister rapping on the door.

The words were still ringing in Louis' ears as he rode in his great state carriage to the Cathedral.

'What is your wish?'

'I wish for the King.'

'The King sleeps.'

There followed a repetition of these words three times, when the Bishop replied: 'We ask for Louis Seize whom God has given us for King.'

So they had led him to his carriage, he feeling *gauche* in the crimson robes with his mantle of silver and the plumes and diamonds in his cap.

How could he help thinking of those monarchs who had gone before him: Charlemagne, St Louis, Henri Quatre, Louis Quatorze – even his grandfather! How different they must have looked to the people from the fleshly, somewhat sullen-faced man who was now their King.

But, as he knelt before the altar and the robes of royal velvet decorated with golden lilies were laid about him, he was swearing that he would never cease to work for his country, that his aim in life should be to restore France to prosperity, that he would give his life if need be in the service of his country.

He looked up suddenly and saw Antoinette. She was in a gallery close to the altar, and he saw that she was leaning forward and that she was quietly weeping.

He paused and she smiled at him through her tears, while many witnessed their exchange of glances, sensing their emotion and the affection in those looks they gave each other. Some wept, and all applauded, crying: 'Long live the King and his Queen!'

It was a moving moment, a departure from tradition; and never, it was said, were there a King and Queen so devoted to one another as this King and Queen.

As soon as he was able he joined Antoinette. She held out her hands to him and lifted her face to his.

'We will always be together,' said Louis.

She nodded mutely, for she, who was much more easily moved than he was, had at this time nothing to say.

The people were calling for them. They must walk along that gallery which had been erected from the Cathedral to the Archbishop's Palace.

'Come,' said Louis, and he drew her hand through his arm.

Thus they walked, and the crowds on either side of the gallery saw the affection in the King's face, saw the emotion in the Queen's.

'God bless them!' the cry went up. 'Long life to Louis and his Queen!'

Thérèse, Comtesse d'Artois lay back on her pillows; she was exhausted but triumphant. She was the first of the royal wives to give birth to a child.

Thérèse had good reason to feel triumphant. She had proved herself fertile, and it seemed probable that neither of her husband's brothers could provide those greatly wished-for *enfants de France*. If this were so, her children might one day wear the crown.

The lying-in chamber was crowded for it was the custom that all who cared to be were permitted to witness the birth of one who might inherit the throne of France.

Her sister Josèphe, she knew, was anxious; as for the Queen, it was said she would willingly give ten years of her life if she might give birth to an heir.

But neither of them was to have her wishes granted; and it was Thérèse, plain Thérèse, who was the fortunate one.

Antoinette was standing by the bed now.

'Why, Thérèse,' she said, 'you are indeed fortunate. The baby is charming . . . charming . . . '

Thérèse's thin lips curled into a supercilious smile, and Antoinette turned from the bed. She knew what Thérèse was thinking. Indeed, everyone present was thinking the same. It seemed to her that the eyes of those whose vulgar curiosity had brought them to the chamber of birth at this time, were fixed on her.

For, thought Antoinette, they have not come to see the birth of Thérèse's child, but to witness the mortification of a barren Queen.

She commanded that the child be brought to her that she might embrace it. There it lay on the velvet cushion, its little face red and puckered, its tiny hands clenched.

'May God bless you, my child,' she murmured.

There was a hush all about her. One of the women from the fish-market called out in her raucous voice: ''Tis your own child you should be holding in your arms.'

This vulgar *poissarde* had merely voiced what all were thinking. Antoinette turned to her and nodded slowly. Then with great dignity she handed the child back to the nurses, and went to the bed to take her leave of Thérèse.

'You need rest,' she said.

Thérèse agreed. She was exhausted, and the room was warm with the press of people.

'It is a barbarous custom, this,' whispered Antoinette. 'So many to stare at a woman at such a time.'

'Yes,' said Thérèse with a hint of malice in her voice, 'but one must endure the inconvenience for the satisfaction of giving birth to a child.'

'I would willingly endure it,' murmured Antoinette; and as she kissed her sister-in-law and turned away, she thought: 'Most willingly.'

The sightseers fell back as she walked calmly to the door. She heard the whispers about her, for what did the common people, whose privilege it was to storm the bedchamber at such times, know of Court etiquette or ordinary good manners?

'One would think she would be ashamed . . .'

'It may be that if she spent less time at her balls and fêtes, and more with the King . . .'

'Yet there she goes, haughty as they make them . . . These Austrians . . . they are not like the French. They are cold, so they say. They do not make good mothers . . .'

'Holy Mother of God,' prayed Antoinette, 'how can I endure it? Why cannot I have a child? If I had a child . . . a

Dauphin for France, I should be the happiest woman in the world. Is it so much to ask? Is it not my due? Why should I be denied what I want more than anything on earth?'

Again she felt that choking sensation in her throat, and she was afraid that she would break down and show her misery to them all.

As she passed through the *salle des gardes* she was aware that the women of the fish-market were walking beside her.

To them she seemed unreal. Their hands were so red and coarse, chapped with handling cold and slimy fish; but those little hands, sparkling with jewels, looked as though they were made of china. The Queen herself looked as though she were made of china. Her golden hair was piled high and dressed with flowers and ribbons; her dress was of rich silk, cut low to show her dazzlingly white throat on which the diamonds blazed; her silk skirts rustled as she walked; and it seemed to the coarse women of the fish-market that such a creature was no more than a pretty doll and that France had need of something more than an ornament on its throne. Beside this exquisite creature they felt coarse, and, as always, envy bred hatred. Many of them had more children than they could afford to feed. They remembered the pain of childbirth, the sickening repetition of conception, gestation and birth. Why should we go through all that, they demanded of themselves, while this pretty piece of frivolity, who looks like a china ornament to be kept in a glass case for fear of breaking, knows how to have all the pleasure in the world and won't even suffer the pain of bearing a child?

'When are we going to see your lying-in, Madame?' one demanded boldly.

'Wouldn't it be a better thing to give a child to France than so many fêtes to your friends?' cried another.

'Oh, Madame is too dainty, too pretty to bear children. Madame is afraid that would spoil her dainty figure.'

She could not look at them; she dared not. What would they say in the streets of Paris if these creatures went back to their stalls and told how the Queen had so far forgotten her majesty that she had wept before them?

So she held her head high; she looked neither to the left nor to the right, and it seemed to her a very long walk from the lying-in chamber of Thérèse to her own apartments.

They misinterpreted her gesture. The high colour in her cheeks, the tilt of her head – that was haughtiness, that was Austrian manners which she was bringing into France.

Their blood was up. Now they spoke to her and each other in the coarsest terms. They told each other crudely why she and the King could not have children. They repeated all the rumours, all the stories, which were circulating in the lowest cafés and taverns of the town.

They would show the proud Austrian that French *poissardes* did not mince their words.

Still she walked on; they were surrounding her and she could feel their hands on her clothes; their hot breath, smelling of garlic, their clothes saturated with the stench of fish, made her fear she would faint.

The Princesse de Lamballe, who walked beside her, was breathing heavily, and Antoinette knew that the Princesse was afraid of the people when they came too close. These women crowding about them reminded Antoinette of the mob she had seen from the balconies at the time of the *Guerre des Farines*. They were the same people who had shouted *Vive le Roi! Vive la Reine!* in Rheims – the same people in a different mood.

The apartments were reached at last. The pages opened the

door. For one hideous second she was afraid the *poissardes* would follow her. In that second it was possible to think other evil thoughts. She was able to picture them, laying their dirty hands upon her, stripping her of her clothes, while their obscene observations became more obscene.

She thought: I am afraid of the people of France.

Then the door was shut and there was peace. She could no longer hear the voices, no longer smell the fish market.

The Princesse de Lamballe, her dearest friend, was beside her.

'They should not upset you,' murmured the Princesse. 'The low rabble . . . what do we care for them?'

'I care, not for them nor their lewdness, their obscenity,' said Antoinette. 'I care only that I am a barren Queen.'

Then she went to her bed and lay there sobbing quietly.

The Princesse de Lamballe drew the curtains and left her to sob out her grief.

❖ ❖ ❖

The Princesse de Lamballe, whom the Queen had selected for her special friend soon after she came to the throne, was a charming young girl, generous and sentimental, truly fond of the Queen, truly distressed to see her unhappy.

As Marie Thérèse Louise de Savoie-Carignan, a member of the noble house of Savoy, she had been married very early to Louis Stanislas de Bourbon, Prince de Lamballe, who was the only son of a grandson of Louis Quatorze and Madame de Montespan. Fortunately for the Princesse her husband had died a year after their marriage, worn out by a life of excessive dissipation; and the Princesse's experiment in matrimony, being so brief, had left her gentle and eager for friendship. She was a little naive in her outlook, young for her years in spite of her experiences, and Antoinette, perhaps owing to her own unfortunate matrimonial experiences, found the girl's company attractive.

Antoinette had bestowed on the Princesse the post of superintendent of her houshold and, as this post had not been held by anyone for over thirty years, it was clearly of no great importance although it carried with it a salary of 150,000 livres. Antoinette wished to keep her charming friend at her side and see her entertain at the Court; therefore it had been her great pleasure to bestow the post upon her.

It was unwise, since there were so many to watch and criticise her actions, but Antoinette shut her eyes to criticism.

After that humiliating and even alarming walk from the lying-in chamber of Madame d'Artois to the Queen's apartments, the Princesse, drawing the curtains about the Queen's bed, stood uncertainly, wondering what she could do to comfort her beloved mistress.

Sensing that Antoinette wished to be alone with her grief she tiptoed to the door and there was met by the little Marquise de Clermont-Tonnerre.

'Rose Bertin has come to see you,' she said, 'concerning a dress. I told her you were with the Queen and that she had no right to come to the château unless sent for. I could not get rid of her.'

The Princesse, glad to have something to do, said that she would go to her apartments, which adjoined those of the Queen, and that Rose Bertin should be brought to her there.

No sooner had she gone there than the *modiste* was shown in.

Rose Bertin, sprung from the lower classes, was a woman of

vigour, imagination and determination. As dressmaker to Court ladies her great ambition was to serve the Queen. She had on many occasions tried to insinuate herself into the château, but the rigorous etiquette imposed on tradespeople had meant that she had never been allowed to speak to the Queen.

Madame Bertin did not know how to take No for an answer. She had applied herself to her trade and knew herself to be the best dressmaker in Paris, but even the best dressmaker needed luck and good friends to achieve the goal she had set for herself.

She had at last made a dress for the Princesse de Lamballe, and she knew that that lady was delighted with her work, as she had intended she should be. She had pictured the Queen's admiration; and the question: 'But who is your dressmaker?' And the answer: 'Oh, it is a little dressmaker from the rue Saint-Honoré. Rose Bertin by name.' And then the Queen's command: 'Send for Rose Bertin.'

But it had not happened, and Rose Bertin was not one to sit down and wait for things to happen.

She had been in the lying-in chamber; had witnessed the departure of the Queen. The *modiste* in her longed to dress that exquisite figure while the business woman reminded herself of the benefits which could accrue from the dressing of a Queen.

She had brought with her a roll of silk to show one of the ladies of the Court who had asked to see it; but, having seen the Queen and the Princesse leave for the former's apartments, she had decided that she would ask for an audience of the Princesse; for if the Princesse was with the Queen, might not the name of Rose Bertin then be brought to Her Majesty's notice?

In the Princesse's presence she unrolled the silk.

'Recently arrived from Lyons, Madame. See the sheen! Oh, the beauty of it. I see it in folds from the waist . . . and a train; and instead of panniers, a new hooped arrangement which I have invented and which none has seen yet. To tell the truth,' went on the garrulous *couturière*, 'there was one I had in mind when designing the new hoop. There is one who is dainty enough to show it to perfection.'

The Princesse smiled, for naturally she thought the woman was referring to herself. Rose Bertin knew this. She was shrewd; she had cultivated a bluff manner which served her well. It was said: 'La Bertin is honest. She is gruff, ill-mannered, but she means what she says.'

'The Queen,' said Bertin.

The Princesse's pretty face was thoughtful for a moment. The silk was delightful, and the Queen was very interested in fashion. Would it take her mind from that dreadful scene in the lying-in chamber if she could be interested in the new hoop?

'Madame has a plan?' prompted Rose.

'Wait here a moment,' said the Princesse.

Rose could scarcely hide her pleasure; her capable hands even shook a little as she folded the silk.

In a short time the Princesse returned. 'Come this way,' she said. 'You must not be over-awed. I am going to present you to the Queen.'

'But this is a great honour!' said Rose, and she could not completely hide the smile of satisfaction; it was so gratifying to an ambitious woman when her little ruses succeeded.

She was determined to make the most of the interview.

The Queen's eyes were a little red and puffy. So she had

162

been upset by the humiliating scene. That was good. She would be more receptive.

What a wonderful hour that was for Rose Bertin. She knew – being Rose – that it was the beginning of good fortune.

The Queen stood in the centre of the apartment and allowed Rose to pin the new silk about her, to explain how effective the new hoops would be.

Rose was an *artiste*. A few deft touches, and she could transform a piece of silk into a magnificent dress.

The Queen was gracious, even familiar.

'But you have real genius,' she said.

'If I could but dress Your Majesty,' added Rose, 'I should be the happiest dressmaker in the world.'

'Who would not be,' said the Princesse, 'to dress a Queen?'

'A Queen!' Rose decided that a little bluntness would do no harm here. 'I was not thinking of the Queen. I was thinking of the most exquisite model to show off my beautiful, beautiful creations.'

'You forget to whom you speak,' said the Princesse.

Rose looked bewildered. 'I crave pardon. I was ever one to speak my mind.'

The bait had been swallowed. The Queen was delighted.

'When the dress is made,' said she, 'bring it to me yourself; and in the meantime bring me sketches of more dresses, patterns of more silk.'

When Rose departed she could scarcely wait to get back to the rue Saint-Honoré.

'The woman did me good,' said Antoinette to the Princesse. 'Oh, dear Marie, I am glad you brought her to me.'

'I am glad she did you good,' said the Princesse, kissing

Antoinette, for there was the utmost familiarity between them. 'It hurts me, more than I can express, to see you unhappy.'

She did not realise that, in bringing the calculating *modiste* to the Queen, she had done far more harm than good.

✣ ✣ ✣

It was after that incident that Antoinette began to live a life of unparalleled gaiety.

Rose Bertin was visiting her apartments twice a week, making dress after dress. The Queen received her in her *petits appartements* much to the disgust of the old nobility. Madame Bertin, shrewd business woman that she was, now made not only for the Queen, with whom of course prices were never discussed, but for other ladies of the Court who were determined to follow the fashions set by Her Majesty.

Rose had now extended her premises and was employing many seamstresses; she set up a sign over her shop: 'Dressmaker to the Queen.' She had her own carriage in which she rode out from Paris to Versailles. She proclaimed herself to be, not only the Queen's dressmaker, but her friend.

This was ridiculous, declared the ladies of the Court. Never before in the history of France had Queens received their dressmakers in their own apartments, chatted with them, and received them as equals.

Rose went her haughty way. She treated the ladies of the Court with her own brand of gruff indifference. 'Oh, I am too busy to see you, my lady. I have an appointment with Her Majesty.' It was unheard of. It was incomprehensible. So were the bills which were sent in from time to time.

The Queen, it was said, chose her friends from strange caprices. She never said: Here is the noblest lady at the Court;

she must be my friend. It was well known that the ladies of highest rank – Madame de Provence, Madame d'Artois and Madame de Chartres – were her greatest enemies. No! She must be charmed by the beauty of some person of little fortune, someone whose manners attracted rather than her rank.

It was thus with the Comtesse de Polignac.

All at Court remembered how that great friendship began. Gabrielle Yolande was the wife of the Comte de Polignac – an enchanting creature, with blue eyes and soft brown curls. The Queen had noticed her at a Court ball and had her brought to her side.

'I have never noticed you before at Court,' she said.

Gabrielle lowered those enchanting blue eyes and murmured: 'Your Majesty, I rarely come to Court. We are too poor – my husband and I – to live at Court or to come often.'

Such honesty delighted the Queen.

'And to whom do we owe this present visit?' she asked.

'To my cousin Diane who is lady-in-waiting to the Comtesse d'Artois.'

'Stay beside me awhile and tell me about yourself.' Antoinette laughed, for she was aware of the disapproving eyes upon her. It was quite wrong, of course, for the Queen to select the most unimportant guest and spend almost the whole evening talking to her. For that reason alone she would have wished to do it.

But apart from that, this little Gabrielle Yolande had proved delightful company.

'You shall have a place at Court,' said Antoinette, 'for I feel that you and I are going to be good friends.'

Gabrielle was not enthusiastic. She had her life in the country, she said.

'And no wish for a place at Court?'

'Madame, we have not the means.'

The Queen smiled. 'A place at Court would bring with it the means.'

She looked at the childish face and thought how pretty was this girl, though she wore few jewels; yet a cherry-coloured ribbon was more becoming in some cases, thought the Queen, than expensive jewellery.

And she prevailed upon this girl to stay at Court; she kept her with her and they were often seen walking in the gardens together – she, the little Polignac and the Princesse de Lamballe.

But if Gabrielle was not looking for advantages, the same could not be said of her relations. They came to Court; they begged little Gabrielle to speak to the Queen on their behalf for this or that favour. As for the Queen, she delighted to please Gabrielle; and in addition to the post she found for Gabrielle's husband, she showered further honours on other members of the family.

Who were these Polignacs? it was asked at Court. What was the meaning of the Queen's passionate friendships, with first the Princesse de Lamballe, and now with this girl? The Queen was unnatural. Why did she not give children to the state instead of frolicking with young women?

She knew of these rumours. She had her friends among the other sex. There were the Ducs de Coigny, de Guines, de Lauzun; there was the Hungarian Count Esterhazy; there was the Comte de Vaudreuil and the Prince de Ligne. Several of these men were devoted to the Queen; they accompanied her frequently and many were the passionate glances they sent in her direction.

Antoinette delighted in their admiration. She liked to remember that she was not only a Queen but a very charming and desirable woman. This failure to get a child filled her with a great desire to have handsome men about her. It was not due to her lack of attraction that the King preferred his blacksmith's shop. She wanted to reassure not only the Court of that but herself.

There was one who was in constant attendance. That was Artois. Louis had his state duties, and his relaxation with his books and locks; Louis liked to retire early to bed and rise early. Provence held himself aloof from the Queen's set. He had his own reasons. He now firmly believed that he would follow his brother to the throne, for he was certain that Louis and Antoinette would never have children. He wanted to show France that he was quiet and steady – and that he would be a good King. He suffered from a disability similar to that which afflicted Louis. He was sterile, and poor Josèphe was as barren as Antoinette.

Artois, the youngest of the brothers, had no such ambitions. He wanted only to enjoy himself. He was high spirited, ready for any adventure; he was already heartily sick of Thérèse, the only one of the royal wives who proved fertile; she was already pregnant again, and Artois believed that his only duty was to make sure that Thérèse was pregnant and then desert her for his mistresses, of whom he had many. The love of gaiety which he sensed in the Queen was his own love of gaiety. He enjoyed her company and he contrived to make himself her constant attendant.

The rumours were soon circulating.

'Artois is the Queen's lover,' said the people of Paris. 'They are often seen together.'

These rumours did not reach the King. None cared to talk to him of his wife's levity. As for Louis, he thought Antoinette the loveliest creature at Court and, because of his failure as a husband, he still felt the wish to indulge her. Provence heard the rumours and delighted in them. He was too shrewd to show his dislike of the Queen; his was a secret brooding antagonism. Many of the rumours were started by himself and Josèphe, but outwardly he feigned friendship.

Thus Antoinette was thrown into the company of Artois – which suited her own mood – and although she looked upon him merely as a convenient companion and brother, rumour persisted that they were lovers.

They were seen together at the Opéra balls; they went together to the races – a new innovation from England. Artois could be seen riding into Paris in his *cabriolet* and returning to Versailles in the early hours of the morning. In the winter he and Antoinette had sledging parties, much to the disgust of the people who declared this to be yet another Austrian fashion introduced by the Queen. They made up parties to see the sunrise. And after such a party, it was said that the Queen disappeared into a copse and remained there for quite a long time with one of the gentlemen.

The days were full for Antoinette and it was a matter of dashing from pleasure to pleasure. She rarely rose before four or five in the afternoon. How could she, when she had been dancing through the night? The ceremony of the rising would begin with her going through her book in which were pinned miniature models of all the dresses in her wardrobe. She would take a pin and place it in the model of the dress she wished to wear for the beginning of her day. There were endless discussions with her favourites, and Madame de Polignac was always nearest to the Queen, and the Princesse de Lamballe not far distant. And while the Queen was being dressed they would chatter together about the night's fête or ball or entertainment. There might be a session with dear Madame Bertin who had become almost as great a friend as Lamballe and Polignac.

One day Antoinette's carriage broke down as she was riding masked to Paris for a ball, and while the driver went to procure another carriage, the Queen saw a fiacre, hailed it and arrived at the ball in it.

Antoinette, delighted with her adventure, immediately began to talk of it. It was so amusing; and she had never ridden in a fiacre before.

This story was hailed with horror by all the Court. What lack of etiquette! What defiance of form!

The people of Paris supplied a sequel. The Queen had had her reasons for riding in a fiacre. Quite clearly she had come from a rendezvous with her latest lover.

This story brought protests from the Empress.

Antoinette must mend her ways. Whither was she going? asked her distracted mother. Gossip abounded. She danced through the night, slept through the day, scarcely saw her husband and had so far failed to give France a Dauphin.

She *must* change her mode of living.

It was a hot summer's day. The Queen's *calash* was speeding along the road past a group of cottages when a child ran out.

There was a wild scream and the boy was lying bleeding by the roadside.

The Queen called at once to the coachman to stop. The *calash* drew up and Antoinette alighted.

Several people came out from the cottages, but Antoinette did not see them; she had picked up the child and was looking with dismay at the blood on his woollen cap.

And as she looked at him he opened his eyes and met her gaze.

'I thank God,' said the Queen, 'he is not dead.' She turned to a woman who was standing near by. 'Could we not take him into his home? He ran out in front of the horses. I feared he might have been killed. Where does he live?'

The woman indicated a cottage.

'I will carry him there,' said the Queen.

The driver of her *calash* was beside her. 'Permit me, Your Majesty.'

But Antoinette, deeply conscious of that emotion which children never failed to arouse in her, held the child tightly in her arms and refused to relinquish him. The boy was gazing up at her and a little colour had returned to his cheeks. Antoinette saw with relief that he was not badly hurt after all.

An old woman had come to the door of that cottage for which they were making. She saw Antoinette, recognised her, and knelt beside her water butt.

'I pray you rise,' said Antoinette. 'This little boy has been hurt. He is yours?'

'He is my grandson, Your Majesty.'

'We must see how badly hurt he is.'

The old woman turned and led the way into the cottage. Antoinette had never before been inside such a place. There was one room only, which housed a big family, and it seemed that there were children everywhere. They were all regarding the splendid apparition with astonished bewilderment.

'Make your curtsys,' said the old woman. 'This is the Queen.'

The children bobbed quaint curtsys which made the susceptible Antoinette's eyes fill with tears.

Oh, the squalor, the unclean smell – and so many children in one small room, when the spacious royal nursery was quite bare! It was heartbreaking.

She laid the child on the table because there appeared to be nowhere else to put him.

'I don't think he is badly hurt,' she said. 'I was afraid when I saw the blood on his face.'

'What was he up to?' asked the old woman. And the Queen noticed that the child cowered away from her. One small hand was grasping the Queen's dress, and it was as though those round eyes were pleading for royal protection.

' 'Twas but natural for a child to run into the road,' said the Queen. 'If we had some water we could bathe that wound on his forehead and mayhap we could bandage it.'

'Odette,' cried the woman. 'Get some water.'

A dark-eyed girl, whose matted hair fell about her face, could not remove her eyes from the Queen as she took a bucket and went out to the well.

'What is the little one's name?' asked the Queen.

'James Armand, Madame,' the woman replied.

'Ah, Monsieur James Armand,' said Antoinette, 'are you feeling better now?'

The child smiled, and again she felt the tears spring to her eyes. There was a fascinating gap in his teeth; she noticed that his hand had tightened on her sleeve.

'Could you stand, my dear, then we shall see if there are any bones broken?' She lifted him up and he stood on the table – a minute little man in the woollen cap and clogs of the peasantry.

'Do your legs feel all right?' asked Antoinette.

He nodded.

'Does he talk?' she wanted to know.

'Oh, he talks well enough. There's no stopping him. He knows he's done wrong though. He's a cunning one.'

'It was not wrong,' said the Queen. 'It was but a childish action.'

The girl had returned with the bucket of water, and the Queen took off the woollen cap and bathed the child's brow. She longed now to leave the cottage. It was so stuffy and malodorous; yet she was loth to leave little James Armand.

The water was cold; there was no cloth, so she tore her fine kerchief into two pieces and damped one with water.

'Does that hurt?' she asked tenderly. 'Ah, I see you are brave, Monsieur James Armand.'

The little boy had moved closer to her.

'You have a large family,' she said to the woman.

'These five are my daughter's,' was the answer. 'She died last year and left me to care for them.'

'That is very sad. I am sorry for you.'

'That is life, Madame,' said the woman with bleak stoicism.

Antoinette tied the dry half of her kerchief about the boy's head. 'There! Now I think you will suffer no harm, monsieur.'

She drew away from the table, but the boy kept hold of her sleeve; his mouth began to turn down at the corners and his eyes filled with tears.

'Let go of the lady,' said the grandmother sharply.

He refused. The woman was about to snatch him away, when the Queen prevented her.

'You do not want me to go away?' asked Antoinette.

'You stay here,' said the boy. 'You stay always.'

'He's a forward little villain, that one is,' said the grand-mother. 'That's the Queen you're speaking to.'

'Queen,' said the little boy, and in all her life Antoinette had never sensed so much adoration as she did now in that small voice.

She made one of her impulsive decisions.

'Let me take him,' she said. 'Would you come with me? Would you be my little boy?'

The joy in his face was the most moving thing she had ever seen. The little hand was in hers now, clinging, clinging as though he was never going to let her go.

The Queen turned to the woman. 'If you will let me take this boy, and adopt him,' she said, 'I will provide for the upbringing of the four who are left to you.'

The woman's answer was to fall on her knees and kiss the hem of the Queen's gown.

Antoinette was never so happy as when she was giving happiness.

'Then rise,' she said, 'rise, my good woman. And have no fear for your family. All will be well, I promise you. And I shall take James Armand away with me now.'

She lifted the child in her arms. She kissed his grubby face; her reward was a pair of arms about her neck – a tight and suffocating hug.

She thought: he shall be bathed; he shall be suitably dressed. James Armand, you are my little boy from now on.

For a long time she was happy.

Each morning James Armand was brought to her; he would climb on to her bed; he would be happy merely to be with her. He asked nothing else. He was not like other children. He was glad of sweetmeats; he liked handsome toys; but nothing but the company of the Queen could give him real pleasure.

If she had danced late and was too tired to be disturbed he would sit outside her door waiting disconsolately. None of her ladies could lure him away with any promise of a treat.

There was only one thing which could satisfy James Armand, and that was the presence of his most beautiful Queen who had by the miracle of a summer's morning become his own mother.

Sometimes he dreamed that he was at the cottage door watching the carriage pass by. There was a heavy gloom in those dreams because in them the royal *calash* had not pulled up and he was still living with his grandmother in her dark one-roomed cottage . . . the miracle had not happened, his enchantress had not appeared.

He would wake whimpering; then his little fingers would touch the fine linen of his bedclothes and he would see the gilded furniture in his room, and he would know that all was well.

Once she had seen the traces of tears on his cheeks and demanded to know the reason.

'Dreamed you did not come,' said James Armand.

Then he was caught in that perfumed embrace, and his happiness was so great that he was glad of the bad dream which had made it possible.

So heedlessly she lived through those gilded days.

The hours flew past, there was never time to be bored; and she dreaded boredom more than anything on earth. She confided this to Artois. It was a fear they had in common. So she must plan more dresses with Rose Bertin; she must give a ball, have firework displays; she would spend an hour or so playing with her dear James Armand who so adored her; she would ride out to Paris, masked for the Opéra ball, as she used to in the old days.

But there was something missing in her life. Her dear friends, Madame de Polignac and the Princesse de Lamballe, could not make up for that. Indeed, those young men who hovered about her, paying their compliments which could be delicate or bold, came nearer to providing it. Madame de Polignac had taken a lover – the Comte de Vaudreuil, a Creole, not very handsome, his face having been pitted by the smallpox, but so witty, so amusing that he was quite charming. Gabrielle Yolande confided in the Queen, and Antoinette felt those twinges of envy for women who could enjoy such a relationship.

Another of her friends, Madame de Guémenée, took the Duc de Coigny for her lover. It was not that Antoinette shared her confidence, nor indeed that she liked her, but she was often at her card parties, for gambling, Antoinette had discovered, was one of the surest ways of driving boredom away. It was purely for the sake of Madame de Guémenée's card parties that the Queen frequented her apartments.

Madame de Guémenée belonged to the Rohan family and the Queen did not feel very friendly disposed towards one member of that family. This was Louis, Prince de Rohan, that Cardinal whom she had never forgotten because he was the first man who had looked at her with that kind of admiration which she now met on every side. He was the young man who had received her in place of his uncle the Bishop in the Strasbourg Cathedral, when she was on her way to France from Vienna.

She had good reason not to forget this man, for she had discovered that he had written disparagingly of her mother in a letter from Vienna, whither he had gone soon after the occasion of his first meeting with Antoinette. She had heard no other than Madame du Barry reading it aloud. And for that, Antoinette had said, she would never forgive Louis, Prince de Rohan. All the same she could not resist his relative's card parties. Moreover Madame de Guémenée was a friend of Gabrielle's and that meant that the Queen must receive her and try to like her.

And so, looking round at her friends and seeing their happiness, she found new emotions being stirred within her. She found herself listening more eagerly to the fulsome compliments of the men about her; she found herself encouraging these compliments.

The Duc de Lauzun was particularly charming and he was known to be something of a hot-head. During those dangerous days he was often in the company of the Queen. With Madame de Polignac and her lover, the Queen and Lauzun would stroll in the gardens, and dance their minuets and gavottes on the grass before the Petit Trianon.

It was beginning to be asked: 'Is the Duc de Lauzun the Queen's lover?'

As for Lauzun he grew more and more certain of the Queen's surrender, and he found it becoming increasingly difficult to remain in her company without attempting to make love to her.

He found her one day alone in her boudoir — that charmingly intimate chamber — where she often received her visitors and where she herself had commanded that ceremony be set aside.

'Antoinette,' said Lauzun, taking both her hands, 'how long can we go on like this?'

She looked at him in astonishment, but they both knew the astonishment to be feigned.

'I do not understand you,' she said in a whisper.

He drew her to him and murmured: 'Then you must . . . for it is more than I can humanly endure to go on like this . . . seeing you day after day . . . so close . . . so near to me . . . and never to kiss your lips . . . never to hold you . . . '

'I pray you stop,' she cried in a panic.

But he would not stop. She had played the coquette so long, so often; she had played at taking a lover as she had played at being a mother to a motherless boy.

This was different. The play-acting had suddenly become a reality. There was no mistaking Lauzun's meaning. He was suggesting that they should be lovers — even as Gabrielle and Vaudreuil were — even as Victoire Guémenée and her lover were.

She felt herself tremble. The blood rushed to her head and drained away again. She was almost fainting with horror.

This must never be.

What if she were to have a child — a child that all would know was not the King's child.

She drew herself up to her full height. She suppressed her raging senses; she would not look into the fiercely demanding eyes of the Duc de Lauzun.

The game had gone too far.

'Never, never, never,' she said to herself. To him she said coldly, 'Go away from here, Monsieur. You must never come here without my permission. You must never be with me alone. . . .'

'My dearest,' began the Duke.

But the Queen turned away. She ran out of her boudoir and shut herself into her bedchamber.

She was trembling with fear and the knowledge that she had needed all her strength to tear herself away from temptation.

✤ ✤ ✤

There were spies even in the ideal kingdom of the Petit Trianon.

Mercy was alarmed. He wrote in haste to Maria Theresa. It was no use remonstrating with Antoinette now. Remonstrances were useless. What had she said when the Empress had begged her to curb her extravagant love of jewels, having heard that she had just purchased a magnificent pair of diamond earrings? 'So my earrings have travelled to Vienna?'

No! Letters were no use. But something drastic must be done to prevent the Queen's rushing headlong into disaster.

The great trouble was the King's disability, brooded the wise Maria Theresa.

She called her son to her.

'Joseph,' she said, 'you must pay a visit to your sister. You must talk to her tactfully. Do not lecture, for if you do so you will make her angry and that will drive her mayhap to greater folly. Try to instil some sound sense in her. At the same time try to strengthen the alliance between our two countries.'

Joseph looked at his mother ironically.

'You have left unsaid the most important part of my mission,' he said.

She nodded.

'I will speak to Louis,' said Joseph, 'and see if an end cannot be made to this sorry state of affairs.'

So Joseph II, Emperor of Austria, came into France.

Joseph was entirely sure of his ability to set matters right for his sister, for Joseph had a very high opinion of his own powers. He looked upon himself as the most important and the most successful ruler in Europe.

Everywhere he went he called attention to himself by his alleged desire for no ceremony. He did not travel as a mighty Emperor might be expected to travel.

'Indeed not,' said Joseph. 'To all on the road from Vienna to Paris I shall be known as Count Falkenstein.'

So through all the villages and towns his servants implored great secrecy.

'Hush!' they said. 'Count Falkenstein demands privacy. Above all he wants no fuss. Make sure that there is complete secrecy as to his arrival.'

'And who is Count Falkenstein?' asked the villagers and townsfolk. In Austria they knew, of course. They had often been made aware of the Emperor's aliases.

The rain was pouring down when he arrived in Paris. He came in an ordinary little open carriage such as any minor nobleman might affect. He sat in it soaked to the skin, greatly enjoying the experience. He had refused to go in state to Versailles where splendid apartments had been offered him.

'No, no, no,' he protested. 'Mercy shall put me up at the Embassy. I want no fuss. My camp-bed will suffice, and a bearskin will serve for a mattress.'

It pleased him greatly – he the mighty Emperor – to live as an ordinary man. He wanted the world to know that he despised physical comforts. Comfort for him was to know he ruled his country well, that his subjects should know he carried their welfare close to his heart.

The day after his arrival in Paris, the news of which he had begged should be kept from the royal family, he set out in a post-chaise from his Paris lodging for Versailles.

'I am most anxious,' he had already written to the Abbé de Vermond, 'to avoid sightseers or any demonstration. When I arrive I wish you to meet me and conduct me with all speed and with no fuss to the *petits appartements* of my sister.'

This was done.

Antoinette had been informed that he was in Paris and, although she had been unsure of the hour he would come to Versailles and in what manner, was not altogether surprised to receive him.

She had made a point of retiring early the night before. She was a little afraid of Joseph, much as she longed to see someone from home. He was, after all, fourteen years older than she was and had always been the domineering elder brother.

'Much as I long to see him,' she had said to Gabrielle, 'I know there are going to be some stern lectures. Joseph could never resist them.'

He came bursting into the apartment wearing with pride his plain brown jacket which he believed gave him the appearance of a humble citizen; and he took one look at his little sister who was seated at her mirror while her ladies were combing her hair. It was hanging round her shoulders, and even Joseph was moved at the sight of so much beauty.

'Joseph!' she cried, and the tears brimmed over and began to fall down her cheeks.

'My little Toinette,' returned Joseph, genuinely moved as he took her into his arms.

'It is so long,' he said.

'Far, far too long, Joseph.'

They held each other at arm's length, looked into each other's faces and both began to speak rapidly in German.

'And how is my dearest mother?'

'As well as we can expect, and longing to hear news of you.'

'She hears too much news of me.'

'I hope to take good news back to her.'

'Oh, Joseph, Joseph! It is so wonderful to see someone from home.'

'You are prettier than I thought,' said Joseph in an unusual rush of sentiment which this reunion had aroused. 'If I could find a woman as pretty, I would marry again.'

That made her laugh and hug him and grimace at his plain brown jacket, and call him Herr Joseph ... plain Herr Joseph.

'I will take you to the King's apartment,' she declared, and she led him there by the hand.

The King was not fully dressed, but Joseph shared a disregard of ceremony with his sister.

He took his brother-in-law in his arms and kissed his cheeks. Then he looked at him with affection which veiled a certain contempt, for Joseph felt old and wise in the presence of Louis.

The King was delighted to see the Queen's pleasure in her brother, and welcomed Joseph on behalf of France.

The Emperor had come to Versailles unheralded, and there would be many who would wish to pay him homage. He must meet the King's brothers, the King's ministers, the noblemen of the Court.

Joseph smiled benignly but with faint superciliousness. He considered all this ceremony, all this gilded splendour, unnecessary to the ruling of a country.

❖ ❖ ❖

The table was laid for dinner in the Queen's bedchamber, and three armchairs had been placed at it for the King, the Queen and the Emperor.

'No, no!' cried Joseph, for now the emotion he had felt at his reunion with his sister had passed and he was himself again, the Spartan Emperor, determined to behave as an ordinary man, determined to excite attention by his desire for anonymity, determined to receive great honour by his disregard for it. 'No chair for me. No chair for me. I am a plain and ordinary man. A stool is good enough for Count Falkenstein.'

'Bring a stool for the Emperor,' ordered the King. 'And since our guest uses a stool, so must we. Let three stools be brought.'

So the chairs were removed and the stools brought, and the King and Queen rested their aching backs against the Queen's bed during the meal, while the Emperor, smiling at their weakness, sat erect on his stool.

'I look forward,' he told the King, 'to meeting your brothers and their wives. I believe we shall have much to say to each other.'

He was already preparing the lectures he would deliver to the King's brothers. Provence did not enter enough into public affairs. Artois was too irresponsible. The King was a poor conversationalist; he should practise conversation instead of shutting himself away with his locksmith. Joseph must therefore have many improving talks with his brother-in-law. He clearly had a great many tasks to perform before he returned to Vienna.

❖ ❖ ❖

'My dear sister,' began the Emperor when they were alone together. 'All this preoccupation with gaiety is causing a great deal of comment throughout Europe. You may be sure it is causing more in France. You are a Queen, and Queen of a great country. I would not suggest that you meddle in state affairs, but I beg of you, try to infuse into your behaviour a greater seriousness. We hear of your extravagance in Vienna – the jewels, the dresses, the way in which you spend your days. We have heard of your expenditure at your country house. It is fantastic'

Antoinette laughed. 'Joseph, this is not Vienna. The people of France wish their Kings and Queens to look like Kings and Queens. They would not appreciate a Spartan Emperor.'

Joseph did not believe that. He was sure that he would be appreciated wherever he lived.

'Your love of gambling could be disastrous,' went on the Emperor. 'You consort with the wrong people. That Madame de Guémenée is no friend for you. Her apartment is nothing more than a gambling den. I was shocked to see that last night in your presence someone was accused of cheating. Do you not understand what lack of dignity there is in that? And look at your hair!'

'What is wrong with my hair? Does this style not become me?'

'Become you it may, but it seems to me that piled up thus it is over-fragile to bear a crown.'

'Joseph, you know not our customs.'

'I know the ways of the world, and I believe that things cannot go on here as they have been going on. I am afraid for your happiness. Things cannot go on like this. You only think of amusing yourself. Have you no feeling for the King?'

He saw the look of pain in her eyes.

'But,' he went on, 'if there were a child it would be different. There must be a Dauphin.'

'Ah, Joseph,' said Antoinette, 'if that were but possible!'

The Emperor's lips tightened. His look implied that, as with God, all things were possible with the Emperor Joseph.

In any case it was concerning this matter of the Dauphin that he had come to France.

✤ ✤ ✤

Joseph walked about the streets of Paris in his plain brown coat, followed only by two lackeys in sombre grey.

He was noticed. It was inevitable, for no one else looked at all like the Emperor.

The citizens of Paris liked him – liked that lack of fuss and ceremony in him; that indifference to formality, which they so deplored in his sister, perversely they found charming in the Emperor.

'Long live the Emperor Joseph!' they cried.

He would hold up his hand deprecatingly. 'My good people . . . my good people, I am sorry you recognise me. I had hoped to mingle among you like an ordinary man.'

'How charming he is!' they said to one another.

Like a plain citizen, he wandered into shops and bought goods. He chatted lightly and good-naturedly; he was always so eager to know about their lives, so very interested in the affairs of ordinary men.

The people of Paris felt more affection towards their Queen for possessing such a brother.

Joseph shut himself in with his brother-in-law.

Joseph, the older man, smiled benignly.

'Well, Louis, my brother,' he said, 'this has been a delightful time for me. It is pleasant to see my sister in her home and to know that she has such a good fellow for a husband.'

'I thank you, Joseph,' began Louis.

But Joseph held up a hand. 'You know, speaking as brother to brother, you would be more of a conversationalist if you practised talking more. You are inclined to let others do all the talking, Louis. You should make one of these ministers of yours listen while you talk. Don't let the people shout you down.'

'I . . . began Louis.

'It's quite simple,' pursued Joseph. 'Shut them up . . . just shut them up. There is one matter which greatly disturbs me, Louis. Now we must be very frank together. Well, after all, are we not brothers? I will make no secret of the fact; it is on account of this matter that you now see me here in France. The Queen is too frivolous, and it is clear that she is plunging into so much gaiety because she lacks more important pastimes. The Queen should be thinking of her children, Louis, not her gambling debts.'

'If it were only possible,' murmured the King. 'It is the great grief of her life . . . and mine.'

'Now, Louis, let us consider this disability of yours. Tell me all about it. Speak frankly. I am your elder brother, you know. Feel no embarrassment. There is too much at stake for embarrassment. There are operations – simple operations, you know – and our doctors have skill, greater skill than ever before. A little circumcision and then . . . all would be well, if what I have heard ails you is the truth.'

The Emperor took his embarrassed brother-in-law by the shoulders and shook him affectionately.

'Now, Louis, have I your word that you will submit to an examination? But of course I have. You cannot so fail in your duty as to fail me . . . and your Queen and your country. We will give orders immediately, and the operation shall be performed.' Joseph gave the King of France one of his hearty *bourgeois* slaps on the back. 'Then I doubt not that all will be well in France.'

And such was the persuasive power of the Emperor that, before he left Paris, the operation had been performed.

It was not long after, that Antoinette was writing to her mother:

'I have attained the happiness which is of the utmost importance to my whole life. More than a week ago my marriage was thoroughly consummated. Yesterday the attempt was repeated. I was in mind to send a special messenger to my beloved mother, but I was afraid this might attract too much attention and gossip. I don't think that I am with child yet, but at any rate I have hopes of becoming so from day to day.'

The Court was seething with excitement.

'Have you heard . . . ?'

'It was that *petite opération* . . .'

'Is it really so?'

'Indeed yes. Have you not noticed the dark circles under the Queen's eyes?'

It was indeed so. The King could not resist talking about it. He was so delighted.

Adelaide was at his side; the other two aunts not far off.

'Dear Louis, but there is a change in you. You are a deeply contented man.'

'I am indeed a contented man, dear aunt.'

'It was . . . perhaps the *petite opération*?'

All the aunts came a little nearer. Three pairs of eyes studied him intently; they were like gimlets trying to probe his head, uncover the thoughts behind his eyes.

'Yes, aunt, yes. It gives me great pleasure.'

'It gives him great pleasure,' said Adelaide to her sisters when they were alone. 'Depend upon it, it will not be long before the marriage is fertile.'

Provence and Josèphe shared a great fear. Could it possibly be true? And if it were, there would be an end to hope, an end to ambition.

'Watch the Queen,' said Provence. 'Watch her as we never watched her before.'

The Spanish Ambassador, the Sardinian Ambassador, the English Ambassador, were writing long letters to their governments.

The whole Court was waiting.

Provence breathed a little more easily. It was becoming clear that the new pleasure, discovered by Louis, did not appeal quite so much as hunting or making locks. A good sign. A very good sign.

Maria Theresa wrote frantic letters to her daughter. 'Make sure that you retire early, at the time the King retires. Do not stay in your single bed at Petit Trianon.'

Then one day there was a certain brooding serenity visible in the Queen's face. She was absentminded when people spoke to her. She had given up dancing through the night; and she no longer seemed interested in cards.

All noticed it, except the King. He was therefore surprised when one morning the Queen stormed unceremoniously into his apartments.

She frowned and stamped her foot.

'I have come, Sire,' she cried, 'to complain. One of your subjects has been impertinent enough to kick me in the belly.'

Louis stared at her in momentary alarm; then great floods of joy swept over him.

The tears sprang to his eyes and he held out his arms.

They kissed, embraced, and kissed again, their tears mingling.

'It is the happiest moment of my life,' said Antoinette. 'There can only be one happier. That will be when I hold our Dauphin in my arms.'

Louis was silent, but that was because words did not come easily to him. His joy was no less than hers.

✤ Chapter VII ✤

MADAME ROYALE AND THE DAUPHIN

That was a happy summer and autumn for the Queen. She spent a great deal of time at her Petit Trianon; now she could watch the children playing on the grass with quiet pleasure, for soon there would be a royal child to play on that grass, to come running to her, to pull at her skirts and demand bonbons. A Dauphin! She was sure the child would be a Dauphin.

There were so many pleasant matters with which to occupy her mind, and she discussed them continually with Gabrielle and the Princesse de Lamballe.

'He shall not be swaddled, my little Dauphin,' she declared. 'That is not good. It is old-fashioned and we shall employ no old-fashioned methods for Monsieur le Dauphin. He shall have everything that is modern. They say that children nowadays should be carried in a light cradle or in one's arms, and that little by little they should be put in the open air and sunshine. And when they have grown accustomed to it they may be in it all the time – little legs and arms free that they may kick at will. That is the way to make them strong. I shall have a little railing built on the terrace, and there the Dauphin will have his own

189

little kingdom. There he shall stand on his dear little legs and walk and grow strong.'

They listened to her; they discussed the garments he should wear; they planned the whole of his days. There was nothing which delighted the Queen more.

'There is only one thing that plagues me,' she said. 'Monsieur le Dauphin, you are so long in coming.'

She could not feel very interested in anything else. When Artois made his customary bow to the stately statue of Louis Quatorze in the Orangerie at Versailles and cried: '*Bonjour*, Grandpapa,' she no longer thought it as funny as she had hitherto. When the Prince de Ligne suggested he should hide behind the statue and, immediately after Artois uttered his greeting, reply to it in hollow tones to give the irreverent Artois a shock, she was only vaguely interested.

It was so difficult to think of anything but the Dauphin.

Little James Armand noticed the change in her. He would stand at her side, leaning fondly against her, his anxious eyes looking up into the beautiful face; for while she caressed his hair he sensed an absentmindedness in those delicate fingers, and a great fear came to him that even while she touched him, even while she smiled, her thoughts were far away.

'Come back,' he would say in panic. 'Come back.'

Then she smiled. 'What do you mean, my dear? Come back? I am here, am I not?'

'You are going far away,' he said.

'You are an odd little boy, Monsieur James,' she told him.

She noticed that his hand clutched her sleeve as it had that day when she had gone into his grandmother's cottage; and she told him about the baby she was to have.

'I have so longed for a baby. And now I am to have one.'

'You have your Monsieur James,' he reminded her. 'Is he not enough?'

She laughed. 'I am so greedy. And I love my Monsieur James so much that I could do with twenty like him.'

That made the boy laugh. But later she would find him standing in a corner, listening to the talk about the expected baby, a faint frown between his eyes.

She would call to him and make much of him, give him sweetmeats, those which he liked best. But he was disturbed, for he wanted more than sweetmeats.

It was during this period that Comte Hans Axel de Fersen came to the Court.

He was brought to her in the salon at the Palace of Versailles while she was with the King and surrounded by members of the Court.

As he knelt before her he saw the sudden recognition dawn in her eyes.

She spoke without thinking: 'Ah, this is an old acquaintance. Welcome to the Court, Comte de Fersen.'

He murmured: 'Your Majesty is gracious.'

The King scarcely noticed him. His mind was occupied with state matters. His enemies, the English, were at this time engaged in war with their colonists in America, and this war could prove of the utmost importance to France.

'It pleases me to see you here,' the Queen told the Comte. She was remembering that night at the Opéra ball and how bold this man had been; how he had snatched off her mask and known her for the Dauphine, as she had been then.

She had thought about him a great deal at the time; then other matters had claimed her attention. She was not surprised, studying him now, that he should have impressed her so deeply.

He was tall and very slender and the Swedish uniform became him well. His complexion was very pale but so clear as to seem almost transparent; his eyes, which were inclined to darkness, were very large, his nose straight and perfectly shaped, his mouth beautifully modelled, and his expression was both manly and tender.

Antoinette could readily understand how he had stirred her emotions at their romantic meeting.

She made him sit beside her and tell her all that had befallen him since their last meeting, of life in Sweden, of his father, the Senator, whom he greatly reverenced and admired.

He said suddenly: 'There is one occasion in my life which I shall never forget: that night when I danced at the Opéra ball with Your Majesty.'

'Did it shock you very much to discover who I was?'

'It was the greatest shock of my life.'

'You exaggerate, Comte,' she told him.

'No,' he said. 'I do not.'

She knew that she should not have kept him beside her talking, but she could not resist the temptation to do so.

'I was a Dauphine then,' she said. 'Now I am a Queen I have greater liberty to do what I please.'

'Queens,' he said, 'have less liberty to please themselves than Dauphines, Your Majesty.'

She laughed lightly. 'I believe you have been listening to tales of me.'

'I have treasured every word I ever heard spoken of you.'

'Evil tales?' she asked.

'Nothing could be evil in my eyes if it concerned you. The fact that it did so would banish evil from it.'

'That is a charming thing to say.' She lifted her fan with the quizzing glass set in it, and looked at him. She was somewhat short-sighted and she wanted to see clearly every line of his face.

'You find me changed,' she said. 'Different from the Dauphine with whom you danced.'

'I find you changed . . . yet the same. I find you perfect, although I had thought the Dauphine that. Should I not pass on now? We are being closely watched.'

'A plague on their watching eyes. They watch me continually. If I dismiss you that would surely be wrong, for everything I do is wrong in the eyes of those determined to condemn me. I merely have to do it to make it so. Therefore I *will* be wrong in commanding you to stay, for I surely should be if I dismissed you.'

'Your Majesty is a very happy woman,' he said wistfully.

'I am to have a child and I have longed for a child. I have been wildly happy since I knew it was to be so. Now . . . an old friend, or one whom I think of as an old friend, returns. That makes me happier still. Do not worry about staying beside me. The King is busy with his ministers. They talk endlessly of this war between England and her colonists in America.'

'French sympathies are with the settlers,' he said.

'Of a certainty. French sympathies are always contrary to English sympathies.'

'Throughout France many are saying, Good luck to those who rise against the English crown.'

'I know. Joseph, my brother who was here recently, was disturbed by such talk. When people praised those who were rebelling against the English crown he would grow a little angry, I must confess. Only, being Joseph, he never showed it. He used to say: "*Mon métier est d'être royaliste*," in his very curt crisp way which seemed to announce: "I, the Emperor, say this; therefore it must be so." Dear Joseph! He is the best brother in the world, but I cannot help laughing at him.'

Fersen laughed with her because her laughter was so infectious.

He told himself then: It was a mistake to come back to the Court. If she were Dauphine then, she is Queen now. She is even further away.

Antoinette kept him at her side until she left the salon for her apartments.

Josèphe and Thérèse were watching. They decided that the very next day they would visit the aunts at the Château of Bellevue where they were now installed. They would be able to talk of the Queen's outrageous behaviour with the Comte de Fersen. It was a pity of course that the Comte had not been in Paris a little earlier. Then they might have started the rumour that the Queen's condition might not have so much to do with the *petit opération* as most people had been deceived into thinking.

Still, it was always pleasant to gossip at Bellevue, where were gathering now all the disgruntled men and women of Versailles who were determined firmly to establish the growing unpopularity of the Queen.

Fersen must be a guest at the Petit Trianon; he must dance with the Queen on the lawn at her informal parties. 'We stand on little ceremony here,' the Queen told him. 'This is our escape from Versailles. We must have our escape. The solemnity of the Court is something I could not endure all the time.'

Therefore dancing on the lawn was yet another reminder to them both of dancing at the Opéra ball in Paris.

Fersen had been deeply attracted by Antoinette from the first moment he had seen her. Within a few days after his arrival at Court he was deeply in love with her.

Antoinette was charmed with him; he was so handsome, so attractive, and so much in love. He moved her to a deeper emotion than Lauzun ever had; but her mind was largely occupied by the child she would have, and she was not by nature a promiscuous woman. Her physical desires were moderate; she had been afraid of her relationship with Lauzun because of the state of affairs between herself and Louis at that time; and the continual reproaches of her mother and those about her, on account of her failure to produce a Dauphin, had given her those *affectations nerveuses* of which Mercy had thought it necessary to write to her mother and which had been mainly instrumental in bringing about the visit of Joseph.

Fersen was wise.

Once before he had disappeared from her life; now he felt that the need to do so was even more urgent.

He spoke to her one day as he sat with her and some of the members of that little entourage of intimates assembled in the garden of Trianon.

'Your Majesty,' he said, 'I shall soon be leaving the Court.'

She was startled and, he was delighted to see, deeply disappointed.

'Monsieur de Fersen,' she cried imperiously. 'You must not leave us. We should miss you too sadly. You must not go back to Sweden. We shall not allow it.'

He lifted those handsome eyes to hers – for she was sitting on her chair which was like a throne, and her courtiers were ranged about her on the grass – and he said slowly: 'Your Majesty, I am not going to Sweden. I am going to America.'

'To . . . to fight!'

'To fight against the forces of the King of England,' he said. 'To help in the fight for freedom.'

'You shall not!' she cried; and tears filled her eyes. She was silent for a while; then she went on: 'But if it is what you wish . . . then you must do it.'

❖ ❖ ❖

She was saddened. Her eyes followed him, and many noticed that they were filled with tears as she did so.

The Princesse de Lamballe begged her not to show her feelings for the young man so openly.

'People are watching you all the time. Your sisters-in-law lose no opportunity of maligning you.'

'I know it,' said Antoinette. 'And they are more angry with me still now that I am to have my Dauphin. But what do I care!'

'You must care,' said the Princesse. 'They can do so much harm.'

'I cannot help feeling sad when I see Axel. He will soon be far away, and I like my friends about me. It is so sad to think that soon he may be dying on some battlefield because he has interfered in a cause which is not his own.'

'He has said that it is the cause of freedom, the cause of righteousness.'

'I believe he is going away because he is afraid of staying here, because of the slander that is being spoken against us.'

'Then he is wise to go,' said the Princesse.

'I am unlucky to be treated as I am,' said Antoinette sadly. Then she laughed. 'But if it is malicious of people to presume I take lovers, it is certainly very odd of me to have so many attributed to me and yet to do without them!'

The Princesse laughed with her; but Antoinette continued sad, contemplating the departure of Fersen.

And even after he had gone she thought a great deal about him until her mind was entirely occupied with her approaching confinement.

During the evenings she would walk on the terrace of the château with her friends. The summer had been unusually hot and Antoinette had spent the days resting, doing fine needle-work while she listened to music and talked of the Dauphin. Therefore it was pleasant in the cool of the evening to walk on the terrace which was illuminated with fairy lights. Music would be playing in the Orangerie; the old custom was that at such times the people of Versailles might have free admittance into the château grounds and even to the terraces.

The Queen, with her ladies, was dressed in white muslin with a big straw hat and veil which were the fashion and were copied by many. Thus, as they sat or strolled on the terrace and the people wandered freely about, many would speak to the Queen without knowing who she was.

One night as she sat there a man came and stood beside her.

'What a beautiful night!' he said, and took a chair next to hers.

'It is very beautiful,' she replied.

She believed that he did not know who she was, for he was clearly of the tradesman class. She did not wish to humiliate him, so promised herself that she would say a few words then murmur that she must go and immediately leave him.

He was watching her intently.

'There is not a lady in Versailles as beautiful as you,' declared the man ardently.

'It is kind of you to say so,' she said. 'Pray excuse me now. I must join my family.'

She rose and looking about her saw her sisters-in-law standing not far off, watching.

'Let us go now,' she said to them.

Josèphe, seeing what had happened, came hurrying up.

'Your Majesty has tired yourself,' she said audibly; and her gleaming eyes were on the man.

She saw the smile touch his lips, and she knew that from the beginning he had been aware of the Queen's identity.

Antoinette took Josèphe's arm and they walked away. Josèphe later was gleeful as she recounted the incident to Provence. It was quite clear that many were beginning to believe in the *légèreté* of the Queen.

❖ ❖ ❖

At last December came, and the whole Court was in a state of great excitement.

Many times during the day the King was making his way to the Queen's apartments at the southern end of the Grande Galerie.

He was demanding to know how she was. Should she not rest more? Was there anything she desired?

He would question her ladies anxiously. Did the Queen seem a little tired? Did they think she was taking enough exercise? Too much exercise? One of them must send the *accoucheur* to his apartment. He wished to question both *accoucheur* and doctors immediately.

'The Queen is in good spirits, Your Majesty,' he was told. 'And all is as it should be.'

But it was difficult for Louis to satisfy himself.

'I could wish,' he told the doctors, 'that we could dispense with the ancient and barbaric customs which prevail at the Court at such times. It is monstrous that the people – not only my own family but any French subject – have the right to enter the lying-in chamber while the Queen gives birth to an *enfant de France.*'

The doctors agreed with the King; but etiquette – and particularly at such a time – must be preserved. The King knew that it was very necessary in this case, for although he had heard less than any of the rumours concerning Antoinette and himself which were circulating throughout the Court and the country, he could well imagine what would be said if he refused to allow witnesses into the lying-in chamber. In view of the long barren years it would surely be said that the child was not the King's and Queen's after all; that there was no royal birth. There had been such rumours before.

'However,' he said, 'I have decided that the screens surrounding the bed shall be fastened with cords so that they cannot be overthrown by the crowds.'

In the early hours of that December morning Antoinette woke and called out to her women that she felt the first of her pains.

The news spread throughout the Palace. All the bells were ringing to summon the relatives of the royal family who were either in Paris or Versailles awaiting the event. Pages and equerries were galloping to Paris and Saint-Cloud to bring their employers to the château.

Antoinette's ladies-in-waiting, headed by the Princesse de

Lamballe and the Duchesse de Guémenée, arranged themselves about her bed.

'Marie,' whispered Antoinette, clinging to the hand of the Princesse, 'as soon as my child is born, let me know if . . . it is a boy.'

'It will be a boy,' the Princesse assured her.

'It must be a boy,' said Antoinette, her face contorted with sudden pain.

'Cling to me,' said the Princesse. 'The doctors and the *accoucheur* will be here very soon.'

'I do not complain of these pains,' said Antoinette. 'I welcome them. It cannot be long now, Marie. Oh, pray that it cannot be long.'

Behind the screen the Princes and Princesses, the royal Dukes and Duchesses, noblemen and women of high rank sat waiting. Behind them the townsfolk crowded in as was their privilege. They stood on chairs that they might see beyond the screens; they jostled each other and shouted.

It was a strange scene – there in that stately room, the ceiling of which was decorated by Boucher and the walls with Gobelins tapestry. The young Queen writhed on her bed, now and then uttering a shriek of agony, and all under the watchful eyes, not only of the members of her family, but any who had been quick enough to force a way into the bedchamber.

Outside the bedchamber in the Salon de la Paix with its beautiful decorations and gilded doors the crowd massed. In the Grande Galerie they pressed against one another and cursed that ill-fortune which had made them too late to get a place in the lying-in chamber itself.

Meanwhile in the chamber, the windows of which had been

sealed and seamed with paper to keep out the December draughts, the crowd waited.

The Queen lay exhausted on her bed, but at last her agony was over, her child delivered.

Antoinette's eyes were on the child – the much longed-for child. She saw it – small, shrivelled, hardly like a human being. It lay still. It did not cry. She looked at the *accoucheur* who had taken it from the doctor. She saw the frightened eyes of the Princesse de Lamballe.

She tried to speak then. But the room seemed to be fading away. She was aware of a great silence all about her. She felt waves of heat sweeping over her; she was gasping for breath, for the air of the lying-in chamber was made hot and fetid by the curious invaders.

She thought she heard the cry of a child. Someone said: 'The Queen! The Queen!'

Then she was lost in darkness.

'It is a girl.'

The cry went up.

'So . . . No Dauphin for France!'

'But a healthy child . . . a girl.'

'And the Queen?'

The doctors were at the bedside. The Queen was lying like a dead woman, and the King had ceased to think of the child now. He strode to one of the doctors and shook him.

'The Queen!' he said. 'Attend to the Queen.'

'This air . . . It is foul,' said the doctor. 'The room should be cleared, and fresh air let in.'

The King acted more quickly than he had ever done in his life.

'Clear the room,' he shouted. 'Clear the room immediately.'

He fought his way through the crowd to the window. He did not wait to tear away the seals, but thrust his elbow through the glass. The cold air rushed into the room.

The spectators looked on in silence. His strength was great, and enhanced by fear he wrenched open the windows.

Then he turned to face them.

'Did you not hear my orders? Clear the room immediately.'

'Sire . . .' began Provence.

But this was one of the rare moments in his life when Louis demanded immediate obedience. Louis was King, as he had been for a short while during the *Guerre des Farines*, and as such none dared disobey him.

The flunkeys were rushing about, turning out the crowds, while the doctors shouted for hot water.

No one had any hot water ready, the servants believing that the most important feature of a royal birth was to arrange for the spectators. It would be some time before hot water could be produced, and the Queen was in imminent danger.

Then one of the doctors lanced the Queen's foot and the flow of blood with the sudden rush of cold fresh air brought her back to consciousness.

'My baby?' she asked.

The Princesse de Lamballe knelt by the bed, her eyes full of tears.

'A little girl, Your Majesty. The dearest little girl.'

Antoinette closed her eyes. So there was no Dauphin. For a

moment she was desolate, for the child of whom she had dreamed over the months of waiting had always been a boy.

She opened her eyes and saw Louis standing by the bed, and she felt a rush of affection for him because he looked so anxious.

'Dear Louis,' she said. 'I have disappointed you. You so hoped for a Dauphin.'

'Disappointed?' said Louis, his mouth twitching with emotion. 'How could that be? You are not going to die . . . and we have a child.'

She held out her hand. He took it and kissed it.

'I want my baby,' she said.

So they brought the child and laid it in her arms.

'My poor child,' she murmured. 'We did not wish for a girl, but you will be none the less dear to me.' She lifted her eyes to those about the bed. 'Why, a son would have belonged more particularly to the State, but you will be mine. You will have all my care, you will share my happiness and assuage my griefs.'

The King came close and looked down at the baby. 'Now you have seen this wonderful child, you must rest,' he commanded. 'Those are the doctors' orders. Come, close your eyes. Have no fear, there are many here to watch over Madame Royale and give her a welcome into the world. Rest well. Your ordeal is over. The father of la petite Madame is as pleased with her as her mother is.'

So she handed the child to the Princesse and sank into contented sleep.

Louis could not tear himself away from the Queen's apartments. He would stand for a long time by the cradle of his daughter, looking down at her and marvelling at the tiny perfection of her hands and feet. He would smile as the little fingers curled about his thumb. He would call to any who came near him: 'Come here. Look at these beautiful fingers. Did you ever see anything so minute, yet so perfect? Is it not wonderful?'

All those called upon to share his enthusiasm would agree that it was.

The Queen would stand beside him, and they would laugh contentedly and ask each other whether they would, if they could, exchange this exquisite creature even for a Dauphin.

No, indeed they would not. Marie Thérèse Charlotte – Madame Royale – was perfect in their eyes and they would not lose her for the world.

Louis, loving husband and devoted father, wanted to show his affection in more tangible terms.

Antoinette loved jewels; he would send for the Court jewellers and command them to make something for the Queen which would delight her more than any piece of jewellery in her possession.

When the summons came to Messieurs Boehmer and Bassenge, the Court jewellers, Monsieur Boehmer rubbed his hands with delight. 'Now,' he said to his partner, 'is the time to dispose of the diamond necklace.'

The diamond necklace was about to be completed. It was the most magnificent ornament ever made, both jewellers were sure, for who in the world could afford in the first place to procure the stones which went into it, and who in the second place would have the skill to make it?

They had taken four years to find stones of sufficient size and perfection and mount them into this necklace. It was, of course, made with the Queen in mind, and the jewellers had not a moment's doubt that she would be so enchanted when she saw it that she would be unable to resist it.

The diamond necklace occupied the thoughts of Messieurs Boehmer and Bassenge all day and often part of the night. Its sale would make them rich men. They were comfortably off now, for business had been good since the Queen had such a taste for diamonds; and the Court followed the Queen. But the necklace was designed to make their fortunes.

The diamonds which formed a choker necklace were enormous, and graduated from the largest in the centre; from this choker necklace hung another looped rope from which was a pendant of diamonds culminating in a huge pear-shaped stone. More clusters hung from the choker; then there was a magnificent rope of double diamonds from which hung four tassels all composed of the finest diamonds in the world.

The jewellers hoped to sell this unique creation at 1,600,000 livres.

So when the King sent for Boehmer and the latter guessed that His Majesty wished to make a present to the Queen, he hastily completed the necklace and took it along to show Louis.

'Your Majesty,' he cried, 'I show you here the finest ornament in the world, of which only Her Majesty is worthy.'

Louis was very impressed by the glittering jewellery, though the price made him flinch a little; but he was eager to show Antoinette and the world that he was a happy husband and father.

'I will speak to the Queen before buying it,' he said.

And the jeweller went away contented and confident.

205

James Armand stood with the Queen by the cradle.

He was looking with misgiving at the baby, for he now knew her to be his greatest rival at Court. It was useless for his beloved Queen to assure him that he was her little boy. He knew differently. She was absentminded now when she played with him. Indeed she played less with him than she had before.

He was frightened. He remembered his grandmother's cottage and all the others there, and how they had refused to let him play with them, how they had shut him out of the games because he was the youngest.

He would go to the Queen when she was holding the baby and her ladies were about her, admiring the tiny creature.

'James Armand is here,' he would announce.

They would all laugh.

'So James Armand is jealous of Madame Royale?'

One of the Queen's ladies said: 'You forget, James Armand. Madame Royale is the Queen's own child.'

'I am too,' he declared hotly. 'I also.'

The lady smiled and ruffled his hair. 'Have a sweetmeat, James Armand. Come, here are your favourites.'

But he only ran away and hid himself.

He would cower in the hangings and watch the Queen with the baby, see her stoop over the cradle and kiss the child.

He heard her say: 'It was the happiest moment in my life when I held my own child in my arms.'

He ran out then. He thought she referred to him; he said: 'It was when you picked me up from the road after the horses had kicked me.'

She gave the baby to one of her women then and put her arms about him.

'You must have no fear, James Armand,' she said. 'You will always be my boy.'

He gave himself up to the pleasure of that embrace, but he could not entirely believe it. There was so much to make him disbelieve.

The Queen was thoughtfully considering the boy, when the King came to her.

'Boehmer has shown me the most magnificent diamond necklace I have ever seen,' Louis told her.

'The necklace?' She smiled. 'I have heard of that necklace.'

'If you would like it, it shall be yours.'

'I believe it would cost a great deal.'

The King raised his eyebrows. 'Since when have you become concerned with cost?'

'Since I was truly a mother perhaps. I am going to change now, Louis. I have been very extravagant. I have wasted so much money. It was because I longed to be a mother; and because I was not, I had to spend the time somehow. Now I have my dearest wish realised. I have my own child, and I shall have more. No, I will not have the necklace. Mother would send complaining letters, and you know how I am continually reproached for my extravagance. I have plenty of diamonds and they do not go so well with the new fashions of muslin and cambric. And I should wear this magnificent trinket only about half a dozen times during a year. No, Louis, I will show you and the world how I have changed. I will not have this diamond necklace. I will not even see it . . . for fear I should be tempted.'

'It costs nearly two million livres – 1,600,000 to be precise. It is a great deal of money. One could build a man-o'-war with that.'

'Then have your man-o'-war, Louis.'

'I should have liked to give you this necklace . . .'

'You have given me our little Charlotte. That is enough.'

He was looking at her with shining eyes of approval. She was right of course. She had been extravagant, and it would be good to show the people that she was so no longer.

He sent a messenger to Boehmer to tell him that the Queen had decided against the necklace.

When Boehmer received the message he was distraught.

'We are ruined,' he said to his partner. 'We have borrowed so heavily to buy the stones. We have wasted four years on the necklace. Unless we can sell it we are ruined. I was counting on the Queen.'

'Who would have believed she could resist it?' cried Bassenge. 'Who will buy it now?'

'God knows! The price of it puts it out of the market. There is no one but the King and Queen who could afford the necklace. Many have seen it and admired it – but of course must consider it right out of their reach. There is only one thing to do if we are to be saved. I must start at once. I must visit all the Courts of Europe in the hope of finding a buyer.'

So the Queen did not have the diamond necklace. Instead a hundred couples, who were about to marry, were given a dowry besides new clothing, and money was distributed throughout the country; pardons were granted to certain criminals and many debtors were forgiven their debts. There were fireworks and illuminations in the Capital, wine flowed from fountains and all were admitted free into the Comédie

Française. It seemed that the popularity of the Queen had been regained, for everywhere she went now she was acclaimed by shouts of *'Vive la Reine!'*

But her enemies were as strong as ever. The aunts continued to receive their visitors at Bellevue.

'And how long do you think this reformation will last, eh?' demanded Adelaide of her sisters.

They waited to hear from Adelaide how long, but they knew of course that Adelaide had already decided it should be of the shortest possible duration.

Josèphe and Thérèse continued to watch the Queen closely. The fond mother would soon become the frivolous Queen again, they were sure. For one thing she still kept her favourites about her. The Polignacs were as strong as ever. Gabrielle was the most favoured person in the whole of the Court.

'In the old days it was the King's mistresses,' said Josèphe; 'now it is the Queen's friends.'

'The people should be told that,' cried Adelaide.

Her sisters nodded. They knew that Adelaide and Josèphe and others with them would see that remark was repeated throughout Paris.

The Comte de Vaudreuil, who was Gabrielle's lover, had lost money in the West Indies owing to the American war, and Gabrielle begged the Queen to help her lover; the result was that the Comte was found a sinecure at Court which was a charge on public funds to the tune of 30,000 livres a year. Gabrielle's lovely young daughter was affianced to the Duc de Guiche. The King must give her a dowry of 800,000 livres because the Queen so wished to please her dear friend Gabrielle; then, of course, the bridegroom must have his gifts also. There must be a command in the company of Guards, an estate and a pension for Monsieur de Guiche.

Gabrielle had been made a Duchesse and had been given estates at Bitche, and ever since she had been known throughout Paris as Bitchette.

Other members of the Polignac family were not forgotten. Even Gabrielle's husband's father, the old Vicomte de Polignac, who was far from brilliant, was sent to Switzerland as ambassador.

The Queen's enemies made sure that the people knew of her follies; they were determined that her new-found popularity should not last. She lost this completely when, after a slight attack of measles, she decided to recuperate at the Petit Trianon.

'This,' she declared, 'is what I must do, for the King has never had measles, so I must keep right away from him.'

'Your Majesty must not be dull during convalescence,' Gabrielle told her. 'That would considerably retard your recovery. I for one shall be with you.'

'If you have not had the measles, Gabrielle . . .'

'Measles or not,' said Gabrielle, 'I shall be there.'

Four gentlemen of the Court came forward to say that they had also had measles. They said it so glibly that it was quite clear that they were not at all sure whether they had or not, but that they considered an attack little to pay for the intimate society of the Queen.

So with the Queen and a few — a very few — of her ladies went the Ducs de Coigny and de Guines, the Baron de Benseval and the Comte Esterhazy; and there at Petit Trianon they made her convalescence merry. Her bedroom was the centre of the gaiety, and it soon became known throughout Paris that the Queen entertained these men in her private bedchamber.

Now all the old scandals were revived. The people in the streets were inventing scandals and singing songs about her once more.

Mercy wrote frantically to Maria Theresa. Maria Theresa's instructions came promptly in reply.

Mercy visited Petit Trianon and, as a result, the four gentlemen were commanded not to enter the Queen's bedchamber after eleven o'clock in the day.

But the damage was done.

The finances of the country were in a tragic state.

Turgot had been replaced by Clugny de Nuis and, when the latter died, by Jacques Necker, the Genevese banker.

Necker was very popular and there was delight throughout the country on his appointment. A great deal had been heard about the Déficit, and it was firmly believed that Necker was the man who would put France on her feet again.

Necker, accustomed to dealing with finance, was horrified to discover that the national deficit was some 20,000,000 livres a year, and that owing to the American war – for France was supporting the settlers – the debt was increasing rapidly. He dared not inflict more taxes for he understood that the people would have risen in revolt if he had. Instead he resorted to loans.

With the borrowed money it seemed that Necker was succeeding. He was cutting down expenses throughout the country. He had believed in the beginning that if he could make France prosperous he would be able to repay the loans when the time came for repayment.

This he failed to do. The war was virtually over and he realised that his only means of repaying the loans was through further taxation. This he could shelve for a little while; so, determined not to throw the nation into a panic, he published a little booklet which he called *Compte Rendu,* and in this he set out details of the national income and the national expenditure. As he falsely included the loans as income he was able to show, instead of a deficit, a credit balance of 10,000,000 livres.

There was general rejoicing and the cry went up: 'Long live Necker! He is the saviour of France!'

Antoinette was joyfully pregnant again.

James Armand stood behind her chair, listening to her talking about the new baby which was coming. 'This time,' said the Queen, 'it must be a boy.'

It was a pleasure now to write to her mother. It was a pleasure to open her letters. Maria Theresa would forget to scold if there was a Dauphin on the way.

It was, however, but a few months after the child was conceived when she had her miscarriage. She was very sad about this, and wept often, but when she was assured again and again by her friends that she would almost certainly be pregnant again, her spirits lifted.

James Armand stood by the bed smiling his satisfaction. At least for the present there would be no other rival to be set beside the little girl in her cradle.

Antoinette laughed at him and told him he was a wicked little subject of the King. James Armand laughed with her. He cared not for the King, he told her; he was the Queen's little boy.

'Now,' she said to Gabrielle, 'there will be more letters from my mother. I shall be told that I must at all costs avoid *le lit à part*. Poor Mother, this will be a great shock to her. Ah, Monsieur James, is it not strange that what rejoices you will fill my dear mother with dismay?'

But the letters from Maria Theresa were coming less frequently.

In the last few years she had grown very fat. She had suffered badly from the smallpox, and Antoinette would not have recognised her if she had seen her at that time. The Empress knew that she had not long to live; and one day, soon after Antoinette's miscarriage, when driving, she had caught a chill. A few days later she was dead.

❖ ❖ ❖

When the news was brought to Antoinette she was prostrate with grief.

The King had sent the Abbé de Vermond to break it to her gently; he himself, guessing how broken-hearted she would be, declared he could not bear to do so. But as she lay on her bed, too dazed for speech, Louis came to her and took her into his arms.

'I cannot believe it, Louis,' she said. 'Mother . . . dead. But she was so vital. I think she believed she would be immortal.'

'We are none of us that,' said Louis.

'Yet she seemed so. And to think I have sometimes put her letters aside because I knew they would contain scoldings. As if she ever scolded when I did not merit a scolding. Louis, who will look after me now?'

'I will,' said Louis.

She smiled at him tenderly. Dear Louis. But Poor Louis. How different he seemed to her from that strong woman to whom she had felt she could always turn.

'I cannot believe,' she went on, 'that she is not there. You see, Louis, she was always there . . . from the moment I first became aware of anything she was there . . .'

He soothed her. She felt closer to Louis than ever before; and in those days of mourning she wished to be shut away from everyone but her husband and her dear friends, Madame de Polignac and the Princesse de Lamballe.

The finances of France were tottering.

Necker had overlooked the fact that when he had made his drastic plans for reducing expenditure, the result would produce unemployment and the dissatisfaction of a great number of people; and that hundreds who had looked upon the service of the nobility as their livelihood would be without means of earning a living.

Necker was idealistic. The state of the hospitals appalled him, so he prevailed on the King to pay secret visits to those of Paris; and Louis, whose great desire was to serve his country, was willing to do so. What Louis saw in places such as the Hôtel-Dieu filled him with horror. Disguised he had wandered through the wards and seen the dying lying in heaps in corners, had seen as many as four people crowded into one narrow bed, all in various stages of misery.

He had come back to the Palace and told the Queen what he had seen; and he and Antoinette had wept together. Something must be done for the hospitals. In the provincial cities they were moderately satisfactory; it was in Paris that they provoked such horror and shame.

The Queen founded a maternity hospital at Versailles; the King bought new beds to be installed in the Hôtel-Dieu. This was admirable; but it cost money. Turgot, Malesherbes and Necker were all reformers, all idealists, but all lacked the means to bring their reforms into being.

Necker was now at the height of his popularity. Only Maurepas, now in his eighties, wise and shrewd, doubted the banker. Maurepas could not believe that the country's financial state was as good as Necker had made it out to be; to Maurepas' practical mind it was an impossibility. Trouble started between Necker and Maurepas when the banker rejected a proposal to strengthen the Navy, which had been put forward by de Sartines, who was then Minister for Naval Affairs and whom Maurepas was supporting.

There was an open rupture in high places. Necker, who was cheered every time he went into the streets, thought to score off the old statesman by demanding the post of Minister of State.

Maurepas then threatened to resign and take the Administration with him, pointing out that Necker was a Protestant and no Protestant had ever held the post of Minister of State since the days of Henri Quatre; but Necker imagined that, since the people believed in him, new rules should be made on his account.

The King and the Queen were reluctant to accept Necker's resignation, but this was forced on them. Necker fell from power; and the men and women in the streets murmured because of it.

There was another disturbing factor. Many French had returned from America, now that war was being brought to a satisfactory conclusion. This sent the citizens of Paris wild with joy. From the beginning they had been on the side of those who called for liberty. They had cheered Benjamin Franklin, Arthur Lee and Silas Deane when they had appeared in Paris some years before to enlist French support. Many had sailed to America under the Marquis de la Fayette.

The King had wanted to remain aloof. It was because he was distrustful of war. He had an uneasy feeling too that, as a royalist, he would be fighting on the wrong side. All Europe was declaring against England in the struggle, not on principle but because they feared that mighty rising Power.

And now the war was over and the Declaration of Independence had been signed. This was success for the settlers, success too for France. The stigma of the Seven Years' War which had so humiliated the French was wiped away. Now they were victorious over their old enemies, the English.

It had been an easy war, as wars which were not fought in the homeland should be. France had recovered her colonies in the West Indies, in Senegal and India. She had hoped to regain Canada, but that country had refused to rise against the English.

It seemed that France was set for glory again as it had been in the days of Louis Quatorze. Here was the beginning of richness, the people told each other.

There were certain things they had forgotten.

The Déficit was greater than ever, for the war had cost forty-three million livres. Those reforms, which Louis had so dearly wished to put into being and in which he had ministers to support him, had had to be put off for the sake of the war.

This was bad; but there was one thing which, for the monarchy, was more dangerous still.

Soldiers sat in the taverns and cafés and talked of the new

country. In the new land there were no Kings. There was more freedom in the New World.

A new cry had replaced 'Long live the King'. It was 'Long live Liberty!'

✤ ✤ ✤

The Queen was oblivious of the change which was coming over the country. Her mind was occupied with one thing. She was again pregnant, and this time she was determined not to lose the child.

She shut herself away from the Court, took the utmost care of her health and saw few people apart from Louis and her dearest friends.

In the streets the people had ceased to talk of the new world and were discussing the coming of the child, for a royal birth was an event to eclipse all others.

The King was firm in declaring that he would not have the Queen submitted to the danger and indignity which she had suffered during the birth of Madame Royale. He proclaimed that only those close members of the family, doctors, ladies-in-waiting and those necessary to the occasion should forgather in the lying-in chamber. He did not forget how the Queen had come near to death by suffocation at her last confinement.

The King called the Queen's ladies to him a few days before the child was expected.

'I am anxious on the Queen's behalf,' he said. 'I remember last time. If the child should be a girl she will be distressed, I know. This fact must be kept from her until she is well enough to learn the truth.'

The Princesse de Lamballe said: 'Sire, if the child should be a boy, shall we not tell Her Majesty?'

'No,' said the King firmly. 'For joy can be as big a shock as grief.'

'And if she should ask, Sire?'

'I shall be at hand. I shall tell her.'

❖ ❖ ❖

She was waiting. She knew it could not be long now. 'Holy Mother of God,' she prayed, 'send me a Dauphin.' She paced up and down her room; she had dismissed her women; she wanted to be alone to think of the child. All was ready, waiting for him. 'Oh, God, let it be a boy.'

If only Mother were alive, she thought. If I have a Dauphin, how happy Mother would be. Perhaps she is looking down on me now, being happy . . . knowing that soon I shall give birth to a healthy boy, the Dauphin of France.

She touched the beautiful Gobelin tapestry which lined her walls. 'If I have a boy,' she said, as though making a bargain, 'I will be quite different. I will no longer gamble. I will do all I can to please the people. I will be quite sober . . . I will be the Queen whom Mother would have wished me to be. Oh, why was I not, when she was alive? What grief I must have caused her! Yet it was so hard . . . I was so bored . . . so utterly bored. I had to do something to stop thinking of the children I wanted. Now I have Charlotte. How I love Charlotte! And if there is a Dauphin . . .'

She would see less of Gabrielle. She was beginning to think she was less fond of Gabrielle. Gabrielle was so absorbed by her lover, and should she, the Queen, faithful wife of the King, accept Gabrielle and her lover as her close friends in the way she did? Gabrielle was a darling of course, but her relations . . . oh, her relations! There were too many of them, and they were

218

too acquisitive. When she thought of all they had had it seemed incredible that they could ask for more. No wonder there were complaints about them. They were every bit as expensive as Grandpa Louis' mistresses had been. The people were right in saying that.

She would spend more time with Madame Elisabeth, her pleasant little sister-in-law. She had always liked Elisabeth, from the moment she had seen her on her arrival in France; and, now that Clothilde was married, she and Elisabeth should be together more.

It was true Elisabeth was a little saintly and consequently a little dull, but she adored Antoinette's little Charlotte and she would be such a pleasant companion.

'Oh, give me a Dauphin and I will see less of Gabrielle,' she prayed. 'I will cultivate the love of Elisabeth; I will be with my children, and soon even the citizens of Paris will have nothing of which to complain.'

She caught her breath suddenly.

Her pains were starting.

She called. Marie de Lamballe, who was not far off and expecting the call, came hurrying to her.

The King was in the bedchamber, and with him were those members of the family whose duty it was to be present.

On the bed Antoinette lay, the doctors and *accoucheur* about her. Not far off hovered the Princesse de Lamballe and the Princesse de Guémenée whose position as *Gouvernante des Enfants* entitled her to be there.

The labour was not long and within three hours the child was born.

As the Queen emerged from the exhaustion of her ordeal she was immediately conscious of the silence all about her, and she was terrified suddenly by that silence.

Her eyes sought those of the Princesse, but Marie de Lamballe avoided her eyes.

Antoinette grasped the sheets. She thought: There is no child. It is born dead. After all these months!

She licked her lips and said: 'You see how patient I am. I ask . . . nothing.'

Louis was at her bedside. He cried aloud, and his voice was like a fanfare of trumpets: 'Monsieur le Dauphin begs leave to enter.'

Antoinette's heart beat uncertainly as the Princesse de Guémenée laid her son in her arms.

There was great rejoicing throughout the country at the birth of an heir to the throne of France. Now would be the time for pageants and merrymaking, and in such festivities reality could be thrust aside.

Everyone was talking of the Dauphin, the King most of all. Every sentence he uttered seemed to begin with: 'My son the Dauphin . . .'

He was continually in the Queen's apartments; he was for ever bending over the cradle.

'Madame de Guémenée, how fares my son, the Dauphin, today?' 'My son, the Dauphin, lies very still this morning. Is that as it should be?'

He welcomed the child's wet-nurse, called Madame Poitrine by the Court – a gruff peasant woman, wife of one of the gardeners, a woman who cared for nothing except the Dauphin, and refused to conform to etiquette or show the slightest respect for her new surroundings.

When asked to powder her hair, she roared in her coarse voice:

'I've never powdered my hair nor will I now. I have come here to suckle the little one – not to stand about like one of those dummies I see all over the place. I'll not have that nasty powder near me.'

She told the King himself this, without a 'Your Majesty' or 'Sire' to accompany the gruff words. The King smiled at her. He knew her for a good honest woman; one who would serve the Dauphin well.

'And my son?' he asked her. 'The Dauphin? His appetite is good to-day?'

'Fair enough,' said Madame Poitrine. 'Dauphins or gardener's sons, they're all the same greedy brats.'

'Take care of my son,' the King begged her.

'Your son's all right. Don't you worry,' said Madame Poitrine kindly, as though the King were another of her children.

Louis would sit by the Queen's bed, and all their conversation was of the Dauphin or Madame Royale.

They were proud parents now, and they could not forget it.

Little James Armand realised, on the birth of the newcomer, that he had had good reason to fear. The Queen rarely asked for him and, when she did, she scarcely seemed to see him.

The ladies laughed together about Antoinette's preoccupation with motherhood. It had been the same when Madame Royale was born. In the middle of a conversation – and this happened even when she talked with the ministers – she would break in with the latest saying of Madame Royale, or explain how the Dauphin chuckled when Madame Poitrine took him up for his feed.

The Grand Almoner presided over the Dauphin's baptism. He was none other than Louis, Prince and Cardinal de Rohan, that man who had welcomed Antoinette in Strasbourg Cathedral when she had first arrived in France.

Antoinette would have preferred another to have officiated, but it was clearly the duty of the Grand Almoner and, since Rohan held this office, he must take charge of the Dauphin's baptism.

She decided she would ignore him. She would have nothing to do with a man who had slandered her mother; she had heard too that he had talked to Joseph of herself when he was in Austria, for Joseph had made a friend of the man in spite of the fact that Maria Theresa had so disliked him.

Provence and Elisabeth stood proxy for the baby's godparents, who were his uncle the Emperor Joseph and the Princesse de Piedmont.

Antoinette found that during the impressive ceremony she could not help being aware of Rohan's piercing eyes; and she believed that, while he went through his duties at the baptismal service, he was thinking of her, pleading with her not to hate him, trying to tell her of some strong emotion which she aroused in him.

It was uncomfortable to be near the man.

The bells continued to ring through the Capital. There were processions and festivities in the streets – all in honour of Louis Joseph Xavier François, the Dauphin of France.

The trade guilds banded together to make their own

offering of thanksgiving, and one day shortly after the birth they came marching to Versailles from Paris. The King, the Queen and members of the royal family stood on the balcony before the King's apartments while the members of the different guilds crowded into the courtyard.

With them came the market-women wearing black silk gowns; and their leader congratulated the Queen, speaking for the women of Paris, on the birth of the Dauphin; she assured the Queen of the love and loyalty of the women of Paris, and Antoinette, forgetting all the cruel slanders concerning herself which these very women had helped to circulate, wept tears of joy and pleasure to see them thus.

Then came the members of the various guilds with their offering for the Dauphin. All wore the best clothes they could muster, and each guild had brought a symbol of their trade to show the King that they would serve the Dauphin as they had served his ancestors. The butchers brought an ox for roasting; the chairmen carried a sedan chair, a glorious object decorated with golden lilies in which sat a model of the wet-nurse holding the Dauphin. The tailors presented a uniform, perfect in every detail, calculated to fit a small boy and give him the appearance of a Guards officer; the cobblers had made a pair of exquisite shoes, and these they presented to the King for the Dauphin; the little chimney-sweeps had built a model of a chimney, and on the top of this was a small boy – the smallest of all chimney-sweeps. They carried it ceremoniously into the courtyard of Versailles to show that the chimney-sweeps were loyal to the monarchy.

Then came the locksmiths. They came proudly, and their leader asked to be conducted to the King.

By this time Louis and the Queen had come into the

courtyard to mingle with the loyal members of the guilds and to express their joy in welcoming them to Versailles.

The chief locksmith cleared his throat and, bowing low, presented a small locked box to the King.

'We have heard of Your Majesty's interest in our craft,' he said, 'and it is our honour to present you with this box with the secret lock. We doubt not that Your Majesty's skill in our craft will enable you to discover the combination in a very short time, and it would be our delight to see you do so here before us all.'

Louis, smiling blandly and deeply moved by all the honour which was done to his son, feeling that his dear people shared his joy this day, declared he was all interest and could not let another moment pass without attempting to discover the secret of the combination.

The locksmiths watched him set to work, nodding with approval, holding their breath with delighted expectation.

In a few minutes the King had found the secret.

There was laughter and cries of delight; then a burst of cheering for, as he opened the lock, a tiny figure sprang out of the box.

It was a model of a Dauphin in steel – a boy in his robes of state.

The King stood still, holding the model in his hand; the Queen, standing beside him, put out a hand to touch it, and those near her saw the tears in her eyes.

The crowd began to cheer wildly, calling 'Long live the King! Long live the Queen! Long live the Dauphin!'

The people love us after all, thought Antoinette. It but needs an occasion like this to show it.

Then she looked up and saw a small party of men approaching. Over their shoulders they carried spades.

'But look,' cried Antoinette. 'Who are these?'

The King, holding the model Dauphin in his hands, looked up with her.

Someone beside them whispered: 'These are the grave-diggers, Your Majesty. They insisted on showing their loyalty with the rest.'

'Welcome,' said Louis. 'Welcome.'

But a certain fear had touched the Queen's heart. She did not wish to be reminded of death on such a day. It was as though a faint shadow crossed her happiness.

She was uneasy, conscious of the grave-diggers as, at the baptismal ceremony, she had been made uneasy by the presence of the Prince Cardinal de Rohan.

❧ Chapter VIII ❧

PETIT TRIANON

*N*ow that Antoinette was the mother of two children she was spending more and more time at the Petit Trianon. But it was not enough to live in her little house like a lady of the manor; she wanted to put into action that plan for creating her own *petit hatneau*. Madame de Pompadour had thought of doing it. Antoinette would do it.

She gathered her friends about her and made them enthusiastic over the project. She would build cottages – ideal cottages; there were many poor families who would be only too glad to come and live in them. They would have a farm and keep real sheep and real cows – the best sheep and cows in the world. She could scarcely wait to put her scheme into practice.

The cost did not worry her at all. The cost never worried her. Madame Bertin's bills, arriving regularly, were never checked. Her dear Madame Bertin might be an expensive dressmaker, but then she was the best dressmaker in Paris.

She told the King of her scheme for a model village, her adorable *hameau*. He listened benignly. 'It will please the people,' she explained. 'There will be many to share my model village. I shall be so happy to see them happy.'

So the work went on. The cottages were built – the prettiest cottages in France; the families were selected to live in them, families who were only too ready to enjoy the delights of that ideal village. There were eight little houses, tiny farms with their hayricks and byres and fowl-houses; and the sheep wore blue and pink ribbons round their necks. The Queen and her ladies, when they were tired of dancing on the grass or theatrical entertainments in the open air, decided they would make butter; they would be little farmers. The cows must be washed before they came into contact with the dainty Antoinette, and they were milked into porcelain vases decorated with the Queen's crest.

It was the greatest fun. The Queen no longer wore rich silks. Rose Bertin must make her muslin dresses and charming shady hats.

Indeed, yes, declared Madame Bertin, but the muslin must of course be the finest, for she would simply refuse to make a dress for so exquisite a creature that was not of the finest material available; and as much skill – nay more – was needed to make a suitable muslin dress as one of silk or velvet. The Queen would understand that with fine fabrics they themselves provided elegance; but the simplicity of a line – ah, that was where skill was really needed.

'You are right, of course, dear Bertin. You are a magician with clothes, I know,' Antoinette told the woman.

And so the muslin dresses were made and the bills which followed them were larger than ever.

Then Antoinette must build a theatre, for now she had discovered a great love for the theatre, and she herself would play the chief roles.

The King came as a guest, for she had decided that in her

Petit Trianon she was the ruler and the only ruler. Louis was pleased to see her so happy, and it was such a pleasure to watch the ladies making butter in dishes stamped with the Queen's monogram, to see the be-ribboned sheep led by charming shepherds and shepherdesses, to see the women picturesquely washing their linen in the stream. It was all so ideal – all as a village should be in a perfect world.

So the Queen arranged special fêtes for the visiting King, which he enjoyed before he left for Versailles that he might be in bed by eleven.

And after he had gone the revelry would grow wilder, so that they were all somewhat glad to be relieved of his presence.

On one occasion Antoinette put the clock on so that he might leave even earlier than usual, so eager were they to continue with those frolics which were too wild to please Louis.

This was remarked and gave the country and the Court another whip with which to scourge her.

So the gay existence continued.

But the citizens of Paris asked themselves what the frivolity of the Queen was costing them in taxes; and in the *oeil-de-boeuf* between the *chambre du roi* and the *chambre de la reine* in the château of Versailles, those men and women, who were deprived of their Court duties because the Queen was no longer at Versailles, complained bitterly.

And thus the nobility and the people were full of complaints against the Austrian woman.

The Duc de Chartres was dissatisfied.

'What,' he demanded of his father the old Duc d'Orléans, 'is happening to the old nobility? We are no longer even rich.

These ministers with their reforms have cut us down to such an extent that we can no longer live as we used to.'

''Tis so,' said the old Duke. 'One wonders whither France is being led.'

It would mean little to him; the old regime would last long enough to see him out. He looked at his son and wondered what the future held for him.

Chartres was handsome and ambitious.

It was a sad thing, thought Orléans, to be so near the throne with no hope of possessing it. This curse had afflicted the whole line of Orléans. Chartres was feeling it now.

The old Duke realised what his son was asking himself. Why should such a one as I – alert of mind, clever, so worthy to wear the crown – have to stand aside and see it on the head of fat Louis, merely because he happens to trace his line from an eldest while I trace mine from a second son? France was in need of a strong king, a firm hand to govern.

Ah, thought Chartres, how much stronger I would be! How much more of a king than poor Louis!

Chartres was approaching his mid-thirties and growing restive.

A restive man in a restive age, thought the old Duke. But I shall not be here to see what he makes of his career.

'There was a time,' said Orléans, 'when you were happy enough to follow the fashion of the Trianon. It was either you or Artois who was at the Queen's side when she was gambling the country's money away or dancing at her masked balls.'

Chartres was silent. It was true; he had found her enchanting, the Austrian woman. She was the loveliest lady of the Court; there was no doubt of that. He had been deeply attracted by her gay and almost childish ways.

He had been a normal young man; he looked for his pleasures in gambling, dancing, daring exploits, hunting – and above all, women.

She angered him. She was coquettish enough; one would think one had a chance. Perhaps deliberately she wished to give that impression. Why not? he had thought. She is beautiful, quite desirable. And the King? . . . All had known of the King's disability. It would have been natural for the Queen to take a lover, and one such as the Duc de Chartres, a Prince of the blood-royal, would have been eminently suitable. And if by chance there had been a child, would that have been the first such? And what harm done? Their child would have had royal blood in his veins.

But she had drawn back. Those bright blue eyes of hers had become ice-blue. 'Oh, no, Monsieur le Duc, I indulge in a little coquetry. A light flirtation, if you will – but no further please.'

She was cold; she had no feeling. That must be so; how else could she have refused the fascinating Duc de Chartres? He was a royal Prince – as royal as she was, he would have her remember, as royal as poor impotent Louis.

Chartres' love was self-love. He needed conquest – not to assuage desire for a certain woman but to placate his own conceit. He saw himself as irresistible; and he grew to hate any who tried to show him to be otherwise.

His father was now looking at him with those shrewd old eyes which seemed to see too much.

'A man grows tired of vanities,' said Chartres.

'I am glad of that,' his father told him, 'for you know, my son, I am finding myself much poorer than of yore and I fear that I can no longer afford to live in this place.'

'You cannot afford to live in the Palais Royal? But this is

our home. The Palais Royal is to Orléans what Versailles is to the King!'

Orléans nodded. 'I could not relinquish the old place altogether of course. What think you of this plan? I have considered opening the gardens to the public, and letting the ground floor – as cafés . . . shops . . .'

'So it has come to this,' burst out Chartres. 'Louis lives in style at Versailles while we must turn over our palace to tradesmen.'

'Do not envy Louis,' said his father quickly.

The young man looked sharply at the elder.

'What do you mean?'

'I am an old man. France has changed a great deal in my lifetime. I have seen these changes – yet I never saw France in the mood she is in to-day.'

'It is the war mayhap,' suggested Chartres.

'Wars put strange thoughts into the minds of men. Why, in the days of Louis Quatorze, I have heard it said, a man dared not speak his mind; in the days of Loius Quinze he whispered what he thought; in the days of Louis Seize he shouts it.'

'The people of France are aware of the power of the monarchy,' said Chartres. 'I noticed the difference when I was in England. I noticed the difference in their mode of government. England is a sane and healthy country compared with France.'

The old Duke smiled at his son. 'You have done nothing but sing the praises of England since you returned. I thought it was the English women who had so enchanted you.'

'They did,' answered Chartres, 'but so did other things. The English parliamentary system is more advanced than ours. I would like to see their methods introduced here. I would like to see parliamentary elections conducted on the lines they are in England. In England, the Prince of Wales appears to lead the Opposition. A Prince on one side . . . a King on the other. I call that healthy politics.'

'It could be unhealthy.'

'Not in England. The people are not afraid to state their views. Can you call our *Parlement* representative of the people? Here the King's will would appear to be absolute. That worked in the past. It will not much longer.'

'As you are so impressed with these democratic ideas,' said the old Duke, 'you will not object as heartily as I thought you would to the letting of the ground floor.'

'Cafés, you say,' Chartres mused. 'If they were cafés like the English coffee houses, where men gather to talk of affairs, I might not object so much.'

'So you plan to bring English customs to the Palais Royal.'

Chartres did not answer. He was looking into the future. He saw himself wandering through those rooms on the ground floor, gathering about him men who were interested in ideas, men who would look up to him as a leader.

Faint lights of alarm appeared in the eyes of the Duc d'Orléans.

Then he shrugged lightly.

He had lived his life. He would not be there to see the great events which he sensed were about to break over France.

The Queen sat in her boudoir at Petit Trianon. She was holding the Dauphin in her lap, and Madame Royal was leaning against Madame Elisabeth who was reading aloud. James Armand had peeped in at the door and gone off again.

232

He was growing up and too old to play with children. Antoinette was not listening to Elisabeth. She was thinking of the Dauphin. He worried her a little; he had not Madame Royale's healthy looks. He was whimpering now.

My little Louis Joseph, she thought, you must not be sick. You must be big and strong like Uncle Joseph. I shall not mind if you think you are so right and all the world wrong – as Uncle Joseph does – if only you will be strong and well and eager for your food, not turning away from it as you so often do, my precious.

One of the ladies came in and announced that the Princesse de Guémenée was asking for an audience with the Queen.

Antoinette frowned. The Princesse had never been a great friend of hers; it was true that she had attended the woman's card parties, but that was largely because the Princesse was a friend of Gabrielle's. Now she herself no longer cared for Gabrielle as she once had. There was another reason why she was not very eager to see the Princesse. She was related to the Cardinal de Rohan; and ever since the baptism of the Dauphin, Antoinette had thought now and then of the man. Those piercing eyes of his disturbed her. He was a fool if he thought she was going to show friendship to one who had made light fun of her dear mother.

'Your Majesty,' went on the woman, 'Madame la Princesse is in great distress.'

Antoinette's sympathy was immediately aroused.

'Tell her she may come to me,' she said.

The Princesse came and threw herself on her knees before the Queen.

'A terrible thing has happened,' she cried. 'And I implore Your Majesty to help me.'

'What terrible thing is this?' asked Antoinette.

'My husband the Prince is so deeply in debt that he has had to declare himself bankrupt.'

'The Prince? But you two have not been together for so long.'

'This affects me even as it does him. His debts are so vast. He owes 33,000,000 livres all over the country, and now his creditors have declared they can wait no longer for the money.'

Antoinette shook her head sadly. 'It is all talk of money nowadays. I do not know what I can do to help. I dare not ask for some post for the Prince which will bring him an income. You know what trouble there has been over the Polignacs.'

'Your Majesty,' said the Princesse, 'my husband owes so much that no post at Court could save him now. I have come to ask you to intercede for him. If you could speak to the Comptroller-General there might be some way of preventing the Prince's creditors making their demands for a little while at least.'

Antoinette immediately forgot her faint dislike of the Princesse. She could not bear to see anyone in trouble.

'I can try,' she said. 'I will speak to Fleury and see what he can do about it.'

'You are indeed gracious,' murmured the Princesse. 'I feel happier now that I know you are on my side.'

'Sit down beside me,' soothed Antoinette. 'Tell me how this terrible situation has come about. What a sad thing it is that there are all these money troubles. I hear constant complaints on all sides – and it is always . . . money.'

The Queen summoned Joly de Fleury to her apartment and told him that she had given her word to help the Guémenées in their trouble.

Fleury looked grave.

'Your Majesty,' he said, 'it is most unwise for you to have your name mentioned in connection with the Guémenées. The Prince is in debt to the tune of 33,000,000 livres. Your Majesty does not realise the import of this. All over the country tradesmen have given these people credit. Now these tradesmen are demanding the money owed to them. They need that money to save themselves from bankruptcy. It is not forthcoming. This is going to be a very bad thing, and not only for the Guémenées, Madame.'

'I know. I know. But cannot something be done? If the tradesmen can be persuaded to wait awhile, mayhap the Prince will retrieve his fortunes. If he is made bankrupt, everybody suffers.'

'Your Majesty, may I presume to offer you a piece of advice?'

She bowed her head a little wearily. There had been so much advice.

'Keep clear of the Guémenées. Do not let their trouble touch Your Majesty.'

He did not understand that she would not dream of standing clear of them – even though they had never been great friends – merely because they were in trouble. It was at such times that she was prepared to be friendly even with those whom she did not like.

'I trust,' went on Fleury, 'that Your Majesty will forgive me, but I can have nothing to do with this case. If you insist that I should, there would be nothing for me to do but to hand in my resignation. The people of France are in an ugly mood and have been for some time. This affair could have very unpleasant results. I beg of Your Majesty, consider well before you allow any to link your name with it.'

But she would not leave it at that. She went to the King. They could not allow the Prince to be declared bankrupt, she insisted. What good would it do? Would the people to whom they owed money receive it? No. Nobody would be any better off.

The King, always eager to indulge her, foolishly agreed that a moratorium upon debts should be imposed.

Triumphantly Antoinette called the Princesse de Guémenée to her, and the Princesse fell on her knees, kissing the hand of the Queen as she poured forth her gratitude.

✤ ✤ ✤

First the carriage-maker went bankrupt. He could not pay his debts. He was an honest man. Where he had gone wrong was to trust the Prince de Guémenée. The glove-makers, the bakers, the butchers – all over Paris, and in the country too, they were going out of business.

They had, every one, allowed the Prince de Guémenée to run up vast debts. They had not thought it possible to do otherwise. Nor had it occurred to them that a connexion of the royal family could default, and while they had the Guémenées' promise to pay they had felt it safe to go on supplying goods.

This was what came of taking the word of a nobleman.

People gathered in the streets – all those who had suffered, and all those whose sympathies were with the sufferers.

'These Guémenées are Princes, are they not?' they cried. 'How much longer shall we allow Princes to ruin us?'

'I hear the Guémenées have retired to their country house; that is very nice. Meanwhile the King takes care that they shall not be bothered. What of poor Lafarge? Oh, it does not matter. He is but a humble tradesman. What of the butcher, the baker? They have been supplying the Guémenées with food these last months. But what matters that? They are only tradesmen.'

'You know why we have all this trouble, do you not?'

'The Austrian woman!'

'She is the one who sets the example for all this extravagance.'

'Remember that song we used to sing:

' *"My little Queen not twenty-one . . ."* '

'Ah, 'tis a great pity we did not send her across the border all those years ago. Much trouble would have been saved our country if we had.'

So the people in the streets grumbled; and they were a little more angry, a little more fierce than they had been before the Guémenée disaster.

⚜ ⚜ ⚜

Fleury was in a panic; he had to raise money somehow. He floated more loans.

It was clear that Necker's *Compte Rendu* had been a very optimistic document; and it seemed to the King that only fresh loans could tide the country over disaster.

But it was not so easy to raise money as it had been previously. More taxes had to be levied.

This sent up a groan from the people; and the *Parlement* declared itself against the levying of more taxes.

So much money, declared members, had been wasted in the past, and the country was in no mood to pay more taxes merely to support the extravagance of certain people. Little jobs with big salaries had been created for some. A great deal of money had been spent on certain houses. This was a direct shaft for the Queen.

The *Parlement* then declared that if these taxes were imposed there must be an Estates-General, a gathering together of a representative assembly of the entire country – which had only been done in the history of France in cases of dire emergency. Fleury decided to try to raise money by other means. He wondered whether it would be possible to create new offices at Court, for which ambitious men would be willing to pay vast sums.

He knew though that the *Parlement* was setting itself against the monarchy.

In the ground-floor rooms of the Palais Royal men and women gathered to discuss the latest events.

Often would be seen walking among them, or sitting at one of the tables, that handsome young man, the Duc de Chartres.

He was a good fellow. He did not seem to mind mixing with them in the least – in fact he seemed to enjoy it. Nothing seemed to delight him more than to sit at a table and chat with a member of the *bourgeoisie*. He would not disagree if any ranted about the aristocracy. He would nod his head slowly and often he would say: ' 'Tis true. 'Tis all true, my friend. I am one of them, and will you believe me when I tell you I am not always proud of that?'

They would shout down his apologies.

'But you, Monsieur le Duc, you are different. Ah, Monsieur, if there were more like you at Versailles!'

'I certainly see things from the citizens' viewpoint,' he would say.

Then he would tell them about the English Parliament – a far more democratic institution than the French *Parlement*.

They liked to listen to him. They were flattered to nod and chat with him, to share a bottle of wine.

'Why should we not have such a parliament in France, Monsieur le Duc?'

'Ah! Why not indeed? We have an absolute monarchy here, that is why. The King is sole ruler. What use is a parliament? It is a different matter in England.'

'But we beat the English in the war, did we not, Monsieur?'

'Poof! Are they beaten? What think you? Who is mistress of the seas? Who is building up the biggest empire the world has ever seen? Not France, Messieurs. No, my heart bleeds to say it, but not our country.'

'And you think this parliament . . . ?'

'The King is my own cousin, Monsieur . . .' The Duke smiled apologetically.

'Monsieur le Duc, you are a good Frenchman.'

'I hope so.'

'Then should the fact that the King is your cousin interfere with your judgement?'

The Duke brought his fist down on the table. 'You are right. You are right. Nothing but justice should determine the thoughts of a good Frenchman.'

'Monsieur le Duc, you have been at Court . . . in the company of the King and the Queen . . . these stories of the Queen . . .'

The Duke stood up. 'I cannot remain, my friends. I cannot listen to scandal concerning the Queen.'

'You could defend her?' suggested someone.

'It is precisely because I cannot, that I will take my leave.'

It was dramatic, but he *was* dramatic. They watched him go.

Monsieur le Duc is a fine man, they said among themselves. He is the finer because he has lived as they have, and seen the folly and injustice of such living. Monsieur le Duc is a leader of men.

The Duke walked in the gardens of the Palais Royal. All sorts of men and women wandered there. The prostitutes came looking for customers. They mingled with the politicians.

The Duc d'Orléans watched his son.

He said to him: 'It would seem you are King of this *demi-monde*.'

King! thought Chartres. Yes, indeed they treated him as such. He was welcome everywhere. The cafés of the Palais Royal prospered largely because so many of the patrons came in the hope of speaking to him or at least of catching a glimpse of Monsieur le Duc.

He was their friend. They talked of him, of what he had said last night, of what he had seen in England. He was in truth King of that *demi-monde*.

Then he began to dream of being King of more than that small domain.

King of France!

Why not? What if the people decided they had had enough of Louis and his extravagant Queen? What if they decided to replace him by King Louis Philippe Joseph?

So he moved among his friends; and he never missed an

opportunity of letting the slow poison of contempt for Louis and his Queen seep into their minds.

Such scandals as the affair of the Guémenées delighted him. He was ready to declaim against the extravagance of the Court set, to remind his listeners that the Princesse de Guémenée had been a friend of the Polignacs – and they all knew the disgraceful story of that family.

Now there was this suggestion of fresh taxes.

Would the people of France be so weak as to accept them? Taxes? For what purpose? To buy pink and green ribbons for the sheep of the little village at Trianon?

Again and again he brought the conversation back to the Queen, for he sensed that in the Queen they saw their true enemy. The King was slow and gentle and kind; he was a man who had been led astray.

And who had led him astray? The foreigner in their midst, the wicked woman from Austria.

❖ ❖ ❖

In the gardens of the Petit Trianon Madame Poitrine rocked the baby. She watched the workmen who were making a new lake where they had built the Fisherman's Tower.

Madame Poitrine thought it strange that they should be putting fish in the lake merely that the King and his guests could come here to take them out again. It did not make sense to her practical mind.

'Come, come, Monsieur,' she said to the baby. 'Suck time!'

Then she shook her head from side to side and frowned over the little one. He was not growing as she would have wished, and it was not due to any deficiency in her milk. Her own was a fine and healthy brood.

'Something in the blood,' she murmured. 'Something wrong with a child who don't cry for his milk and has to have it forced on him.'

She surveyed the tower with its twelve columns, and clicked her tongue.

The Dauphin began to suck.

'That's better, my pretty. We'll make a strong little man of you yet.'

She began to sing in a soft voice which was quite different from her everyday one, and which she kept for her babies.

'Malbrook s'en va-t-en guerre . . .'

And her eyes had a far-away look as they rested on La Tour de Marlborough, which they called this new tower they were building.

✳ ⚜ ✳

Antoinette was angry.

The people had begun to hate her again.

'What have I done?' she would demand of Madame Elisabeth. 'Such a short while ago they were cheering me. That was when the Dauphin was born. What have I done since then?'

Elisabeth shook her head sadly. 'The people are unaccountable.'

'Unaccountable indeed,' said Antoinette angrily. 'Stupid. Foolish. There is only one way in which to treat them. Ignore them.'

'If it is possible,' said Elisabeth.

'I shall make it possible.'

She was sad suddenly.

'You care about the people,' said Elisabeth. 'You care very much.'

'I wanted to be loved. I've always wanted to be loved. I thought they did love me. When I came to Paris Monsieur de Brissac said that all Paris was in love with me.'

'Times change,' said Elisabeth sadly.

'Is it my fault the Guémenées are bankrupt? They blame me. They blame me for everything. It makes me unhappy.'

'Pray,' said Elisabeth quietly. 'Pray to God.'

Antoinette glanced impatiently at her sister-in-law. Elisabeth was so mild; she found such comfort in her religion. She would never marry, thought Antoinette. Joseph had thought about asking for her hand; but the reports he had had on her appearance, had not encouraged him to do so. Antoinette was glad, which was selfish of her, she admitted. She wanted to keep Elisabeth with her. But perhaps it was not so selfish – remembering Joseph; and Elisabeth was the sort of person who would be happier in the single state.

It was not easy to talk to her of what was in her mind. Antoinette knew that if she ventured out into the streets she would hear songs about herself – about her extravagance, her wickedness, her imaginary immorality. It seemed that nothing they could think of would be too bad. Every innocent escapade of her girlhood seemed to have been remembered and made into a song, that the people on the streets might slander her.

Pamphlets were being written about her. These pamphlets, were illustrated, and she knew that the buyers would be disappointed if she did not figure in every illustration.

It was unbearable to contemplate these things. She would be

pictured in compromising situations which would be explained in the lurid text.

They were even smuggled into the palace; she would find her ladies hastily thrusting them into the pockets of their gowns if she came upon them suddenly. The fact that they touched such things, read such things, and could do so with interest instead of indignation, made her wonder whether they were truly her friends.

Yesterday, when she and Louis had entered their box at the theatre and they had stood for a while acknowledging the cheers of the audience before sitting down, she had noticed that while many called *"Vive le Roi!"* few cried *'Vive la Reine!'*

And as they had stood there, she had caught sight of the paper pinned on the balustrade in front of the King's seat and had seized it while the King was bowing and smiling. She was glad that his short-sighted eyes had failed to notice it. She herself was short-sighted, but these pieces of paper were very familiar to her.

The cruel verse had unnerved her temporarily. It was addressed to the King but, as usual, it vilified the Queen.

> *'Louis, si tu veux voir*
> *Bâtard, cocu, putain,*
> *Regarde ton miroir,*
> *La Reine et le Dauphin.'*

She knew that her enemies were all about her. There were very few whom she could trust. She knew that the aunts at Bellevue, Provence in the Luxembourg, and most of all Chartres in the Palais Royal, were her enemies. Whom could she trust? Louis? Certainly Louis. And Elisabeth. Mild

Elisabeth who would have been happier in a nunnery than at the Court!

The Princesse de Lamballe was her friend. Who else?

Then there returned to the Court one in whom she knew she could put her whole trust.

The war had changed Axel de Fersen. His face had lost that pale yet healthy complexion; there were lines under the handsome eyes; but it seemed to Antoinette that the man who returned to Court was more charming than the handsome boy who had gone away to fight the English in America.

She could not help showing her pleasure in his return.

'You have been away for a long time,' she murmured to him.

The eyes which met hers were passionate and angry – not angry with her, but with the fate which had made her a Queen.

He had gone away, he wanted to remind her, not because he wished to, but because he feared to stay.

He was a Swede among Frenchmen, he was less voluble than they; he did not show his feelings; his emotions were locked away within him but it would seem that they went deeper because of that.

He told her: 'I have been away so long, but I have never ceased to think of you. I have heard many rumours about what goes on at Court and, because it occurred to me that you might be less happy than you once were, I wanted to come to see you for myself.'

'It was good of you to come,' she said. 'There are times in one's life when it is pleasant to know real friends are near.'

He had heard of the stories about her which were circulated

throughout France; he had seen many of the pamphlets. 'There will be many to watch us,' he said. 'We must be careful.' He knew that his name had already been linked with hers, that many knew of that very first meeting at the Opéra ball. They knew that she had watched him leave for America with tears in her eyes. There were so many spies about them.

'You must come to Petit Trianon,' she said. 'Yes, you must visit me in my little home. There I enjoy some privacy.'

He looked at her with tenderness. There was much she did not understand. There was little privacy in her life; and it was her activities at Petit Trianon which had called forth the most cruel of the gossip.

But what could he do? He had stayed away so long; he had thought of her during the campaign – thought of her continually. There had been others of course. Charming American girls, but the *affaires* had been of short duration; he had forgotten them; he had indulged in them merely to forget the charm of the Queen who was out of reach.

So he went to Petit Trianon. He walked with her in the pastoral surroundings; he danced; he joined in the butter-making; he rode in the forest, and each day it became more and more difficult to hide his feelings from the Queen – and others.

He would entertain the company with talk of his adventures as aide-de-camp to La Fayette. He told how his contingent and the insurgents beat the English, and how they had forced Lord Cornwallis to sign a capitulation which was more humiliating to the English than that of Saratoga; and how George Washington, when he received the sword from O'Hara, who had taken Cornwallis' place, was really accepting his country's independence.

It was a stirring story, and Fersen with his quiet method of understatement – so different from that of the French – was regarded as a hero and one of the most welcome visitors to Trianon. The Queen was finding it difficult to do without him, and those about her were excited by his visits because it was so amusing to watch the passionate friendship between the Queen and the Swedish Count.

Rumour seeped out, Fersen's father wrote from Sweden demanding to know what was detaining his son so long at the Court of France.

In desperation and seeking to turn his father's suspicions from the real reason, Fersen declared that he was seeking to marry the daughter of Necker, the ex-minister and millionaire.

It was very pleasant to forget the storms outside Petit Trianon, to walk about the gardens, with a company of intimate friends which must always include Axel. Antoinette would watch Madame Royale playing in the gardens, and the little Dauphin, now two years old, tottering about on his rickety legs.

If, thought Antoinette, Axel were my husband and King of France, if my little son were strong and healthy . . . why then I should be perfectly happy.

She rarely asked what had become of James Armand. He did not come into her presence now. He was so jealous, she had been told, of the Dauphin.

'Foolish child!' she murmured. 'I must reprimand him.'

But she always forgot.

James Armand must be growing up. She had forgotten how old he was, for she was forgetting so much about him since the birth of her children. Madame Royale was now five years old, and Antoinette had adopted James Armand before the girl's birth. He must be quite ten years old. Quite a little man. Ah, he did not want the company of women and children now. He had been so charmingly fond of her once, but doubtless now he found boys of his own age with whom to play.

James Armand had indeed found interests. He was often with the servants, listening to their talk; sometimes they took him to the cafés in the Palais Royal. There he listened to the talk. He discovered a new emotion – hatred of Madame Royale and the Dauphin. In the Palais Royal there were gathered others who knew how to hate. They hated the Queen more fiercely than any, and James Armand began to consider that hatred.

Meanwhile Axel's father was alarmed. He approached his King and asked that his son might be recalled to Sweden; and the result was a summons from King Gustavus.

Axel went to the Queen and begged a private interview, and as soon as she looked into his eyes she saw his distress.

'What is it?' she asked fearfully.

'A summons home.'

'Oh, no! We must prevent that. You *must* not go from here.'

She held out her hands impulsively and as impulsively he took them; he kissed them fervently.

She smiled through her tears. 'There are times,' she said, 'when even Swedish reserve may be broken down.'

He said: 'How shall I endure the days without seeing you?'

Her answer was quiet but as impassioned as his. 'How shall I endure mine?'

'Antoinette,' he said. 'You know . . .'

'Yes,' she said. 'You love me. I know it, and it delights me because I love you also.'

'This summons, to come now!'

'You must stay here. A post must be found for you.'

248

'This summons comes from my King.'

'Then there shall be another from a Queen.'

'You are impulsive,' he said. 'Were you not ever so? Oh, if I stayed what would become of us?'

She cried: 'I do not ask for anything . . . only that you stay.'

He smiled at her tenderly. 'To see you thus before me . . . confirms me in my belief that I must go.'

'If you stayed

'We should be lovers in very truth. That is an impossible situation. You . . . the Queen of France! All eyes watch you. Do you not know that?'

'I have been innocent.'

'Innocent you must remain. What if you were . . . guilty?'

'I would not care,' she cried. 'Why should I care? They have falsely credited me with so many lovers. Why should I not have one in truth?'

'Your Majesty is distraught.'

'I will not let you go. Why should I let you go? I love you. Why should I not know this pleasure, as others have? For years I have been frustrated . . .'

'There is the King.'

'Oh, the King. My poor Louis! I am fond of Louis. Who could help but be fond of Louis! In the beginning . . . You do not know. I will not talk of that. But how could I love Louis as . . . I now know love?'

'Antoinette,' he said, 'the people must not have a chance to spread new slanders.'

'They spread them in any case. Let me give them just cause for once.'

'No. No. Never forget you are Queen of France, Antoinette.'

'Axel, what sort of a lover are you? You tell me you love me, and forbid me to love you in the next breath.'

It was too much for him. He held her in his arms. But he was so much wiser than she was. He had recently come from the conflict of war. He had learned much about greed and cruelty, malice and envy – particularly envy. He saw the Queen – the woman he loved – as a target for her enemies, a fragile target. He knew that he dared not disobey his King; he knew that for Antoinette's sake he must not stay another night in France. He took his leave, and that night he left for his own country.

The Queen was preparing to make the journey to Notre Dame that she might give thanks for the recovery from her confinement. It was a year since Axel had gone away, and a great deal had happened in that year.

He had been right, of course, to go. If he had stayed, neither of them would have been able to stem that passion which was between them. Its fruition must have been as inevitable as its beginnings. Axel was a man whom she could love; he was strong; he was competent; and beneath his calm was an ardent passion; he had everything that she would wish for in a husband, all of which Louis lacked.

And now she had another child, who did much to soothe her. He was a boy, and it was clear from the first that he was as healthy as a young peasant. She thought sadly of the child's elder brother who grew more wan each day. She feared that he was a victim of the wasting disease which from time to time attacked the Bourbons.

Dear little Louis Joseph! She prayed for him constantly. The rude health of little Louis Charles, while it delighted her, yet saddened her because it must remind her of Louis Joseph.

And now she must ride to the cathedral of Notre Dame; and she was beginning to dread her excursions into Paris. This time the birth of a son would not regain for her her lost popularity. There would be many in the streets to repeat that wicked verse against her and the new child. Whose child this time? they would be asking.

At such times she longed fiercely for Axel. If he had remained and they had become lovers, she would have been glad. She wanted to shout at those who slandered her, 'Yes, I have a lover. You are right. I have a lover.'

But all she did was to pass among them, her head high, never for once losing her look of haughty disdain which infuriated them more than anything.

What a long year it had seemed since he had gone. And when would he return? Would he ever return?

At first there had been nothing to do but seek to be gay. The days had been so dreary: to sit for her portraits by Madame Elisabeth Vigée le Brun who painted her and her children so charmingly and in so many different poses; to play with her children; to dance a little, to gamble. She had been glad she had her theatre. There was forgetfulness to be found in watching the comedies and tragedies enacted before her eyes. There was great fun too in taking part in them. Often she and Artois would play together, for her younger brother-in-law was not unlike her in temperament. She was glad of his company during that time, although of course the rumours concerning their relationship were revived.

Yet, whoever she had with her, there would be scandal. She was reputed to be not only the lover of men but of women. Madame de Polignac and the Princesse de Lamballe had not escaped the scandal which accompanied the Queen wherever she went.

Calonne had been appointed to the ministry; he was a friend of the Polignacs. His idea for the recovery of the country's finances was further loans; he believed that all France needed was confidence in her position, and that the spending of money on public services would give this confidence. 'We are prosperous,' people would say to one another; and the baker would spend with the candlestick-maker, and the butcher with the tailor. Hence prosperity would return to France. When he decided to build roads and bridges, the people were impressed. But that winter was harder than ever before, and there was a great deal of suffering throughout the land.

Necker wached the new minister's activities with a sneer. Borrowing was not the way to success. He published a new book: *Administrations of the Finances of France*. In it he deplored Calonne's policy, and so Calonne prevailed upon Louis to exile the banker.

Necker left, but the people's suspicions were then thoroughly aroused. They began to distrust the glib Calonne and, as soon as they did so, they remembered that the man whom they had praised when he was spending borrowed money for public works, was a friend of the Polignacs.

Now they cried: 'Calonne! He is the Queen's man!'

When the Grand Duke Paul of Russia visited France he was delighted with the French theatre and expressed a desire to see acted on the French stage a play he had recently read. This was Beaumarchais' *Le Mariage de Figaro*, a play which Beaumarchais had already tried to have played, but which had been banned by the King, for Figaro, the pert barber and central character, was the mouthpiece of Beaumarchais' views on existing society in France, and many of the King's advisers had been astute enough to see that the playwright was making fun of the nobility; and that if the sober citizens of Paris saw the play and brooded on Figaro's observations, they would certainly come out of the theatre with less respect than ever before for those whom tradition had taught them to believe were their betters.

'Keep Figaro off the stage,' Louis had been advised; and he had accepted that advice.

The Polignac faction, always anxious to show its power with the Queen, and never more than now when they felt they were losing it, had declared in favour of the piece, and they implored Antoinette to use her influence with the King.

Louis read the play through with her, pointing out the allusions to the government and the nobility. Antoinette was disappointed that he would not give his permission, and Artois, who thought of nothing but frivolous pleasure, longed to see the play performed. He fancied himself in the role of Figaro. He declared that the King often changed his mind, and suggested that plans for production should go on.

Louis, however, was determined to be firm in this instance, and stopped the show a few hours before the curtain was to rise.

Then Vaudreuil and his mistress, Gabrielle, determined to do the play privately; and this they did at Vaudreuil's château at Gennevilliers. The Queen, much as she would have liked to attend, and much as she wanted some such pleasure to turn her mind from her longing for Axel and her fears for her son, decided that since the play was being performed against the wishes of the King she could not do so. Artois came back to Court and with Vaudreuil and Gabrielle began to sing the play's praises.

Antoinette then sought out the King. 'If you do not allow this play to be played either in Paris or Versailles they will say that you are a tyrant. Many have heard of its success at Gennevilliers and are asking for it to be played here.'

Louis, who always saw himself as the indulgent Papa, wavered; the play was read again, and four out of six judges declared it fit to be played, for Beaumarchais had pretended to make cuts of the speeches objected to, and believing this to have been done, the judges agreed that it might safely go on.

And so on an April day *Le Mariage de Figaro* was played at the Théâtre-Français, and the crowds had waited in the streets all during the previous night to make sure of getting seats.

The Parisians applauded the sentiments of the impudent barber, particularly where they saw references to certain members of the Court.

They stamped their feet, laughed and applauded; but after the show they stood about outside the theatre and considered the daring remarks of the comic barber.

Antoinette had enjoyed the play and had shared Artois' feelings about it. It would be amusing, she had said to him, to put it on in the lovely gilded theatre she had had built at Trianon.

Artois was enthusiastic. He pranced about the apartment, quoting the merry barber.

But in the weeks following the showing of *Le Mariage de Figaro*, there had been more pamphlets than ever before; when she sat at table Antoinette would find them beneath her plate, and the King would discover them among his papers.

It was unfortunate that the purchase of Saint-Cloud should have been made so public. She had been worried about the Dauphin's health and, when repairs to the château of Versailles were necessary, had not wanted to take him into Paris. She had often visited Saint-Cloud, which had belonged to the Orléans family since the days of Louis Quatorze, and she had thought that they, complaining as they did of their poverty, would have been glad to sell at a reasonable price, or perhaps take one of the royal houses in exchange.

Chartres, with whom it was necessary to deal, the old Duke being so ill now that he could not live much longer, had prevaricated and Calonne, who was handling the transaction on behalf of the King and Queen, was prevailed upon to pay a very large sum for it.

The news was out. In the streets they were talking about the further waste of money, the great extravagance of the Queen. Rumours immediately began to circulate. It was declared that the Queen planned to spend money at Saint-Cloud as she had at Trianon.

'What is all this talk of a deficit?' demanded the people. 'What is this deficit? What does it mean?'

The answer to that was: 'There is one who can answer that question, for she is Madame Déficit.'

Now in the pamphlets she had a new name: Madame Déficit.

Everything I do, she told herself, is turned to my disadvantage. The Emperor Joseph had asked the Dutch to open the Scheldt and so bring prosperity back to the Netherlands which were under Austrian dominion. The Dutch had refused to do this, and flooded their country, as they had done before in order to save it from the invader. Louis and his ministers, realising that a European war was about to break out, offered mediation between the two countries, with the result that the Scheldt was to remain closed but the Austrians were to be paid a sum of money by the Dutch as compensation. As the Dutch were unable to find this money, the French came to their rescue. This was no altruism on the part of the French; a conflict so close to them could have involved them in war, and one thing France's tottering financial structure could not endure at that time was participation in a war; therefore 5,000,000 florins seemed, to the ministers of France, a small price to pay for peace.

But it was not possible to expect the people to understand this.

'Déficit! Déficit! Déficit!' they cried. 'We are nearly bankrupt. So what do we do? We send money to the Queen's family. For what purpose? Oh, that they may build Petit Trianons in Austria, that they may have their little farms and houses and theatres . . . just as *l'Autrichienne* does in France. What matters it? The French pay. Ask Madame Déficit.'

'It matters not what I do,' she told herself. 'Nothing I do could be good in their eyes.'

She went down to her gilded coach which was to take her into the Capital.

Josèphe was already waiting for her. The years had not improved Josèphe. She was even more sour than she had been when she had first come to France; though it would have been difficult at the time to believe that was possible. She was barren of children and of hope, for now that the King of France had two sons she believed her husband would never be King.

As they made the journey from Versailles into the Capital, Antoinette knew that Josèphe was delighted at the cold reception given the Queen.

The crowds were there to watch, but they did not cheer. They merely stared at her as she passed.

She knew they were calling her haughty. If she had unbent they would have called her frivolous.

Ah, she thought, when they have determined to hate a sovereign as they have determined to hate me, there is no hope of gaining their affection.

The ceremony over, she emerged from Notre Dame.

Now she must make her way to Sainte-Geneviève. She must enter the church and endure further ceremony, for Sainte-Geneviève was the patron saint of Paris.

'Why should I?' she asked herself. 'I am weary of their ceremonies. Why should I do my part when they will not do theirs? Why should I prolong the ceremony simply because it is their patron saint they wish me to honour? The people of Paris do not honour me.'

The coach had slowed down and the Abbé of Sainte-Geneviève had come out to greet her.

She answered his greeting with warmth and charm, and told him that she would be late for the banquet which was being given at the Tuileries and that she would therefore be unable to enter the church.

The Abbé bowed his head. The people gasped.

'It is an insult to our Patroness!' they murmured. 'It is an insult to Paris.'

Josèphe was smiling, well pleased. It always pleased her to see the foolish frivolous creature make her mistakes.

'You are well pleased, Josèphe,' said Antoinette as they drove to the Tuileries.

'Like you,' said Josèphe demurely, 'I am glad the tiresome ceremony is over.'

'We but exchange one tiresome ceremony for another,' said the Queen wearily.

She thought how pleasant it would be to sit on the lawn before her dear little house watching the children play, dressed in one of her muslin dresses, a shady hat on her head.

But the ceremonies must go on. There must be the banquet at that cheerless palace. Even the performance at the Opéra, which followed, raised her spirits very little, although the audience did not treat her with the same contempt as that which she had received in the streets, and there were a few lukewarm cheers.

After the Opéra she and the King went to supper at The Temple, Artois' Paris home.

She shivered as she entered the place. 'It's so ancient,' she complained to Artois. 'Why do you not rid yourself of the place and build yourself something modern?'

Artois bent his mischievous face close to hers and whispered: 'How would it be if I asked Calonne to arrange to buy Saint-Cloud from you?'

They laughed. She could be gay in the company of Artois. He refused to take anything seriously. The people of Paris were grumbling about the purchase of Saint-Cloud. Let them grumble! was Artois' way of thinking. Who cares for the people of Paris!

When she was with him she could share that insouciance, and it was as though they were young again, arousing the wrath of the people with the Austrian habit of sledging, and riding back to Versailles in the early hours of the morning.

'All the same,' she said. 'I find the Temple a gloomy residence. I command you, brother, change it for another.'

Artois bowed over her hand. 'The Queen commands,' he said and lightly kissed her fingers.

Chapter IX

THE DIAMOND NECKLACE

Artois was in the Queen's apartment. He was pacing the floor, his eyes ablaze, his impish smile illuminating his rather handsome face. Antoinette smiled at him. She had always been a great deal fonder of him than of his brother Provence.

He was saying: 'But why not, 'Toinette? Why not indeed? It would be a wonderful show. A perfect play for the Trianon Theatre. I tell you it is better than *Le Mariage de Figaro*. The barber is more amusing, more witty, more impudent than ever in this play. We must do it. Come, 'Toinette, say you will allow us to play *Le Barbier de Seville* in your theatre.'

'As you are so earnest . . .' she began.

He was beside her, kissing her hands, putting his arm about her and dancing with her about the apartment.

'It is well that there are only those whom we trust watching us,' she said.

''Toinette, we should never trust any, and there will always be those to watch us whom we do not trust.' He struck an attitude and declaimed: ' "Since men have no choice other than stupidity or madness, if I can't get any profit I want pleasure at

259

least. So hurrah for happiness. Who knows if the world is going to last three weeks?" That,' he continued, 'is Figaro. What a character! My dearest Queen, you must play Rosine. "Imagine the prettiest little woman in the world, gentle, tender, lively, fresh, appetising, nimble of foot, slender-waisted, with rounded arms, dewy mouth; and such hands; such feet; such eyes!" There! That is Rosine. And you, my Queen, must play Rosine. I swear if you do not I'll not play the barber, and what will the play be like without me as the barber?'

'You are growing old, you know, brother. You should show more seriousness.'

'Ha! Look who commands me.'

'And you a father!'

'Fathers must have their fun, 'Toinette.'

'You have not forgotten, I trust, that it will soon be your eldest son's birthday. That reminds me – I have such a charming gift for him. I hope it will please young Monsieur le Duc d'Angoulême.'

'If you chose the gift, it surely will,' said Artois. He went on: 'Vaudreuil would wish for a part, I am sure.'

She was determined to tease him, although she was interested in the Beaumarchais play.

'I have some diamond epaulets and buckles for your son,' she said. 'They are certainly charming. I wonder if they are here. I will show them to you.'

'Let us settle this matter of the play first.'

'There is time for that.' She called to one of her women. 'Henriette, has Boehmer brought the diamonds for the Little Duke?'

'Yes, Madame. I have them here. The jeweller left a letter

for you with them. He was somewhat agitated. He was so anxious that you should have the letter.'

'Bring them to me. I wish to show the ornaments to the Comte.'

Henriette de Campan brought the jewels and the letter. Antoinette showed the trinkets to Artois and, while he was examining them, she opened the letter from the jeweller.

She read it and frowned.

'This surprises me,' she said.

Artois came and looked over her shoulder, and they read the letter together.

'Why so?' asked the Comte.

'Because I have no notion what the man is talking about. Henriette,' she called.

Madame de Campan came hurrying to her side.

'How was Boehmer when he left the letter?'

'Strange, Madame. Agitated.'

'Do you think he is . . . sane?'

'Sane, Madame? How so?'

'He writes such a strange letter. I have no notion what he means. He says he is very satisfied by the arrangements and that it is a great pleasure to him that the most magnificent diamonds in the world are now in the possession of the most beautiful of Queens.'

'He's hoping for business,' said Artois.

'A strange letter to write. What does he want to sell me now? Thank heaven it is not that necklace of his!'

'The famous necklace,' mused Artois.

'You've heard of it?'

'Who has not heard of it? Didn't the man roam the world trying to sell it?'

'Yes. He declared that if he did not succeed he would be ruined. He came to me one day and implored me to have it. He made quite a scene before Charlotte. I told him to break up the stones and sell them separately. It was a foolish idea to make the necklace in the first place. I was delighted when he sold it. Who was it bought it, Henriette?'

'The Sultan of Constantinople bought it for his favourite wife, Madame,' said Madame de Campan.

'I was quite relieved when I heard it,' said Antoinette. She looked at the letter again, laughed and held it up to the flame of the candle. Then she threw it from her into the fireplace. Dismissing the matter, she called to Madame de Campan to put the little Duke's present away and gave herself up to the pleasure of discussing the proposed performance of *Le Barbier de Seville*.

❖ ❖ ❖

The Queen was rehearsing her lines. There was no doubt about it; Beaumarchais had surpassed himself with the Barber. She really believed with Artois that it was a better play than *Le Mariage de Figaro*.

Her role was – apart from that of the barber – the most important, and she was eager to acquit herself with honours. It should be one of those occasions such as she loved. The King and all the most noble people at Court should be in the audience. Meanwhile rehearsal followed rehearsal.

She found it a little difficult to concentrate on rehearsals, for on the previous day the jeweller Boehmer had presented himself at Trianon and begged an audience. She had refused this. She sent her woman to say that she was in no need of new jewels and, if at any time she decided she needed more, she would send for him.

The woman had reported that the man had been very disconsolate and had told her that Madame de Campan had suggested he see the Queen as soon as possible.

'Madame de Campan!' Antoinette had cried. 'Where is Henriette? Is she not visiting her father-in-law?'

'It is so, Madame,' Antoinette was told.

'Then the man is clearly not telling the truth. It is some plot of his to obtain an audience and then show me some magnificent pair of earrings which he has made especially for me. It will be like the affair of the necklace all over again.'

Nevertheless the matter worried her. Could it really be that the man was going out of his mind? That letter he had written about the satisfactory arrangements – what could it mean? It really seemed as though he were, to put it kindly, a little unbalanced.

The rehearsal went on, and afterwards everyone declared that Antoinette would make a charming Rosine – a perfect foil to Artois' barber. Oh, yes, this was certainly going to be the finest production ever seen at the Trianon Theatre.

When her women were helping to dress her after the rehearsal, one of them mentioned that Henriette de Campan had returned from her visit to her father-in-law, and that she was anxious to speak to the Queen privately as soon as Antoinette would receive her.

'Leave me now,' said Antoinette, 'and tell her to come to me at once.'

When Henriette came, Antoinette immediately saw that something had happened to cause her grave anxiety.

'Henriette,' cried the Queen, 'what is wrong, and why did you send that absurd man Boehmer to Trianon?'

'It is about the necklace. The diamond necklace.'

'That trinket . . . the one which was sold to the Sultan of Constantinople?'

Henriette was looking at her mistress with bewildered eyes. 'Boehmer says, Madame, that it was not sold to the Sultan, but that it was sold to you.'

'Then he is mad. I feared it. So that is what he wished to see me about. Speak up, Henriette. What are you thinking? What has he told you? It is a lie if he says I bought the necklace. You know very well that he sold it to the Sultan.'

'Madame, I must tell you what has happened. He was at my father-in-law's house. He said he must talk to me about this matter, for he found it difficult to get an audience with Your Majesty. He said he was surprised that I did not know you had bought the necklace. He felt sure that I must have seen you wear it on some occasion.'

'But he himself said it was sold to the Sultan.'

'I told him this, Madame. He said that he had had instructions, which came indirectly from you, to *say* that the Sultan had bought it. I did not believe this, for I remembered you had referred to the matter quite recently — when you had Boehmer's letters. I asked him when you had told him that you would buy the necklace. He answered that he had not had dealings with you personally about the matter.'

'Ah!' cried Antoinette. 'Indeed he has not. So he spoke the truth there.'

'He declared that the transaction was made through the Cardinal de Rohan.'

'The Cardinal de Rohan! That man! I loathe him. Does

Boehmer think that I would allow him to transact any business for me?'

'Your Majesty, he has documents. He says your orders were passed to him by the Cardinal. These orders were signed by you, and he has shown them to various people in order to obtain the credit he needed. He says that you have received the necklace through the Cardinal, and that it is to be paid for in four instalments at four-monthly intervals.'

'This is preposterous!' cried the Queen. 'I have never had the necklace. I have had no dealings with the Cardinal de Rohan. The man must be mad. Send at once for Boehmer.'

Boehmer came to the Queen. He was apprehensive.

'What is this ridiculous story you have to tell?' demanded the Queen.

'Madame,' said Boehmer. 'The diamond necklace was handed to the Cardinal de Rohan who was able to show me the order which was signed by Your Majesty.'

'Where is this order?'

'I have it here.'

The Queen seized it. It was written in a poor imitation of her handwriting, and it was signed 'Marie Antoinette de France'.

'That is not my writing,' said the Queen. 'And you know, do you not, that Queens never sign their names in that way. I always sign simply "Marie Antoinette", never "of France". Surely that should have shown you that this is a preposterous forgery.'

'Madame, the Cardinal assured me that his orders came from you. I am distracted. The first payment was due on the 1st August. I cannot ask my creditors to wait any longer.'

'It's a lie. You know that you sold the necklace to the Sultan of Constantinople.'

'That was the story which Your Majesty wished to be put about, because this transaction was to be so secret.'

'I never heard such a ridiculous story.'

'Madame, I swear I handed the necklace to the Cardinal, and that he assured me that it was at your command.'

'I do not see the Cardinal. I will not see the Cardinal. I have not seen him since the baptism of the Duc de Normandie, and then I did not speak to him.'

'Madame, he assured me that the go-between was a lady – a very dear friend of yours.'

'What lady?'

'The Comtesse de Lamotte-Valois.'

'I have never heard of the woman. The whole thing is a plot by the Cardinal. Pray go now, Monsieur Boehmer. I promise you this matter shall have my immediate attention – and that of His Majesty.'

The jeweller took his leave and, when he had gone, Antoinette went at once to Louis' apartments.

'Louis,' she cried, 'I must speak to you alone . . . at once.'

Louis dismissed all his attendants, and she burst out: 'That man, that wicked man who so maligned my mother, has determined to humiliate me also. He has contrived some absurd plot – some frightful plot – to . . . to do me some harm. Though I cannot quite clearly see what. He has been to the jeweller and, according to Boehmer, bought on my account that diamond necklace which he was always talking about and urging us to buy.'

'Bought it . . . on your account? But the Cardinal . . .'

'Exactly! I have not exchanged a word with the man for

years. And now it seems he has been to the jeweller and told him that I have begged him to buy the necklace on my behalf. There are forged documents – documents said to have my signature on them. Look at this. This is supposed to be my order. You can see for yourself that it is a forgery. "Marie Antoinette de France"! As if I would sign myself thus. And do you mean to tell me that Rohan did not know this for a forgery?'

Louis was bewildered; he could only stare at the paper in his hand.

'What does it mean, Louis? What does it mean?'

'You . . . have not bought the necklace?'

She looked at him with deep reproach. 'You . . . even you . . . ask that! Indeed I have not bought the necklace. Would it not have been noticed immediately if I had worn it? Why should I keep it a secret? There has been a terrible fraud . . . a fraud to humiliate and insult me and involve me in – I know not what . . .'

Louis said: 'Be calm. We will sift this matter, and we will discover what it is all about.'

✦ ✦ ✦

It was Assumption Day and the courtiers thronged the Salle de Glace and the Oeil-de-Boeuf waiting to accompany the King and Queen to Mass.

Louis, Prince and Cardinal de Rohan, who, as Grand Almoner to the King, was to officiate, was also waiting there. He was excited – as he always was on those occasions when he had an opportunity of being near the Queen. She never gave a sign that she noticed him; but recently, since the affair of the necklace, he had convinced himself that she had her reasons for behaving thus. She was by no means indifferent to him: Jeanne de Lamotte-Valois had assured him of this.

He was obsessed by the Queen. He had thought of her constantly since he had first seen her – a young, so innocent girl, a little frightened, leaving her native country to come to a new one where she was to be called upon to play such an important part.

He had been a fool, he often accused himself, to write slightingly of her mother. But who would have thought it would have been allowed to get to the Queen's ears that he had done so? That was bad luck.

She had been very disdainful towards him since, and never given him so much as a glance. Perhaps that very attitude of hers had inflamed his passion, for he was a man of deep sensuality, and the fact that he wore the robes of the church had never been allowed to interfere with his amorous adventures. But these had begun to pall; there was one woman with whom he wished to share them, and she had been completely out of his reach until Jeanne de Lamotte-Valois had come along and informed him to the contrary.

Then the exciting and incredible adventure had begun. There had been letters from the Queen; there had even been a brief meeting in the gardens of Versailles. The Cardinal had begun to believe that the Queen was far from indifferent to him and that if he were a little patient she would become his mistress.

To show how absolute was her faith in him she had entrusted him with that transaction with the jewellers and he had procured for her the diamond necklace which, he had been told, she wished to buy secretly as the King would not buy it for her; he had even lent her money.

At any moment now the doors would be thrown open and she would appear with Louis. Poor Louis! Who cared for Louis? No wonder the enchanting creature must have a lover.

Now was the moment. The doors were flung open.

But the King and Queen did not appear. Instead a lackey stood where they should have been.

'Prince Cardinal de Rohan!' called the lackey.

The Cardinal went forward.

'The King commands you to go at once to his private apartments.'

❖ ❖ ❖

The Queen was with the King in his private apartments. Rohan gave her a quick look; but she did not seem to see him. Also present was the Baron de Breteuil, the Minister of State.

The King said: 'Cousin, have you recently bought diamonds from the jeweller Boehmer?'

'Yes, Sire. I have.'

'Where are they?'

Rohan looked anxiously towards Antoinette, who stared beyond him with the utmost haughtiness. He presumed now that the King knew the necklace was in the Queen's possession, and that no good would come of trying to hide this fact.

'I think they have been delivered to the Queen,' said Rohan.

'By whom?'

'By the Comtesse de Lamotte-Valois who brought me instructions from Her Majesty, whose commands I then carried out.'

Antoinette cried angrily: 'Do you think, Monsieur le Cardinal, that I, who have not spoken to you for years, would ask you to arrange such a commission, and that it is possible that this should be through a woman I do not know?'

Rohan was bewildered. The King saw this and was sorry for him.

'There must be some explanation,' said Louis kindly.

'I believe, Sire,' murmured Rohan, 'that I have been most cruelly deceived.'

'I am awaiting your explanation,' said the King. 'Where is this necklace?'

'I have handed it to Madame de Lamotte-Valois. She assured me that she had passed it on to the Queen. I have letters, which, I was told, were written by the Queen.'

'Show me,' said Louis.

The Cardinal produced one, and the King looked at it. 'Marie Antoinette de France,' murmured Louis. 'You should know, cousin, that no Queen would sign herself thus. Leave us now. This is a matter which it will be necessary to sift, that we may know the truth. The Queen's good name is involved, and I would have you know, cousin, that makes this a matter of first importance to me.'

The Cardinal retired. In the Salle de Glace and Oeil-de-Boeuf people were asking each other why Mass was being delayed. They saw the Cardinal walk out of the King's apartment, his face quite white, his eyes glittering.

He had taken but a few paces when Breteuil appeared behind him and shouted an order to one of the guard who was stationed in the King's ante-room.

'Arrest Louis, Prince and Cardinal de Rohan.'

There was a breathless silence as the tall and handsome Cardinal was conducted to one of the guard-rooms in the lower part of the Palace.

The performance of *Le Barbier de Seville* was given at the Trianon Theatre on the 19th August, four days after the arrest of Rohan.

The audience was a little absentminded, because they were thinking of this preposterous affair of the necklace. Already the people in the streets were talking of it, calling it 'The Queen's Necklace', asking each other what fresh extravagance was this. 1,600,000 livres squandered on one necklace to adorn that proud neck, while many in Paris had not the necessary *sous* to buy their bread. And it was a secret transaction too! The Queen had called in her latest lover to buy the necklace for her. What next?

They waited eagerly to find out.

The truth was that an amazing fraud had been perpetrated, and the victims of that fraud were the Queen and the Cardinal de Rohan. The person who had planned the whole affair was a wily and extremely handsome woman who called herself Jeanne de Lamotte-Valois, claiming that she was of the royal house because an ancestor of hers had been the illegitimate son of Henri Deux.

Jeanne had had a hard childhood and had often been reduced to begging in the streets; but she was clever and, when only seven years old, had presented herself to the Marquis de Boulainvilliers and told her story of possessing royal blood so pitiably that the Marquise had taken the girl and her younger sister into her household and educated them; finally, when Jeanne married a Captain of the Guards, she insisted that he must assume the title of Comte, that he might be worthy to mate with a descendant of the Valois; and she added Valois to their name so that they were known as the Comte and Comtesse de Lamotte-Valois.

Jeanne soon tired of her husband, but with the help of the Marquise de Boulainvilliers she made the acquaintance of the Cardinal de Rohan, that notoriously sensual prelate. Jeanne was a very handsome woman and it was not long before she became his mistress. To be the mistress of an exalted Cardinal was pleasing, but Jeanne was too worldly not to know that her triumph was ephemeral; she was too strong-minded to accept a minor role in any partnership, and immediately began to wonder how she could make herself rich and independent.

Obsessed by the thought of the royal blood of which she boasted, she determined to see if she could make her way at Court; and the only way she could think of in which she could call attention to herself was by fainting in the apartments of Madame Elisabeth. This lady, saintly by nature, was known to be good of heart and to have a very soft spot in it for the poor. Jeanne made sure that there should be friends at hand to explain that she was descended from the Valois – who were as royal as the Bourbons – and that she had fainted from starvation. The result of this was that Madame Elisabeth had her taken to her home and gave her a sum of money. Jeanne repeated the fainting fit, once in the apartments of Madame d'Artois and once in those of Antoinette. On each occasion she was given financial help, but no one seemed interested in her story.

Jeanne however could not resist talking about her experiences at Court, inventing stories of how the Queen had received her and made much of her, calling her 'dear cousin'.

In the rue Neuve-Saint-Gilles, where Jeanne had her lodgings she became a person of importance. Each day she went to Versailles – to call on the Queen, she said. Many flocked to her house, bringing her presents, for they felt it would be wise to win the favour of one who was so well received at Court, and they had heard that the Queen chose her friends from all classes. Take for instance Madame Bertin the *couturière*. She was a friend of the Queen and consequently had become a person of great influence. And what was she but a dressmaker? Yet Madame Bertin could procure all sorts of jobs for her friends, and was queen of her little circle. Jeanne became queen of hers.

She would wait in the Galerie at Versailles to see the Queen pass; she would study her well; and all the time she was turning over in her mind how she could make herself rich, respected, and received at Court.

Jeanne had a lover – a cunning man, Retaux de Villette. They schemed together as they lay in bed at night.

'You should not neglect your good friend the Cardinal,' Retaux warned her. 'He is too rich and influential to be neglected.'

This was true. Often Jeanne called at the Episcopal Palace to see her old benefactor and to remind him of times past.

The Cardinal fascinated her. She knew him well. He was a Prince, a relation of the royal family; he was cultured and of high rank in the church, and yet it seemed to Jeanne that the Cardinal was in some ways a fool.

He was, for one thing, completely under the influence – perhaps control – of a strange man, Joseph Balsamo, who called himself the Comte de Cagliastro but was in reality the son of a converted Sicilian Jew who had died when Joseph was a boy. In their home at Palermo the young Joseph had been apprenticed to an apothecary. He was a strange boy, and had declared from the first his belief in occult powers; he developed certain tricks, and was both a conjurer and a ventriloquist. Of striking appearance, he was undoubtedly possessed of certain hypnotic powers which he developed. With all these gifts he had at an early age set out to make his fortune.

During the first stages of his career he had been in trouble more than once when he had been accused of being a common thief and swindler, but later he became a Freemason and was received with honour in the various countries he visited. It was thus that he came to be regarded as a man of superhuman powers and there were many who were ready to listen to him.

One of these was the Cardinal de Rohan whom he had completely fascinated. Cagliostro now lived in the Cardinal's palace and was deferred to by all therein. There he worked at his crucible and declared that he could make gold and precious stones.

Cagliostro, some said, had exerted his powerful influence over the Cardinal so that in him de Rohan could see no wrong.

'Have a care, Monseigneur,' warned his friends. 'This man whom you harbour in your house will make great demands upon you.'

'He asks me nothing . . . nothing,' declared the Cardinal. 'He will make me the richest prince in the world, and he asks nothing for it. He is divine. There are times when I think Cagliostro – who has lived through many centuries – is God himself.'

Truly the Cardinal was bewitched.

And if he could be bewitched by a sorcerer, thought Jeanne, why should he not be bewitched by a clever woman?

Jeanne made the acquaintance of Cagliostro who was so interested in the young woman that he would occasionally walk with her in the gardens of the Episcopal Palace and, on one memorable occasion, he discussed the Cardinal.

'Monseigneur has two great desires in this life,' Cagliostro told Jeanne.

'And they are, Master?'

'Why should I tell you?' asked Cagliostro, turning his brilliant gaze upon the woman at his side. 'But methinks I will. For I shall then have the pleasure of seeing what you make of the knowledge. But indeed I know; for, my child, all things are known to me.'

Even a practical woman such as Jeanne could not but be affected by the man. He walked beside her, his wide nostrils flaring with that passion which seemed to be pent up within him; with his olive complexion and rather prominent and piercing black eyes the man was striking enough; his hands were folded behind him and his taffeta coat, which was trimmed with gold braid, was open to show his scarlet waistcoat, embroidered with gold; his red breeches and his stockings were of many colours which were also touched with gold. He wore many jewels – diamonds flashed on his fingers, rubies as buttons adorned his waistcoat; his watch-chain was composed of diamonds; and all these stones were enormous. It was said he had made them himself. Some said they were paste; yet they seemed to sparkle with a brilliance greater than that of other stones. Some said that Cagliostro put a spell on all those who looked at his jewels, so that they saw them as he wished them to.

'Yes,' he went on, 'I will tell you of the two wishes which are dear to the Cardinal's heart. He has brooded much on other

Cardinals who have played their part in the history of his country. There are times when he tells me the secrets of his heart and knows not afterwards that he has spoken of them. He talks much of Cardinal Richelieu. He talks of Cardinal Mazarin; and he dreams of the day when men and women will talk of the great part Cardinal de Rohan played in the history of his country.'

Jeanne said: 'Yes, Master. I know it.'

'Yes, you know it, my child. You know it even as I know, for I have willed that you should know it. And know you this. He thinks constantly of the Queen. He believes that if he were the lover of the Queen there would be nothing to stand between him and his desires. He longs to be the lover of the Queen; he constantly searches for the means of winning her favour.' Cagliostro turned his prominent eyes on Jeanne. 'You, my child, tell us you have found favour with the Queen. You tell us that she receives you and calls you cousin.'

Jeanne shivered. He knows I lie, she thought. He must know. The Master knows everything.

She felt the white fingers touch her shoulder. She did not look down but she was aware of the flashing diamonds, the ruby that was almost the size of an egg.

'Since you tell us the Queen receives you,' said the strange man, 'mayhap you could speak to her on the Cardinal's behalf. That, my child, would do you much good with the Cardinal.'

Then he left her; and Jeanne pondered. She thought of the flashing diamonds of the sorcerer, and it was then that she conceived the idea.

276

So Jeanne talked to the Cardinal of her triumphs with the Queen. Rétaux, who was by profession a clerk, had a gift for adapting his handwriting to various styles, and he produced a flowing feminine one in which he wrote a letter addressed to 'My dear cousin Valois', signed as by the Queen.

The Cardinal read the letter, and as he read it Jeanne was aware of the shadow of Cagliostro passing the window. Jeanne was trembling, for she feared the Cardinal must recognise the forgery. It seemed incredible that he – a Prince accustomed to royal documents – should not have recognised a clerk's clumsy hand in this, but he did not.

'I have spoken to Her Majesty of your Excellency,' Jeanne said. 'She has at times felt hatred towards you for what you said of her mother, but she has whispered to me that it is unchristian to preserve such hatreds for ever.'

The Cardinal, seeming bemused, was enchanted with this news; yet Jeanne was aware of a certain bewilderment which crossed his features, and she said quickly: 'I think that if I assured Her Majesty of your desolation at the rift between you, and that it is your greatest desire to serve her, she might give some sign of her changed feelings for you.'

'Bring me this sign,' said the Cardinal.

In a few days Jeanne returned with a letter which she said the Queen had entrusted to her for delivery to the Cardinal.

It ran:

'I am delighted that I need no longer regard you as blameworthy. It is not possible to grant you yet an audience such as you desire, but I will let you know when circumstances permit this. Meanwhile be discreet . . .'

And this extraordinary document was signed 'Marie Antoinette de France.'

The Cardinal, in his delight, showered gifts on Jeanne – the clever go-between through whose favour he might win the Queen's.

How to turn this amazing situation to greater advantage occupied Jeanne and her lover day and night. Jeanne was a bold schemer and she believed so fervently in her own astuteness that she never hesitated to put into action her most outrageous plans.

She now told the Cardinal that the Queen was short of money and was asking him to show his esteem by lending her 50,000 livres, which should be handed to her dear friend the Comtesse de Lamotte-Valois. The Cardinal showed signs of suspicions, so Jeanne hastily declared that the Queen would meet him for a few moments in the gardens of Versailles. This meeting must be very secret. She could not explain why, but he would know later when Antoinette was able to receive him openly.

The Cardinal, overjoyed, borrowed the 50,000 livres from a moneylender and gave the money to Jeanne; this was riches in the household in the rue Neuve-Saint-Gilles, but both Jeanne and Retaux realised that unless they could procure a 'Queen' to meet the Cardinal it would be the last of their pickings.

They were bemused by their success; they had come to believe that they could do exactly what they liked with the gullible Cardinal, so Retaux discovered a *modiste* who was a prostitute in her spare time, a very pretty, fair young woman in whom many noticed a faint resemblance to the Queen.

They brought her to the house in the rue Neuve-Saint-Gilles and offered her what seemed to her a fabulous sum if she would do exactly what they wanted. They rehearsed her in what she must say, dressed her in muslin such as the Queen

wore for her simple country life at Trianon, and took her one
starry night to the grove of Venus in the Versailles gardens
where the trees were so thick that it was impossible to see
clearly the faces of those who sheltered beneath them. There
Mademoiselle d'Oliva waited, nervously clutching a rose and a
letter which she was to give to a tall gentleman who would
come to her and converse for a few seconds only. With her was
Retaux in the livery of a royal servant which he had managed
to procure, and also Jeanne who would help her if she needed
help.

The tall handsome man came to the rendezvous; he was
wrapped in a great cloak and, as soon as he saw the little
prostitute, he knelt and kissed the hem of her muslin gown.

Mademoiselle d'Oliva whispered: 'You may hope that the
past will be forgotten.'

The dark man was on his feet. He had taken her hand.

She proffered the rose which he took eagerly.

At that moment Jeanne whispered in a voice of great alarm:
'Come away . . . quickly, Madame. Someone comes this way.
You must not be discovered.'

Only too glad to have played her part, Mademoiselle
d'Oliva turned and hurried away with Jeanne.

After that incident it was easy to draw more sums from the
Cardinal.

Then to Jeanne came the great idea of making herself rich
for ever.

She was entertaining lavishly on the money which the Cardinal
had provided; her friends were certain that she had some high
place at Court. Several times a week they saw her ride out in

her carriage for Versailles. There she would alight and wait with the crowds in the courtyards or the Galerie, and whenever possible study the Queen. She could then go home and describe to her friends what the Queen wore, what she looked like that day – in fact, with the aid of her memory and her vivid imagination, she was able to give credibility to this story of her friendship with Antoinette.

And to one of her parties a friend brought Boehmer the Court jeweller. He was very deferential to the Comtesse de Lamotte-Valois, and asked if he might speak to her alone.

'Madame,' he said, 'I find myself in great financial difficulties. There is a diamond necklace which I made in the hope that the Queen would buy it. I have put myself and my partners deeply in debt in order to procure only the finest stones; and the skilled workmanship which has gone into the making of this necklace is the best in the world. But if the Queen cannot be persuaded to buy this necklace – and no one else in the country could afford to do so – I and my partner are ruined men. Now you are the Queen's dear friend. If you could persuade her to buy this necklace, believe me, dear Comtesse, I should be ready to offer you a very big commission.'

Jeanne considered this. It would have been a pleasant way of earning money, *if* she had known the Queen, *if* she had been in a position to persuade her.

She said she would do what she could, and the jeweller went away somewhat relieved.

She continued to think of the necklace, and eventually asked the jeweller if he would bring it to her house and show it to her.

As soon as she set eyes on it her fertile mind began to work. She dreamed of the necklace. She did not see the beauty of those magnificent stones and their clever setting; she saw 1,600,000 livres – a fortune.

She paid a visit to the Cardinal.

'I have news, Excellency, of Her Majesty.'

The Cardinal's handsome eyes gleamed with excitement.

'The Queen needs your help. She says that if you will help her in this matter she will know you are truly her friend. She wishes to buy a diamond necklace. The King will not buy it for her, so she must do it herself; and this means doing it secretly.'

'I will do all in my power . . .' murmured the Cardinal.

'These are the Queen's instructions. You are to visit the jeweller and tell him that you have the Queen's order to purchase the necklace for her. The price is 1,600,000 livres, and the Queen finds it difficult to raise this large sum; so she wants you to arrange that it shall be paid in four parts . . . the first of these to be payable on August 1st. The necklace should be handed to you on February 1st. Would you agree to make this transaction for the Queen?'

'There is nothing on earth I would not do for the Queen.'

'Then if you will write out the agreement I will submit it to Her Majesty for her approval.'

The Cardinal sat down at once and drew up the document.

Jeanne took this, and a few days later returned to the Cardinal.

'Her Majesty is satisfied with this document and agrees to abide by the terms,' she said. 'She asks that you take it to the jeweller, who will give you the necklace. Then she wishes you to hand it to me that I may take it to her at once.'

The Cardinal hesitated.

'You do not wish to undertake this transaction for the Queen?' asked Jeanne quickly.

'I wish to please Her Majesty in every way. But this is a very big undertaking. It involves a great deal of money. I feel that the jeweller will wish to see Her Majesty's signature on the agreement.'

Jeanne could hardly suppress a sigh of relief. Her Majesty's signature – what could be easier than that? She took the document home and Rétaux signed each clause: 'Approved, Marie Antoinette de France.'

It was so simple that it was almost unbelievable that it could have worked out so easily.

Rohan took the document to the jeweller, and the next day the necklace was in Jeanne's hands.

❖ ❖ ❖

How they gloated over it – she, her husband and Rétaux. Their fortunes were made. The most magnificent diamonds in the world were in their hands. They immediately set about breaking up the necklace. They disposed of some of the diamonds in Paris but, as they were so startlingly magnificent, this caused a little questioning; Rétaux was able to tell the police that he had been charged to sell them by the lady whom he served. She was the Comtesse de Lamotte-Valois. The royal name allayed the suspicions of the police; but after that it was decided that it was too dangerous to sell the remainder of the jewels in Paris, so the Comte de Lamotte-Valois took them to London to dispose of them there.

Now the Comtesse began to live up to her royal name. She had a carriage and four English mares to draw it; she had her servants dressed in royal livery. On her berline she had engraved the royal arms of Valois, not forgetting the lilies of France and the inscription 'From the King, my ancestor, I derive my blood, my name and the lilies.'

Meanwhile the Cardinal was restive.

There was no message from the Queen to say she had received the necklace and that she was delighted with it; she never wore it at any state ceremonies at which, as Grand Almoner, the Cardinal was present. It seemed strange that she who had been so eager to possess the necklace should never wear it. When he questioned her Jeanne's answer was: 'The Queen has told me that she will not wear the necklace until it is paid for. She hesitates to let the King know she has bought it, until she can say that she has made the last payment.'

This sounded reasonable, but the Cardinal was still impatient; it seemed to him that the Queen should show some sign of gratitude to a man who had arranged such an unusual transaction for her; yet at all functions she was as haughty as ever.

But even the carefree Jeanne could not hold back time, and the 1st of August was near. The jeweller would demand payment on that date and, since he had been told to put about the rumour that he had sold the necklace to the Sultan of Constantinople (Jeanne had told him the same story as she had told Rohan, of the Queen's not wishing it to be known that she possessed the necklace until it was paid for) he might begin to grow suspicious if he were not paid, and go to the Queen.

'We must hold out a little longer,' said Jeanne to her accomplice. 'I will tell them that the Queen thinks the price too high and demands a reduction of, say, 400,000 livres. They will not want to agree to that, and I shall then tell them that the Queen will return the necklace if they do not. That will involve a great deal of argument and put off the day of payment.'

Rétaux was worried. 'But can you put off the day of payment indefinitely, and what if they refuse to make the reduction?'

'They are bound to argue. Then if necessary I shall explain the whole thing to the Cardinal. He will find some means of paying the jewellers because he will not dare do otherwise.'

'He will denounce us.'

'Not he! He is too deeply involved. To denounce us would be to show the world what a fool he is to have been so duped. Don't be afraid. We are safe enough.'

But Jeanne's good luck was beginning to desert her. When she visited the Cardinal's palace she saw Cagliostro in the distance; he did not seek her out; she fancied that he was smiling in a satisfied way, as though something he had desired had fallen straight into his lap.

She thought then: Did he plan the whole thing? Why? Is it because he likes to make us dance to his piping? Is he really a sort of god?

The jewellers, in desperate need of the money, immediately agreed to reduce the price of the necklace, so that there was no delay on account of the argument which Jeanne had hoped for.

She then went to the Cardinal and told him that the Queen could not raise the money, but wished him to arrange with the jewellers that there should be a double payment on the 1st October instead of the first being paid on the 1st August.

The Cardinal was alarmed. Jeanne began to see great cracks in her scheme. She had planned from move to move; and now she saw only one left to her.

She went to the jewellers.

'Monsieur Boehmer,' she said, 'I am worried. I have reason to believe that the Queen's signature on the contract may have been forged.'

Boehmer was pale with terror; he began to tremble.

'What shall I do?' wailed the jeweller. 'What can I do?'

Jeanne said almost blithely: 'You must go to the Cardinal. He will look into this matter, and if he finds there has been fraud . . . well, the Cardinal will never allow it to be said that he has been the victim of such a disgraceful fraud. Have no fear, Monsieur Boehmer. The Cardinal will pay you your money.'

Jeanne thought that she had slipped gracefully out of the difficulty. She had the château she had bought at Bar-sur-Aube; so she retired to the country.

There she would stay for a while; then perhaps she would join her husband in London where he was disposing of the diamonds.

But the jeweller did not go to the Cardinal. Instead he went to Madame de Campan and through her reached the Queen.

Jeanne was dining in state in her country home when a messenger arrived at her château.

'Madame,' he cried, 'Monsieur le Cardinal de Rohan was arrested at Versailles this day.'

Jeanne was alarmed. It seemed to her that for the first time luck had gone against her.

She retired hastily to her bedroom where she burned all the letters which the Cardinal had sent to her regarding the transaction.

She felt better after that.

She went to bed and tried to compose herself; she was

already making plans to join her husband in London. It would be safer to be out of the country for a spell.

At five o'clock in the morning there was a disturbance in the courtyard. She rose and threw a robe about herself. Her maid came hurrying to her.

'They come from Paris,' she stammered.

'Who?' demanded Jeanne.

But they were already on the staircase. They marched straight to her bedroom.

'Jeanne de Lamotte,' they cried, 'you are under arrest.'

'By whose orders, and on what charge?'

'On the order of the King, and for being concerned in the theft of a diamond necklace.'

In the Queen's theatre was played that delightful comedy, *Le Barbier de Seville* – the Queen playing Rosine enchantingly, looking exquisite, tripping daintily across the stage in a delightful gown made for the occasion by Madame Bertin at great cost. Vaudreuil played Almaviva with great verve; and Artois strutted across the stage, an amusing Figaro: 'Ah, who knows if the world is going to last three weeks!'

The glittering audience applauded, but between the acts they were saying to one another: 'What does this mean – this matter of the necklace? Is it true that the Cardinal was the Queen's lover? There must be a trial, must there not? Then who knows what we shall hear!'

They were certain that what they heard would be of greater interest than the play they had come to Trianon to watch.

In Bellevue where, under Adelaide, those older disgruntled members of the nobility gathered, they talked of the latest scandal. 'What this matter will reveal I would not like to prophesy,' declared Adelaide, looking sternly at Victoire. (Sophie had died some years before.) Victoire knew what she was prophesying and that she would be greatly disappointed if it did not come to pass.

In the Luxembourg, Provence's friends gathered about him. They confessed themselves astonished with this newest scandal, and they asked one another how the children of such a woman could possibly become good Kings of France. For one thing, how could it be certain that they had any *right* to be Kings of France?

In the cafés of the Palais Royal, men and women were thronging in greater numbers than ever before. A diamond necklace, they murmured. 1,600,000 livres spent on one ornament while many in France starved. Their hero, Duc d'Orléans (Chartres had assumed the title on the recent death of his father) went among them, his eyes gleaming with ambition. 'This cannot go on,' murmured the people. 'It cannot go on,' echoed Orléans. 'And when it is stopped . . . what then?'

And throughout the Rohan family and its connections there were many hurried conferences. A member of their family was in danger. They must all rally to his side. Connected with the Rohans were the houses of Guémenée, Soubise, Condé and Conti, some of whom declared they had already been slighted by the Queen.

They would all stand together; and they determined that all blame should be shifted from the shoulders of their relative. And the best way of doing this was to place it on those of a more eminent person.

So, as the affair of the necklace became the topic of the times, the Queen's enemies began to mass on all sides.

Antoinette lay on her bed. She was pregnant and in two months' time was expecting the birth of a child. She had had the curtains drawn about her bed because she wanted to shut out reminders of that tension which she sensed all about her.

Everyone in the Palace, everyone in Versailles and Paris was eagerly awaiting the verdict in the necklace trial.

She had heard that all day the people had been crowding into Paris, that every important member of the Rohan family and its connexions had come to the Capital. They paraded the streets of the city dressed in deep mourning, all their servants similarly clad; they were clad in mourning on account of their innocent relative. It was preposterous, they implied, that a noble Prince, a Rohan, should be made a prisoner merely because he had been selected as a shield behind which the lascivious, acquisitive and wicked Austrian woman might cower.

'Why must they go on and on about this matter?' Antoinette had asked Louis wearily. 'The necklace is stolen, the stones have been broken up and sold. That should be an end to the matter. Why not let it rest?'

'Your honour is at stake,' said the King sadly. 'We must defend it.'

'Do they think that I stole the necklace?'

'They will think anything until we convince them to the contrary.'

Then she had thrown back her head and declared: 'Well, if they want this thing made public, so let it be. Let us have this matter tried by the *Parlement*. Then my complete innocence will be proved, and all France must acknowledge it.'

So on this May day, nine months after the arrest of the Cardinal, the case of the Diamond Necklace was being tried by the *Parlement* of Paris.

The judges had entered the great hall of the Palais de Justice. The crowds who had gathered in the square cheered them as they went in. The streets, the river banks, the taverns and cafés were full; all who could had come to Paris on this May day that they might immediately hear the verdict on the most notorious case of the age.

Among the prisoners was the fabulous Comte de Cagliostro, for Jeanne's quick mind had searched about her for someone on whom she could fix the blame. She remembered an occasion when she had walked in the gardens of the Cardinal's palace with Cagliostro, and she made herself believe that the Count had put the idea of fraud into her head. She therefore accused him of the theft, and as a result he was arrested.

Now, in alliance with the mighty members of the Rohan family were the Freemasons, one of the most powerful societies in France and throughout the world. Cagliostro was Master of a lodge, one of the leading men of the movement, and it was inconceivable that the mighty Cagliostro should be treated as a criminal.

There were two minor prisoners involved – Rétaux the forger and Oliva the *modiste* prostitute. Jeanne's husband had, fortunately for him, been in England when the arrests were made, and there he stayed and the diamonds with him.

This meant that the diamonds could not be produced, and the rumour which found most favour was that the Queen had been behind the whole thing, that the Cardinal had destroyed her letters to him out of gallantry, and that the Queen kept the necklace in a secret jewel box.

Trembling before the judges the little Oliva told of her meeting with the Cardinal in the Grove of Venus. The Cardinal told how he had been duped, and as he spoke he kept his eyes on the commanding figure of Cagliostro, seeming to draw as much strength from him as he did from his assembled relations who, dressed in mourning which they had been wearing ever since the arrest of this member of their family, presented a formidable company.

The sixty-four judges and members of the *Parlement* knew that they were expected to declare the Cardinal and Cagliostro innocent; they were also aware that they were dealing with more than a case of theft. The verdict they would give would be more than one of guilty or not guilty; it might be an indictment of the monarchy, for Joly de Fleury, in the name of the King, had made it clear that even if the Cardinal were acquitted as a dupe in the affair, he had been guilty of 'Criminal presumption' in imagining that the Queen would meet him in the gardens of Versailles. Unless a verdict of Guilty was given, the Queen must surely be exposed as a woman of light reputation, since a Cardinal who was also a Prince could imagine she would meet him thus; and on this incident was based the whole structure of the case.

The Contis, the Condés, the Soubises and the Rohans, the Freemasons, all the friends of the aunts, and the Queen's sisters-in-law, all those who congregated in the Palais Royal to talk of liberty, were determined on one thing: whatever the sentence passed on those concerned in the Necklace affair, the Queen should not escape unscathed.

And after long arguments the verdict for which all waited

was given. The minor actors in the drama were quickly dealt with. Oliva was acquitted as a dupe, a prostitute who was accustomed to do what was asked of her for payment; this she had done in this instance and merely followed her trade. She was guiltless, and freed. Rétaux was banished from France. Cagliostro was quickly admitted to have no hand in the affair whatsoever. His cool and almost indifferent answers to their questions, together with the pressure of the Freemasons, made it necessary for him to be quickly acquitted.

As for the other three – their cases needed greater consideration. The Comte de Lamotte, who was absent in England, was sentenced to the galleys. He could laugh at the sentence because he was not in their hands that they might carry it out.

Jeanne was found guilty of stealing, and her sentence was a violent one. She was to be taken to the prison of Salpêtrière, where she would be whipped and branded on the shoulder with the letter V, thus proclaiming her *'Voleuse'* to the world; then she was to be imprisoned for life.

But it was the verdict regarding the Cardinal which was so significant. He was declared innocent of every indictment. And as he came out into the streets of Paris, those who had gathered together all during the day went wild with joy.

'Vive le Cardinal!' they cried. And there was laughter in Bellevue and the Palais Royal.

The verdict meant that the judges considered the Queen a light woman, since the Cardinal had quite reasonably supposed that she might leave the Palace in the darkness to come out and meet a man in the Grove of Venus.

Crowds went in a body to the prison of Salpêtrière and there saw Jeanne de Lamotte stripped and beaten; they saw her wriggling and screaming as the irons were heated with which to brand her, twisting in the arms of her tormenters so that instead of receiving the V on her shoulder it was implanted on her breast; they saw her carried away fainting to her prison, where she was sentenced to spend the rest of her days dressed only in sackcloth and sabots, and to exist on black bread and lentils.

'And what of the woman behind all this?' was being asked. 'She will be living in one of her many palaces; she will be dressed in her silks and velvets, made by that arrogant Madame Bertin; she will be feasting on the fat of the land and mayhap peeping into her jewel box at a diamond necklace to gain which she has brought suffering and misery to so many.'

The Queen was furious when she heard the news.

She raged up and down her apartment. The Princesse de Lamballe and Madame de Campan in vain tried to soothe her.

'You should lament with your Queen,' cried Antoinette, 'who has been insulted and sacrificed by cabal and injustice.'

The King came in. He was angry and bewildered.

'You have reason to be sorrowful,' he said. 'This is an insult to the crown.'

'What will you do about it?' demanded the Queen.

Louis shook his head. The verdict had been given. They had been wrong to have the affair tried by the *Parlement*. They had given too much publicity to the matter. It would have been better to have quietly paid the jeweller and said nothing.

'Nay,' said the Queen. 'My honour was tarnished. We had to do all in our power to throw light in these dark and secret places. But this verdict is iniquitous.'

'The Freemasons were against us,' declared the King, 'and with them the Rohan family.'

'You are the King, are you not?' cried Antoinette.

The King wondered if it would not be wiser to let the matter rest; but he had to placate his infuriated wife, so he ordered the Cardinal to resign from his position as Grand Almoner, and signed a *lettre de cachet* which exiled him to the Abbéy of Chaise-Dieu in the mountains of Auvergne. As for Cagliostro, he banished him from the country.

These gestures were typical of Louis' timidity. They did not go far enough.

Had he disbanded the *Parlement*, he would have shown his strength, and at that time the powerful members of the Rohan family would have had to come to heel.

But his tepid action merely aroused the wrath of the *Parlement;* and there he had created a dangerous situation. There was now a wide rift between King and *Parlement*. The people went to the Salpêtrière prison and watched Jeanne de Lamotte taking her exercise in the courtyard.

'Poor woman,' they said. 'She is bearing all the blame in this matter of the necklace. Is this justice?'

The murmuring against the Austrian woman grew. The pamphlets were distributed in increasing numbers and they became more obscene.

Pictures were passed round the cafés and smuggled into the Palace; they still found their way into the apartments of the King and Queen. And in all of them was depicted the woman – her hair looming ridiculously above her haughty face; she was referred to as 'Madame Déficit', and about her neck there would always appear a magnificent necklace of diamonds.

❧ Chapter X ❧

THE FOURTEENTH OF JULY

*D*isasters came thick and fast in the year which followed. The baby, who had been born a few weeks after that terrible day when the verdict on the Diamond Necklace affair had been given, was a girl. Antoinette called her Sophie Beatrix; she lacked the strength of her sister, Madame Royale, and was going to be as sickly as the little Dauphin.

Antoinette was so unhappy about this child that she ceased to brood on the implication of the verdict; she ceased to care what the people said of her.

Her anxieties over her son and daughter had sobered her considerably. No more did she act on the stage of her gilded theatre at Trianon. She would sit with the sick child in her arms, staring bleakly before her.

And less than twelve months after her birth little Sophie Beatrix died in her mother's arms.

There was another death that year in the royal family. Madame Louise, the Carmelite nun, passed piously away that November, crying as she did so: 'To Paradise, quick, at full gallop!' She believed that a special coach had been sent from heaven to convey her there. Mesdames Adelaide and Victoire still lived on at Bellevue, vindictive, never losing an opportunity to vilify the Queen.

'Oh, Elisabeth,' said Antoinette to her sister-in-law who had helped her nurse the sick child, 'sometimes I wonder whether I shall ever be gay again.'

Elisabeth wept with her; Antoinette was beginning to realise that her quiet little sister-in-law was the best friend she had, and one of the very few whom she could trust.

Her unpopularity was growing every day. She was aware of the gathering malice all about her. Once someone called after her as she passed through the Oeil-de-Boeuf to the King's apartments: 'A Queen who does her duty should keep to her apartments and concern herself with knitting.' Madame Vigée le Brun was afraid to hang her portrait of the Queen in the Salon lest it should be the signal for riots; and Antoinette had realised that it was best for her not to appear too often in the Capital.

During the months of sorrow it was beginning to be clear to her that the affairs of the country were in a dangerous state. As she pondered these matters a change came over her, so that she felt impatient with the giddy person she had been. She remembered that she was a Habsburg and that the Habsburgs were rulers; she thought often of her mother, and she began to wonder whether in the years ahead of her she might not grow a little like her. The King she saw as kindly but very weak; and what France needed now was a strong ruler. Louis – Poor Louis – even in his magnificent robes of state could not look like a King. His appearance was against him no less than his character.

Calonne was bringing further disaster upon the country

with his policy of borrowing; the yearly deficit was now over 100,000,000 livres. It was impossible to keep the true state of affairs from the King any longer, and when Louis heard this alarming news he was filled with horror.

Calonne, ever optimistic, ever ready with schemes (never mind if there was no possibility of carrying them out, they were still schemes with which to lull the fearful) decided to gather round him a body of men from the nobility and clergy who should help him to govern. These he called the 'Notables', and he gave out that he expected great things from them. The announcement was received with scorn by the people, who promptly gave the new assembly the Anglo-French title of 'Not-Ables'. They had little power, since only the Estates-General could impose taxes; and after a great deal of argument and no achievement Calonne begged the Notables to adjourn; after which he himself was dismissed from office.

The country was calling for Necker, but the King was against his recall and firmly refused to have him back.

Antoinette, who had been watching the struggle with growing understanding, thought that the Archbishop of Toulouse, Lomenie de Brienne, would be a good man to take Calonne's place. He was therefore appointed to the Treasury, but the people were against him from the start, merely because he had been recommended by the Queen.

He dissolved the Notables, who returned to their estates and lost no time in informing all those with whom they came into contact that the exchequer was verging on bankruptcy.

The *Parlement* determined to oppose every scheme which Brienne laid before it. The minister made one great mistake. He declared that the Queen should have a place at the meetings of the Council and thus help to govern.

The people were outraged. 'We are being governed by Madame Déficit,' they cried. And the rumours increased; the affair of the Diamond Necklace was discussed and garnished with fresh libels. In Bellevue and the Palais Royal it was said: 'It is not the King who is at fault. It is the Queen.'

Everywhere a cry went up for an Estates-General. Brienne started borrowing again; he planned to float new loans; the *Parlement* would not agree.

The King then rose and declared: 'I command you to carry out what you have heard.'

Orléans leaped to his feet and, knowing that he had more than the support of those who nightly gathered in the Palais Royal behind him, assured the King that what he had said was illegal.

Louis, angry and weary with the continual conflict, lost his habitual calm for once and shouted: 'You are banished, Monsieur d'Orléans. You will leave at once for your estates in Villers-Cotterets.'

That was a sign. The rift between the King and the *Parlement* was now an open one.

But if he had subdued the *Parlement* of Paris, this was not the case with the provincial *parlements*. They stood firmly beside the Paris *Parlement;* they refused to accept the edicts proposed by Brienne, and rioting broke out all over the country.

The demand for an Estates-General was renewed. This time a promise had to be given that it should be elected and called for the following year.

The people were calling for the return of Necker, and in this also the King had to give way.

Those were days which seemed to be oppressive with foreboding.

Antoinette had at last begun to understand the need for reform. Now that she took her place as a Privy Councillor she was beginning to see – even more clearly than did the King – what great danger the country was in.

She set about reforming her household, and when Madame Bertin presented herself she was sadly received.

'I shall not be sending for you often,' Antoinette told the dressmaker. 'I have many dresses in my wardrobe. These will suffice for a while.'

'But Your Majesty is joking,' cried the dressmaker. 'We have the honour of France to uphold. I have here a delicious velvet . . .'

'No,' said the Queen. 'Go now, my dear Bertin. I will not discuss dresses now. If I should need your services I will send for you.'

Inwardly fuming with rage Madame Bertin left the Palace. She saw her lucrative business being snatched from her. 'What is this new fad?' she demanded when she returned to her workroom. 'What is that empty-headed idiot up to now?' Then she laughed. 'She'll be calling for me to-morrow. She'll not be able to resist the new velvet.'

And when the Queen did not call for her, Madame Bertin's rage was beyond her control. She spat out insults against the Queen, who had been so good to her; she chatted in *les Holies* with the market-women; and she vilified the Queen as loudly as any of them.

Antoinette then called the Duc de Polignac to her and told him that she must relieve him of his post as Director-General of her horses. For this she had paid him 50,000 livres a year and, as it had been necessary to fill her stables with horses in order to make the post something more than a sinecure, this had been a further expense. Polignac was deeply hurt. The Queen would ruin him, he declared. 'It may be necessary for some of us to be ruined,' Antoinette told him, 'in order to save France.'

She summoned Vaudreuil and told him that he must give up his post of Grand Falconer, which was not exactly essential.

Vaudreuil was horrified.

'I shall be bankrupt,' he declared.

'That may be,' answered Antoinette sadly, 'but it is better that you rather than your country should be so.'

This was outrageous, this was unthinkable. Was the Queen deserting her friends?

'I hope that is something I shall never do,' she told them. 'But the times are dangerous. Have you not heard of these riots? Do you not know that an Estates-General is to be called? We must cut down expenses everywhere . . . everywhere.'

'The Queen has gone mad,' said Vaudreuil to his mistress Gabrielle.

It was not often that Antoinette appeared in public now. She always dreaded such appearances.

But there had come a request from the Opéra House, where a gala performance was to take place. How could there be a gala performance without the presence of the King and Queen?

'I dread going,' she told Louis. 'It is always the same. It is I whom they hate. You they accept and excuse. You are the King and a Bourbon. They cannot forget that I am a Habsburg and a foreigner.'

'We are expected to go,' said Louis.

She knew it was a duty she could not evade.

She rode to the Opéra House with the King. There were some in the brilliant assembly there to cheer them; but the cheers were for the King, and Antoinette's ears were alert for the whisper, which could grow to a shout, of 'Madame Déficit'; she was trying to catch the hisses among the cheers.

And as she stepped into the royal box she saw what had been pinned there. It was a placard and on it had been scribbled in huge letters:

'Tremble, Tyrants. Your reign is nearly over.'

A servant hastily removed it but all during that performance it seemed to dance before the Queen's eyes, and wherever she looked, from the stage to the glittering audience, she saw those words, 'Tremble, Tyrants'.

And she did tremble.

✣ ✣ ✣

The terrible sense of foreboding stayed with her.

Soon the members of the Estates-General would be in Versailles; with this new foresight, which had come to Antoinette in her new mood of seriousness, she had begged Louis to hold the assembly in some provincial town, somewhere far distant from Paris, where storms were not so likely to blow up. But Louis was adamant. He was bewildered by what was happening, but he continued to look upon himself as the father of his people, and if he showed no sensitivity to the rising storms, neither did he show fear.

Certainly the Estates-General must come to Versailles and the Capital.

'The Estates-General are elected members from all classes of society,' she reminded him. 'It is the first time men have been elected from the lower ranks of society to take a part in the country's government. Louis, it is a complete turnabout. It will rob you of your power.'

'It was necessary,' said the King.

And she was afraid of the Estates-General.

But there was one matter which caused her greater sadness. The health of her eldest son was rapidly failing.

The little Dauphin was subject to sudden attacks of fever; one of his legs was shorter than the other, and his spine was twisted; he was unable to stand, for he suffered from that complaint which had affected so many Bourbons: rickets.

Each day his mother sat beside him and wondered whether it would be his last. Often she would remember how Louis loved their children, even as she did; how kind and gentle he always was to them. She said to Madame de Campan: 'Do you remember how the King used to sit up with me night after night when Madame Royale was a baby and she was sick?'

Madame de Campan remembered.

'The King is a good man,' said Antoinette. She put out a hand suddenly to Madame de Campan. 'I will go to my rest now,' she said. 'It is a big day to-morrow.'

The Princesse de Lamballe said: 'You will wear your dress of violet, white and silver. It is a beautiful dress, one of the best Your Majesty ever had.'

Antoinette did not answer.

'And your ostrich plume headdress is so becoming,' went on the Princesse.

But still Antoinette was not listening. 'Light my candles,' she said. 'I will go to bed now.'

They lighted four candles on her dressing-table and as they

took off her elaborate headdress one of them went out. Madame de Campan relighted it, but almost at once the second candle went out.

'What is wrong with the candles to-night?' said the Queen.

'There is a draught coming from somewhere,' replied Madame de Campan.

'Pray shut the windows. I do not like to see the candles going out like this. It frightens me.'

The windows were shut and the room seemed very quiet, and then the third candle went out.

The Queen turned suddenly to the Princesse and caught her in an embrace. 'My misfortunes make me superstitious,' she said. 'I am afraid of something . . . something near me . . . something evil. I feel that the candles are warning me to-night. I believe that if the fourth candle goes out it will be an omen of overwhelming evil.'

'You are distraught,' said the Princesse. 'It is the ordeal of to-morrow of which you think. But be assured, dearest, that it will soon be over and . . .'

The Princesse had stopped. The three women were all looking at the fourth candle which had gone out.

✦ ✦ ✦

'Maman,' said the Dauphin, 'how beautiful you are!'

She smiled and danced daintily before him in the violet, white and silver gown.

'Kneel down,' said the Dauphin, 'that I may see your feathers.'

So she knelt, and he tried to put up a thin arm to touch them. She caught his arm and kissed it; then she held him pressed against her, that he might not see her tears.

'Maman,' he said, 'I wish I were strong. I wish I could ride in the carriage beside you to-day. You look so pretty . . . all the people will love you.'

She shook her head and tried to smile.

'But they will,' he told her. 'You are so pretty.'

She began to bargain then. Let him get well and I will not complain whatever they do to me. Let them vilify me; let them hiss me . . . shout at me . . . but let my baby be well and strong.

He said: 'Maman, could I not see the procession?'

'My darling, you are not strong enough.'

'It will be wonderful,' he said. 'All the horses, and you and Papa in the state carriages; the horses with their plumes . . . the beautiful coaches and all the postilions in their gay uniforms. Will you ride with Papa?'

'No, he will ride in the first coach with your uncles; I shall follow him in the second one.'

The boy's lustreless eyes brightened a little.

'I remember other ceremonies. The Cardinals in their red robes and Bishops in violet. Papa will be in cloth of gold, will he not? How I should love to see him! But you . . . you will be more beautiful than anybody. I wish I could be part of the procession.'

'One day you shall.'

'One day,' he repeated. That was how she had consoled him in the past. 'One day you will be strong enough.' He always believed it, even as each day he grew weaker.

'Maman, if I could but watch you . . . I should be so happy. Could I not . . . perhaps from the balcony?'

She kissed his forehead. 'We will arrange something. You shall see us pass by.'

He smiled. 'One day,' he said, 'I'll be there, and I'll ride in your carriage, Maman. I'd rather be in your carriage than anywhere else.'

'One day,' she said.

And she gave orders that he should be warmly wrapped up, and that a little bed should be put for him on the veranda over the royal stables. From there he could watch the procession pass by.

✤ ⚜ ✤

The carriages drove out from the château – the King in the first with his brothers; the Queen in the second; and following were the noblemen and women of royal blood.

They came to the church of Notre Dame where a short service was held; and from Notre Dame they walked in procession to the church of Saint Louis, where Mass was to be celebrated.

It was a brilliant sight with the banners flying and the clergy and other dignitaries of Versailles leading the processions. All carried wax candles – the members of the Tiers Etat in tricorn hats, black coats and white muslin cravats; the nobility followed, their garments of cloth of gold, and their plumed hats making a marked contrast with the soberly clad members of the Tiers Etat. Among the noblemen one stood out because of the plainness of his dress. The Duc d'Orléans had allied himself with the common people by refusing to wear the garments of his rank.

When he appeared there were loud cheers: *'Vive le Duc d'Orléans!'* And that cry was louder and more insistent than that of *'Vive le Roi!'*

The Cardinals in their scarlet robes and the Bishops in their violet cassocks made a splash of colour. They preceded the Host carried under a canopy by four Princes; immediately behind this came Louis, dressed as the noblemen, his candle in his hand.

The Queen looked up, for she could see in the distance the stables and the little bed there; she smiled and she thought she saw a movement as though the little Dauphin had seen her and recognised her.

She was thinking of him, so that she did not realise how deadly was the silence as she passed through the crowd.

Then suddenly a group of women close to her shouted: *'Vive le Duc d'Orléans!'*

She understood their meaning. They were telling her they hated her in her beautiful garments which were such a contrast to those affected by the Duc d'Orléans.

Yet she could hear their shouting now: *'Vive le Roi!'* It was only the Queen they hated.

She knew that those about her were watching her anxiously.

She held her head a little higher. She looked very majestic in her beautiful gown, the plumes of her headdress swaying gracefully as she walked – haughty and beautiful – the Queen who remembered only her royalty and cared nothing for the insults of the *canaille*.

Antoinette knelt by the bed of her son.

His fevered hands were in hers; his wish was that she should not leave his side.

'Maman,' he said, 'do not be sad; one day, you know . . .'

Her lips said: 'One day'; but she could not stop the tears falling from her eyes.

'You cry for me, Maman,' said the Dauphin. 'Am I so very ill?'

She said: 'Do not speak, my darling. Save your breath for getting well.'

He nodded. 'I will get well, Maman.'

She lifted her eyes to the doctors. What could they do but shake their heads? It had been obvious for many months that the Dauphin would not live.

Louis was beside her, his hand on her shoulder.

Poor Louis! Dear Louis! He suffered even as she did.

The little boy was lying back on his pillows; his breathing was stertorous; desperately he was fighting for his life.

But he was going, little Louis Joseph.

Antoinette knelt by his bed and buried her face in her hands, because she could not bear to look at her son in his last moments.

The King brought her other children to her – Madame Royale who was just past her tenth and little Louis Charles who had had his fourth birthday.

'Comfort your mother,' said the King.

And Antoinette, opening her eyes, found great balm from those little ones.

❖ ❖ ❖

Now the conflict had grown more wild. The nobility and the clergy banded together against the Third Estate; and the Third Estate was in conflict with the Estates-General.

The Third Estate began to call itself the National Assembly, with Jean Sylvain Bailly its President; they decided that they would draw up a Constitution which was to make understood by all how much power was in the King's hands.

Necker urged the King to agree to certain reforms, and drafted a speech for the King to deliver. The King was persuaded to alter this, which infuriated Necker who realised fully how desperate the situation was. Louis wanted to make it clear that he understood he must give up a certain amount of authority, but he was determined to keep the privileged classes in control of the country's affairs; and he could not agree that the Estates-General should have the power to alter the social life of the country. Privilege must be maintained; that was to be the theme of the King's speech.

This was received with anger, and when the King dismissed the assembly, Mirabeau, the most dynamic member of the Tiers Etat, retorted that they had held their office by the power of the people and would not leave except at the point of the bayonet.

Bailly, the President, pointed out more diplomatically that the nation once assembled could be dismissed by none.

The King, alarmed, ordered that more troops be brought into Paris and Versailles. He now realised that the National Assembly which had sprung into being was his bitterest enemy. He determined to form a new government from which he would dismiss all with liberal ideas. He called in de Breteuil and dismissed Necker – the one man in whom the people had faith.

Necker, weary of the struggle and seeing disaster very near, took his leave of Versailles and went to his native Switzerland without delay.

The people watched the arrival of the troops with sullen eyes. The rumour spread that the King's intention was to lodge the newly elected representatives of the common people in the Bastille.

Louis assured the assembly that he was merely taking precautions on account of certain signs of unrest in the Capital. Food was scarce owing to last year's bad harvest; and at such times, as had been proved in the past, it was necessary to take these measures. He wanted no repetition of the *Guerre des Farines*.

He sensed, he said, that the Assembly was uneasy, so he would then arrange for its members to leave for the provinces.

Louis and the nobility congratulated themselves. They had countered the rebellious notions of the common people. There should be no new Constitution with a manacled monarchy. The old regime should continue.

It was the 12th of July – hot and sultry.

The National Assembly heard that Necker had been dismissed, and they knew then that all hope was lost. Necker was the only King's man on whom they had pinned their hopes.

'Necker gone.'

'Necker *dismissed*.'

The news reached the fevered streets of Paris; and it was like the match applied to the fuse.

During those hot days of July Orléans, from the windows of his apartments at one end of the square which formed the Palais Royal, looked down on astonishing scenes; and looking was filled with gratification and ever-growing excitement. The Gardens of the Palais Royal were crowded day and night. Between the tables outside the cafés the prostitutes walked among the men who argued fiercely against the monarchy; agitators had stationed themselves under the trees to harangue the people. Throughout the evening and far into the night could be heard the shouts against religion, and most of all against the aristocrats. The wildest rumours were bred in the Palais Royal. And Orléans was King of this little world made up of merchants, beggars, vagabonds, prostitutes, certain aristocrats who believed that their safety lay with Orléans, and certain politicians who believed that the way to fame and fortune lay with him.

Many able men were with him. Choderlos de Laclos was a useful man. His novel, *Liaisons Dangereuses,* had aroused anger in many because of his descriptions of the depravity of society; he was a General who, when he left the army, had become *secrétaire de commandements* to Orléans. He could write a pamphlet which could rouse the masses to fury – a very useful man. There was Mirabeau, an aristocrat himself, become bankrupt through many years of dissolute living, but a man of immense powers, could he but use them; and now, having reached the mature age of forty, he desired to use them; he longed for power; and he saw in France's present position a means of attaining it. There was Camille Desmoulins, a fiery journalist and protégé of Mirabeau. There was Danton, the paid agitator.

And there was Théroigne de Mericourt. Orléans was not sure that Théroigne was not as useful as any of the men. He had first met Théroigne when he was in England. She had been called Anne Terwagne in those days; she was a Belgian, and the Prince of Wales had mentioned her to Orléans. She had become one of Orléans' mistresses and he had brought her to France with him, where she had quickly set up house and become one of the most sought-after courtesans of Paris society. She adopted the name of Comtesse de Campinados and found several rich protectors with whom she travelled in the utmost luxury throughout Europe.

But Théroigne was clever. She had heard rumours. She knew of the trouble which was brewing in France; and she knew that many looked to Orléans as the leader of it. If Orléans was to lead a new society in France, if he were to become King of France, which she knew had been a secret ambition of his, she wanted to be at hand to share his triumphs.

That was why Théroigne was in Paris; that was why she had established her salon in the rue de Bouloi where she gathered writers, politicians and disgruntled aristocrats, and served revolutionary ideas with her wine.

It was therefore pleasing for the Duc d'Orléans to sit in his apartments and watch the rising excitement.

Mirabeau had laid his plans. When the moment was ripe the people should rise against the King; they should appoint the Duc d'Orléans Lieutenant-General of the Kingdom. And from that, mused Orléans, it should be an easy step to the throne.

Then came the news that Necker was dismissed.

It was the sign, and Mirabeau was ready. It was true that when Necker had been in office he had sneered at the man, called him the Genevese sou-snatcher, the clock that was always slow; and he had indeed been preparing a speech to deliver to the Assembly in which he was going to demand his dismissal and accuse him of being concerned in the famine which was the result of the failure of the previous year's harvest.

What did that matter? The King had dismissed Necker; the time was ripe, the mob were ready; the weather was hot, and so was the blood of the people. Necker would serve very well as an excuse.

Camille Desmoulins leaped onto a table outside one of the cafés in Palais Royal.

'Citizens,' he cried, 'you know the nation has asked for Necker to be retained, and he has been driven away. Could you be more insolently defied? To arms, Citizens! To arms! I call you, my brothers, to liberty.'

The mob crowded about him; some carried sticks, some had pistols, some hatchets, some brooms – anything that would do for a weapon.

They seized Desmoulins and carried him high on their shoulders; they surged about the Palais Royal, crying 'To arms! Citizens, throw off the shackles of slavery! Liberty, Citizens! We will fight for liberty.'

Desmoulins produced effigies. One was of Necker; the other of the Duc d'Orléans.

Through the streets of Paris the people marched carrying those effigies high, shouting 'To arms, Citizens! Liberty!'

✤ ✤ ✤

Disorder had burst on Paris. Gangs roamed the streets; the tradespeople barricaded their shops, for many of the brigands who were rioting and looting were strangers to Paris. They spoke with accents which did not belong to the Capital and its environs; they were wilder, lacking completely the grace of the Parisian which was evident even in the most humble. The Parisians were the most cultured people in France; and France had been the most cultured country in the world. They liked to sit outside the cafés and talk; they were less eager to act. They were idlers by nature, preferring the adventures of the mind to action. These coarse crude people certainly did not belong to Paris. It was becoming clear to many of the peace-loving citizens of the Capital that these hordes who roamed the streets shrieking of their ills and demanding liberty, were hirelings. This filled them with alarm.

During those two or three days and nights which preceded the 14th, the sober men and women tried to found a band of guards who would protect them from these brigands who went about the streets shouting: *'Des armes et du pain.'* Behind the barricaded houses parents stood over their children in the utmost anxiety, praying that the sound of shouting in the streets should not come their way.

On the 13th the disorders had increased. Gunsmiths' shops had been raided, and the wild men and women now were armed. The Hôtel de Ville had been broken into and more ammunition stolen.

The citizens of Paris were seriously alarmed. Determined to protect their city from the marauders, the magistrates held meetings in the Hôtel de Ville; several men came forward to offer their services, arms were handed to the protectors of Paris, and bands were formed which were to patrol every district.

One or two of the rioters were seized and hanged; but the ring-leaders escaped. The streets grew quieter as the day wore on, but there was great uneasiness. It was remembered that the troops, having been instructed by the King not to fire on the people, had been useless in the riots, and their presence in the city had caused only uneasiness and panic.

Evening came and the agitators were standing on their tables in the Palais Royal and on the street corners, reminding the people of their wrongs.

Georges Jacques Danton was the cleverest of all the

agitators; he knew how to fire the people to anger while he was making them laugh.

He shouted: 'Shall we use the green cockade as our colours, Citizens? Never! Those are the colours of the Comte d'Artois, and the Comte d'Artois is one of those accursed aristocrats who snatch the bread from our mouths, Citizens, that they may parade in their glory. Nay, let our colours be those of our friend Monsieur d'Orléans – the tricolor, Citizens – blue, white and red! I have a list here, Citizens. It contains the names of those who are traitors to their country. Artois is in that list. Shall we use his colours?'

'No!' screamed the crowd.

'Then let it be the tricolour.'

'Long live the tricolour!'

❧ ❧ ❧

The 14th July dawned, a day of blazing heat and blazing emotion, a day that was to be remembered for ever after.

Crowds gathered about the Palais Royal.

The plan was ready, but the people of Paris did not know this. Word was sent through the city.

'Troops are advancing on Paris. Citizens are to be bombarded by the guns of the Bastille.'

'Citizens, will you stay in your homes and do nothing? Will you allow the guns of the Bastille to murder your wives and children and yourselves? You have seen the price of bread . . . rising . . . rising . . . and you have dared to complain. Those to whose interest it is to see the price of bread rise now wish to murder those who raised their voices against tyranny. To arms, Citizens! There is one way to defeat our enemies. To the Bastille!'

The people were crowding into the streets. They assembled around the Hôtel de Ville and in the Place de Grève.

'What means this?' they asked of one another.

And the good citizens mingled with the cut-throat hirelings. They had seen the guns on the battlements; those guns could be brought to bear upon the surrounding streets with devastating results.

Many people had passed the great fortress with its eight pointed towers and its dry moat; they had passed the gate which opened into the rue Saint-Antoine; they had looked at the two drawbridges, one the Pont de l'Avancée which opened on the Cour du Gouvernement, and the other on to the prison.

The prisoners of the Bastille were mostly political prisoners, and it was said that conditions therein were more comfortable than those of the Châtelet or the Salpêtrière.

'We must take the Bastille,' shouted the agitators. 'Thus only can we prevent the guns of the fortress being used on the citizens of Paris.'

The cry went up: 'To the Bastille!'

And on that hot 14th July, the people marched, brandishing sticks, rakes, guns, anything to which they could lay their hands; and in all the preceding days there had never been such tension, such rising excitement as there was that day.

❧ ⚜ ❧

The drawbridge chains had been cut. The defenders of the Bastille, on orders from the King, had not fired on the people . . . and the people were in command.

Through the streets they marched, singing in triumph; before them held high on a pike they carried the bleeding head of the Marquis de Launay, the Governor of the Bastille.

It was the night of the 14th when the Duc de Liancourt came riding in haste to Versailles.

'I must see the King,' he declared. 'Without delay. There is not a moment to lose.'

'His Majesty has retired for the night,' the Duke was told.

'Then he must be awakened,' was the grim answer.

'Monsieur le Duc . . . I tell you the King has gone to his bed!'

The Duc de Liancourt had thrust aside those who would detain him; he had marched into the King's bedchamber and drawn back the curtains.

'Sire,' he cried, 'the people have taken the Bastille and de Launay's head is being carried on a pike through the streets with the mob howling about it.'

Louis sat up and rubbed the sleep out of his eyes. He said: 'This would seem to be news of a revolt.'

'No, Sire,' said the Duke. 'It is news of a revolution.'

❧ Chapter XI ❧

THE OCTOLBER DAYS

The people were demanding the recall of Necker, and at the same time declaring that if the King did not come to Paris they would go in a body to Versailles, destroy the Palace, drive away the courtiers and bring the King to his Capital that they might 'take good care of him'.

There was consternation at Versailles. Artois had heard that his name was on a list of those who were to be executed. The King embraced him. 'You must make immediate preparations to leave,' he said.

The Polignacs and their friends had been the butt of lampoons and pamphlets for years. They too were near the top of the list.

'I would not detain you here,' said Antoinette. 'It is too dangerous. You should get out of France with all speed.'

She went to the King and stood trembling before him. She was amazed at the calm of Louis. Was it courage, she wondered, or was it that it was as impossible to arouse him to fear as it was to ardour?

'I shall go to Paris,' he said.

Antoinette, looking at him, thought of all the years they had been together, all the kindness of this man, all the indulgences she had received from him. She thought of how his children loved him, and threw herself into his arms and implored him not to go to Paris.

'Do you know that they have said that if I do not go to them they will come here?'

'Do not go,' said Antoinette. 'They intend to kill you as they killed de Launay.'

'They will remember that I am their King and they are my children.'

Antoinette shook her head; she could not speak; the lump in her throat was choking her.

He heard Mass and took the sacrament, made his will and set out for his Capital.

✣ ✤ ✣

Antoinette watched him from the balcony of his apartments.

'Good-bye, Louis,' she said. 'Good-bye, my poor dear King and husband.'

She did not see the King in his carriage; she waved automatically. She could not shut out of her mind the thought of the bloody head of the Governor of the Bastille, and she imagined another head on the pike those howling madmen carried – that of Louis.

The Princesse de Lamballe was beside her.

'You too should be leaving us,' said Antoinette. 'Gabrielle will be gone this day. You too, dear Marie, should go with them.'

The Princesse shook her head.

'I am afraid,' said the Queen. 'I am beginning to think that I never really knew fear until this moment.'

'The King will be safe,' said the Princesse. 'The people love him. They will never forget that he is their King.'

'I know not what will become of him. It may be that I shall never see him again. Oh, Marie . . . I think of my children . . . my poor children. I will go to them now; come with me.'

Madame de Tourzel was with the children. She was to be their *gouvernante* now that Gabrielle, who had held that post, was preparing to leave.

The children ran to her smiling. Thank God, she thought, they know nothing. Madame Royale, quiet, gentle and so pretty, would be a comfort to any mother. The little Dauphin gave her some anxiety. He was a charming little fellow, quite strong and healthy, but he had a certain nervous tendency which gave rise to fear bordering on hysteria. He would wake screaming if some strange noise upset him, and would tell grotesque stories of what had happened to him. He hated his lessons and loved to play the sort of games in which he could imagine himself older than he was. Most of all he delighted in being a soldier. He made speedy friends with all the Palace guards, and it was a pleasure to see their delight as the audacious little Dauphin strutted beside them. He was full of high spirits and the most affectionate of children. He adored Madame Royale, and could not bear to be separated from her; he loved his father dearly and with great respect; his mother he worshipped.

And what will become of these children? wondered Antoinette.

She was determined as she went to the royal nurseries that day, that she must place their welfare above everything else. Louis was the kindest of men, but he lacked imagination and he saw all men as himself. He did not believe in malice, and cruelty would have to be perpetrated right under his eyes for him to believe anyone capable of it. Those men and women who had stormed the Bastille, those who had cut off the head of de Launay and carried it dripping through the streets were in the eyes of the King poor misguided children.

'Maman,' cried the Dauphin, 'what has happened? Why has Papa gone to Paris, and why is Madame de Polignac too busy to speak to us?'

'The people have called your Papa to Paris, my darling,' said the Queen.

She met the lovely eyes of her daughter, and felt an urgent desire to confide in her. But no! She would not disturb the serenity of the sweet child. Let her remain happy for a little longer.

'We may have to go to Paris soon,' she said. 'I am going to have clothes packed for us and carriages made ready. So do not be surprised if we leave soon.'

'How soon?' asked Madame Royale.

'That I cannot say. But be ready.'

"Will the soldiers go with us?' asked the Dauphin.

'I do not know.'

'I do hope so.' The Dauphin held an imaginary musket on his shoulder and began marching about the apartment.

She left them, for she feared that if she stayed she would break down and tell them of her fears.

She had made up her mind: she would beg sanctuary for herself and the children from the National Assembly. She would ask that they might be with the King.

And all day long there were whispered rumours throughout the château. Had the mob taken the King prisoner? Was the King wrong to have delivered himself into their hands? Was it true that the stormers of the Bastille were already marching on Versailles?

* ✤ *

Louis rode into Paris. He was astonishingly calm, and those who saw his carriage pass could have believed that he was setting out on some ordinary state occasion, and that his guards had been taken from him and replaced by the ragged army of men with guns and lances, scythes and pick-axes, dragging cannons with them; there were women too in that assembly; they danced and shouted and waved branches of trees which they had tied with ribbons.

When this strange procession entered Paris, Bailly, the new Mayor, was waiting to receive the King. In his hands he held the cushion and the traditional keys.

He said in loud clear tones which all could hear distinctly: 'I bring Your Majesty the keys of your good city of Paris. These were the words which were spoken to Henri Quatre. He reconquered the people; here the people have reconquered their King.'

Louis showed no sign of annoyance that this contrast should have been drawn between himself and that King whom the people of France had always lauded as their greatest sovereign. He graciously accepted the keys and smiled benignly at the ugly crowd who insisted on keeping close to his carriage.

It was in the Place Louis XV that the shot was fired. It missed the King but killed a woman. No one took any notice of her as she fell, and in the tumult Louis was unaware of how narrowly he had escaped death.

They had come to the Hôtel de Ville and there they halted. The King alighted from his carriage and, under an archway of pikes and swords, he entered the building. The Mayor led the King to the throne, and the people crowded into the hall after him.

Louis took his place on the throne and that strange calm was still with him. It was as though he said: 'Do what you will with me. I cannot hate you.' He was like a benign father, scarcely saddened by the pranks of his children because he loved them so, and knew them to be only children – his children.

'Do you accept, Sir, the appointment of Jean Sylvain Bailly as Mayor of Paris, and Marie Joseph Gilbert Motier de La Fayette as Commander of the National Guard?'

'I do,' said Louis.

He was then handed the blue, white and red cockade, which he accepted mildly, and, still in the mood of indulgent parent playing the children's game, he then took off his hat and affixed thereon the tricolor.

The people all about him, unable to resist falling under the spell of that benevolent paternity, cried: *'Vive le Roi!'*

Then the Comte de Lally-Tollendal, who was a member of the Royalist Democrats, a party which sincerely wished for reform to be brought about in a constitutional manner, cried:

'Citizens, are you satisfied? Here is your King. Rejoice in his presence and his benefits.' He turned to the King. 'There is not a man here, Sire, who is not ready to shed his blood for you. This generation of Frenchmen will not turn its back on fourteen centuries of fidelity. King, subjects, citizens, let us join our hearts, our wishes, our efforts, and display to the eyes of the universe the magnificent sight of its finest nation, free, happy, triumphant under a just, cherished and revered King, who, owing nothing to force, will owe everything to his virtues and his love.'

The applause broke out. Now there were tears in the King's eyes. He said in a voice vibrant with emotion: 'My people can always count on my love.'

The people were pressing close to him; they kissed his hand; they kissed his coat; and one woman from the market threw her arms about his neck; she declared that he was the saviour of his country; there was bloodshed and murder everywhere, but Louis, the little father, had appeared, and all was well.

The King prepared for his journey back to Versailles. How different was the journey back. In his hat the King wore the tricolor.

'Long live the King! Long live the little father!' shouted the crowds. And those who had called 'Murder him!' now cried 'Honour him!'

It was eleven o'clock when, surrounded by the shouting multitude, his carriage drove into the Cour Royal.

Antoinette heard it; she ran down the great staircase and threw herself into the King's arms.

He was back. He was safe. There was then a little respite.

She looked into his face, saw the marks of fatigue under his eyes, the stains on his clothes, his twisted cravat – and the tricolor in his hat.

She was frightened then. But the King was smiling blandly.

'Not a drop of blood has been shed,' he cried triumphantly. 'I swear that it never will be.'

In the courtyard the carriages were waiting. Those who had been the intimate friends of the Queen would soon be leaving Versailles and making their way with all haste to the frontier – Artois and his family, Condé, Conti, Esterhazy, Vaudreuil,

Lauzun, the Abbé de Vermond, all those who had been the companions of her carefree days in the Trianon. The Polignacs were ready to leave. They would be the first to go. They knew that if ever the rabble marched to Versailles theirs would be the first heads to be placed on pikes.

They remembered de Launay, the Governor of the Bastille who had lost his head. There were terrible tales coming from Paris. Foulon, a former Minister of Finance, had met a violent death. The people hated him because they blamed him for the taxes he had imposed, and it had been whispered that he had once made the inhuman statement that if the people were hungry they should eat hay. They hung him upon a street lamp and stuffed his mouth with hay, before they cut off his head and paraded with it through the streets. The same fate was meted out to Foulon's son-in-law, Berthier de Sauvigny.

The mob was determined to deal savage deaths to those it hated.

So the Polignacs must go. Antoinette was anxious on their account. 'I shall know no peace until they have left,' she said. 'I shall not be happy until I know that Gabrielle has crossed the frontier.'

She sent 500 louis to her friend with a tender note: 'Adieu, my dearest friend. What a sad word is good-bye, but I have to say it. Here is the order for the horses. I have only strength left to send you my love. I will not try to put into words the sorrow I feel at being separated from you. We are surrounded by misfortune and hardship and ill-starred people. Since all are deserting us, I am in truth happy to think that those in whom I am chiefly interested have had to depart. You may be sure however that adversity has not lessened my strength and courage. These I shall never lose. My troubles are teaching me prudence.'

When Gabrielle had left, disguised as a servant, the Queen sat alone in her apartment and, although she covered her face with her hands, she did not weep. Now that great sorrow, great foreboding was upon her, she did not weep so easily as she had in the carefree days.

Gabrielle was thinking of the Queen as the berline carried her and her relations towards the Swiss frontier. Poor Antoinette, to remain in that place of terror. Gabrielle shivered. She had been fond of the Queen. She would have been content to be her simple little friend if there had not been so many making their constant demands upon her.

'The King and Queen should be with us,' she said suddenly. 'They are foolish to stay there. They should escape while they can.'

No one answered her. The Polignacs had no time to think of the Queen. They were nearing the Swiss frontier. There they would be safe. But until they passed that frontier they could think of nothing but their own safety.

At the town of Sens, while the horses were being changed, their coach was surrounded by a mob. Gabrielle drew back into her seat as unkempt heads were thrust into the carriage. She trembled and waited for disaster.

'You come from Paris?' asked one of the intruders. 'Then tell us, are those wicked Polignacs still at Court?'

Gabrielle tried to speak, but she found she could not do so. The Abbé Balivière, who was travelling with them, said quickly: 'The Polignacs! Those evil leeches! I could swear they are not at Court now. I heard the Queen had rid herself of them.'

'That is well,' said the man. He turned to the crowd. 'The Polignacs have left Court,' he cried.

'We'll search every coach till we find them!' shouted someone. 'Then . . . off with their heads!'

But the berline was allowed to go on; and thus the Polignacs, who had done so much to enhance the Queen's unpopularity, passed safely across the border, leaving Antoinette behind to bear the results of her unfortunate friendships.

❖ ❖ ❖

Gloom hung over Versailles. There was silence in the Galerie des Glaces and the Salon de la Paix. There were no more balls, no banquets during those terrible weeks of July and August. Each morning the King and Queen with their children heard Mass; then they would spend long hours closeted with the ministers, all desperately seeking some solution to the alarming situation.

One by one the courtiers were deserting and, as their carriages drove out of Versailles, fresh and more terrifying news arrived each day.

There was revolt in the country towns and villages, where peasants were rising against the Seigneurs. Châteaux were pillaged; carriages making their way across the country were suspect and stopped by howling mobs, who might decide that the occupants were fleeing aristocrats; sometimes they imprisoned them; at others they killed them on the spot. No one any longer paid taxes. In the big towns, houses and shops were closed; their occupants had secretly left the country. Many of those who had served the rich were unemployed and starving in the streets. The country revolts meant that no grain was coming to Paris. Crowds massed daily outside the shuttered bakers' shops, demanding bread.

In the meantime the leaders of the revolution never ceased to work upon the people, inflaming them to greater activity. Desmoulins wrote in those newspapers which continued to appear. Men and women walked about the streets, flourishing the *Patriote Français* and discussing the latest light which was being thrown on the callousness of the aristocrats, and the wrongs endured by the people.

Paris had acquired a new sport. Massing in the streets, marching in a body to the house of some ill-fated man of whose behaviour in the past they had read in the articles of Marat or Desmoulins in the *Patriote Français* or the *Courier de Paris et de Versailles*. They would haul him from his house, lead him to the Place de Grève, shouting insults and threats, almost tearing him to pieces before they hung him on a lamp-post, then sliced off his head and paraded with it through the streets.

It was said that the English were planning to attack France now that the revolution had brought her low; defences were put up in the Channel ports. And who, it was asked, had escaped to England? Who was giving information to this enemy of France? The aristocrats. The *émigrés*. Then to the lamp-post with a few more.

Those terrifying days in Versailles would never be forgotten. There were few left now to comfort the Queen. There was her good friend the Princesse de Lamballe who refused to leave her, and there was Madame de Tourzel who refused to leave the children.

'What will the end be?' the Queen often asked herself. For the first time in her life she was concerned for the future, and for the first time she was truly afraid.

326

One day the Princesse came to her and said: 'There is someone to see Your Majesty. He has just arrived at Versailles. He craved audience and, knowing that you would not wish to wait, I have brought him here to you.'

The Queen lifted her eyes and stared at the door where he was standing. He had changed. He was no longer debonair, no longer the handsome young man he had been at their first meeting.

She could not stop the cry of pleasure which rose to her lips as he strode across the room to her. He took both her hands and covered them with kisses.

'Axel,' she said, 'you should not have come. You should not have come.'

He lifted his head and she knew in that moment the depth of his love for her and, in spite of the threatening gloom about her, in spite of all that had happened and which she feared was yet to come, she was conscious of a happiness such as she had never before experienced.

She sought to control her emotions.

'This is not the time to arrive in Versailles,' she cried. 'Do you not know what is happening here? Everybody is leaving us.'

'I know,' he said. 'And that is precisely why I have come.'

What peace there was in the Trianon. There it was possible to believe that cruelty and violence were far away; there was the ideal village she had built, where she could wear her muslin dresses, her shady hats; there she could escape for long hours at a time – escape to forgetfulness.

Only her intimates were with her, only those whom she

could trust. Now, she often thought, I know whom I can trust, because all those whom I could not have long deserted me.

Fersen came to Trianon. Each day he called. They would walk together in the French and English gardens, by the lake and the stream; they would sit in the boudoir like two cosy happy people. They shut out the world. It was the only way to escape.

And each moment of every day was precious because it must be lived as though it were their last. For who could be sure that it would not be?

And there, in those terrifying August days the Queen seemed to lead two lives: one of horror and foreboding in Versailles, one of love and passion in the Trianon.

She would cry in her lover's arms and beg him to make her happy, beg him to shut out the hideous world.

'It must be, it must be,' she cried. 'For how could I endure my life unless I had this love?'

Sometimes she would think how ironical was life. She loved this man who seemed to her all that a man should be. He was strong, he was resourceful. His was a quiet dignity, which was born of great courage.

And in this fairy palace, with its model village clustered about it, with its air of complete unreality, Antoinette could shut herself away, and for a few brief hours forget all else but love; and so she found the courage to live through the anxious days.

The King was aware of what was happening.

They did not speak of it, but he knew. He would regard her sadly, for he understood. He had failed as lover; he knew that. His nature was such that, apart from that disability of the first years of his marriage, he must always be cold. He was fond of the Queen as he was fond of his children; he was the kindest and most tolerant of men.

His failing was that he was perhaps too kind, too tolerant. He was always able to see every side of every problem; thus he could rarely make up his mind how to act effectively, and his hesitation cost him dearly. He lacked the fire of men like Mirabeau, Desmoulins, Marat, Robespierre.

The Queen had a lover, and this Swedish nobleman, who was every inch a hero, was giving the Queen the courage she so desperately needed during these days of terror.

So the King was silently sad and never forced himself upon her.

When he saw the cruel pamphlets directed against her, when he heard the threats and libels, when he realised how she had been chosen for a scapegoat, he said to himself: 'How could I make her life more burdensome by reproaching her?'

There were so many problems for Louis to face during those weeks, so he stood aside and allowed the Swedish Count to comfort Antoinette.

On the first of October a new regiment arrived at Versailles and, in accordance with the old tradition, a banquet was given by the regiment already garrisoned in the château.

It was agreed that the banquet should be given in the Palace theatre. This was a grand occasion such as those of the old days. The King and Queen with their children were present, and when they appeared the Guards – every man among them – rose and cheered them until they were hoarse. The band played some of the old songs which rang with fervour and loyalty to the crown. The cheers were ecstatic, for the Guards wished their sovereigns to know that they were loyal.

They had all arrived wearing the white cockade – the pledge of loyalty.

It was possible during that day, to believe that there had been no riots, no fall of the Bastille, no revolution.

That night and the next day the atmosphere of Versailles seemed to have lightened.

It was as though the laughter of the guests and the shouts of loyal men lived on.

✤ ✤ ✤

In the streets of Paris the banquet was discussed. Crowds gathered at the Place de Grève and outside the Palais de Justice. In the gardens of the Palais Royal the agitators were at work.

'Citizens, while you starve there is plenty at Versailles. These pigs of aristocrats sit at their tables which sag under the weight of so much food. You wait in vain outside the bakers' shops for bread. Shall you stand aside and touch your caps and cry: "So be it!" No, Citizens. You are not made of ice; you are made of proud flesh, and good red blood flows in your veins. Have done with this injustice. Come, Citizens. Arm yourselves and then . . . to Versailles!'

So they marched through the city, brandishing knives and broken bottles. They passed through the poorest streets calling to the men and women: 'Come! Join us. We go to Versailles. To the lantern with Madame Déficit! There is one head we shall bring back to Paris. The hair will be dressed three feet from the forehead, Citizens, and the neck adorned with a diamond necklace which will keep you all in bread for a year.

To the lantern with the Austrian strumpet! To the lantern with the foreign whore!'

And so they marched out of Paris, rioting and stealing from the shops as they went. At their head marched the 'women' – big broad figures, all wearing dirty mob caps as the best means of disguising their masculine features.

La Fayette, commanding officer of the National Guard, was afraid of the rabble when he saw them in their present mood.

He, the hero of the American war, tried to reason with them.

'Wait, my good people,' he cried. 'You demand justice, and you are right to demand justice, but this is not the way in which to enforce it . . .'

The leaders of the mob laughed at him. They were out for plunder; they were out for blood, and they would not look too kindly on any – hero of the American war, head of the National Assembly or not – who tried to detain them.

'A *bas La Fayette!'* cried some.

But there were many who were not ready to see La Fayette's head on a lamp-post. They shouted: *'A Versailles!'*

'My friends . . .' began La Fayette.

He was interrupted by a cry: 'All good patriots march to Versailles this day.'

On marched the rabble.

And behind them, sick at heart, shamed and undignified, rode La Fayette with 20,000 men behind him.

It was a pleasant afternoon. The leaves were turning russet and gold.

'How can I endure this château on such a day?' said Antoinette to the Princesse. 'I feel I must go out. I am going to walk over to Trianon.'

'When shall we leave?' asked the Princesse.

'I wish to go alone. I shall merely take a footman to carry what I require. I want to be alone, Marie.'

The Princesse nodded. The Trianon was full of memories – memories of recent joys to overshadow those extravagantly splendid days of the past.

'It may be that I will sketch awhile, or perhaps I will read. It is too pleasant a day to stay within walls.'

How lovely was the Trianon that day. She remembered how she had enjoyed seeing the little Dauphin – the Dauphin she had lost – playing there in the pleasant meadows of her perfect village.

She thought: Perhaps Axel will come to see me here. Marie will tell him where I am. We could walk together out to Cupid's Temple and make each other believe that we are the only people in the world.

She sat on the terrace in front of her house, the sketch-book held idly in her hand as she looked out over the tree-lined meadow. The autumn wind ruffled the fichu at her bodice and her hair beneath her white hat.

And as she sat there she saw a page running towards her. He was clearly agitated.

She rose and went to meet him, and she saw as she came near to him that he carried a letter.

He cried breathlessly: 'Your Majesty! Monsieur le Comte de Saint-Priest sent this letter. He begs you to read it at once.'

She opened it and read: 'Return without delay. The mob is marching on Versailles.'

'The carriage is waiting, Your Majesty,' said the page.

'I will walk back through the woods,' she answered.

The young page shook his head. 'Madame, I was commanded to beg you to take the carriage. It may be that some of the mob have already reached the woods. Madame, you are in acute danger.'

She smiled. 'Come,' she said. 'We will take the carriage.'

She turned for one fleeting instant to look at the charming village she had created. Then she hurried after the page.

❖ ❖ ❖

At Versailles there was confusion.

The King's ministers were all about him, arguing, putting forward plans which were hastily discussed, discarded and discussed again.

'Your Majesty should put himself at the head of his dragoons and march out to meet the rebels,' said one.

The King was loth to do that. 'These are my people,' he said. 'How could I take up arms against them?'

Another cried: 'There is but one thing to do. Take the Queen and the royal children, say to Rambouillet. From a safe place it would be possible to treat with the leaders of the revolution. It is hopeless to parley with the mob.'

Horses and carriages were brought into the courtyard, but the King prevaricated. He could not make up his mind, and the minutes of indecision grew while the rioters drew nearer to Versailles.

Then in the courtyard was the sound of galloping hoofs.

A man leaped from his horse, threw the reins to a startled groom and strode into the Palace.

Antoinette felt immense relief when she saw him.

He cried: 'The mob is marching on Versailles.'

'We know it,' he was told.

Fersen could only look at Antoinette, and his fears for her safety were apparent to them all. But he was there; he would remain near to her; he was there to defend her with his life against the bloodthirsty mob.

✦ ✦ ✦

Now the rabble was in the Cour Royal, and the violent shouting echoed through the corridors of the château.

Fersen had insisted that the Queen shut herself away with her children in her apartments. To everyone's surprise the Swedish nobleman had seemed to take charge with a firmness which the ministers had failed to show.

The King was insistent that he himself should speak to his people. Louis was amazing in that moment; he was quite calm, even bland; he appeared to have complete faith in the goodness of all. He was sure that when he explained certain matters they would understand; then all would be well.

Word was passed among the mob that the King would be willing to receive a deputation from the women of Paris and listen to their grievances. There was that in the King of France, that benevolent calm, that firm belief that his subjects were his dear children, that almost always when they were in his presence they must feel his estimation of them to have some truth in it. And they who had come armed with knives and broken bottles agreed to the deputation being sent. They chose little Louise Chabry, a flower-seller, to talk to the King, because she was young, innocent and pretty. Louise was nervous but, urged on by the mob, she dared do nothing else but obey, so accompanied by a few of the more presentable women – those who were truly women and not men dressed in women's clothes – was taken to the King's audience chamber.

Louis, seeing the nervousness of this young and pretty girl, told her gently she must not be afraid of him.

Louise, overcome by the splendour of her surroundings and the kindly graciousness of the King, fell on her knees and mumbled apologies for disturbing the King's peace.

She found it difficult to speak, and one of the others, less susceptible – but only slightly less – told the King that the people of Paris were starving, and it was for this reason that they were marching on Versailles.

Louis declared that the suffering of his people was *his* suffering, and he was going to give orders that bread must be found somewhere and sent to Paris without delay.

The deputation, uncertain what to do now, for they had expected haughty arrogance and had found charming civility, declared themselves satisfied and honoured. As for little Louise, she fainted at the feet of the King, so overcome was she by the presence of royalty.

'Bring my smelling salts,' cried Louis to one of his attendants. 'And bring wine. The young lady must be revived.'

The wondering deputation then saw the King himself kneel by little Louise and hold the smelling salts to her nose. Then he himself held the glass of wine to her lips.

'Come, my dear,' he said, 'all this excitement has been too much for you.'

And Louise, opening her eyes, looked into the benign face of her sovereign and wept for all the harsh things she had said of this man.

Those of the deputation who watched said: 'But how could we hate such a good man? He is indeed the father of us all.'

The deputation returned to the mob. The King had promised to do something for Paris. The King was kind.

The mob murmured, but night was beginning to fall and it was raining, so they decided to find shelter in some of the houses and shops close by, in the Place d'Armes, in the barracks and the hall of *Menus Plaisirs*.

They muttered to one another: 'The King has bewitched our deputation. What now?'

The leaders had deliberately selected the deputation for its innocence. They had not wanted it to consist of blood-thirsty men dressed as women, or foreigners hired to kill and loot, or those of the south who had marched north determined to bring revolution to Paris. The deputation did not represent the mob.

Now they reminded each other that they had determined to bring the King to Paris. And this they would do. They had determined to have the Queen's head on a *lanterne*. Why should they be prevented by a gullible deputation's impression of a tyrant?

Meanwhile in the château the conference continued.

Fersen cried to the Queen: 'You must leave at once. I have horses ready. I have planned a route we can take. You . . . the children . . . and a few of the ladies. I will take you across the frontier into safety.'

The Queen looked at him; his eyes were alight with purpose. How could she help comparing him with the indecisive Louis? She had never loved Fersen so much as she did in that moment; she had never wanted anything so much as to ride with him away from Versailles, out of France, to some peaceful place where she might never again feel the menace of the mob.

But she shook her head. 'I am the Queen,' she said; 'and where the King is, there must the Queen stay.'

The lovers looked at each other and loved each other for what they were. They knew that death was in the air that night; and they were glad that they had given each other such joy.

La Fayette had arrived at the château with his men. The King received him with relief, for La Fayette was a nobleman who possessed some loyalty for the King, yet was respected by the mob.

La Fayette posted his men about the château and went to find a bed in the Hôtel de Noailles.

A fine rain was falling and it was cold. The smoke from a bonfire which had been made in the Place d'Armes choked him and he could smell the roasted flesh of a horse which the mob had killed and were eating. He could hear the sound of drunken singing, and he knew that those terrifying hordes had been looting the wine shops on the road to Versailles.

The mob were restive. They were cold and hungry; they were tired of waiting. It was five o'clock in the morning when pandemonium broke out.

'What are we doing here?' they demanded. 'We have come to kill the Austrian and take the King to Paris.'

'What are we waiting for?' cried one of the men, lifting his skirts above his knees so that for a moment his great boots were visible. 'Come . . . to the château! To the Austrian woman! Are we going to let the traitor Antoinette live?'

In a body they marched through the Place d'Armes, the

crowd growing in numbers as they marched. They came to the gate of the château which was manned by the National Guards.

'Let us through. Let us through,' they cried.

One of the Guards protested, and an axe was raised in a strong masculine arm.

Now they had their mascot, their emblem; now they were happy. They had the head of one of the Guards to carry before them on a pike. They had seen blood flow; and they longed to see more. But *royal* blood this time, the blood of the woman they had reviled for years because she was a foreigner, because she was rich and beautiful and because they envied her riches and her beauty.

They broke into the Palace; they climbed the *escalier de marbre*, killing two Swiss guards who barred their way; they battered through to the Queen's ante-room.

They shouted as they went: 'Give us Antoinette. We want the head of that traitor. Give us the Austrian bitch and we'll tear her to pieces. We want to take the King back to Paris. And we want the head of Antoinette.'

Now they had more heads to adorn their pikes. They looked at them with satisfaction. But there was that other head which they desired most of all, and on that morning of the 6th October, the *canaille* – the prostitutes, the hirelings, the seekers after power – were determined to have it.

⚜ ⚜ ⚜

Madame de Tourzel and the Princesse de Lamballe were standing at the Queen's bedside.

'Wake . . . wake . . .' they cried. 'The mob is at your door.'

Antoinette started up. She had only an hour before fallen

into a deep sleep. She stared about her as though she were still in a nightmare.

'Quick . . . quick! There is not a moment to lose. I can hear them hammering on the door.'

Antoinette was out of bed, a shawl about her shoulders, her shoes in her hand; and with her two friends beside her she ran through the Oeil-de-Boeuf and the chambre de Louis XIV to the rooms of her husband.

To her horror she found that the door of that room was locked. She hammered on the door in desperation. What agony she lived through then! Now she could hear the drunken shouts coming nearer; she heard them screaming her name. 'Death . . . death to Antoinette! Death to the Austrian! Death . . . death . . . We'll have her head on a pike . . . to show Paris. Death to Antoinette!'

'Oh God,' she cried, 'let me escape them. Let me die, but not this way . . . not in their filthy hands. Oh, God, help me.'

'Open! Open!' she screamed. 'For the love of God!'

But help was long in coming. The King and his attendants had not heard the noise in her wing of the château. The door had been barred that night, as all doors had been barred, and the mob was coming nearer.

She owed her life that night to the cupidity of the mob, who, even for the sake of Antoinette's head, could not resist plundering the rich rooms through which they passed.

And at length a slow-footed servant heard the hammering on the door, heard her screams, and carefully the door was opened.

Louis who, sleeping soundly as he always did, had heard nothing until this moment and had believed that after he had talked to the deputation of women all would be well, was now hurrying to her side.

The door was again barred and bolted; Louis put his arm about her; and into the courtyard rode La Fayette with his soldiers.

La Fayette – nicknamed Général Morphée – who was never on the spot when needed, saw now the disaster which had taken place, saw his murdered guards and realised that he should have foreseen what would happen; and as he forced his way through the mad mob and saw the rich tapestries and gold and silver ornaments which they carried, he knew that it was not he and his soldiers who had saved the life of the Queen – and perhaps of the King.

With him came Orléans and Provence, and for these two the mob made way respectfully. They were conducted to the King's apartments where the Queen sat erect, her children on either side of her.

It was now clear to everybody – even to the King – that there could be no parleying with the mob.

Orléans, who many suspected had more to do with that night's work than he would wish to be known, Provence, whose eyes were gleaming with speculation, and La Fayette, were all certain that the King must obey the mob who, even now, could be heard shouting outside the Palace: *'Le Roi à Paris.'*

❖ ❖ ❖

'I will speak to them,' said the King. 'I will do my best to explain.'

'They will kill you,' warned La Fayette.

'They will not dare to kill their King,' said Louis.

He stepped onto the balcony. He was bareheaded, and that in the eyes of the crowd seemed a gesture of humility.

They shouted: *'Vive le Roi!' 'Vive Louis,* the little father!'

Louis smiled at them and raised his hand. They were the masters though. They would not listen to him. He must not think he could speak to them. They were going to take him to Paris, and he must obey, but meanwhile they were content to shout: *'Vive le Roi!'*

Then a voice in the crowd cried: 'Let the Queen show herself.'

Fersen had stepped to the side of the Queen. 'It would be unwise,' he said.

Antoinette looked at him, remembering tender moments in the Trianon, thinking: This may be the last time I see him. They will surely kill me when I appear. They have guns, and they have been calling for my death.

The shouts continued: 'We want Antoinette. Let the Queen show herself.'

La Fayette said: 'It is necessary, Madame, in order that you may placate them.'

She rose then. She looked pale but very lovely in her stateliness. Never had she looked more queenly than she did in that moment.

'No!' said Fersen.

She turned to him and smiled. 'Yes,' she said. 'As Monsieur de La Fayette says, it is necessary.'

She went to the balcony. Fersen had thrust the hands of the children into hers. He believed there was some hope of safety in doing this. Those people down there had cheered the King; they would surely not risk the life of the Dauphin.

With her head held high, all dignity, all courage, she

341

stepped on to the balcony. There was a hush; then someone cried: 'Send back the children.'

'Go back,' she said to them quietly; and they, too terrified to do anything else, obeyed.

Now she stood there alone, waiting. She looked down on those ugly faces beneath the unkempt heads, and she thought: This is the end of my life. I came from Austria to France for this.

And she folded her hands across her breast and waited.

The crowd gasped. Many of them had never seen her before. In her flowing dress she was infinitely graceful; her fair hair was falling about her shoulders, for there had been no time to dress it; those beautiful white hands, crossed on her breast as though protecting her, gave her a look of helplessness which mingled strangely with that calm dignity, that complete absence of any show of fear.

The hush lasted several seconds. Then La Fayette, despising himself for his negligence of the previous night, and overwhelmed by his admiration of this brave woman, stepped on to the balcony; with a courtly gesture he bowed before the Queen, took her hand and kissed it.

There was a startled cry; then the strangest thing happened. Someone in the crowd cried: *'Vive la Reine!'*

And the cry was taken up by those who, but a short while before, had vowed to have her head on a pike.

⚜ ⚜ ⚜

The victory was brief; the mob had determined to take the King to Paris.

Louis stood on the balcony and addressed them.

'My children, you wish that I should follow you to Paris,

342

and I consent to do this, but on the understanding that I shall not be separated from my wife and children; and I ask for the safety of my bodyguard.'

'*Vive le Roi!*' cried the crowd. '*Vive les gardes du corps!*'

And so began the most humiliating hours which Antoinette had yet lived through.

In the first coach Antoinette rode with the King and her children, Madame Elisabeth, Madame de Tourzel and Provence. Behind them came the carriages containing other members of the Court. Before the coaches, behind them and all about them, were the mob, peering into the carriages, shouting insults at the Queen, spitting at the Queen – always the Queen.

Before the procession a band of prostitutes marched, led by Théroigne de Méricourt, prancing, dancing, singing obscene songs about the Queen.

Past the royal carriage pikes were carried; on them were the bleeding heads of murdered guards.

'We have the baker, the baker's wife and the baker's boy,' they shouted. 'We are bringing them to Paris. Citizens of Paris, come and meet the baker, meet the baker's wife and the baker's boy.'

Madame Royale and the Dauphin cowered close to their mother who had them on either side of her, her arms about them; she scarcely moved during that long ride, sitting erect, only now and then lifting a hand to take the head of the Dauphin or Madame Royale and hold it tightly against her breast, that they might not see sights too horrifying for their young eyes.

'Papa,' said the Dauphin, 'who are these people? What are they going to do to us?'

'There are evil men,' said the King, 'who have stirred up the people against us. But we must not bear a grudge against the people. They are as little children and not to blame.'

'They will not kill you, Papa?' enquired the Dauphin.

'No, my son, they will not kill me.'

'You are a good man, Papa, so they will not kill you.'

'No, my son. They will not kill me.'

'Nor will they kill my mother,' said the Dauphin; and he smiled up at her. He kept looking at her, for when he did so he was not afraid.

It was seven o'clock in the evening when they reached the Hôtel de Ville. Bailly greeted the King.

'It is a good day,' he said, 'which has brought you to Paris, sir.'

'I come,' answered Louis, 'with joy and confidence to the people of Paris.'

'What says the King?' cried the crowd.

'That he comes with joy to Paris.'

Antoinette said in loud tones: 'You have forgotten, sir, that the King said "with confidence".'

'To the Tuileries!' shouted the crowd.

The carriages rumbled on.

How desolate seemed the old Palace after the glories of Versailles. There were few beds and few furnishings; and a dank coldness pervaded the atmosphere.

'This is an ugly place,' complained the Dauphin. 'I do not like it. Let us go home now.'

'Why, my son,' said the Queen briskly, 'your great ancestor, Louis Quatorze, used to live here. He liked it very well. So you must like it too.'

'Tell me about him,' begged the Dauphin.

'Some other time,' said the Queen.

'Tell me why the people shout in the streets.'

'Because they love to shout.'

'They love us,' said the Dauphin. 'They love Papa because he is good, and you because you are good, and my sister because she is good, and me because I am good. They would never kill us, would they?'

'We are safe here,' said his mother gently. 'Safe in the old Palace of Louis Quatorze.'

But that night the Dauphin woke in his hastily improvised bed, screaming that he saw men in his room, men with heads on pikes, and they were marching all round him.

His mother had him brought to her, and she kept him beside her. Madame Royale slept on the other side of her.

Only the King slept soundly, the sleep of exhaustion.

And lying in that grim old Palace, splendid no longer, damp, unlived in, full of foreboding, Antoinette felt that she was a prisoner – a prisoner whom the people had condemned to death.

❧ Chapter XII ❧

MIRABEAU

Through that dreary winter the royal family lived, shut off from the world, in the ancient Palace of the Tuileries. How different this from the glories of Versailles, the charm of Trianon! Antoinette's apartments were on the ground floor, those of the King and the children on the first floor; and these apartments had their own private staircases – dark and smelling of damp, as were all the passages of the Palace; and even during the day they were lighted by oil lamps which smoked and gave out a foul smell. All these passages, staircases and apartments were patrolled by the National Guard, so that the royal family were not allowed to forget for one waking moment of the day or night that they were the country's prisoners.

But that almost unnatural calm of the King, allied with the stately courage of the Queen and the youthful innocence of their children, created an atmosphere of royalty even in this dark prison. Antoinette was able to ignore the presence of her guards; to Louis they were, as were all his subjects, his dear children, playing a game of which he did not altogether approve but which he accepted as a childish vagary; as for the

346

children, Madame Royale had her mother's dignity, and the Dauphin was soon on good terms with the soldiers.

Each day was very like another. Antoinette spent a great part of the morning with her children. She liked to be present while they had their lessons; again and again it was necessary to call the Dauphin's attention to that which the Abbé Davout was trying to teach him. His thoughts strayed and were often with the soldiers who could always be seen from the windows.

Every day the family attended Mass; and they had their midday meal together, like any family of the *bourgeoisie,* while the children prattled and their parents smiled at each other over their artless talk. Antoinette had never felt that she belonged so intimately to her family as she did in those days at the Tuileries.

After the meal, the King would slump in his chair and doze, or go to his apartments to do so. Antoinette would retire to her apartments where she would talk with her friends. Fersen was a frequent visitor, but she did not see him alone. Their passionate love-making belonged to the Trianon, and each was aware of the longing in the other to return there. The Tuileries offered them no opportunities.

Fersen was continually anxious for Antoinette's safety. He, even more than Antoinette, found it difficult to forget that terrible drive from Versailles on October 6th, and his active mind was concerning itself with one thing: escape.

Antoinette knew this; and in it was her comfort.

The family took their supper together; and with them would be Provence and Josèphe, Adelaide and Victoire (strangely subdued these days) bewildered, clinging together, wondering what was happening to their world.

The Queen often suggested a game of cards or billiards –

anything to prevent those fearful silences, those sudden bursts of conversation which would often end in the hysterical tears of Adelaide and Victoire.

Then early to bed – the King to his apartments, the Queen to hers. They had not shared a bed since Fersen had become her lover.

Louis slept soundly, for no disaster could rob him of his sleep or his appetite; but in her bed Antoinette lay sleepless, listening to the tramp of the guards, afraid to sleep lest she dream of those hideous shouts, lest she see in her fantasy those leering faces close to hers; afraid to sleep lest they should come upon her while she was unaware, as they had at Versailles. Always waiting, listening, wondering what that night and the day which followed would hold.

❖ ❖ ❖

The Parisians were ashamed of the march from Versailles, for it was soon realised that those screaming hordes did not represent the people of Paris. The *poissardes* and the women of the Market even went so far as to present a petition to the Tuileries in which they firmly stated that they had no part in the outrage, and that they considered justice should be done to those who were responsible for it.

It had become clear to many of those who sincerely wished for reforms that the revolution, which they had hoped to bring about by peaceful means, was in the hands of the rabble. Some of these, including Lally-Tollendal, left the country because they did not wish to be involved in shameful massacres.

La Fayette, suspecting the march to Versailles to have been organised by Orléans, declared that he was an ardent supporter of liberty and he believed that if Orléans were successful there

348

would be no liberty in France. There was no point in replacing one absolute monarch by another.

He sought out Orléans and, in the blunt way of a soldier, told him of his suspicions.

'I suspect,' said La Fayette, 'that you, Monseigneur, are at the head of a formidable party which plans to send the King away – perhaps worse than that – and proclaim yourself Regent. I am afraid, Monseigneur, that there will soon be on the scaffold the head of someone of your name.'

Orléans professed his utmost surprise. 'I understand you not,' he said.

'You will now do your utmost to have me assassinated,' retorted La Fayette. 'If you attempt this, be sure you will follow me an hour later.'

'I assure you that you wrong me. I swear this on my honour,' said the Duke.

'I must accept that word,' said La Fayette coolly, 'but I have the strongest proof of your misconduct. Your Highness must leave France or I shall bring you before a tribunal within twenty-four hours. The King has descended several steps from the throne, but I have placed myself on the last. He will descend no further, and to reach him – and the throne – you will have to pass over my body. I know you have cause for complaint against the Queen – so have I – but at such a time we must forget all grievances.'

'What proof have you of my complicity in the events of October?' demanded the Duke.

'Ample proof. Aye, and I can get more. I know, Monseigneur, that you had a hand in organising that rabble which marched to Versailles – mostly men dressed as women, not good Parisians, but hirelings, foreigners and rough men of the South, your paid agitators. It has been suggested that you were with them to guide them to the Queen's apartments.'

'This is absurd.'

'Then stand before the Tribunal and prove it.'

The Duke shrugged his shoulders. The events of those October days had failed; he saw that. The King was still the King; the Queen was still alive; they were prisoners in the Tuileries, it was true, but the Tuileries was now the Court; and many good citizens had become disgusted by the methods of the mob.

He said: 'These are dangerous days. Any man may be accused of he knows not what. I will leave the country for a while if that is necessary.'

La Fayette then went to the King, who was very distressed to hear of the suspected perfidy of his cousin.

'A member of my own family,' he murmured. 'Is it credible?'

'It can be proved,' said La Fayette, 'that certain cries were heard among the October mob. Not only *"Vive le bon Duc d'Orléans"*, Sire, but *"Vivre notre roi d'Orléans"*. You are most unsafe while Orléans lives.'

'He is my cousin,' said Louis helplessly.

'He would have seen your head on the *lanterne*, Sire.'

Louis shook his head. 'Let him be sent to England. He is fond of the English, and they of him. He will then be out of our way. And let it be said that he goes on a mission for me. I would not wish it to be known that I suspect a member of our family – my own cousin – of such conduct.'

So with the exile of Orléans, and with him the writer Choderlos de Laclos whose writings had done so much to stir the people, there was quiet in the city – though a brooding quiet – pregnant with smouldering danger.

There remained one formidable leader of the Orléans group: Mirabeau.

❖ ❖ ❖

The events of October had had their effect on Honoré Gabriel Riquetti, Comte de Mirabeau. He was an aristocrat by birth and it was because, in view of his past, he had been rejected by the nobility, that he had offered his services to the Third Estate. His great energy, which he liked to remind people was equal to that of ten men, and his powers as both speaker, writer and diplomat, had been at the service of Orléans. Now Orléans was exiled, and Mirabeau believed he saw a way of welding the King and the people together; and he determined to use all his vast energies to this purpose. Believing that he alone could save France, he wrote to the King offering his services.

'I should,' he wrote, 'be what I have always been, the defenders of monarchical power regulated by the laws, and the champion of liberty as guaranteed by monarchical authority. My heart will follow the road which reason has pointed out to me.'

The King did not answer his letters. Antoinette had seen them and she remembered that Mirabeau had been one of those men who had helped to foster the revolution and bring to the royal family much humiliation and terror. She reminded the King of this and pointed out that such conduct, by a man of noble birth, was doubly treacherous.

Mirabeau waited for his replies. He was now obsessed by his plan to save France and was becoming more and more convinced that he was the only man who could do so. He thought of his past, of all the years of loose living which lay behind him. He remembered all the poisonous obscenities which he had written; he thought of the numerous mistresses who had loved him in spite of his somewhat terrifying appearance (his face was hideously marked by smallpox, and his thick hair stood out in an untidy thatch about it); he remembered his reckless extravagance and numerous bankruptcies; and desperately he wished to make his mark upon the world before he died. He also wished to satisfy his creditors. He was suffering from a life of excesses and in spite of that unflagging energy he knew he had not long to live. He was obsessed by his desire to set right what he had helped to start. He wanted to turn the bloody revolution into a peaceful one.

And it occurred to him that there was one person who was preventing this: the Queen.

For she was now the King's chief adviser, and Mirabeau knew that the King with his high ideals was not the man to make the necessary decision.

Mirabeau thereupon began courting the Queen's attention, and the letters he wrote to Louis were intended to flatter her.

'The King has but one man to support him,' he wrote. 'That is his wife. The only safeguard for her lies in the re-establishment of royal authority. It pleases me to fancy that she would not care to go on living without her crown; and of this much I am certain, she will not be able to save her life if she does not save her crown. She must show moderation and must not believe she will be able, whether by the aid of chance or intrigue, to overcome an extraordinary crisis with the help of ordinary men and ordinary measures.'

Still his letters were ignored.

He knew this was due to the Queen. The winter passed; the

spring came; the brooding quiet continued, but Antoinette – a prisoner in the Tuileries – did not believe that it had come to stay.

With the coming of the summer it was decided that the royal family must leave the Tuileries, for the hermit-like life they were leading was having its effect upon their health. The King had grown fatter and more unwieldy; he did not hunt now, and a daily game of billiards did not give him the exercise to which he was accustomed. The Queen was pale, and the children had suffered from the many colds they caught in the draughty lamp-lit corridors.

There was only a little protest when it became known that the family intended to go to Saint-Cloud for the summer. The Orléanists made an attempt to rouse the mob, but this failed and, when the carriages left the Tuileries for Saint-Cloud, the people gathered about them, shouting: *'Bon voyage au bon Papa.'*

There was respite at Saint-Cloud. There was a new freedom. Fersen was with the royal party. He talked long and earnestly to the King and Queen.

'You must escape,' he said. 'You cannot go back to the Tuileries. From a distance you could come to terms with the revolutionaries. I am certain that it is wrong to allow yourselves to be the people's prisoners.'

Louis, who could never make up his mind about most things, was adamant on this point. He would not run away. He would stay with his people.

The Queen looked at him sadly. 'Where the King is,' she repeated, 'there must the Queen remain.'

Fersen was indefatigable. He roamed the countryside, sounding opinion. He made plans for escape, always hoping that Louis would accept them.

The city of Rouen, he discovered, was loyal. Why should not the King go to Rouen, set up his Court there and in dignity set forth the conditions on which he would return? He should take with him loyal soldiers. Fersen was for action; and again and again Louis let his chances slip through his fingers.

Fersen was now urging the Queen to receive Mirabeau.

'He is the cleverest man in France,' he declared. 'He can do much for you. I beg you, do not continue to ignore him. Do not turn such a man, who offers friendship, into an enemy.'

'Have you forgotten that he was one of the leaders of the conspiracy? Have you forgotten the October outrages?'

'I shall never forget those days as long as I live,' declared Fersen. 'But, my dearest, this is not the time to remember past slights. Your life is at stake.'

'And yours,' she said quietly, 'while you stay with us. What need is there for you to stay here? You are not even a French man. You can go where you will . . . No one will question you. Why do you stay here, daily risking your life?'

'I think you know,' he answered.

'Oh, go, Axel . . . please go. Let me know that you are safe.'

'When I go,' he said, 'I shall take you with me.'

She could only feel exultation. There had always been that about Axel which gave her new courage.

'See Mirabeau,' he insisted. 'Ask his help. He will work for you with all that knowledge of events, all that brilliance which he once gave to others. Let me arrange a meeting. I think it should be secret. Mirabeau wishes to see you before he sees the

King. He is sure that if he can succeed in persuading you, you will persuade the King.'

'You have arranged this meeting?' she asked.

'Yes, I have arranged it. He will come in secret to the gardens of Saint-Cloud, for it will not do for your enemies to know that he is with you yet. Let it be in the Palace grounds at a lonely spot at eight on this Sunday morning, when the Palace sleeps.'

'You would arrange my life,' she said.

'I love you,' said Fersen. 'At this time there is one thing I care more about than anything else in the world . . . your safety.'

'Do you know,' she said, 'when I am with you, I can even believe that one day I shall be free from my troubles. You have decided that it shall be so, and you could not fail.'

✦ ✧ ✦

She came out into the Palace grounds that sunny July morning. It was very quiet, and she was able to slip into the copse without being seen. She thought then: If Louis had wished it we could have escaped from Saint-Cloud. But of course Louis did not wish it. He would not run away.

The man was waiting for her. She shuddered with horror when she saw his face. That extremely ugly countenance, that look of brute strength, reminded her of faces she had seen about her carriage during the October ride.

'Your Majesty,' said Mirabeau, bowing deeply, 'at last I have this pleasure, this chance to tell you all that I can do to bring you back your royal dignity.'

She did not want to look at his face and he was aware of this, for even those women who eventually loved him so passionately had been horrified by his looks in the first instance. In time the Queen would be accustomed to his ugliness, and it would mean as little to her as it did to him.

But if his face was ugly, his voice was golden; he was an impassioned speaker; he had again and again swayed the Tiers Etat to his way of thinking; now he used all his persuasive charm on the Queen. He did not seek to cover up the terrible position in which the royal family was placed; he discussed possibilities – hideous possibilities – with frankness which made her flinch, and which she realised were no exaggeration.

The result of that meeting was that he pledged himself to fight on two fronts. He would continue to speak to the National Assembly. He would work for the King and the Nation; and because he was a man of superhuman powers he would weld the two together.

When he went back to his coach he said to his nephew who, disguised as his coachman, had driven him to Saint-Cloud: 'The Queen is good and she is noble. I can save her, and I will.'

✤ ✤ ✤

As soon as the summer was over, the people demanded the return of the royal family to the Tuileries. They suspected there were plots for their escape, and wished to keep them close.

Adelaide's spirit was broken, and her sister followed her in this as she had all her life.

Victoire would wander about the gloomy corridors murmuring: 'We used to say "Poor Sophie!" "Poor Louis!" But it would seem that they were the fortunate ones. They have gone to Heaven, and we are left behind.'

Antoinette went to the King and said to him: '*We* cannot go

356

from here, Louis. I understand how you feel about that. But is there any reason why the aunts should stay?'

'No,' said Louis after a pause. 'I do not think it is necessary for them to stay. They shall go.'

'If the people will let them,' she added grimly.

She went to the aunts and said: 'Louis thinks you should not be forced to stay here if you wish to go.'

Adelaide's eyes lighted up. 'Is it possible?'

'You could try,' said Antoinette.

'When could we do this?'

'Very soon. The Comte de Fersen will arrange everything for you.'

Adelaide did not look at the Queen. She was remembering all the scandal she had helped to circulate about Antoinette and the Swede.

Victoire too was remembering.

'I never thought,' said Adelaide, 'that I should be so happy at the thought of leaving France.'

'Nor I,' cried Victoire, and they both began to weep.

Antoinette put her arms about them.

'You forget . . . so easily,' said Adelaide.

Antoinette knew what they meant.

'When there is little joy in remembering, it is better to forget,' she said.

'You are so changed . . .' stammered Adelaide. 'We are so changed.'

'Life changes us all,' said the Queen.

'If . . .'

But Antoinette would hear no more of their remorse. It was enough that they felt it, and she was ready to be their friend.

So the carriages were in the courtyard, and the mob saw them and began to clamour round them.

'What is this?' they demanded. 'Who goes away?'

The two old ladies came out into the courtyard with a few of their servants, and Victoire kept close to Adelaide as they climbed into the carriages.

'Shall we let them go?' cried a voice in the crowd.

There was no answer; and during the lull the coachman whipped up his horses and drove away.

The people continued to stand about in the Tuileries. 'This is the beginning,' they declared. 'Go after the Mesdames! Bring them back to Paris.'

But the carriages were already on their way out of the city, and Victoire and Adelaide held each other's hands tightly, fearfully, as they rode, saying nothing.

The crowd stopped them at Fontainebleau.

'What coach is this? What does it contain? *Emigrées!* Let us take a look at them.'

Ugly faces peered at the two frightened old ladies.

'Who are these?' it was asked. 'They are not Antoinette and her family. That's clear.'

And while the old ladies shivered, the people of Fontainebleau decided to let them pass as they were such old ladies and could certainly not be the Queen disguised.

On they went through Burgundy, and again there was a halt, when they must leave the carriages, and be taken before the Commune while it was discussed whether or not Les Mesdames should be allowed to leave the country.

What wretchedness they lived through during those hours of indecision! They did not speak to each other; but Adelaide saw in Victoire's eyes that question, that fear:

'Did we, in our malice, help to bring ourselves to this pass?'

Adelaide believed then that she would never again dominate Victoire, for Victoire had seen her stripped of her sisterly authority, Victoire had doubted the wisdom of her malice; they were two sisters now, shorn of royalty, shorn of everything but the relationship between them, two frightened old ladies.

'Let them go,' said the Burgundians. 'They can do little harm.'

So on went Adelaide and Victoire, to Rome and to Naples where the sister of the Queen whom they had so fiercely hated received them with affection and the ceremony due to their rank.

Adelaide and Victoire were safe; and there they stayed as guests of Maria Carolina, Queen of Naples and sister to Antoinette.

And to Maria Carolina they talked of the sadness of Antoinette, of the courage of Antoinette, and how they had good reason to love her.

Orléans made good use of his time in London.

A year or so after her imprisonment, Jeanne de Lamotte had escaped from the Salpêtrière. She had good reason to believe that the Duc d'Orléans might have had some hand in that escape. Clothes had been smuggled in to her and, with the kindly help of the guards and sentries who, it seemed, had been paid well to look the other way, she slipped out of her prison and made her way to the Seine where a boat was waiting to take her out of the city. She at length reached the frontier and journeyed through the Netherlands to London.

There she joined her husband. The sale of the diamonds had made them rich and, when it was discovered that she was that Jeanne de Lamotte-Valois who had played such a big part in the notorious case, she was welcome in several houses, for she had such amusing stories to tell of the Queen of France; and Jeanne told her stories, making them more and more outrageous with each telling; if ever she felt a little ashamed of her lies, she merely had to let her fingers touch the angry-looking V on her breast, and then she felt that nothing she could say would be too bad.

Now the Duc d'Orléans was seeking her out.

'How would you like to return to France?' he asked her.

'Return to France!' Jeanne firmly shook her head. 'To the Salpêtrière?'

'Certainly not to the Salpêtrière – to a house of your own where you could receive your friends.'

'It would not be safe. I should not wish to suffer again what I have endured at the hands of those unjust rogues.'

'You would not.'

'But I escaped from prison, Monsieur le Duc. I was sentenced for life.'

'Have you not heard, Madame, that the people have stormed the Bastille? Do you not know what they say now of Antoinette? No! You would run into no danger if you returned to Paris. I would give you an *hôtel* in the Place Vendôme.'

'In exchange for what?'

The Duke took her by the chin and kissed her lightly.

'All Paris would be interested in your little stories of Antoinette.'

Jeanne smiled.

'There is no place like Paris,' she said.

'Then . . . return to your home. There is work for you to do.'

The Queen paced up and down her apartments.

'Louis,' she said, 'how can we endure this life? We had a little respite at Saint-Cloud, and now we are back ... back here in this dreary place. How much longer shall we remain prisoners here?'

Louis shook his head sadly.

'We should seek help from outside,' she cried. 'There is my own country. Ah, if only Joseph were alive!'

Joseph had died recently, and her brother Leopold was now Emperor. Leopold had his own difficulties; they would not include fighting in his sister's cause.

Antoinette's plan was that the Austrian armies should march to the frontiers of France, and that Louis should muster as many men as he could and go to meet them; and that the might of Austria should show the French that Austria disapproved of the way in which they were treating their monarchs.

But there was no help coming from Austria.

Orléans had returned to Paris, and La Fayette was afraid to raise the matter of his exile, for fresh demonstrations were now occurring in the Palais Royal.

Moreover that criminal and jewel-thief, Madame de Lamotte, was now established in the Place Vendôme, and libel after libel poured out from her pen. There was a new story of the necklace – Madame de Lamotte's version. No story was too vile to be attached to the Queen.

✢ ✣ ✢

There was one man who was keeping the revolution at bay. This was Mirabeau. He was now using his considerable gifts to the limit and was serving both the National Assembly and the monarchy, deftly keeping the balance between them, working with his tremendous powers to weld the two together.

The King had offered to give him promissory notes to the value of a million livres, to be paid when Mirabeau had brought about that which he had set out to do. This was to bring the revolution to an end and place the King firmly on the throne. Mirabeau's debts would be settled, and he would be left affluent. He was determined to earn the money and at the same time win for himself fame with posterity.

He could do it; he knew he could do it; he firmly believed that he held the fate of France in his hands.

Brilliantly he played his game. Eloquently he spoke in the National Assembly; he was working for the new constitution; and at the same time he intended to save the King and Queen. He was a master of words and rhetoric. He could sway the assembly, he could persuade the King.

Such brilliance was certain to bring him enemies. He was threatened with the cry *'Mirabeau à la lanterne!'* But he snapped his fingers. Marat accused him of working with the enemy. He snapped his fingers at Marat.

His plan was to stop the violence of the revolution with greater violence, and he said to the King: 'Four enemies are marching upon us: taxation, bankruptcy, the army and winter. We could prepare to tackle these enemies by guiding them. Civil war is not certain, but it might be expedient.'

He was like a giant possessed. Civil war! Law and order armed to fight the murderous mob!

The King was horrified. Was Mirabeau suggesting that he should fight against his dear people!

'Oh, excellent but weak King!' mourned Mirabeau. 'Most

unfortunate of Queens! Your vacillation has swept you into a terrible abyss. If you renounce my advice, or if it should fail, a funeral pall will cover this realm; but should I escape the general shipwreck, I shall be able to say to myself with pride: I exposed myself to danger in the hope of saving them, but they did not want to be saved.'

Realising the danger which threatened the King and Queen in Paris, he consulted with Fersen, for he saw that the Swede's plan to get them out of Paris was a good one.

Rouen would be useless now; they must go farther towards the frontier, where the Marquis de Bouillé was near Metz with his loyal troops.

Fersen made the journey to Metz and returned with the news that the King and Queen should leave Paris without delay, for Bouillé was not so sure of the loyalty of his troops as he had once been and he feared that disaffection was spreading.

Still the King hesitated.

'Then,' cried Mirabeau, 'must Your Majesty come out of retirement. You must show yourself in the streets. The people do not hate you. Have you not seen that, though they shout against you, when you appear they call you their little father? They have always had an affection for you. Are you not Papa Louis? But you shut yourself away, while your enemies spread evil tales concerning you.'

Fersen was terrified of the Queen's appearing in the streets, but Mirabeau was impatient.

This was not the time to hesitate. It seemed to him that nobody but himself realised all that was at stake.

He, Mirabeau, could save France; he, Mirabeau, would be remembered in the generations to come as the man who had averted the destruction of the monarchy; the man who had saved his country from anarchy.

It was Mirabeau who had stood beside Orléans and helped to raise the storm; it should be Mirabeau who cried: 'Be still!' and for whom the rising tide of bloodshed should be called to halt.

But he could get no help. The King would not countenance a civil war; he would not show himself to his people; he would not escape.

So Mirabeau continued deftly to keep his balance. He swayed the Assembly and he worked for the monarchy.

'Mirabeau is shaping the affairs of France,' said Marat, said Danton, said Robespierre; and said Orléans.

And one day, when his servant went to call Mirabeau, he found that his master was dead.

Mirabeau had suffered from many ailments, which were largely due to the life he had led. Was it the colic which had carried him off, or that kidney trouble which had afflicted him?

'Death from natural causes,' was the verdict.

But many people believed that the Orléans faction had determined to put an end to the man who had once been their friend and was now working to destroy all that they hoped for.

There were many in the streets to whisper of Mirabeau's sudden death: 'Oh, a little something in his wine. He lived dangerously, this Mirabeau. He thought he was the greatest man in France. Then death came, silent and swift.'

In the Tuileries fear descended. The King and the Queen now realised how much they had depended on Mirabeau.

✤ Chapter XIII ✤

ESCAPE TO VARENNES

*T*he death of Mirabeau greatly increased the danger to the royal family. In the Palais Royal men and women were demanding action. This was at the instigation of the Jacobins – members of that Club des Jacobins which the Club Breton had become. Club Breton had been the first of the revolutionary clubs, and many of its members were Freemasons or members of secret societies. It consisted mainly of partisans of Orléans – who was very much under the influence of Freemasonry – and the name of the club had been changed when it set up its Paris headquarters in the convent situated in the rue Saint-Honoré, for the headquarters of the convent which they had taken over was in the rue Saint-Jacques.

The purpose of the Jacobins was to press on with the revolution.

Soon after the death of Mirabeau, the King and Queen, feeling the need of a change, decided that they would go to Saint-Cloud for Easter. Their plans soon became known to the Jacobins, as one of the Queen's women, Madame Rochereuil, had a lover, a member of the Club, and he had assured her that the way in which she must serve her country – or herself be suspected of treachery – was to spy on the Queen.

So Madame Rochereuil lost no time in telling her lover of the intended visit to Saint-Cloud.

There was to be no secret about this visit; the carriages would arrive in the courtyard and the King and Queen would get into them; people would see them leave, and perhaps shout after them as they had when they had left for Saint-Cloud last year: *'Bon voyage, Papa!'*

But the fact was that the Jacobins had intended to prevent the King's and Queen's departure last summer, and they had only failed to do so because they had insufficient time to organise a riot.

Now, thanks to the work of Madame Rochereuil, they were warned in time of the royal intentions; and Danton arranged that the rioters should be mustered in good time, made drunk, reminded of their wrongs, and incited to revolution that they might give as good a performance as they did in October.

So on the day of the departure the Jacobins were busy. Laclos, disguised as a jockey, harangued the crowds. 'Citizens,' he cried, 'the King is running away from you. He will join Artois and the *émigrés;* he will plot against you and bring armies to conquer you. Citizens, will you allow the King to escape?'

The carriages were waiting. The King, the Queen and the royal children with their attendants and servants, came out and took their seats. But the rabble surrounded them.

'You shall not pass,' they cried.

And again Antoinette saw those leering drunken faces near her own, again she was forced to listen to the obscenities and insults.

La Fayette rode up with his soldiers and demanded that the mob stand clear and the carriages be allowed to drive on.

But what cared the mob for La Fayette? They jeered at him; they flung mud at him; they took the horses from the carriages and demanded that the King and Queen, with their family, return to the Tuileries.

✤ ✤ ✤

Antoinette said: 'We are truly prisoners now. They have determined that we shall not leave the Tuileries.'

Even Louis was abashed, and there was a worried frown on his brow.

Antoinette went to him and put her arm through his. 'Louis, we cannot go on like this. I cannot endure this life.'

He looked at her sadly and shook his head.

'I think perhaps,' he said, 'that you are right. I think perhaps there is nothing we can do while we remain their prisoners.'

Fersen begged an audience. He had come from Saint-Cloud where he had hoped to meet the Queen; but news had reached him of the mob's decision not to let them leave the Tuileries.

'Your Majesty must see,' he cried passionately to Louis, 'that this state of affairs must not go on.'

Louis looked at his wife's lover; and in that moment he felt a glimmer of understanding as to why Antoinette loved this man; he saw in Fersen all that he himself was not, and in a sudden moment of clarity – which was gone almost as soon as it came to him – he realised that his indecision had brought him to this pass, that there had been moments in the dangerous road he was travelling when he might have said, 'Halt. I will take my stand here'; when he might have turned and taken the offensive. Who could say that, had he been blessed with the boldness of this man, with the boldness of Mirabeau, his position might not have been different from what it was to-day, and France not the tortured nation she was fast becoming.

'You are right,' said Louis.

'Your Majesty will consider my plans for your escape?'

The King nodded.

✤ ✤ ✤

Now there was great activity in the Tuileries – secret activity. They missed the brilliant Mirabeau, but they were certain they could do without him.

Fersen planned like a lover, worked like a lover. He lived for one purpose – to remove Antoinette from danger. He needed money and he must procure it in such a way that it would not be noticed, so he provided it himself by mortgaging his estates. He was already in correspondence with several foreign countries; he had General Bouillé on his side, for it was General Bouillé with whom Mirabeau had planned the royal escape. Bouillé was still prepared to help, although he warned Fersen that every week's delay was dangerous, as each day the cavalry under his command was being indoctrinated with revolutionary ideas.

Fersen knew full well that if one little hitch occurred in his plans, if one of the numerous letters he was constantly writing went astray, it would be *'Fersen à la lanterns'*, and hideous death would await him. The thought imbued him with a reckless courage.

Fersen was truly in love.

Every day he was at the Tuileries and, in order not to attract too much attention, he often came disguised. Each evening he would join the King and Queen, and in hushed voices they would discuss the plans for the escape.

He would look at the Queen with glowing eyes.

'I have ordered a berline to be built,' he said. 'It is a comfortable vehicle . . . very wide, and the springs are good. I have seen to that myself, so that Your Majesties will travel in the utmost comfort.'

They listened eagerly. It sounded miraculous.

'The passport I have had forged is made out in the name of Madame de Korff – a Russian lady. Madame de Tourzel, who of course must travel with the children, will be Madame de Korff. Her Majesty the Queen will be the governess, and His Majesty the King, the lackey; there will be three women servants. Madame Elisabeth will of course be one of these.'

'And there will be room for all these in the berline?'

'Indeed yes,' said Fersen. 'There was never such a berline as this which is being built for the flight, but it will be necessary for Your Majesty to send some of your clothes and jewels in advance.'

'I will send them to Brussels,' said the Queen. 'Monsieur Léonard will take them. I shall not need him to dress my hair while we are on the journey.'

'Indeed not. You must not forget that you are the governess.'

The Queen smiled. Already her spirits were lifted. It was due to the thought of escape from the dreary Tuileries; it was due to the joy of planning with Fersen.

'I have arranged with Bouillé and the Duc de Choiseul that troops shall be posted along the route, so that once we are out of Paris the greatest of the danger will be past.'

'That is wonderful,' cried Antoinette. 'And you . . . Comte?'

'I shall be disguised as your coachman. I shall drive you to the frontier.'

Louis looked at them sombrely, and he thought: They love each other.

There was the man he might have been; and had he been that man, handsome, distinguished, a man of action, Antoinette might have loved him as she loved Fersen.

He did not blame Antoinette; he did not blame Fersen.

But he was in danger of losing his kingdom and his wife, and suddenly he felt an unusual emotion; mingled with it was anger against the Swede. Why should the man arrange their lives; why should he take charge of this adventure? Why should Antoinette look at him with those adoring eyes?

No. He must accept Fersen's help but, once they were out of Paris, the escape should be his own achievement. He was the King; and he would be in command.

'Monsieur le Comte,' he said, 'I think you might accompany us to Bondy. There another shall take over the berline and you shall ride on by a different route to the frontier.'

Fersen was bewildered. 'But, Sire,' he said, 'I have been over the route. I have made all the arrangements ... I ... I have planned this ... '

Louis' face was quite expressionless. 'I would wish you to leave us at Bondy.'

Fersen looked at the Queen. She said; 'The King is right. The risk ... if we were discovered ... would be too much for you to take. The mob would tear you to pieces if they discovered who you were and all you had done for us.'

'But I must beg of you to listen to me,' said Fersen.

Louis was a King in that moment, who did not give reasons for his decisions.

'I wish it,' he said.

Fersen bowed.

370

The plans were ready. The 6th of June was fixed for the day of escape, and all details were completed. Fersen had arranged everything. The King and Queen were to leave the Tuileries separately; they were to cross the square to where he would have an old-fashioned fiacre waiting for them. When they were all assembled, he would drive them out of Paris to where the berline would be waiting for them; in that he would drive them to Bondy, where he would leave them. They must make with all speed to Châlons-sur-Marne, for once they were through that town they would find the soldiers waiting for them, half an hour's drive ahead at Pont de Somme-Vesle; and so they would make their way to Montmédy, which was but ten miles from the frontier. Fersen would be impatiently waiting at Montmédy; and once they had reached that town they would be safe.

The most difficult part of the operation was slipping out of Paris. They talked of it continually, rehearsing what they would do.

✦ ❖ ✦

It was inconceivable, of course, that the Queen should leave her jewels behind. She visualised her arrival in a foreign Court. She must be adequately dressed. She must not let her friends think that she came as a beggar.

Fersen had realised this, and the berline itself was the most magnificent of its kind ever built. There had never been such a large carriage; this was necessary, Fersen declared, as it had to carry so many.

Fersen had put all his love into the building of the berline.

Continually he thought of the comfort of the Queen. He had built into it a cupboard for food, and this was to be packed with chicken, wine and various delicacies for the journey; there was a clothes-press, for the Queen had always been fastidious about her clothes; there was even a commode – everything for the comfort of the travellers.

Fersen, who had planned every detail to perfection, failed to realise that the building of such a magnificent vehicle could not be kept entirely secret; and although his story was that it was for a Russian baroness, rumours soon started from the coach-maker's workshop.

Provence and Josèphe were to leave the Tuileries at the same time, but Provence was arranging his own escape and proposed to travel to Montmédy by a different route; there they would meet.

Provence had different ideas from those of Fersen, and decided that he and Josèphe would travel in a shabby carriage without attendants.

✤ ✤ ✤

The Queen was packing her jewels, in her apartment, preparing them for Monsieur Léonard to take into Brussels, when she became aware of Madame Rochereuil standing in the doorway, watching her.

Antoinette swung round, and with difficulty prevented herself from crying out.

'Yes, Madame Rochereuil?' she said coldly.

'I wondered if I might help you, Madame, with the packing.'

The woman's eyes were on the jewels spread out on the sofa.

The Queen said: 'There is nothing you can do.'

Madame Rochereuil left her, but the Queen was anxious. She called Madame Elisabeth to her.

'That woman is spying on us,' she said. 'That woman knows we plan to go.'

'Could we not rid ourselves of her?' asked Elisabeth.

'That would be to call suspicion on us. I have discovered that Gouvion, a member of the Jacobin Club and a rabid revolutionary, is her lover. She watches all we do, and reports it to her Jacobin friends. Elisabeth, she knows!'

'She cannot know when. No one knows when . . .'

'But she will be spying on us. How can we ever leave as we planned? You know how careful we shall have to be . . . And she will be watching us all the time.'

And so it seemed, for at odd moments Madame Rochereuil would be near them, smiling quietly, alert, watchful, knowing herself to be recognised as a spy, the spy of whom they dare not rid themselves.

'We cannot leave on the 6th,' said Antoinette to Fersen. 'The wretched woman, Rochereuil, knows we intend to go. She saw me packing my jewels. I told her that they were a present to my sister, but I could see she did not believe me.'

'We must wait awhile,' said Fersen uneasily.

It became clear that they were wise to do so, for shortly afterwards an article by Marat appeared in the *Ami du Peuple*. 'There is a plot,' he wrote, 'to carry off the King. Are you imbeciles that you take no step to stop the flight of the royal family? Parisians, you stupid people, I am weary of telling you that you should have the King and Dauphin under lock and key; you should lock up the Austrian woman and the rest of the family. If they escaped it might mean the death of three million Frenchmen.'

Marat was afraid that, if the King escaped from Paris, he would gather forces together and there would be civil war throughout France.

'We cannot go yet,' it was decided in those secret meetings in the Tuileries. 'We must wait until suspicions are lulled.'

Fersen fretted; so did Bouillé and the Duc de Choiseul. Everything had been arranged to the smallest detail. But Marat had aroused the suspicions of the people and Madame Rochereuil was watchful.

So during the days of that June it was necessary to infuse a listless air into the Tuileries. Never for one instant must they forget the watching eyes of Madame Rochereuil.

'We *must* leave on the 19th,' said Fersen desperately. 'We dare not delay longer.'

So the escape was fixed for the 19th.

But on the evening of the 18th Madame de Tourzel came to the Queen and said: 'Madame Rochereuil will not be in atendance on the 20th. She has asked leave to go and visit someone who is sick. I believe this to be true, because I heard from another source that Gouvion is unwell.'

'This is a heaven-sent opportunity,' cried the Queen. 'We will leave on the 20th. Not on the 19th.'

It was late to make alterations, but she was sure that it would be folly to attempt to leave the Palace under the spy's watchful eyes, when they could do so the next day in her absence. She called Monsieur Léonard to her and sent him off with the jewels. He would meet the cavalry on the road; and he was to tell their leader that the royal party would be twenty-four hours late.

Léonard left.

The 20th dawned. This was the day of escape.

The day seemed endless. Antoinette was certain that never before had she lived through such a long day. In the late morning, to the great relief of the Queen, Madame Rochereuil went. She was sure now that if they had been suspected of trying to escape earlier in the month, they were no longer; for if this had been so surely Madame Rochereuil would never have been allowed to leave her post.

Louis was as calm as ever. Louis was fortunate, as he never showed emotion.

Often during that long day Elisabeth and the Queen exchanged anxious glances, each aware of the other's thoughts. Will the time never pass?

They stood at the windows, looking out. The sun was shining. That was fortunate; it was one of those lovely summer days which would draw the people out of the streets away to the open country.

Antoinette saw that Elisabeth's lips were moving silently in prayer.

There was Mass to attend, and after that the family had their midday meal together. Antoinette was amazed that Louis could eat with his usual appetite. She had to force herself to appear normal, so did Elisabeth, and even Provence was more silent than usual. Antoinette was glad she had been able to keep their plans from the children.

She said to the King: 'You are going to your apartment to rest? I shall go to mine, I think. I wish to work on my tapestry.'

She had not been in her room more than five minutes when a servant announced the arrival of Fersen. She received him in her apartment with only Elisabeth present.

'The woman is not here?' he asked.

'No. She is having a short holiday.'

'I wish she had taken it yesterday.'

'Do not worry. You worry too much,' said the Queen tenderly.

'I am thinking of the soldiers waiting at their posts.'

'But Monsieur Léonard can be trusted. He will reach them at the appointed time and tell them that we shall be twenty-four hours late.'

'I would that I were driving you all the way.'

The Queen did not meet his eyes. 'It is the King's command,' she said.

'Is everything ready now?' asked Fersen. He looked anxiously at the gilded clock on the wall. 'Does it seem to you that time stands still?'

Antoinette nodded.

'When I leave the Palace,' he went on, 'I shall take a look at the berline, to make sure everything is ready. I shall have the wine and food packed into it, and then it will be sent to wait for us beyond the Barrier. We shall then change vehicles, and away. You will not forget your parts.'

'No,' said the Queen. 'I am the governess to my children, employed by Baroness de Korff – my dear Tourzel – the King is the lackey, and Elisabeth the companion; then dear Madame Neuville and Madame Brunier are servants, are they not? And that completes our little party.'

'Is it necessary to take them? There seem so many of us,' said Elisabeth.

'I must have my maids,' said the Queen. 'I shall need them to help me with my toilet.'

'They are trustworthy,' said Fersen; 'and they may leave an

hour before you do, and can join the party later on. No one will
stand in the way of *their* going. The difficulty will be to get you
two ladies, the King and the children away without suspicion.'

'I know,' agreed the Queen.

'Take care.'

He put out his hands, and Elisabeth did not look at them as
for a moment they clung together.

Then Fersen was taking his leave.

When he had gone the Queen and Elisabeth took Madame
Royale and the Dauphin for a drive in the Tivoli pleasure
garden; when they returned the children went to bed and the
King and Queen took supper with Elisabeth, Provence and
Josèphe. After the meal they retired to the great drawing-room
and, huddling together far from the doors, discussed the last-
minute plans.

Every now and then they would glance at the clock and
comment on the slow passage of time.

Privacy was never of long duration. The royal family
must not excite suspicion by remaining too long in the
private drawing-room. They made their way to the great
salon where the members of the Court were gathered. Some
talked; some were engaged in card games. The great test was
beginning. There among those courtiers the impression must
be given that this night was no different from countless
others.

The King was calm, enough. He sat on his chair, looking
sleepy, as he usually did during the evening. He was discussing
the latest phase of the revolution in the way he discussed such
things every night.

377

It was ten o'clock when the Queen rose and remarked that she wished to write a letter and would shortly return. With madly beating heart she slipped through the gloomy corridors to the children's apartments. Madame de Tourzel was waiting for her.

'You are ready?' breathed the Queen.

'Yes, Madame.'

Antoinette went to her daughter's bed. Madame Royale opened her eyes and stared at her mother. 'You are to get up quickly. Ask no questions. Dress at once. Madame de Tourzel will help you.'

Madame Royale obeyed instantly.

Antoinette went to the Dauphin's bed.

'Come, my darling,' she said. 'We are going on a journey.'

The Dauphin sprang up. 'Now . . . Maman? Now? Where do we go? Are the soldiers coming with us?'

'We shall go to a fortress where there are many soldiers. Come now. I will help you to dress. Be quiet, for it is late and there is not a moment to lose.'

'These are girls' clothes!' cried the Dauphin in dismay. Then gleefully: 'Is it a masked ball, Maman?'

'I said, be quiet. It is important to be quiet.'

'Are you coming?' he whispered.

'Yes . . . but later. Do as I say, or you will be brought back and there will be no journey. Do not say a word until you are told you may.'

The Dauphin nodded conspiratorially and allowed himself to be dressed in a girl's gown and bonnet.

'Now,' said the Queen. She led the way swiftly through silent rooms, down a private staircase to that exit at which Fersen had made sure no sentry should be placed.

The Queen went ahead of her children and looked out. Almost immediately a cloaked figure appeared from the shadows. It was a coachman, and Antoinette recognised him by his gait. She could have wept with joy and gratitude. She might have known he would not fail.

No word was spoken. Fersen took the Dauphin's hand; Madame de Tourzel was holding fast to Madame Royale. Fersen led the way to where the fiacre was waiting, and Antoinette returned to the salon.

✤ ✤ ✤

At eleven the Queen intimated that she was tired and would retire for the night.

Her women undressed her, and never had they seemed so slow.

'Pray,' she said to one of them, 'order the carriages for tomorrow morning. If the weather is as good as it has been to-day I should like to go for a drive.'

'Yes, Your Majesty.'

The Queen yawned.

'Your Majesty is tired?'

'It is the heat, and the conversation in the salon seemed even duller than usual.' While they removed her headdress she watched them through half-closed eyes. She wanted to shriek at them: 'Be quick. Every moment is important.'

At last they drew the curtains about her bed, and she heard the door close.

Immediately she was out of bed; she dressed herself in a simple grey silk dress and put on a black hat with a thick veil. Her fingers were clumsy, for she was unused to dressing herself. She wondered how Elisabeth was faring. But Elisabeth would be calmer than she was. No doubt Elisabeth was already joining the fiacre in the rue de l'Echelle.

She wondered about Louis. He too had to make ready for his escape. He would find it even more difficult. La Fayette would pay his nightly visit to the Tuileries and would spend some time with the King. A good deal depended on how soon the King could dismiss La Fayette without arousing his suspicions.

But she must think only of her own escape which would need all her care.

Fully dressed now in the hat with the heavy veil, she was unrecognizable. She drew the curtains about her bed again and slipped out through the private door, down the private staircase.

As she came to that door through which the children had left, she saw the tall figure of a guardsman. She caught her breath in a moment of fear, although she knew she was to meet such a man who would conduct her to the fiacre. What if they had misjudged their man? What if he, like Madame Rochereuil, was a traitor after all?

His voice was soft as he whispered: 'All is well, Madame. Follow me.'

Her heart leaped. She could trust Fersen to have made all the arrangements.

Louis was yawning effectively, letting La Fayette see that he was weary of his company; but it was not as easy as it had been to dismiss a general. La Fayette talked, and Louis must not draw attention to his desire to go to bed. Marat's article might be remembered, in which case La Fayette might consider it expedient to double the guard.

But at length La Fayette, in consideration of the King's yawns, took his leave; but Louis' troubles were only just beginning. He must submit to his *coucher*, for the etiquette of the Court had not been so far forgotten as to allow the abandonment of such a traditional ceremony. So Louis was put to bed and, according to the old custom, his valet must sleep in his bed chamber, with a cord attached to his wrist and to the King's bed-curtains, so that if the King needed him, all he had to do was reach for the curtains and jerk the man awake. How to escape from the valet, who was a man who could not be trusted with the secret, had occupied the minds of them all for many nights. It had been arranged that the King should go to his bed, have the curtains drawn as though he wished to settle down to immediate sleep, and while the valet went into his closet to undress, dart out from behind the curtains into the Dauphin's bedchamber which adjoined his. There he would pick up the clothes which were ready for him in the Dauphin's room – a lackey's suit and hat, and a crude wig, and then tiptoe down the secret staircase with these to one of the lower rooms where Guardsman de Maiden who was in the secret would help the King to dress.

So the King of France, barefooted and in his nightgown, escaped from his valet and, being dressed in these humble garments, walked calmly out of his Palace across the courtyard past the guards who mumbled a sleepy good night, and out into the streets, across to the Petite Place du Carrousel to the rue de l'Echelle and the fiacre.

It was disconcerting to find that the Queen, who should have left the Palace earlier than the King, had not yet arrived.

Antoinette followed the guardsman.

They had escaped from the Palace, and her spirits were rising. Never again, she thought, shall I live a prisoner in that gloomy Palace.

The guardsman was a little way ahead; she hurried to keep up with him. Who would have believed that escape could have been so easy? In five minutes, she thought, I shall be with the children. They are safe . . . safe with Axel.

It was strange to be out walking in the streets of Paris. She realised then how little she knew the city. I should never have found the fiacre by myself, she thought.

Suddenly she saw that the guardsman had halted, and in a second she understood why. Coming towards them was a coach before which walked the torchbearers. The guardsman was signalling her not to come forward, and looking about her, she saw an alley and slipped down it. The light from the torches shone on the dark wall of the alley. She lowered her head for she had recognised the livery of La Fayette's men and she knew that the General would be in his coach.

The coach passed so close to her that she saw La Fayette sitting in it. For an instant her heart felt as though it would choke her. Holding the veil tightly about her throat, she turned and began walking slowly down the alley.

The sound of the carriage wheels had died away and then she heard footsteps behind her. She dared not turn. Her heart was beating madly. 'Oh, God,' she prayed, 'let me reach the fiacre. Let me reach my children.'

'Madame.' She felt she wanted to shout with relief, for it was her guide. 'That was a near thing. If the General had seen Your Majesty . . .'

'He would not have recognised me,' she said, for the man was trembling.

'Madame, it is not easy for you to disguise yourself.' He was frowning. 'Let us go another way to the rue de l'Echelle. I am afraid that if we take the route we planned we may meet more carriages.'

'You are right,' she said. 'Let us do that.'

So they walked and, after ten minutes, the man admitted that he was not sure where he was. He was not so well acquainted with this part of Paris, and these back streets were such a maze.

'They will be waiting,' she cried frantically. 'They will think I have not escaped. We must find them . . . quickly.'

But they were lost in that maze of streets and, when they tried to retrace their way to that spot where they had met La Fayette's carriage, they could not do so. For half an hour they sought to find their way and, when they finally reached the rue de l'Echelle, it was to discover that the others were in despair, having been waiting for almost the whole of an hour.

Antoinette took her place in the ancient fiacre; she felt too emotional for words; all she could do was take her sleeping children in her arms and hold them against her.

Fersen climbed into the driver's seat and whipped up the horses. Precious time had been lost, and in an endeavour such as this each minute was important.

Through the narrow streets went the fiacre, Fersen alert for any sign that they were followed. The occupants of the fiacre scarcely dared speak to each other. Many possibilities occurred to them; they would feel greatly relieved when they had left Paris behind them.

At length they came to the Barrier, but the berline was not at the spot where Fersen had arranged that it should be waiting for them.

He drew up and looked around him in consternation. There was silence all about them. Fersen descended and went to the door of the fiacre.

'Something must have happened,' he said. 'There may have been an alarm which caused them to move from this spot. I will leave the fiacre here and search awhile. It cannot be far away.'

After half an hour Fersen found the berline; it was about half a mile away and it had not been visible because the lamps were covered up. The driver had been alarmed by the long delay and, when horsemen had ridden past, had felt it necessary to move from the appointed spot. Fersen then drove the fiacre to the berline and the royal family moved from one to the other.

They were now ready to continue the journey; but it had been an uneasy beginning, and they had planned to leave Paris at midnight; it was now two o'clock.

Fersen drove full speed to Bondy where it was necessary to change horses, and while this was being done, Fersen examined the berline, made sure that everything was in order; then he came to the door and said his farewells. His eyes were on the Queen, hers on him.

She said in a quiet voice: 'This could never have happened but for you.'

'You have your parts to play,' he said. 'Do not forget, Your Majesty, that you are the governess.'

'If we return,' said the King, 'we shall not forget you.'

'When we return,' corrected the Queen.

Fersen stood back from the berline; he called in a loud voice: 'Adieu, Madame de Korff.'

The berline moved forward; Fersen lifted his hat and turned the horse, which he had arranged should be waiting for him at Bondy, towards Le Bourget.

Antoinette thought: In two days' time we shall meet at Montmédy, but as the first light of dawn showed her his retreating figure she was conscious of foreboding. This had been *his* endeavour; without him, she did not feel the same confidence, the same certainty that all would be well. Only two days, she reminded herself. But a great deal could happen in two days.

The children awoke.

'I'm hungry,' announced the Dauphin. 'Are we nearly there?'

'Not long now,' answered the Queen. 'And we shall have our picnic now.'

'A real picnic? In the fields?'

'No, in the carriage. I will see what we have in the cupboard. No,' she smiled at Madame de Tourzel who had risen and was about to open the cupboard door, 'I shall do this. And Elisabeth shall help me. Do not forget that Elisabeth is the maid and I am Madame de Rochet, the governess. Madame de Korff, I beg you sit still and let your servants wait upon you.'

Madame Royale looked bewildered, but the Dauphin lifted his shoulders with delight.

'You see,' said the Queen, 'it is a new sort of masque. You are a little girl, my darling, do not forget that. And I am your governess. You must be a little afraid of me, I think, for I am very stern, and when you speak to me you must not forget to address me as Madame Rochet.'

'Madame Rochet. Madame Rochet . . .' crooned the Dauphin.

Elisabeth brought out the silver platters which Fersen had had put into the coach, for he had deemed it inconceivable that the Queen could eat off anything but gold or silver; the Queen brought out chicken while the King found the wine.

The children laughed merrily. This was indeed a good way to enjoy a picnic. They picked the meat off the bones and threw them out of the window. The Dauphin pretended to be very much afraid of Madame Rochet and, throwing himself whole-heartedly into the game, insisted on Madame Royale's playing it with him. But Madame Royale, who was thirteen years old, could not be so easily duped, and the tension did not escape her.

At Claye, they picked up the two ladies-in-waiting who had already been there some hours and were delighted to see the berline, for the delay had made them very anxious. The horses were changed and the journey continued.

The King studied the maps, following the route and pointing it out to Madame Royale and the Dauphin.

'Here, you see, we have left Paris behind us . . . and been through Bondy and Claye. Now we come to La Ferte. Then we shall go on to Châlons-sur-Marne . . .'

Oh that they were there! thought the Queen, for after Châlons the worst danger would be over since the cavalry, promised by the Duc de Choiseul and Bouillé, would be waiting for them beyond that town. Then their journey to Montmédy would begin, and at Montmédy Axel would be waiting.

As the journey continued the heat in the berline became oppressive.

The Dauphin began to whimper. 'Oh, Maman . . . I'm too hot. I want to get out now.

'You must be patient,' soothed the Queen. 'Do not forget that I am your stern governess, Madame Rochet.'

'No, no,' said the Dauphin. 'You are my maman, and I am too hot.'

As the coach began to labour up a hill, Madame de Tourzel suggested that she and the children should walk. It would be good for them to have a little exercise and they would not be much slower than the coach which they could rejoin at the top of the hill.

This seemed an excellent suggestion and the berline was halted while Madame de Tourzel alighted with the children. The berline reached the top of the hill first, for the Dauphin had wanted to linger in the fields, and half an hour or so was lost at that point; but no one felt this was of any great importance because the little boy was so much less fretful, and after another meal he leaned against his mother and went to sleep.

It was early afternoon when they came to Petit Chaintry – a small village close to the main one of Chaintry – for Fersen had deemed it wise that they should change horses at the smaller hamlet. The postmaster's son-in-law was spending the day with his wife's family in Petit Chaintry; he was an innkeeper who travelled now and then to Paris, and there he had seen the King.

While the horses were being changed, this man, Gabriel Vallet, strolled out to look at the extraordinary vehicle which was such as he had never seen before. It was quite magnificent.

The travellers must be very rich indeed, he guessed. He touched the berline and nodded sagely. Oh, yes, a very fine piece of work, perfectly sprung; then he caught a glimpse of the damask lining of the coach.

Émigrés, he thought. Now I wonder who? Important people doubtless. It must be hot inside that coach. Why do they not get out and enjoy a little fresh air while they can?

He strolled past the window of the berline, and caught his breath. Could he be mistaken? The wig was rough, and the hat that of a lackey, but the face beneath it – that plump long-nosed face? Surely he was not mistaken. Two children and a woman dressed as a governess. A governess! Not even during the revolution, when all classes had discovered that they were equal, could a governess learn that air of dignity.

Vallet drew his father-in-law to one side.

'You have distinguished callers, Papa,' he said.

'So?' said the old man. 'And who are these?'

'Only the King, the Queen, the Dauphin, Madame Royale and some others.'

The old man was overcome with surprise and pleasure at serving the King; he went out to the berline and, bowing low, said: 'Your Majesty, this a great honour and one I shall remember to my dying day. We are humble folk, but all that we have is at Your Majesty's service.'

Louis, touched as ever by the devotion of one of his dear children, murmured to the Queen, who was looking horrified: 'Have no fear. We are far from Paris, and these dear people are our friends.'

Vallet appeared and bowed, as his father-in-law had done. Then his wife came out with her mother and her sisters. They were flustered with excitement.

'We have a goose just ready to serve, Your Majesty. If you would honour us by eating it . . . we should consider ourselves your most fortunate subjects.'

Louis decided that to refuse the hospitality would be churlish. So they left the berline and took refreshment in the house of these people; and the Queen found gifts from the treasures she had brought with her to bestow upon them. The Dauphin recovered his spirits, and Madame Royale, who now understood that they were in flight from the gloomy Tuileries, was equally joyful.

Vallet asked a special boon. If he could act as postilion on the berline as far as Châlons he would be honoured. He begged the King to accept his service.

The King did not see how he could refuse this request, since he had accepted the homage and hospitality of Vallet's family; and they set out from Petit Chaintry in good spirits. They had lost some time by stopping there, and they had never made up the initial loss. Vallet, determined to serve the King with all his heart, tried to get too much out of the horses, with the result that two of them fell and there was some damage done to the traces.

This had to be repaired, which naturally involved more delay; but at length they came into Châlons.

Here the secret of their identity must be kept, for Châlons was no little village. They were all in good spirits. They were well on their way, and once through Châlons they would soon make contact with the cavalry. Moreover the people of this wine-growing country were not so deeply concerned with politics as the Parisians. They must have seen many *émigrés* escaping to the border. Why should they give special attention to one little party?

There was the fact though that, if they had seen many departing *émigrés*, they had never yet seen any travelling in such style, and the berline with its six horses and its magnificent outward appearance would attract notice wherever it went.

Vallet, the proud postilion, determined though he was to keep the secret, betrayed the fact that he nevertheless had a secret; the townsfolk, who liked to stand about near the posting stations to talk to travellers, were greatly impressed by the berline. They inspected it, glancing in at the occupants. Two children. That was suspicious in itself. Who were the mysterious strangers? People of high rank. Why, it might be . . . Why should it not be . . . ?

And there was Vallet, striding about, looking as though he could tell a good tale of he would, if he were not bound in honour to keep a secret.

One knowledgeable vagabond whispered to the postmaster as he changed the horses: 'Who do you think this is, eh?'

'They have not let me into their secrets,' murmured the postmaster.

'They have a royal look, it seems to me . . .'

'What do you suggest?'

'Louis and Antoinette.'

'Pish!' said the postmaster, who disliked responsibility. 'My job is to change horses, not to invent trouble.'

The horses were changed; the berline was ready to leave. A crowd gathered to watch it go, and in that crowd it was already being whispered: It is the King and his family.'

The berline drove out of Châlons.

The King smiled and looked reassuringly at his family.

'That was the testing place,' he said. 'We all decided, you

remember, that once through Châlons we should be safe.'

He closed his eyes. He was ready for a little nap.

The Queen listened to the clop clop of the horses' hoofs. Soon Axel . . . soon, she was thinking.

❖ ❖ ❖

Soon they would reach Pont de Somme-Vesle, and there they would find waiting for them the Duc de Choiseul and his cavalry; he would accompany the berline until they joined up with Bouillé's troops. 'Then,' said the King, 'all will be well, for if any try to stop us, they will have my loyal soldiers to face.'

The Dauphin was pointing to the green fields.

'Papa, Papa, let us get out and pick some flowers.'

'Should we not go on?' said the Queen. 'We are already late.'

'We have passed the danger,' Louis assured her. 'A few minutes at the roadside will do us no harm and will placate Monsieur le Dauphin.'

So the berline pulled up at the roadside, and the Dauphin and Madame Royal ran about shrieking with joy.

Antoinette sat back fanning herself.

'It was pleasant,' she said, 'to be with loyal people again.'

'That man Vallet was touching,' murmured the King, 'quite touching . . . in his desire to help us.'

In the distance they heard the sound of galloping hoofs, and they came nearer and nearer. It was a solitary horseman who slackened his pace a little as he approached the berline.

Antoinette and the King looked out of the window and they saw his face – excited and strained. He shouted: 'Have a care. Your schemes are known. You will be stopped.'

Then he was gone.

The King and Queen looked at each other in horror.

Then Antoinette called sharply to Madame de Tourzel: 'Bring the children back to the carriage. We must leave here at once.'

❧ ❧ ❧

They came into Pont de Somme-Vesle. The place seemed deserted. The outrider, who had ridden on ahead of them to make sure that fresh horses would be ready, met them with a worried expression.

The cavalry were not there.

While the horses were being changed there was great dismay in the berline, and eventually a single cavalryman appeared in the distance.

The King put his head out of the window and shouted to him: 'Where is the Duc de Choiseul?'

'He left, Sire, with his hussars.'

'Why so?'

'Sire, it was due to the fact that you did not arrive at the appointed time. It is three hours since you should have been here and, owing to the confused message of Monsieur Léonard, Monsieur le Duc de Choiseul thought that you had not been able to leave when you planned to do so.'

'He had orders to await our coming,' cried the King.

'Yes, Sire, but he greatly feared trouble. He had been asked questions. Many people passed along the road and wanted to know what the presence of troops in the district meant. Monsieur de Choiseul's reply was that he was guarding bullion which was to pass along the road to Paris. But there was a rumour, Sire, that you and the Queen were coming this way with the royal children, and the mayor was afraid that the peasants would rise against the soldiers and prevent your passing. Then there was a little trouble between some of the peasants and the soldiers. Monsieur de Choiseul thought he could do great harm by staying, and so moved off towards Clermont. He has sent messages by Léonard to the Marquis de Bouillé, explaining what he has done.'

The Queen said: 'It will be necessary for us to go on without the escort, and that we should do with all speed. Choiseul and his hussars have been unable to meet us, but there will be the dragoons waiting for us at Sainte-Ménehould.'

She sat back, determined not to show the others how alarmed she was becoming.

In the town of Sainte-Ménehould the rumours were wild. Something was afoot. All day the town had been filled with dragoons, who stood about as though waiting for some important event. They had swaggered into the inns; they had drunk very freely and they had gambled with the local inhabitants. Something was about to happen in Sainte-Ménehould, and it was to be kept a secret from the inhabitants. This was not right. But what could they do about it? They could guess! The soldiers, when plied with liquor, found it difficult to keep silent. Some important persons were coming this way and they were to escort them on their journey. Oh, depend upon it, it was a very important party.

'Mayhap it is the Prince de Condé or someone of that rank?' said the innkeeper.

'Mayhap. Mayhap.'

The soldiers strutted about the streets. Their commander,

the Comte de Damas, was alarmed. He saw that many of them were ready to be very friendly with certain young men who ostentatiously displayed the blue, white and red cockade.

Léonard arrived in the town with a confused message. The little hairdresser was distressed. His business was to create new styles for ladies' hair, not to ride about the countryside delivering verbal messages which he did not understand.

What was the exact message he had received from Monsieur de Choiseul? He could not quite remember. But he knew that Monsieur de Choiseul had thought it better to move from Pont de Somme-Vesle because the inhabitants of that place were suspicious of him.

Damas considered. He decided to send most of his troop to a spot five miles distant, where they could camp for the night. He himself would remain at Sainte-Ménehould, greet the King on his arrival, and tell him that he had had to divide his soldiers because of the growing rumours.

So when the berline arrived at Sainte-Ménehould it was to find again no escort waiting for them.

But Damas was there and it was good to see him. He was able to explain the position. His dragoons were not far off, and after passing Les Islettes the berline would take the quiet road to Varennes, and not far distant from that town they would meet Bouillé and his army.

It had been arranged that fresh horses would be waiting for them at the little villages where there would not be posting houses, and this would be ideal, for there would be no inquisitive people to wonder who they were.

There had been some delay and some misunderstanding, but, Damas assured the King and Queen, they were almost on the road to safety.

Among those who watched the handsome berline while the horses were being changed and who saw the respectful way in which the officer of the dragoons addressed the occupants of the coach, was the postmaster's son, Jean Baptiste Drouet.

He was a young man of strong revolutionary feelings, and he knew that the occupants of that carriage were *émigrés;* more than that they were persons of high standing, for who but the very rich would escape in such comfort?

He watched the berline take off and, as he did so, Guillaume, one of his friends, came up to him and said: 'Do you know who that was, Jean Baptiste?'

'It's some of those cursed aristocrats,' said Jean Baptiste. 'Why should we let them pass? It is our duty to detain them.'

'Someone rode in from Châlons. He says it is the King and Queen.'

Drouet brought his hand down sharply on his thigh. 'The King and Queen! And we let them pass!'

He leaped onto the wall of his father's house and shouted: 'Citizens! Do you know what has just happened? The King and Queen have passed this way. They are escaping to the frontier.'

A crowd gathered. They smiled. 'Oh, 'tis Jean Baptiste again. He's a firebrand, he is. He ought to go to Paris and tell them how to run the revolution.'

'Citizens!' cried Jeane Baptiste, 'what will you do? Will you wait here and bring the venom of France upon your shoulders?'

'What can we do?' asked one old wine-grower. 'Run after the fine carriage?'

'My God,' cried Jean Baptiste, 'somebody must. Come, Guillaume. They are on their way to Varennes. I heard it said.

We'll get there ahead of them and we'll raise the town against them. They must not pass beyond Varennes. Now we know why there are soldiers hereabouts. They'll be advancing on us . . . destroying the vines . . . destroying our homes. Come, Citizens!'

The people of Sainte-Ménehould shrugged their shoulders. Guillaume was reluctant. 'Don't make a fool of yourself,' said the wife of Jean Baptiste.

But Jean Baptiste was a son of the Revolution. He demanded that Guillaume go with him; and how could Guillaume refuse a command from such a good son of the Revolution?

They saddled their horses.

'They've had a good start of us,' said Jean Baptiste, 'but we know the short cuts to Varennes.'

✤ ✤ ✤

So the berline came into Varennes. Worn out with the day's adventures the King was dozing; the Queen had her eyes closed but she was not sleeping; she was too anxious to be able to sleep. Not until I reach Montmédy shall I be able to feel at rest, she told herself. Then Axel will be there. If Axel had stayed with us, surely all these mishaps would not have overtaken us.

It was ten o'clock; darkness had fallen and clouds obscured the moon.

The berline was now passing under a church which had been built above the street forming an archway; thus the way was very narrow; and as it slowed up to pass beneath this arch there was a cry of 'Halt!' and the berline came to an abrupt stop.

A man with a gun was at each window.

'Your passports?' said Jean Baptiste Drouet.

Madame de Tourzel produced the forged passport. 'I am travelling to Russia with my children and my servants,' she explained.

Jean Baptiste examined the passports; he was trembling with excitement. This was the greatest moment in the life of a country revolutionary. If the flight of the King and Queen were arrested, he, Jean Baptiste Drouet, would have the honour of bringing about this great event.

Had he not ridden with Guillaume into Varennes! And he had had to force Guillaume to accompany him, so Guillaume should not take more than his share of the triumph! Had he not forced the citizens of Varennes to sound the tocsins and waken the townsfolk! Had he not forced the revolutionary young men of Varennes to rise and prepare to help him in this matter! He was a good member of the Jacobin Club; and this was his hour.

'I fear,' he said, looking at that woman who was called Madame Rochet but whom he knew to be another, 'that you cannot pass.'

'My passport is in order,' protested Madame de Tourzel.

'I must take it,' said Jean Baptiste; 'it must be examined by the solicitor of this town. And you must accompany me to his house. Drive on,' he commanded the driver. 'You will be led to the house of Monsieur Sausse.'

The Queen looked out of the window and caught her breath with horror; she saw that the berline was surrounded by young men, and that many of them were wearing the badge of the revolution.

Monsieur Sausse, mayor, solicitor and shopkeeper of Varennes, was a man who did not like to make trouble. His sympathy was with the royalists, but if necessary he was prepared to keep that to himself.

He knew of the turmoil in the town; he resented the intrusion of this young firebrand from Sainte-Ménehould. He examined the passport. 'This passport is in order,' he said.

'Then let us go,' said the Queen. 'We are in a great hurry.'

They turned and made their way out to the berline.

But Drouet had taken Monsieur Sausse by the arm and shaken him.

'Are you mad? I tell you this is the King. Will you let him escape? You will be a traitor to France. You know what they do with traitors.'

Monsieur Sausse knew. He had seen what happened to them here in Varennes; he had heard even more terrible tales from Paris.

Meanwhile the bells were ringing and the people of Varennes were running into the streets.

Monsieur Sausse was not a brave man.

He followed the travellers out to the berline.

'I am afraid,' he said, 'that you cannot be allowed to leave Varennes to-night. You would not, I am sure, wish to travel by night. Allow me to offer you the hospitality of my house.'

The King looked at the Queen. There was resignation in the King's expression. There was desperation in that of the Queen. Both knew that they had no alternative but to obey.

So into the humble home of Monsieur and Madame Sausse went the King and Queen with their children, Madame Elisabeth and the two ladies-in-waiting.

And while Madame Sausse, overcome by the grand manners of her guests, hurriedly set about cooking and borrowing beds for them all, the news went through the town: 'The King and Queen are in Varennes.'

And in the square, Drouet gathered his revolutionaries. They came with their farm implements – their pitchforks and scythes.

And Drouet spoke to them, shouted at them, reminding them of their duty to the revolution.

✤ ✤ ✤

The King was the only one who was able to make a good meal, but the children, worn out by their exhausting day, were soon fast asleep.

Now that the Sausses could no longer be in doubt of the identity of their guests, they treated them with the utmost respect; and it was clear to the *émigrés* that if their hosts could have their way they would help them to escape.

But what could they do? The shouting filled the streets. Drouet had organised bands, armed with scythes and pitchforks, to guard the house and see that the prisoners did not escape.

While the King was eating, there was a commotion from without and two officers, de Damas and Goguelat fought their way through the crowds about the house and demanded to be taken to the King.

De Damas explained that he had planned to fight a way out of the town, but when he had explained his project to his men, many of them had deserted declaring themselves to be for the Nation. Goguelat had had the same experience.

Antoinette was in despair; she wondered how Louis could remain so stolid. Did he not care that all their plans had gone for nothing? She did not believe that he felt this as deeply as she did. He had fought for a long time against the plan to escape. He hated to run away from 'his children', as he insisted on calling these people who were determined to bring him low.

Oh, Louis, she thought. Had you been different we should not now be in this sorry plight.

Fresh hope came with the arrival of de Choiseul. De Choiseul, with some of his loyal men, fought his way through the crowds, wounding some of them as he did so.

De Choiseul had a plan.

'I suggest, Your Majesty,' he said, 'that we fight our way out of this town. Warning has now gone to Bouillé and it cannot be long before he joins us. If we can fight our way out of Varennes we can take the road to Montmédy, and on the way we shall be sure to meet Bouillé and his army.'

'If we went,' said the King, 'there would be fighting.'

'Sire, my soldiers are ready to fight.'

'My soldiers fight against my people!'

'They will learn that there are still men in France ready to fight for the King.'

'I cannot have bloodshed,' said Louis, shaking his head. 'What if the Queen were hurt? What if the Dauphin were killed? I should never forgive myself.'

De Choiseul bowed his head. He thought the King foolish in the extreme, because it was clear that he was throwing away one of his last chances of achieving freedom. But de Choiseul was a soldier accustomed to take orders, and the King's orders were that they stay.

Louis brightened. 'Before morning,' he said, 'Bouillé must be here. The sight of such a force will make all these people go quietly into their houses.'

'That is so, Sire,' said de Choiseul. 'All should yet be well if Bouillé and the army arrive in time.'

Antoinette listened; she felt drained of all strength. Her heart was beating an uneasy tattoo.

Bouillé must arrive in time. He must!

❖ ❖ ❖

It was half past six. The terrible night was over, and still Bouillé had not come. Into the town of Varennes two horsemen came riding; they leaped from their sweating horses and, surrounded by the men and women who had thronged the streets all that night, demanded to know whether a magnificently equipped berline had passed through the town.

It had arrived, Drouet told them; and it was here still; and the occupants, whom all now knew – owing to his astuteness – to be the King and Queen, were lodged in the house of Monsieur Sausse, the mayor.

'Conduct us there!' said one of the men. 'We are messengers from the National Assembly; we have come from Paris in the wake of the King, having received instructions to do so as soon as the flight was discovered.'

They were taken to the house of Monsieur Sausse, and into the presence of the King and Queen who were with their sleeping children.

'Sire,' said Bayon, one of the men, 'we come from the Assembly with this decree.'

The King took it. It declared that his rights as monarch had been suspended and that the two men who brought the decree had been instructed to prevent his continuing his journey.

The King turned to Antoinette. 'They are determined,' he said, 'to take us back to Paris.'

He threw the paper onto the bed in a mood of utter dejection. The Queen picked it up, screwed it contemptuously into a ball, and threw it on the floor.

The King said: 'Are you aware that Bouillé is marching on the town? If he should arrive while you attempt to force us to return, there will be bloodshed in Varennes.'

'Sire, we have had our orders from Monsieur de La Fayette and the National Assembly.'

'Do the orders of your King mean nothing to you?'

One of the men – Romeuf – looked shamefaced; the other boldly spoke up. 'We must obey the Assembly.'

'You do not understand,' said Louis. 'I merely wish to gather loyal troops about me, and then I shall parley and come to terms with those men who are making revolution. Wait until the arrival of Bouillé. He will be here in a short time. I am sure of that.'

Romeuf, who had often guarded the Tuileries and had been impressed by the courage of the Queen, looked anxiously at his companion and said: 'We had no instructions as to when we should make the return journey. We could wait for Bouillé.'

Bayon's answer was to stride from the room. He stood at the door of the house, and there was silence throughout the crowd assembled there.

Then Bayon shouted: 'They want to wait here until Bouillé arrives with his army. Bouillé is against the revolution. He will cut you to pieces; he will bring bloodshed to Varennes. He has trained soldiers at his command, armed men. And what have you but your pitchforks and scythes and a few guns which will not help you? We must set out for Paris as soon as we can arrange it . . . and we must take the royal family with us.'

'*A Paris!*' shouted someone in the crowd, and the others took up the cry.

In the room Romeuf looked anxiously at the Queen who had scarcely glanced at him since he had entered the house. Antoinette knew how to imply her disgust merely by making those who had displeased her feel that they did not exist at all as far as she was concerned.

Romeuf was very sorry that he had been selected for the task.

He said: 'Madame, I tried . . . I did all in my power . . . to delay our journey. When we passed through the towns on the route and I heard that such a magnificent berline had passed that way, I did everything in my power. . . . '

The Queen turned to him and her smile was very charming. 'I am sorry,' she said. 'I misjudged you. You are their slave . . . even as they would make us.'

'There is one thing you must do, Madame,' said Romeuf, almost happy now. 'Delay the return. Do not let them take you to Paris. . . . Do anything . . . but stay here . . . until Bouillé arrives. The mob can be scattered with a few shots, and your enterprise will have succeeded.'

Bayon returned to the room.

'I must ask Your Majesties to make ready at once for the return to Paris.'

'The children are not yet ready,' said the Queen. 'They must not be frightened. They are still sleeping, you see.'

'Then rouse them and prepare them at once, Madame.'

Madame de Tourzel and Madame Neuville wakened the children and dressed them. The Dauphin asked eager questions and was delighted to see the uniforms of Bayon and Romeuf. 'So we have soldiers,' he chuckled. 'Are you coming with us on our picnic?'

'Yes,' said Bayon grimly, 'we are coming with you, Monsieur le Dauphin.'

'I like soldiers,' confided the Dauphin.

Madame Royale was silent, understanding that they were all in acute danger.

'We must eat before we begin the journey,' said the King. 'We have had an exhausting night and are in no fit state to travel.'

Madame Sausse said she would prepare food. And she murmured to Madame de Tourzel: 'I shall take my time about it. I pray that the troops will arrive in time and save Their Majesties from these terrible revolutionaries.'

'Yes, do please be a long, long time preparing the meal,' said Antoinette.

Madame Sausse turned to her with troubled eyes. 'I will do my best, Madame, but I dare not delay too long. If we were suspected of trying to help you, I dare not think what would happen to us. Terrible things have happened, Madame.'

Antoinette put out a hand and grasped that of Madame Sausse. 'I know you will do your best.'

The meal was eventually prepared; but only the King and the children were able to eat. And when they had finished, still Bouillé had not come.

"What can we do now?' cried Antoinette. 'He *must* be near at hand. Oh God . . . what is keeping him?'

Madame Neuville suddenly slipped to the floor and began to writhe and thresh about with her arms and legs.

The Queen knelt down beside her. She cried to all those

looking on: 'Do not stand there. Fetch a doctor. We cannot travel with the lady in this state.'

Madame Neuville opened one eye. The Queen bent over her. 'You were very good,' she whispered. 'It was a very convincing fit.'

But the doctor was brought all too quickly, for he was in the crowd outside the Sausses' house, and five minutes after the Queen had called for help he was bending over Madame Neuville.

He gave her a potion which he declared would put her absolutely to rights, and he added that she was quite fit to travel without delay.

The mob was suspicious. 'No more waiting,' they cried. '*A Paris!*'

Still Bouillé had not come, and there could be no more waiting. The royal family got into the berline; the townsfolk of Varennes marched beside it, and behind it, in front of it and all around it. They would accompany it on the first stage of its journey until more ardent revolutionaries were ready to take their place.

'*A Paris!*' '*A Paris!*' shouted the crowds; and the Queen lay back exhausted, humiliated, bitterly wondering what was happening now at Montmédy.

✤ ✤ ✤

Almost an hour later Bouillé and his men came riding to the outskirts of Varennes.

They knew they were too late. The bridge had been broken down and there was no ford. All along the road they saw people armed with pitchforks; they heard them singing the songs of the revolution.

He was too late to overtake the berline. The people were in an ugly mood. It seemed to Bouillé that there was nothing he could do but go back the way he had come; he did not want to provoke a civil war.

Helpless, mortified, he retired from the scene.

✤ ✤ ✤

Then began the terrifying journey to Paris, which was much slower than the journey to Varennes had been.

In each town through which they passed crowds gathered. They had made it an occasion for revelry. The drunken peasants were waiting for the berline as it came along the road; they followed it for miles, peering into the windows, screaming insults at the family, reserving most of their insulting obscenities for the Queen who, more than any of the others, annoyed them because of the calm and haughty way she sat there, seeming not to see them.

'*A bas Antoinette!*' they screamed. '*A la lanterne!*' And they came to the window of the berline; they clung to it, brandishing their knives. Still she did not look at them; and her very dignity unnerved them, so that they fell away murmuring feebly: '*A bas Antoinette!*'

The heat was intense; the closed berline stuffy; the journey seemed interminable. There were two representatives of the National Assembly to guard them in the carriage; one was Petion, the other Barnave. Petion, one of the Jacobins, could not resist talking to the royal family, and he addressed most of his remarks to the Queen, for he felt she was more worthy of his interest than the others. They discussed the establishment of a republic, the aims of the Assembly.

'You must not think, Madame,' said Petion, 'that we of

the Assembly are like these rough people who peer in at you and shout insults. We have our reasons for demanding a change.'

He explained the sufferings of the people, and the Queen listened intently.

She said: 'Ah, if we could have talked together more often; if we could have understood each other's needs, mayhap this terrible thing would not have come upon us.'

Both Barnave and Petion were changing their views regarding the royal family as they travelled. Who were these people? Flesh and blood just as they were. Both Petion and Barnave would hold the little Dauphin on their knees, for the carriage was now very cramped by the extra passengers, and try as they might they could not help falling under the charm of the little boy as they had under that of his mother.

The Dauphin noticed the buttons on Barnave's uniform and demanded to know what the words on them meant.

'Can you read it?' asked Barnave.

The little boy slowly did so. *'Vivre libre ou mourir.'*

'That's right.'

'And will you?'

'We will,' said both of the men.

'What does it mean . . . live freely . . . ? I know what dying means.'

The Queen took the Dauphin from them. She smiled at Barnave. 'These matters are too deep for him,' she said.

And so the journey continued.

❖ ❖ ❖

Those interludes of sane conversation were rare. Continually they were subjected to indignities by the mob, who were all round the berline; their shouts rang through the quiet countryside.

Was there to be no respite?

Antoinette drew the blinds that she need not see those distorted faces.

'Draw up the blind!' shouted the raucous voices. 'We want to see you.'

The Queen sat still as though she did not hear.

'Draw them up,' said Elisabeth in terror.

'We must preserve some dignity,' said Antoinette calmly. 'We must have a little privacy.'

She was eating calmly as she spoke. The King was eating with his usual stolid enjoyment. Elisabeth was too frightened to eat. The mob continued to shout for a while, and then gave up shouting; and when the meal was finished, Antoinette drew up the blind and threw the bones out of the window.

Those who had been pressing about the carriage fell back in astonishment at such calm. They did not know that inwardly she was quaking with terror.

La Fayette was waiting for them outside Paris.

Inside the city the people lined the streets. Notices had been posted on the walls since it was known that the King and Queen were coming back.

'Whoever applauds the King shall be flogged; whoever, insults him shall be hanged.'

La Fayette was eager to avoid trouble, and he had arranged that the berline should make a circuit so that it need not traverse the densely populated streets.

The silence was dramatic. No sounds came from that dense

multitude as the berline crossed the Champs Elysées and made its way to the Palace.

Into the gardens of the Tuileries they went, back to their gloomy prison.

The berline drew up; and it was immediately surrounded by the mob. Still none spoke; the notices which had been posted throughout the city must be respected.

The National Guard was in position for the protection of the prisoners.

The King alighted and went on ahead. The Queen followed; and as she did so she saw in the crowd a face she knew well.

It was that of James Armand. Very prominently he wore the blue, white and red cockade.

Meanwhile Provence and Josèphe, travelling quietly and inconspicuously, had arrived at Montmédy and, having heard of the King's bad luck, crossed the frontier into safety.

Chapter XIV ❧

ALLONS, ENFANTS DE LA PATRIE

Back to prison. Back to the gloom of the Tuileries. They had tried and they had failed; and because of that failure they had taken yet a further step along the road to destruction.

Antoinette thought of Axel – continually she thought of him. Had he escaped? He must have, or she would have heard by now. She had learned from the guards who had travelled with them that it was known what part he had played in the escape. A price was on his head. If he ever set foot in Paris again he would be running great risks.

Shall I ever see him again? she wondered. What will be the end of all this misery?

She could not resist writing to him.

'Let me assure you; we are still alive. I have been terribly uneasy about you, and I am distressed because I know how you will suffer if you get no news of us. Do not return here on any pretext whatsoever. They know that you aided our escape, and we are watched night and day. I can only tell you that I love you. Do not be uneasy about me. I crave so much to know that you are well. Write to me in cipher. Let me know where I am to address my letters, for I cannot live without writing to you. Farewell, most loved and most loving of men.' Letters? What poor consolation!

❖ ❖ ❖

It was February in the Tuileries – eight weary months after the humiliating return to what could only be called captivity.

Life had been harder to bear than before the escape. There were guards in the Palace; they filled the gardens; they were determined not to let the King and Queen escape again.

Always the Queen's mind was busy with plans for escape.

'I have been foolish,' she declared again and again to her dear friends, the Princesse de Lamballe and Madame Elisabeth. 'When I might have learnt of state matters I danced and gambled. Now I find myself ignorant.'

'You are learning quickly,' said Elisabeth.

'And bitterly, little sister.'

It was true. That September following the return, the King had been forced to accept the Constitution. This meant that not only was absolute monarchy finished but that the King was shorn of all power. Government was to be by an elected body of men.

Louis had held out as long as he could, but he realised that if he accepted the Constitution there would be no reason for continuing with the revolution. It was true that when he gave way there was a lull in the riots.

But the Jacobins were not pleased at this turn of events. Their great desire was to continue with the revolution and, knowing that the King would not agree that *émigrés* should be recalled to France and sentenced to death if they did not return, they began to agitate for this.

The law was passed that November, but Louis, thinking of his two *émigré* brothers, and knowing that they would not return refused to have the death penalty pronounced on them. He applied the veto; and soon the whole of Paris – inflamed by the Jacobins – was calling out against a King who dared veto the desires of the government. Monsieur Veto, they called the King; and of course Madame Veto was blamed for the King's refusal to submit.

Meanwhile the *émigrés*, including Provence and Artois, talked of raising forces against the revolutionaries, and so angered the people of France. Antoinette cried out against them – for neither Provence nor Artois were in a position to help – and even Louis agreed that they were doing more harm than good to him and his family.

The Queen was now in despair. She was writing to Fersen and receiving letters from him. She was stunned by the behaviour of her husband who seemed unable to arouse himself from his lethargy. Again and again she thought how different their lives might have been if Louis had but possessed a little initiative, if he would only act, and could conquer the vacillation which seemed to beset him on every important occasion.

She wrote to her brother Leopold, who had succeeded Joseph, and implored his help. The countries of Europe, while not prepared to risk much on behalf of the King and Queen, were anxious that the monarchy should be preserved. They feared the rot might spread to them.

Leopold and Frederick of Prussia met and issued a call to other European nations to get together and save the French monarchy. Meanwhile Fersen was using all his powers to persuade his King, Gustavus, to come to the aid of the royal family.

The people in the streets were now saying that the Queen was sending secret messages to the foreign Princes imploring them to destroy the French. She was distraught. She knew for once that what was said of her was true.

'Nothing but armed force can set things right again!' she cried to Louis.

'I do not wish for bloodshed,' said the King.

'I believe,' she cried passionately, 'that you would see your crown trampled in the dust – I believe you would go smiling to your death, if they bade you.'

'My life is in their hands,' said Louis. 'I would be King through their love or not at all.'

She cried out in exasperated anger: 'Yes, I see. I see it is this meekness of yours that is bringing us to ruin.'

Then she burst into tears and flung herself into his arms. Louis comforted her.

'It is too much for you to bear,' he said. 'You must rest. You must let things take their course.'

'Louis . . . Louis . . .' she cried. 'How can we know what to do? I ask Leopold to put himself at the head of the armies and lead them across our borders. I tell him the revolutionaries would be terrified if he did because of what they have done to us. Then I am afraid. If Leopold marched, what would become of us? They would put our heads under the knife. What can we do? What *can* we do?'

Louis could only shake his head. Of what use was Louis? She went to Esterhazy who was about to leave for Sweden.

She cried: 'You are going to see someone who is a friend of us both. Tell him that although we are miles apart nothing can separate our hearts. It is a torment to have no news of those we love. Take this ring to him. I have always worn it. Now I would like him to wear it and think sometimes of me.'

There was an inscription on the ring; she read it for the last time: 'Faintheart he who forsakes her.'

And no sooner had she sent the ring than she was afraid. Would he see in it a reproach? Would he come to her – he for whom the French were waiting?

She wrote to him immediately and despatched the letter by yet another messenger.

'You must not attempt to come here. Your coming would ruin my happiness. I have a great longing to see you, do not doubt that, but you must not come here.'

He wrote to her. He thanked her for her gift. 'I live only to serve you,' he wrote.

She had received that letter on a cold day a week ago, and she re-read it and cherished it; and she thought of him, pleading her cause with Gustavus, begging Gustavus to act. But what cared Gustavus for Louis and Antoinette? He cared though for the preservation of the monarchy. He had said he did not care whether it was Louis the 16th, 17th or 18th who reigned in France. But the rabble should not be allowed to sweep away a throne.

I am foolish, she thought. My tragedy is that I learned what life was, too late. For so many years I thought it was made up of dancing and beautiful clothes, extravagant balls; then when it was too late I found that this was not so.

She smiled faintly, thinking of her beautiful Trianon. Ah, Trianon, shall I ever see you again?

It was easy to drift into dreams – and so pleasant; for only in dreams of the past was there happiness for her.

She heard a sound in her room suddenly. She did not move.

She knew that someone had silently opened a door. She had heard the turning of a key. She was alone in her apartments, and her rooms were on the ground floor. She dared not move. All through the days and nights she was tense, waiting . . . never knowing who would come upon her suddenly.

And now . . . someone was in her room.

'Antoinette.' She did not look round. She dared not. She thought, Oh, God, I am dreaming. It cannot be.

'Antoinette!'

He was coming towards her. It was a dream of course. She was delirious. In truth it could not have happened.

She turned and saw the familiar figure; the rough wig he wore, the all-concealing great-coat could not hide him from her.

She flew to him and threw herself into his arms. She let her fingers explore his face while the tears ran silently down her cheeks.

'It is a dream, I know,' she cried. 'But, oh Holy Mother of God, let me go on dreaming.'

'It is no dream,' he said.

And he wiped the tears from her cheeks.

'It is not truly you?'

'But it is. I have come to you – all the way from Sweden.'

'But why . . . why?'

'To see you. To hold you thus. Does not the ring say "Faintheart he who forsakes her"?'

'Oh, give me the ring, give me the ring. I should never have sent it. It has brought you here . . . to danger . . . to God knows what. Axel . . . my love . . . you are truly here. You are in this room, are you not? Oh, foolish one . . . foolish one to come and risk your life to see me.'

'Of what use is life to me when I do not see you?'

'Hold me tightly, Axel . . . for a little while. I wish to dream. I call you foolish . . . and foolish you are, to come here. But I am the greatest fool in the world because I have called you here, because I have brought to danger the one I love.'

'It is well that, in danger, we should be together.'

'At any moment you could be discovered. At any moment the guards may be at my window. They are all about us . . . Do you know there is a price on your head? There is nothing these beasts, this *canaille*, want more, than to find you. They know it was you who took us to Varennes . . . they know that if you had stayed with us . . . if you had not left us at Bondy . . . all would be well with us now, and ill with them. Axel . . . go . . . go quickly. But how did you come? But let us not stand here where any might see us; come into my little dressing-room. There we shall be safer. There is only Lamballe and Tourzel, and mayhap Elisabeth, who would see you. No other must, Axel. It is foolish to trust any . . .'

She drew him into the dressing-room. She lifted her hands to take off the wig. She ran her fingers through his thick hair.

'Let this minute go on and on . . .' she said. 'If it is a dream . . .'

'It is not a dream.'

'But how did you get here?'

'I had the key. You remember I had it when I came to get the children on that night. I have kept it. I walked past the guards. There are so many who look as I do . . . rough wig . . . great-coat . . . I was not even challenged.'

'And if you had been?' she asked, breathless at the thought.

'I have a good passport . . . forged, of course. I am supposed to be travelling to Lisbon on a mission from my King,' he said.

'That is my story. 'Tis true I am on a mission . . . It is this: I shall get you out of France and this time I shall do it thoroughly. I shall be with you the whole of the time. Nothing on earth will make me give up my part until you are safe across the frontier.'

'Axel . . .' she cried. 'What heart you put into me! What you set out to do . . . you do.'

'I have planned everything,' he said. 'I have come here to lay those plans before you and the King.'

The mention of Louis brought Antoinette back to reality.

'Louis will never go.'

'We must persuade him.'

'I fear we cannot. I have tried to persuade him. He has some idealistic notion that his place is with his people.'

'A people who do not want him.'

'He will not believe that.'

'We must persuade him. I hear terrible stories. You have been safe so far. Do you think you will go on being safe? Your life is in danger. How I wish you were not a Queen. How I wish you were only my love. Then I would not listen to protests . . . I would take you with me . . . whether you were willing or not.'

She lay against him. 'I like to hear you say that, Axel. It is fantastic, but it is beautiful. How I would love you to take me with you!'

Fersen said: 'If the King should refuse . . .'

She answered quickly: 'And the children?'

'You and the children . . .'

She let herself contemplate such a solution for she was still living in her dream. He had come to her, her lover, and he talked of taking her and her beloved children out of this hell.

417

This was a magic night, a night in which it was possible to believe anything. It was as though she had conjured up his image out of her longings. On such a night anything, however fantastic, could be true.

The Palace was quiet; now and then they heard the sound of the guards marching by. But in her little dressing-room they were safe.

She locked the door, shutting them in.

And that night she was alone with her lover, and they loved frantically, desperately, as though each feared that they might never love or meet again.

✣ ✣ ✣

The next day she went to Louis. She whispered to him: 'Fersen is here.'

'Impossible!'

'I thought so too. He has come disguised; he has plans.'

'What plans could there be?'

'You must see him. Come to my apartments at six this evening. Then it will be dark and there will be few people about. He cannot come to you, for fear of the guards.'

'There is nothing he can do,' said Louis.

✣ ✣ ✣

Louis came to the apartment. Fersen was in the dressing-room, and Antoinette took the King to him there.

Fersen kissed the King's hand and Louis confessed his amazement that he should have been able to get into the Palace.

'I come with plans, Sire,' said Fersen.

'It will be a hundred times more difficult to escape now,' said Louis; 'and the last attempt failed.'

'Sire, we learn by our mistakes. It was wrong to have travelled all together. We should have broken up the party and travelled more simply. I realise now the folly of the way we did it and yet, with a little luck then, we should have succeeded.'

'I have misused my chance of escape,' said the King. 'It is no longer possible.'

He did not look at Antoinette. She was standing, pale and tense, her arms folded across her breast. Oh, God, she thought, Louis will be defeated because he accepts defeat.

She loved them both – so much and so differently. She wanted to run to Axel and beg him to take her in his arms, never to leave her, but she wanted to cradle Louis' head in her arms and comfort him.

Fersen argued. It was at least worth an attempt. While the King was in Paris, while he accepted the new Constitution, it was difficult for the European countries to come to his aid. Once he was out of the country he could defy the Constitution; he could call loyal men to his aid, and he could fight for his throne.

Louis faced Fersen and said quickly: 'I could never try to escape, and for this reason: I have given my word to the National Assembly that I will not do so again.'

'But these men are your enemies.'

'It matters not. I have given them my word.'

Fersen knew that he was defeated. Louis, who could never make up his mind as to what action he should take in most circumstances, was firmly resolved on this.

He had given his word.

The King said: 'I will leave you now. Take care when you leave the Palace. Take care while you are in Paris. You risk your life to come here.'

Fersen bowed. 'My pleasure is to serve Your Majesties.'

Louis nodded. But he understood.

He went away and left them together.

✤ ✤ ✤

It was the last embrace; he held her as though he could never let her go.

She murmured: 'If I could but die at this moment . . .'

'Do not speak of dying,' he said roughly.

Then he released her and turned away, only to turn back and take her in his arms once more.

But he must be gone. Every moment he spent in the Palace was a danger.

She would be expected to appear in the salon, to talk, to seem as usual, and all the time her thoughts would be with him. Where is he now? Is he safe?

What had become of her life which had once been so gay, when the newest hair-style arranged by Monsieur Léonard had provided such excitement in her life?

Why should there be such violent contrasts in the life of one woman?

'You must not stay,' she said. 'You must go . . .'

'One day,' he said, 'I'll be back.'

She thought of the little Dauphin, who had said 'One day.' She thought of his dying in her arms.

'Don't say that,' she said. 'It frightens me. Whether we meet again or not I have this night to remember.'

'For ever . . .' he said.

She was alert. 'I hear the sentry. He is coming this way. Oh, go quickly . . . now, or it will be too late. He may look in. He may decide to search the apartment. Oh, go . . . my love . . . go quickly.'

He kissed her hands. She pushed him from her. She longed to keep him, and yet a greater need demanded that she send him away.

He was gone. She stood at the door, watching his figure swallowed up in the darkness.

Then she returned to her apartments. She heard the sentry marching past her window; and she covered her face with her hands as though to hold in her emotions.

The uneasy months were passing. Summer had come. In the streets a new publication was being sold. It was *La Vie Scandaleuse de Marie Antoinette*. Madame de Lamotte had supplied a great deal of the material which went into this and other compilations.

The Assembly had brought forward a proposal that priests who refused to swear to be loyal to the Constitution should be expelled from France. Louis, who was a devout Catholic, declared he could never assent to such a law. In all other matters he had given way. He had even declared war on Austria at the command of the Assembly – Austria, the country whose aim was to restore his monarchy.

It was characteristic of Louis that he should choose his weakest moment to stand out against the Assembly.

Monsieur and Madame Veto had dared attempt to oppose the Assembly, had dared to try to stem the tide of revolution.

It was hot June and the people gathered in the streets; life at the Tuileries had been lived too peaceably since the King and Queen had been brought back to Paris after their ignoble flight. It was time they were taught a lesson, since they had not yet discovered that the Assembly would not allow them to raise their voices in protest against the people.

'*Ça ira!*' was the song the people were singing as they gathered in the squares.

'*A bas le veto!*' they shouted.

They marched to the Tuileries, carrying banners to which had been nailed the symbol of a pair of ragged breeches – the sign of the *sans-culottes*, the name given to the revolutionary bands who had roamed the streets in their ragged clothes demanding bread and the downfall of the monarchy. They massed in the Place du Carrousel and the narrow streets which intersected it; they streamed along the Terrasse des Feuillants; and forced an entrance into the Palace itself.

Louis heard them. He said calmly: 'My people wish to see me. They must not be disappointed.'

'Do not be afraid, Sire,' said a member of the National Guard. 'Remember, Sire, they have always loved *you*.'

Louis took the man's hand and placed it on his heart. 'Feel if it beats more quickly than usual,' he said.

And the soldier was amazed, for the King's heart-beats were quite steady.

Elisabeth was with him. There was one fear in Louis' mind. 'Do not let them find the Queen,' he whispered.

Antoinette had hurried to her husband's apartments but was told to keep away.

'I will be with my husband,' she said.

'It is unwise, Madame. Your presence will inflame the people against him. Wait here in the Council chamber, while the King talks to them.'

She had the children with her; at such moments Antoinette had little fear for herself because all her alarm was for them.

Into the King's apartments the mob had burst. They paused and looked at Louis and Elisabeth who stood side by side, outwardly calm.

Many of them had never seen the royal family before, and they immediately mistook Elisabeth for Antoinette.

'The Austrian woman!' they cried.

Elisabeth had one thought. She believed they had come to murder Antoinette, and she stepped forward crying: 'Yes. I am the Austrian woman. You have come to kill me. Do so quickly . . . and go.'

One of the guards said: 'It is not the Queen. It is Madame Elisabeth.'

The mob fell back. They had turned their attention to Louis, and two of the guards escorted Elisabeth from the room.

Once again that complete calm of the King baffled them. If he had shown one sign of fear, one sign of haughty rancour, they would have fallen upon him and done him to bloody death. But the benign calm puzzled them. They stood back a little. They could only growl: *'A bas le veto!'*

One or two of the guards had placed themselves beside Louis. 'Citizens,' one cried, 'recognise the King. Respect him. The law demands it. We shall die rather than let any harm befall him.'

A butcher stepped forward. 'Listen to us, Louis Capet,' he cried. 'You are a traitor. You have deceived us. Take care! We are tired of being your playthings.'

'Down with the veto,' shouted the crowd.

'My people,' said Louis, 'I cannot discuss the veto with you.'

'You shall! You shall!' cried the crowd, and one or two men advanced threateningly.

Louis did not flinch. He stood on a stool and addressed

them. 'My people, I shall do what the Constitution demands of me, but I cannot discuss the veto with you.'

One of the men pushed forward his pike on which he had stuck the red Phrygian cap which was the symbol of liberty. Louis, with one of those inspired gestures which came to him naturally at such times of danger, took the cap and placed it on his head.

They stared at him. Someone cried: 'Long live the King!' The hard faces relaxed. Louis had once more saved his life.

❖ ❖ ❖

The mob had broken into the Council chamber in their search for the Queen.

They found her there. She was standing erect behind the table. Madame Royale was beside her; and on the table sat the Dauphin. Antoinette had turned his face towards herself so that he should not see the mob. Several ladies stood with her, including the Princesse de Lamballe and Madame de Tourzel.

A group of loyal guards stood about the table.

There was a shriek of delight. 'The Austrian woman!' Here she was at last. The woman of a hundred fabulous stories, the woman who had lived the most scandalous life of any woman in the world – according to the rumours rife all over the country. Antoinette – *l'Autrichienne*.

And there she stood, pale, handsome, looking beyond them as though they did not exist, showing no twitch of lips or eyes which might have betrayed the slightest nervousness.

It was the demeanour of the royal family which baffled the crowds whenever they met it. The sight of her standing there, the children beside her, must make the most sanguinary revolutionary pause. Madame Royale, so pretty, so charming, so gentle, so clearly adored this woman of a thousand evil rumours. The little boy – their own Dauphin – was clinging to her for protection.

But they must not forget that she was Antoinette.

They shouted insults and obscenities. Several of them held miniature gallows made of wood, from which dangled rag dolls. Cards were attached to these on which was written in red letters *'Antoinette à la lanterne!'*

A tricolor rosette was thrown at her. The Queen looked at it disdainfully as it fell on the table. 'Take it,' someone screamed.

'Oh, take it, Mama, please,' whispered Madame Royale; and to soothe her daughter, Antoinette placed it in her hair.

'A cap of liberty for the Dauphin!' cried another.

'No,' said the Queen.

'Madame, it is unwise to refuse,' murmured one of the guards; and a woman stepped up and crammed the cap onto the Dauphin's head.

He began to cry, for the cap stank horribly, and it had slipped down over his face.

Fortunately one of the revolutionaries, seeing that the little boy was in danger of suffocation advanced and removed the cap.

Red-faced and gasping, the little boy flung himself into his mother's arms.

Meanwhile the crowds filled the room, wrecking the furnishings, shouting insults, only kept from attacking the Queen by the fixed bayonets of the guards.

The heat of that day was intense; and the stench of the sweating bodies nauseated Antoinette. For three hours she was stared at and threatened; and every moment of that period was pregnant with danger.

A woman forced her way to the table and, disregarding the soldiers' bayonets, began to repeat some of the hideous stories she had heard of the Queen; she called the Dauphin and his sister bastards; she knew she was safe because, if the guards so much as touched her or any one of the mob, the crowd would tear them to pieces.

The Queen leaned forward suddenly. 'What have I done to you?' she asked softly. 'Have you ever seen me before? They have deceived you about me. I am the wife of your King, and the mother of your Dauphin. I am French as you are French. Tell me what wrong I have done you.'

'You have caused misery to the nation,' said the woman.

'That is what you have been told. I would never consciously harm France. I was happy when the people loved me.'

The woman's fierce expression collapsed suddenly.

She stared at Antoinette and burst into tears.

'You see,' said Antoinette, 'when you come face to face with me you know these tales of me to be false.'

There was a short silence. Then the weeping woman dropped a curtsy before she was dragged back into the crowd.

'She is drunk,' they cried and the vilifying continued. '*Antoinette à la lanterne!*' The Queen continued to stand. The Dauphin, his face hidden from the horror behind him, clutched at the lace of her bodice with hot and fearful hands.

But some fire had gone out of the mob. Their cries were less fierce. To see her there, so haughty, so very much the Queen, made it impossible for them to accept the lies which had been told of her.

And, after three hours of this terrifying ordeal, a shout went up that the Mayor of Paris had arrived with a detachment of the National Guard.

The crowd dispersed; and there was quiet in the pillaged Palace of the Tuileries.

She wrote that night to Fersen: 'I am still alive, though it seems I am so by a miracle. The ordeal was terrible. But you must not be anxious about me. Have faith in my courage to live through these terrible days.'

The men of the south were marching into Paris. Ragged, unkempt, and fiercer than the men of the north, these were the men of Marseilles, and their aim was to depose the King and end the monarchy for ever.

Relentless, ruthless, as they marched they sang a song which had been composed by one of the officers, and which they had adopted as the hymn of the revolution.

Into the capital they came, welcomed by the Jacobins, cheered as they assembled in the Champs Elysées.

And on the lips of all was the hymn of revolution:

> *'Allons, enfants de la patrie,*
> *Le jour de gloire est arrivé,*
> *Contre nous, de la tyrannie,*
> *Le couteau sanglant est levé . . .'*

The terror of life at the Tuileries had increased. There were more spies in the household. Each night mobs gathered outside the Palace and shouted threats at those within.

Antoinette wrote often to her lover. Fersen was desperate; he travelled from Sweden to Brussels, spending long hours at the Courts doing all in his power to urge the monarchs of Europe to unite and go to the aid of Louis and Antoinette. The Duke of Brunswick, the commander of the Austrian and Prussian armies, was preparing to cross the frontier. Fersen, irritated by the delay of this old soldier who refused to be hurried, was terrified that the Queen would be murdered before help reached her. He urged Brunswick to issue a manifesto threatening Paris with destruction if the royal family came to any harm at its hands.

The people congregated in the Place du Carrousel, in the Palais Royal and the Champs Elysées – indeed any spot where they could gather to talk about the manifesto.

❖　❖　❖

The hot weather continued and the tension increased. Elisabeth and the Princesse de Lamballe stayed with the Queen even during the night.

'I feel it in the air,' said the Queen. 'They are gathering against us now . . . and this time there will be no respite.'

They did not go to bed at all that night. They started at the sound of the tocsin; they listened, alert to the distant sounds. And all the time they were waiting.

They knew that the guard was being corrupted; and without the guard they would be brutally murdered, with the revolutionaries in their present mood.

The morning came. Sleepless, his hair unpowdered, his cravat loose, Louis came into the Queen's apartment.

'Louis, what next?' asked the Queen.

Louis shook his head. Antoinette thought: Even he is shaken at last.

Outside the window the guards were drawn up.

'Louis,' said Antoinette, 'you should show yourself. You should review the troops. You should let them see that you are a leader.'

The King turned to the window and looked out. Then, as though in a dream, he left the Queen.

A few minutes later she saw him from the window – unkempt as he was – walking between the lines of the troops.

'I have confidence in you,' he was saying. 'I know I can trust you.

Antoinette heard a jeering laugh from one of the men. She saw several of them break from their ranks and imitate the slow and somewhat ungainly walk of the King.

For what could they hope from such guards?

⚜ ⚜ ⚜

The Attorney-General of Paris came in haste to the Tuileries. He demanded to see the King, and was shown at once to the King's chamber where Antoinette was with him.

'The crowds are massing,' he said, 'for an attack on the Tuileries. It is necessary for you to leave at once.'

'For where?' asked Antoinette.

'You will be safest in the *manège*. The Assembly is in session, and the mob will not attack you while you are there.'

'We have troops to protect us,' said Antoinette.

'I fear not, Madame,' said the Attorney-General. 'All Paris is marching, and with Paris are the men of Marseilles. You dare not hesitate. You must think of the children of France.'

'We will accompany you,' said Louis.

Antoinette ran for her children and brought them to the King's apartment.

'We should leave at once,' said the Attorney-General. 'The *faubourgs* are on the march.'

Antoinette held the Dauphin's hand very firmly in hers and, as they came through the gardens, the little boy kicked the leaves at his feet. He was laughing. There were too many alarms in his life for him to take them seriously any more. As long as he was with his mother and the dirty people did not try to suffocate him with their red caps, he was happy.

'The leaves have fallen very early this year,' said the King in a melancholy voice.

There were already crowds gathered outside the Palace. They saw the royal family through the railings, and shouts of derision went up.

The little party reached the Assembly Hall in safety, and the King cried to all those present: 'Gentlemen, I come here to prevent a crime. I think I and my family cannot be safer than with you.'

The President's reply was that the Assembly had sworn to protect the Constitution, and the King could count on its protection.

The royal family were then placed in the box where the reporters usually sat. It was small and the heat was intense. The family sat there, and those who had escaped with them crowded about the box.

Outside there was murder and bloodshed such as had never been seen before during the whole of the revolution. Houses were looted; men and women dragged into the streets and cruelly murdered. Shots were fired; voices shouted in exultation and screamed in horror. The *faubourgs* were in revolt; the smell of burning was in the air.

Murder, rapine, pillage stalked the streets of Paris on that day. It was a day to remember with that of the St Bartholomew two hundred years before.

The Tuileries was looted. The Queen's apartments in particular were desecrated. The streets echoed with the terrible cry *'A la lanterne!'*

And all over Paris could be heard the triumphant song:

> *'Allons, enfants de la patrie . . .'*

In the crowd which was raiding the Tuileries was a young man who did not join in; he stood a little apart. His attitude was cold and detached.

Another man, too old to share in the violence of his friends, came up and stood beside him. 'Great days for France, Citizen,' he said.

'Great days,' agreed the young man.

'We are seeing the passing of an old regime which has lasted in France for many years.'

'Old regimes must pass,' said the young man. 'There must be new ones.'

'It is the way of life, and we must accept it.'

'We need not accept,' said the young man. 'We can make our own world.'

'Louis Capet has little hope of doing that.'

'Louis Capet could have done it,' said the young man. He paused and then went on: 'What imbeciles! How could they allow that *canaille* to enter? They should have swept away four or five hundred of them with cannons and the rest would still be running.'

'You are not in the riots, Citizen. You are not fighting for liberty. I see you are not a Frenchman.'

'I am from Corsica,' said the young man.

'Ah, it is for that reason that you remain cold.'

'Adieu,' said the young man. 'I'll be on my way.'

The old man looked after him. A strong face, a strange young man. Was it true, what he said?

Meanwhile Napoleone di Buonaparte turned his back on the riots and contemplated the power of arms appropriately used.

The family was homeless now. The Tuileries was unfit for human habitation.

Where should they go now?

It was decided that the Temple, that medieval palace which had once sheltered the Knights Templar, should be their home.

Antoinette cried out in protest when she heard. She had always hated the place. But it was not for her to protest. She must be grateful that a shelter was provided for her, grateful that she and her family were alive to need it.

The rioting had died down, and carriages were brought to the Assembly Hall. The postilions no longer wore the royal livery and their hats were decorated with the tricolor.

The carriage made a slow journey from the Assembly Hall to the Temple, the crowds shouting after it as it crawled along.

And so they came to the new home – ancient and gloomy, a more fearful prison than that of the Tuileries.

Chapter XV

THE KING ON TRIAL

Those who had been set to guard the King and Queen found it impossible to dislike them.

The Queen's aloofness, her determination to show no fear, aroused their respect. As for Louis, how could they call this man a tyrant when he was so gentle?

In the Temple they saw him accept the life of an ordinary man. He never complained; he ate heartily, took his exercise in the grounds, and was often seen walking in the courtyard with the Dauphin, the little boy's hand in his.

Watching the King and his son together they saw how human was this man, how indulgent, how unselfish. He would abandon himself to the Dauphin's game, and when he taught the boy how to fly his kite, it would seem that the most important task possible was the maintenance of that kite. They would measure the distance with their steps in the courtyards, and the Dauphin's shrill voice could be heard consulting with his father.

It was impossible for ordinary human beings to hate this man or see him as a tyrant, except when they were intoxicated by wine or the words of violent revolutionaries.

When they first arrived at the Temple certain alterations had been allowed to be made in the place for their comfort. Four rooms were made into the King's suite and another four were refurnished for the use of the Queen, Madame Elisabeth, Madame Royale and the Dauphin.

But although the Assembly had saved the lives of the royal family they wished them to understand that Court life, as they had once known it at Versailles, was over. They accordingly removed the Princesse de Lamballe and Madame de Tourzel to another prison. The royal family must live simply.

Antoinette had been greatly saddened at parting with these two. Marie de Lamballe had been her great friend for so long that it seemed an unnecessary hardship to do without her now.

'It would seem,' said Antoinette, on bidding farewell to her friend, 'that they look about them and say "What would hurt her deeply?" And they do that. There are times when I am terrified . . . terrified of the future.'

She had had a strand of her hair put into a ring, and the inscription engraved on it: 'A tress whitened by misfortune.'

'Keep it, dearest Marie,' she said, 'in memory of me.'

Now they must live simply, as humble people, the King adapted himself with ease; so did Madame Elisabeth. She had always wanted the quiet life and had often thought of going into a nunnery. Life at the Temple, she told Antoinette, could not be unlike life at a convent.

'All about a convent there is peace,' said Antoinette. 'All about the Temple there is terror.'

She gave herself up to her children – playing with them, teaching them. Sometimes, when they laughed at their play, she would laugh with them; but always she was straining her ears for those sounds in the streets which could grow to a roar; always she was waiting for the next terrifying ordeal.

✤ ✤ ✤

Jacques Rene Hébert, Deputy Public Prosecutor of the Commune, was in charge of the Temple. He was the worst kind of revolutionary leader, inspired by no feelings but greed and envy. An unscrupulous criminal, he had been poor when the revolution began and had seen in it, as had so many, a means of profit and glory. Now he was a man of power. He had established his own newspaper *Père Duchesne*; and in this he vilified the monarchy.

As soon as he took charge of the Temple there was a subtle change in the place. No one dared show leniency towards the King or Queen for fear that in Hébert's eyes they would be suspected of having royalist leanings.

He would watch the Queen whenever he could; she gave no one outside the Temple the opportunity of seeing her; she never ventured out; she could not endure the indignity of being shouted at by the mob.

Hébert, deeply sensual, could not keep his eyes from the Queen. For all her sufferings, she was still a beautiful woman; she had preserved her dainty charm; and the whiteness of her hair accentuated her fine clear skin even as it had in the days of its golden beauty.

He showed her some civility and asked that he might speak with her.

He had tried to explain to her that the revolution was for the good of France.

'I do not think,' said Antoinette haughtily, 'that you and I could agree on these matters.'

435

'We could discuss them,' Hébert had suggested.

'I prefer not to,' said the Queen.

She rose and left him staring after her with lustful eyes.

In his paper that day he asked why fat Louis and the Austrian strumpet should be allowed to live at the country's expense. Was it not time for the employment of the national razor?

⚜ ⚜ ⚜

On a warm September day the people began pouring into the streets.

'Have you heard? The enemies of France are advancing.'

'The Prussians are across the border.'

'Verdun has fallen. The Prussians swear that ere long they will be in Versailles to drink the health of the Austrian woman.'

'It shall not be.'

'*Antoinette à la lanterne!*'

They were mad with the lust for blood. They ran into their houses to snatch up weapons. They congregated in the Place du Carrousel and the Champs Elysées.

'Citizens, to the *lanterne* with all these accursed aristocrats! It is they who have massed the world against us. Why should we wait, Citizens? Why should we wait?'

Their inhuman yells filled the streets as they marched together.

'*Allons, enfants de la patrie . . .*' they sang, and the words inspired them with greater lust to kill.

A crowd had assembled at La Force prison. 'We want justice,' they cried. 'Bring out the prisoners. Let them be tried.'

They knew of one exalted prisoner in La Force prison. It was the Princesse de Lamballe.

They insisted on breaking into the prison and dragging her before the tribunal, which was presided over by Hébert.

He looked at the woman; the proud tilt of her head reminded him of the Queen, and a savage fury possessed him.

'Are you acquainted with the plots of the Palace?' he asked.

'I know of no plot,' answered the Princesse.

'Swear to love liberty and equality. Swear to hate the King, Queen and royalty.'

The Princesse did not answer. Like an accursed aristocrat, thought Hébert, she stood, haughty and unmoved by his threats.

He shook her. 'Swear . . . swear . . . if you value your life,' he demanded.

'I will take the first oath,' she said coldly. 'I could not take the second. I should merely lie if I did so.'

Hébert looked about the court; the mob was pushing its way into the room. He could put her in safe keeping or he could send her back to prison. The latter would be to send her to certain death – and violent horrible death – for the mob were waiting for her and they would spare her nothing.

She had been an intimate of the Queen. The Queen had kissed her often.

'Take her away,' he said.

He had the satisfaction of hearing the gasp of demoniacal glee from the crowd as she stepped into the street, a guard on either side of her. But what were two guards in such company? He saw a knife raised; he saw the red blood of an aristocrat. The Princesse had fallen swooning to the ground and the crowd were upon her.

Outside the Temple the crowd was calling for Antoinette.

'Come to your window, Antoinette. See what we have here for you.'

The shouts and blood-curdling screams filled the Temple.

The King went to the window, and started back in horror at what he saw.

'Antoinette! Antoinette! Come to the window, Antoinette!'

The shouts continued. 'Come and see your dear little friend. Come and kiss her lips now.'

Antoinette was behind her husband.

'No,' said Louis. 'No . . . no! Go away.'

'I must see. I must see . . .' cried the Queen.

But Louis had seized her and forced her back into the room.

Elisabeth was with them. Her horrified eyes went to the window; the head of their dear friend was scarcely recognizable. It was fixed on a pike, covered with mud and blood; and behind it on other pikes came the remains of the once beautiful body of the Princesse de Lamballe.

'Come and kiss the lips of the Lamballe,' chanted the crowd. 'Come, Antoinette! It is your turn now . . .'

Antoinette did not see that ghastly sight, thanks to the intervention of Louis who for once was prompt. But she understood. She fell fainting to the floor.

Later that night a ring was smuggled in to her. Someone had managed to tear it from the finger of the murdered Princesse and return it to the Queen.

Engraved in the ring were the words 'A tress whitened by misfortune'.

It did not seem to matter to the Queen that the National Guard had managed once more to save the royal family from the mob.

438

'I feel my heart is broken,' said Antoinette that night. 'I feel that I have reached the very dregs of sorrow. I know that all feeling will be soon drained from me and that I shall wish only for death.'

Three weeks later there was more shouting in the streets. This time the shouts were of joy.

'The monarchy is abolished,' cried the people. 'The man in the Temple is no longer Louis Seize. He is Louis Capet.'

Now it was the delight of all in the Temple to show the Capets that they were ordinary folk. The lowest servant would sprawl on a chair and put his feet on the table in the presence of the Queen. An uncouth couple named Tison were brought ostensibly to keep the cell clean, but their main work was to spy on the family. Any who were likely to come into contact with them were ordered to address them as plain Monsieur and Madame; and to take off a hat when addressing them would be considered an insult to the new France wherein all men were equal.

The family went about its daily life with quiet dignity, teaching the children, playing with the children, subdued, a certain hopelessness manifest in their faces.

The children were charming, and even the rough servants could not help softening towards them. This was particularly so in the case of the Dauphin. Even the grimmest of their captors – even Hébert – was not quite immune from the Dauphin's charm.

Then came that terrible day when Louis was ordered to make ready to leave his family.

'Where are you taking me?' he asked.

'To other quarters.'

'In this building?'

'Yes, in this building.'

Louis was less distressed. They were not to be entirely separated then.

He had to learn that his jailers had no intention of leniency for, although he was kept in the same building, he was not allowed a sight of his wife or children, nor was he given any news of their health.

Antoinette lost her control when he prepared to go.

'No,' she said, 'this is too cruel. In all our misfortunes we have been together.'

'Have courage,' said Louis.

'I cannot let you go. I cannot.'

'Remember the children. We shall meet soon. They cannot separate us for long.'

She kissed him fervently, remembering all his goodness, and she was filled with remorse because she had loved another man more than this kind Louis.

'It is more than I can bear,' she cried. 'I would they would kill us and put us out of our misery.'

But the children were coming in, and they must hide their grief.

'Papa,' said the Dauphin, 'where are you going?'

'Away for a little while, my son. I'll be back.'

And with a kiss for them all, and a pat on the head for the Dauphin, he went.

Antoinette received no news of Louis. She could only wonder what was happening to him.

'Oh, Louis . . . Louis . . .' she would cry into her pillows at night. 'Where are you? Why do they torture us?'

She was allowed no newspapers. The woman, Tison, watched her every move. Everything she said, everything Elisabeth or the children said, was falsely recorded, was twisted . . . written down to be used against them.

❖ ❖ ❖

During that December of the year 1792 Louis stood on trial for his life. The revolution was victorious. The French had turned the tide of war in their favour. Their enemies had evacuated Verdun and retired across the frontier.

France would show the world that it cared nothing for the rattling sabres of the King's friends.

Louis was accused of treason, of assembling armed forces to attack Paris.

He protested but mildly. 'I have always had the right of ordering troops,' he explained patiently, 'but I never had the intention of shedding blood.' And when they continually referred to him as Louis Capet, he mildly reproached them. 'Capet is not my name,' he said, 'it is the surname of one of my ancestors.'

They continued to call him Capet; and they continued to call him traitor.

'The tree of liberty grows when it is watered with the blood of tyrants,' said one.

'I vote for death,' cried Robespierre.

'I vote for the death of the tyrant,' declared Danton.

There was another who voted for death; the Duc d'Orléans.

The voting was over, and the President announced the result.

'365 have voted for death,' he announced; '286 for detention or banishment; 46 for death after a delay, as an inseparable condition of their vote; 26 for death, while expressing a wish for the sentence to be revised by the Assembly. I declare, therefore, in the name of the Convention, that the punishment pronounced by them against Louis Capet is that of death.'

There was silence in the great hall; and the man who seemed less disturbed than any was the King himself.

There was one last interview.

She had known, as soon as she had been told that she might see him. She threw herself into his arms and clung to him, weeping bitterly and calling down curses on the men who had condemned him to die.

'Nay,' he said, stroking her hair, 'remember the children. And you must not blame these men. They thought they did their duty. You must forgive them, Antoinette, as I do.'

The Dauphin cried: 'Where are you going, Papa? Why do you say good-bye?'

And Louis took the little boy onto his knee and told him gently that he was going away and that they would never meet again.

'They have decided that I must die, my son. One day you will understand; and never, my dear boy, try to avenge your father. Try to forgive all those who have sent me to my death, for only in this forgiveness can there be peace in our country. One day, if God is willing, you may be King of this country. Remember, my dearest boy, that a King is the father of his people. He must never set himself up as their executioner.'

'Papa, I do not want you to go. I want to fly our kite together . . .'

'Ah, my son, that is of the past. Promise me what I ask. Promise me now, for there is little time.'

'I promise,' said the Dauphin.

'Make the sign of the cross, that it may be a sacred promise.'

The Dauphin did so.

'Love your mother well. And be a good Catholic. Then you too, as I do, will find great comfort in your faith.'

Madame Royale was kneeling at his feet, weeping quietly, and Louis, knowing that his presence with them could do nothing but increase their grief, left them.

He went to his confessor and as they sat together he said to him: 'Why must one love and be loved?'

❧ ❧ ❧

He did not see the Queen again. 'It would be too painful for her,' he said.

His hair was cut and he was prepared for his journey.

Those who watched him go were shaken. 'Such courage in the face of death is not human,' they said.

He stood on the scaffold. He unbuttoned his shirt himself, and his fingers showed no sign of trembling. He lifted his hand suddenly and said in a loud firm voice:

'Frenchmen, I die innocent. I pardon my enemies, and I pray God that my blood may not fall back on France.'

That was all.

When it was over the executioner held up the head of King Louis XVI, and a few cried: 'Long live the Republic!'

But the cry was half-hearted; the crowd could not forget the calm acceptance of his fate by the man who had been their King.

The Duc d'Orléans was smitten with a terrible remorse such as he had not believed possible and when, on his return to the Palais Royal, his little son, the Comte de Beaujolais, came running to meet him, he could not bear to look at the boy.

'Go away from me now,' he said to the astonished child, 'for I do not think I am worthy to be your father.'

And all that day there was a silence throughout the Capital as though of mourning.

Chapter XVI

THE WIDOW IN THE TEMPLE

She sat in her prison – the widow Capet – and there were those among her guards who were stirred to pity.

In the streets there were still many who called for her blood; but those who came into contact with her could not but respect her. There were some who were incapable of pity. There was Simon the rough cobbler, uncouth and of the gutter, who had been chosen by Hébert because he feared the compassion of the more cultured. Simon was brutalised; it amused him to spit on the floor of the Queen's prison. There was Madame Tison, asking herself a hundred times a day: 'Why should I be poor and she be rich? Why should I have lived in a garret while she lived in luxury in that wicked Trianon?'

But there were others.

There was François Toulan, one of the guards of the Temple. He had been as eager as any to fight for the revolution; he had been among those who had stormed the Tuileries and shouted for the blood of the King and Queen. It was a different matter when he saw the Queen every day.

'How she suffers!' he would murmur to himself as he stood on duty. The Dauphin came close and looked at him.

'What's that medal?' he demanded.

And Toulan had invented some story, for he was ashamed to say he had won it for pillaging the Tuileries and bringing distress to the boy's family.

Toulan longed to do something to make up for his conduct on that June day, so he stole the King's belongings which had been put in the security of the Commune – there was a locket containing some hair of Madame Royale's, a watch, a seal and a ring – and took them to the Queen, for it was easy to reach her now, far more easy than it had been when the King was alive.

'Madame,' he said haltingly, 'I have brought you these.' For some seconds Antoinette would not look, expecting mockery. He thrust them into her hands, and when he saw the sudden rush of tears he turned quickly away. But she knew then that she had a friend.

✣ ✣ ✣

Toulan could not rest now. He longed to set the Queen free. Greatly daring he asked for a private interview with a General who was an official in the War Office. He knew that General Jarjayes was a secret supporter of the monarchy, and he suggested to him that, with the help of one of the regular guardians of the Temple such as himself, and the money which such as General Jarjayes could provide, the Queen's escape could be brought about.

The General was ready to consider this plan and asked Toulan to keep his eyes open and see how it could be brought about.

The Queen and Elisabeth sat in the small room with the bars across the window. They were working on a piece of embroidery. It was good to keep the hands busy although, as Antoinette had said, that did not prevent the thoughts from going their own way.

They had heard news this day; it was news which made the Queen very thoughtful.

She had heard that James Armand had been killed fighting for the French last November at the battle of Jemappes.

'Poor James,' she said. 'I shall never forget seeing his face close to mine . . . he was a member of the mob then . . . one of our enemies. Little James, whom I had nursed and kissed so often. You remember how he used to call himself my little boy?'

'He was a jealous child,' said Elisabeth. 'I remember seeing him look at little Louis Joseph as though he could kill him.'

'Poor James Armand! Monsieur James, I used to call him, do you remember? It was my fault, you know, little sister. I forgot little James when I had my own children, I used him as a substitute for my own. You cannot use people like that. What a pity such knowledge comes to us too late.'

They were interrupted by the arrival of the *illuminateur*.

'We are trying our eyes,' said Antoinette, 'and did not realise it. Let us put our work away now. To work by the light of the lamp tires me.'

The *illuminateur* went straight to the lamps but his two little boys, who always accompanied him, came to stand before the ladies and stare at them.

'And how are you these days?' asked the Queen.

They did not answer. They just smiled and nudged each other. Antoinette wondered what they had heard about her.

The little boys always came and, knowing they were coming, she saved delicacies from her meals for them. She in any case had little appetite.

'Have you come to see what I have for you to-day?'

They smiled and nodded.

'Then see here . . .'

She watched them eat. They did so with relish, looking at her and Elisabeth as they did so, smiling and nudging each other.

Antoinette was reminded with a bitter pang of those days at Trianon when the children had gathered round her and she had given them bonbons. These children were grimy; the oil of the lamp was on their trousers, smocks and big floppy hats; their faces were none too clean. But she had always been fond of children and she liked to see these each day.

The *illuminateur* did not speak to her; he was afraid of appearing royalist.

Toulan looked in. He said: 'Oh, it is the *illuminateur*. And the children. Ah, Monsieur *l'Illuminateur*, you bring your children that they may learn your trade and soon do your work for you.'

'They could,' said the *illuminateur* briskly, hoping that Toulan might find jobs for the boys in the prison. 'They're bright and old enough.'

Madame Tison came in; her eyes narrowed when she saw the children.

'Here, what's that you got?' she demanded.

'She gave it to us,' said one of the boys, pointing to the Queen.

'What else she give you, eh?' The woman Tison was feeling in their pockets, her mouth tight, her eyes shining; she was hoping to find some message on the boys which the Queen had given them. Disappointed she said: 'Well, don't stand there looking as though you are in the presence of the Almighty. We're all equal now, you know.' The Queen smiled at the boys as though the woman had not spoken; and Toulan continued to look at the boys.

✤ ✤ ✤

The next day the lamplighter came alone. The Queen was disappointed. She had liked to see the children.

She noticed that he fumbled with the lamps, and when she looked at him more closely she saw that he was a new man.

The woman Tison was in the next room and the lamplighter moved closer to the Queen. He whispered: 'Your Majesty, Toulan persuaded the lamplighter to allow me to come in his place. We bribed him. I told him that I was eager to see the prison and the Queen. He is now enjoying himself in a tavern. I had to see you for myself to make certain that I could trust Toulan.'

'You are . . .'

'Jarjayes.'

'My dear General . . .'

'Madame, it is my earnest wish to free you from this place. I have been in touch with the Comte de Fersen. He will not rest until you are free.'

In that moment the Queen felt again a desire to live. The thought of possible escape lifted her spirits and it seemed to her that life could still hold some meaning for her.

'We have to work this out with the utmost care. Toulan

thinks that Lepître, the commissioner of the prison, may help. Everything depends on this man and whether he is amenable to bribes.'

'I understand,' said the Queen. 'Have a care. The Tison woman watches continually.'

'Ask me questions about my children and we will talk under cover of that.'

The Queen did so, and Jarjayes answered, interspersing his answers with an account of what they planned, keeping his eyes on the door while he talked, for fear Madame Tison should make an appearance.

It might be possible for the Queen and Madame Elisabeth to leave the prison disguised as municipal councillors, with large hats, cloaks, big boots and of course the sash of the tricolor. They would need not only forged passports but the co-operation of Lepître, the only man who could conduct them out of the prison.

'My children . . .' murmured the Queen.

'I would come as the lamplighter, bringing clothes for the Dauphin and Madame Royale, so that they would look exactly like the lamplighter's children. I should lead them out with me.'

'And the Tisons?'

'We should have to find some means of drugging them.'

'They take snuff,' said the Queen.

'Drugged snuff would be the answer. I dare stay no longer. Be ready. I trust it will be soon.'

❖ ❖ ❖

Lepître had been a schoolmaster before the revolution. He was a sick man, pale, delicate from childhood, and he longed to get away from the town and live in the country; but he needed money to do this.

It was a daring scheme and Lepître was not a daring man. If he were discovered leading the two most important prisoners out of the prison, what would happen to him? When he considered that, he trembled with fear.

He dared not do this thing. Yet if he had the money, if he escaped with them, he could live in quiet in the country for the rest of his life. He was not a violent man; he could not endure violence. He visualised a little cottage far away from the big towns, where at any moment frightening things could happen.

It should not be difficult. They had the guard Toulan to help them. The Tisons could easily be drugged. All he need do was walk out of the prison with confidence – for who should challenge him, who could suspect that the two *municipaux* were the Queen and Madame Elisabeth? Waiting outside the prison would be two carriages, and in the second of these he would be driven out of Paris.

And for that night's work he was offered a lifetime of peaceful living in the country.

'I will do it,' said Lepître.

A great deal of money was needed for the enterprise, and Jarjayes found it difficult to raise it. It was necessary to wait awhile until he could sound those whom he could trust with the plan.

They needed forged passports. Lepître could provide these, but Lepître was nervous, and he was showing signs of strain.

Madame Tison noticed it. She said: 'And what's the matter with you? You look anxious this morning, Citizen.'

'It's my leg paining me,' Lepître answered, indicating his lameness.

Madame Tison nodded grimly. 'This is a different job from teaching a lot of children, eh?'

The ex-schoolmaster agreed that it was; he tried to talk of the old days, but all the time he was conscious of Madame Tison's watching eyes. She was alert. There was no doubt of that. She hated royalty; she was a passionate exponent of equality, and her passion seemed to give her an extra sense. How could one be sure what she suspected?

The money was found at last, and passports were prepared. Lepître liked the feel of good money in his pockets. It was so simple really. The drugged snuff would not be so very difficult for him to administer. He would go into the Tisons' room and, sitting over a bottle of wine with them, offer them his snuffbox; he would stay with them until they nodded and slipped off into unconsciousness. Everything would be ready, waiting. The General would come in, disguised as the *illuminateur*, and with him he would bring greasy smocks, trousers and floppy hats; the royal children would be hastily dressed in these garments; and Jarjayes would calmly lead them out of the prison to where the carriage was waiting. Meanwhile Lepître would arrive in the Queen's cell with the garments for the Queen and Madame Elisabeth; and when they had donned them he would conduct them out of the prison. In less than an hour after that they would be driving out of Paris.

It was the day before that arranged for the escape. Lepître called on Madame Tison. 'I must have a talk with you both to-morrow evening,' he said. 'Then your husband will be there, eh?'

'Yes, if you wish it,' said Madame Tison.

'I'll be along about dusk, I should think. See that he is here then, that I may talk to you both.'

The woman nodded.

'Have a glass of wine now you're here, Citizen,' she said.

So he went into her room. It would be well to rehearse what should happen on the next day.

He would sit at her table as he was sitting now. He would drink a glass of wine, talk of what he had seen that day in the Place du Carrousel or the Place de la Revolution; he would talk about the prisoners.

'Your wine is good, Madame Tison.'

She grunted: she was an ungracious woman.

'All is well with your prisoners, I trust?' he went on.

Again she grunted. 'They make little trouble. How could they? We're the masters now, eh, Citizen?'

'We are the masters now,' he said with the air of a good patriot. 'Are the children playing with them now?'

'The boy is in the courtyard, playing with that stick of his . . . prancing about, pretending it's a horse and he's riding it. A difference, eh, Citizen, from the old days! A stick now, instead of a horse all fitted up with gold and silver embroidery.'

'A great difference. And the girl?'

'Quiet she is . . . I don't trust her . . . never did trust people who were too quiet.'

It seemed to Lepître that her eyes were boring into him. He found it difficult to repress a shiver.

He drew out his snuff-box. 'You like a pinch of snuff, I understand.'

Her eyes gleamed. She was rapacious; she would never refuse anything; and Tison was the same. That was why they could be relied on to take the snuff.

This was exactly how it should happen to-morrow evening.

'Why, you don't keep the box still, Citizen.'

So she had noticed his shaking hands. He fancied there was a malicious look about her eyes.

She took a liberal pinch appreciatively.

'Did you hear, Citizen Lepître,' she said, still keeping her eyes on him, 'how the *émigrés* are falling into our hands? It's like swatting flies, they say. They're trying all manner of means to get out of the country. It makes me laugh.' Madame Tison rocked in her chair with amusement. 'Trying to get over the frontier . . . and some of them have been managing it. Do you know how? Forged passports . . . There have been more people caught with forged passports these last weeks, Tison tells me, than during the last two years.'

'F . . . forged passports!' stammered Lepître.

'Well, there's no need for you to look alarmed. We're catching them, Citizen. We're catching them.' The woman leaned towards him. 'They tell me they recognise these forged passports at a glance. Then . . . they drag 'em out of their fancy carriages . . . and it's to the *lanterne* without delay. I'll take another pinch of snuff, Citizen Lepître. Why . . . what's wrong? You got the ague? You're shaking so.'

He stood up; his fear seemed to form a haze about him so that he could not see her clearly.

She knows, he thought. She has found out.

'I'll be getting to my own quarters, Citizeness,' he said. 'I feel a little dizzy. This leg of mine has been paining me and I've had one or two of my sick turns lately.'

'I should go to your bed, Citizen; and I'd stay there for a day or so.'

❖ ❖ ❖

He spent the night pacing up and down his room. He brought the uniforms of the municipal councillors from the chest in which he had hidden them. He felt so terrified that he could scarcely stand. Sweat poured down his face; he lay on his bed trembling.

I can't do it, he thought.

And in the morning he went to Jarjayes.

'I suspect the woman Tison,' he said, 'and I cannot do it. I dare not.'

And without Lepître it was impossible to carry out the plan.

There was no hope, thought Antoinette. Everything that was begun failed to reach fruition.

'We are doomed,' she said to Elisabeth.

There was another plot, but this time she did not have high hopes. She knew that there were several royalists in the prison and these were constantly working for her escape. Toulan had been suspected of being too friendly with the Queen, for Madame Tison had reported that he visited the Queen's cell frequently and had conversations with her; therefore Toulan was removed. Jarjayes, in view of Lepître's fears, had thought it wise to leave Paris.

It seemed to the Queen that many of the battalion who had been set to guard her had royalist sympathies. The commander, Cortey, had let her know that he was working with friends to bring about her escape. There was the Baron de Batz, the hero of many fantastic adventures, who was plotting to save the family and proclaim the Dauphin as Louis Dix-sept.

It was a simple plan, as all these plans seemed before it was attempted to carry them out. The Queen, Madame Elisabeth and Madame Royale, dressed in the uniform of the soldiers, were to walk out of the prison with loyal members of the guard. The Dauphin was to be hidden under the heavy cloak of one of the officers, and they would all march together.

The day was fixed; the uniforms were ready; but they had reckoned without the spies with whom they were surrounded.

A word in the right quarter and, when the conspirators were ready to leave the prison, they found that one of their jailers, the uncouth Simon, was there to prevent them.

Antoinette could wish afterwards that there had been no attempt. Now she was more rigorously watched; she and Elisabeth were not allowed to do their embroidery. Madame Tison said that in her opinion all those stitches 'meant something'. There was some code in the needlework by which they conveyed those thoughts which they dared not put into words.

Madame Tison denounced Toulan, so there was one faithful friend removed; she also declared her suspicions of Lepître and he was taken away.

Antoinette was coming to the conclusion that she would never escape. Moreover the Dauphin had come in crying from his play, having hurt himself by falling over the stick which he rode as a horse.

It was necessary to have a doctor to dress his wound; and, as he lay whimpering beside her, she forgot everything else but the need to soothe the boy's pain.

Hébert said to Madame Tison: 'What ails the boy Capet?'

'Oh, Citizen, he fell over a stick. He's hurt himself. The

doctor has bandaged him. He said it was a bad wound . . . in a tender spot.'

She laughed and nudged him. We're all equal now, she implied.

Hébert believed he was the equal of the Queen, but not that Madame Tison was equal to him; but he did not notice her crude manners then. He had an idea.

⚜ ⚜ ⚜

It was ten o'clock at night. The Dauphin was sleeping and there were traces of tears on his face, for his wound had had to be dressed and he had cried a little.

The Queen was sitting by his bed when the door was opened and six members of the *municipaux* came into the room.

She did not look at them, and as they stood awkwardly before her, one of them found his hand going to his hat; he had to restrain himself from taking it off.

'We have come to take Louis Charles Capet to his new prison,' said one of the men.

The Queen gave a sharp cry of alarm which brought Madame Elisabeth and Madame Royale running to her side.

'I beg of you,' said the Queen, 'do not take my son from me.'

'These are our orders,' said the leader of the party. 'He is to be put in the care of his new tutor, Citizen Simon.'

'No!' cried the Queen, thinking of the brutal cobbler. 'Please . . . do anything . . . anything . . . but do not take my son away from me.'

Madame Royale stared at the men with imploring eyes; they would not look at her.

'Wake him up,' said one of the men, a stonemason. 'Come on. We're in a hurry. Either you do, or we will.'

457

'He is not very well. He injured himself recently. Please let me keep him with me. He is not very old.'

One of the men came close to the bed. The Queen, with Madame Elisabeth and Madame Royale, barred his way.

Another of the party, a clerk, said: 'We're sorry. But we're given orders and we have to obey them.'

The Dauphin had awakened, startled out of his sleep. 'Maman, Maman, are you there? I had a dream . . .'

He sat up in bed and saw the men; a look of fear crossed his face.

'Come on, Louis Charles Capet,' said the stonemason. 'You're moving from here.'

The boy drew the clothes about him. 'I . . . I shall stay with my mother,' he said.

One of the men seized him. The Queen ran to his side.

'I beg of you . . . I beg of you. Remember he is my son. You have taken his father . . . murdered his father . . . Is not that enough?'

The Dauphin tried to seize his mother's hands, but he was snatched away.

'Come on, let us get going,' said the clerk.

The Queen ran after the men who carried her son; the other men held her back and pushed her not ungently into the arms of her daughter and sister-in-law.

The door shut. The Queen stood as though dazed, listening to the piteous screams of the Dauphin as they carried him away.

✤ ✤ ✤

They kept the Dauphin in the Temple, in rooms below those occupied by his mother, Madame Elisabeth and Madame

Royale. He was so near, yet so far away, for she was never allowed to see him.

Piteously she would demand news of him from all those who came into contact with her; but they had received stern orders not to discuss the boy with her.

She discovered that on some days he was taken into a courtyard which she could see from her barred window; and for hours she would stand there hoping to get a glimpse of him.

Elisabeth tried to comfort her, as did her daughter; but during those days there was no comfort which life could offer Antoinette.

Madame Tison, coming into her cell, would jeer at her. 'This is a bit different from Versailles, eh? This is a bit different from that Trianon!'

But one day when Madame Tison jeered at her something in the dejected attitude of the Queen brought a catch to the woman's voice which sounded odd and unlike her. Madame Tison turned angrily away, put a startled hand to her cheek and found a tear there.

She tried to excuse herself.

'It's that child,' she murmured under her breath. 'It's taking him from her . . . seems a bit cruel. That Hébert, it's his doings. Who does he think he is? He gives himself the airs of an aristocrat.'

Madame Tison continued to jeer at the Queen, but now there did not seem to be much point in those jeers. The Queen was indifferent to them and Madame Tison no longer uttered them with the same enthusiasm.

Then she ceased to jeer; and oddly enough she discovered new feelings in herself. She would lie awake at night, and sometimes she would awaken out of dreams sobbing, and the Queen always figured in those dreams.

'You going crazy?' asked Tison.

Madame Tison would shiver and stare into the darkness.

❖ ❖ ❖

The Dauphin lay sobbing in his new apartment.

Simon bent over him, shaking him. Simon shook the boy with relish. This was the child who one day might have been King of France. Who would have thought that he, Simon, who had known such dire poverty, would have the opportunity of boxing the ears of the future King of France?

Simon was filled with ecstasy at the thought. It showed what the revolution could do for a poor man. This boy who had had everything he could want – luxury, food, fine garments, people bowing wherever he went – was now the prisoner of Simon.

Citizen Hébert had spoken earnestly to Simon. 'We want to make Louis Charles Capet a son of the people, you understand. He is but a boy. We want to make him a true son of the revolution. We want to make a man of him . . . you understand me? A man of the people.'

Simon was illiterate. He had once had a low-class eating-house in the rue de Seine, but he had not made a success of it. He had lived in utter poverty. He had done all sorts of things besides being a cobbler, in the hope of getting a living, but he had always been a failure until the revolution came. He was crude; he spoke the language of the *faubourgs*; he had lived with the lowest. He was the sort of man who Hébert needed for the task which lay ahead.

Now he leaned over the Dauphin and shook him roughly.

The child looked up at him, too wretched to care about anything but his own misery.

'Here, what's the matter with you, eh?'

'I want my mother,' said the boy.

Simon bandaged his wound for him.

'How did you get this?'

'I was riding on a stick.'

'That's a queer thing to do . . . ride on a stick. What do you want to do that for?'

'Pretending it was a horse.'

Simon spat over his shoulder in disbelief.

The boy was uncomfortable to be exposed before the eyes of this crude man.

'Here,' said Simon, 'you don't need to be so particular. We're all alike, you know. Some of us knows a bit more than others. I reckon I could show you a thing or two.'

'What?' said the boy.

Simon winked.

He then taught the boy how to masturbate. It was all part of the duties outlined to him by Hébert.

'Who taught you that?' demanded Simon.

'You did,' said the boy.

'That's a lie.'

'But you . . . you did . . . You know you did!'

A blow sent the Dauphin reeling across the room. He was startled. He had never been treated in such a way before. He stared in astonishment at Simon.

461

'Now, not so many lies,' said Simon. 'You've got to tell the truth like a patriot.'

'I was telling the truth.'

Simon caught the boy by his ear.

'When I say who taught you that, you give me the truth. You say, my mother.'

The boy flushed scarlet. 'My mother . . . But . . . she . . . she must not know of this. She . . . she would be . . . very angry. She would be ashamed of it.' His lips trembled. 'Please let me go back to my mother.'

Simon shook the boy's head to and fro, still gripping his ear violently. 'Didn't I tell you I wanted the truth?'

The boy looked bewildered.

'Listen here,' said Simon. 'Your mother taught you that. When you slept in the bed with her.'

The boy was silent, the pain in his ear made him want to scream.

'Yes, you used to lie between her and your aunt, and they used to say, do that . . . and they laughed at you, while you did it.'

The boy shook his head. It was too fantastic. His mother to do such a thing! His saintly aunt! He longed to be with them; he longed to return to sanity.

'And I'll tell you something else your mother did, shall I? She used to hold you tight against her . . .' Simon released the boy's ear and put his foul mouth against it.

His whispering words made the boy feel that he had stepped into some fantastically horrible world which was quite outside his comprehension.

Simon finished by saying: 'Now that's what really happened. Is it not so?'

'It . . . it couldn't,' said the Dauphin.

Simon shook him until his teeth chattered and the room swung round him.

'I tell you it did.'

'It didn't . . . it didn't . . . it *didn't*!' sobbed the Dauphin.

Simon's foul face was close to the boy's. He said: 'I'm going to teach you to speak the truth . . . no matter what I have to do to you.'

The Dauphin stared at him with horrified eyes. This was like one of his nightmares coming true. He shook his head dumbly.

But Simon was not perturbed. A few beatings . . . a few days all alone . . . on black bread and lentils . . . then they would see.

Simon would not disappoint Hébert. They would make the boy admit anything they wanted him to. After all, he was only eight years old.

✦ ✦ ✦

Madame Tison dreamed terrible dreams. She dreamed that her bedroom was filled with headless corpses which marched towards her, getting nearer and nearer. They carried their heads before them, and the eyes in their heads accused her while the lips chanted: 'Madame Tison, your turn will come.'

Often she dreamed of the Queen, the Queen with her arms outstretched, the Queen crying for her son.

When she saw the Queen standing at the window hoping for a glimpse of the Dauphin, she shared her misery.

Her husband was brutal to her; he struck her once or twice. 'What's come over you? Do you want to lose us our job? We're in clover here. Do you want to get us turned out of the prison?'

She was sent for that she might be questioned.

'Go on,' said Tison. 'What are you waiting for?'

'I do not want to tell them,' she said. 'I do not want to be their spy.'

Her husband advanced, his arm lifted to strike her. 'You'll go,' he said, 'and you'll tell them about that new guard we saw talking to Elisabeth.'

So she went and, as though under a spell, she told.

When she returned to the prison she burst into the Queen's quarters. Madame Royal was sitting at the table staring ahead of her; Madame Elisabeth was praying; and the Queen was at the window, hoping for a glimpse of the Dauphin.

Madame Tison ran to the Queen and threw herself at her feet; she took the hem of her dress and looked imploringly up at Antoinette.

'Madame, forgive me,' she cried. 'I am going mad. I am a miserable sinner. I have spied on you . . . They are watching you all the time, because they want to murder you as they murdered the King . . . Madame, I beg your forgiveness for what I have done.'

The Queen's face softened immediately. 'You must not be distressed. What have you done you have been made to do. And you have lately been very kind.'

'I am going mad . . . mad, Madame. These terrible dreams. . . . I cannot live with them. They haunt me . . . they will not leave me . . .'

The guards came in. They seized her and took her away.

That night the news went round the Temple: 'Madame Tison has gone mad.'

464

The Queen was at the barred window. He could not see her but she could catch a glimpse of him now and then. How he had changed! He no longer seemed like her little boy. His clothes were stained and greasy; his hair was unkempt.

He shouted as he ran about the courtyard. That gross man, Simon, played games with him . . . rough games.

They sang together. Antoinette recognised the revolutionary song *'Ça ira'*. It was strange to hear those words on the lips of a son of the royal house.

But was he well? Was he happy?

If only she might speak to him, have his own assurance that all was well with him.

'My darling boy . . .' she murmured.

Then she heard the thin reedy voice of her son singing in the courtyard below.

'Allons, enfants de la patrie . . .'

'They have taken him from me completely,' she told herself. 'What does anything matter now? Surely I have touched the nadir of all my sorrows.'

But she was wrong. A greater sorrow awaited her.

It was decided that the time had come for the Queen to stand her trial.

One August morning a carriage came to the door of the Temple. With resignation Antoinette said good-bye to Madame Elisabeth and Madame Royale.

She seemed dazed as she walked out of the Temple; and as she passed under the low porch she forgot to stoop, and knocked her head on the hard stone.

'You have hurt yourself,' said one of the guards, overcome by compassion.

'Nothing can hurt me now,' she answered.

She stepped into the carriage and was taken to the Conciergerie.

✤ Chapter XVII ✤

THE LAST RIDE

There was little comfort in the Conciergerie.

She was taken to a small room with barred windows recently vacated by an old General who had left that day in a tumbril for the Place de la Revolution.

Moisture trickled down the walls of the cell and it was impossible to keep the mattress dry.

The Conciergerie was known throughout Paris as the prison of doom. Few left it nowadays except for that last journey to the guillotine.

Hébert was inflaming the people against the Queen. It was time, he said, that she tried on Samson's necktie. It was time the executioner should play ball with the she-wolf's head. She should be chopped into mincemeat to pay for the blood she had on her conscience.

But the military commanders were not eager for the death of Antoinette. The war was going less satisfactorily, and it was felt that alive she could be used to bargain with the Austrian enemy.

Fersen was in despair when he heard of her removal to the Conciergerie, and at the root of his fear was his feeling of helplessness.

He wrote to his sister: 'Since I have heard that the Queen is in the Conciergerie, I have no longer felt that I am alive, for it is not life to exist as I do and to suffer the pains which I now endure. If I could do something to bring about her release my agony would be less. It is terrible that all I can do is to go about imploring others to act. I would give my life to save her. My greatest happiness would be to die that she might live. I reproach myself for breathing this pure air while she is in that loathsome place. My life is poisoned, so that I veer from pain to wrath and from wrath back to pain.'

But Fersen was powerless. He could only mourn.

✤ ✤ ✤

There was more kindness in the Conciergerie than there had been in the Temple. Was this because the place was known as the 'ante-room of death'?

The jailer's wife, Madame Richard, was a kindly woman. She was charmed by the Queen's graciousness and did all she could for her comfort. She made her husband fit a piece of carpet over that part of the ceiling through which the water dripped onto the bed. And when Madame Richard's little boy came into the cell, the Queen embraced him because he was as fair-haired as the Dauphin was, and of the same age.

'You see, Madame Richard,' she said, 'he reminds me of my own son.'

Madame Richard turned away to hide her tears, and after that she asked the police commissioner, Michonis, who had been a lemonade-seller before the revolution and was now an inspector of prisoners, if he would discover and bring news of the Queen's children. 'For what harm can that do to the Republic?' she asked. 'And look what good it can do to a poor mother!'

So Michonis, who was a good-hearted man, brought little bits of news about Madame Elisabeth and Madame Royale. The Dauphin was well and not unhappy, he said. 'These young children,' he added, 'they are resilient. They recover from griefs more quickly than we do.'

Then there was Rosalie, the young servant girl, who adored her mistress, and who cleaned the cell as she cleaned no others; she brought in a box so that the few clothes the Queen possessed might be folded carefully and kept as well as possible. Every morning she would scrape the mildew from the Queen's shoes, for it would gather during the night in that damp cell.

The Queen had aged considerably. Her hair was white now; there were rheumatic pains in her legs so that some days she found it difficult to stand. She was suffering from haemorrhages which made her very weak.

These good people took it upon themselves to smuggle comforts into the cell – some warm blankets to keep out the damp, some new sheets, a new mourning cap. Madame Richard and Rosalie did little jobs for her when they could, such as washing and mending her clothes.

One day Michonis came to inspect her cell, and with him was a stranger, a man who, he explained, wished to see what the inside of a prison was like.

Antoinette looked at this man and believed she recognised him. He was carrying a nosegay such as was generally carried by visitors to prisons and such places where the foul air might provoke disease.

He threw this nosegay behind the Queen's stove, and when he had gone the Queen picked it up and found a note inside it. On this was written: 'I shall try to find some means of showing my zeal for your service.'

She remembered the man now. He was the Chevalier de Rougeville, and she guessed that he had been inspired in this by Fersen.

Thoughts of the man she loved gave her new hope. Fersen! He had seemed invincible. She had believed in the old days that he would save her and take her to happiness. She found that belief revived.

She must answer the note. How? She had no pens, but she had a scrap of paper, and she had a needle, for since she had come to the Conciergerie her good friends there had provided her with one.

She pricked out an answer. Now, how to get it to the Chevalier? She could ask Madame Richard or Rosalie to pass it on, but she remembered then what had happened to poor Toulan. No. If anything went wrong they would be the first to be suspected.

She dared not involve those who were so close to her and who were already suspected of being too friendly.

At length she decided to give it to Gilbert, one of the gendarmes who seemed a trustworthy fellow.

She could give him nothing, she said, but the gentleman to whom he delivered the note would reward him with 400 louis.

The gendarme was tempted – both by his desire for the money and his desire to help the Queen; but when heads were being severed in the Place de la Revolution every day it made a man wary.

He showed the note to Madame Richard, who was terrified and asked Michonis' advice.

It was one thing to have sympathy for the Queen; it was another to work against the Republic.

Michonis took the paper from Madame Richard and told her to say no more about it.

But the gendarme could not forget it. He mentioned it to his superior officer, with the result that an inquiry was immediately set in motion.

✤ ✤ ✤

Michonis was terrified. He knew that the note would be demanded of him, and he dared not destroy it. In a brave attempt to save the Queen he added more pinpricks to it, so that it did not make sense.

He was brought before the tribunal and produced the note.

The Queen, when questioned, determined to save Madame Richard and Michonis. She did not tell them that Michonis had brought the Chevalier into her cell.

But after this the Commune determined to take greater care of their prisoner and to bring her to speedy trial. Michonis was dismissed from his post; the Richards were imprisoned; the Queen had a new jailer and was removed to a smaller room. But the new jailer and his wife were as sympathetic as the Richards had been, and they brought comforts into her cell. They brought her books and, for the first time in her life, she found great pleasure in reading; thus only could she cut herself off from the unendurable present and live in a world of her imagination. She found pleasure in the adventures of Captain Cook; she could imagine herself on voyages of exploration, and thus passed the long days and nights.

And on the 12th October 1793 she was summoned to the council chamber to face her trial.

❖ ❖ ❖

In the Temple the Dauphin was sitting on a chair by the table. His feet did not quite reach the floor.

With him were three men: Chaumette, the *syndic*, Hébert and Simon. They had brought his sister, Madame Royale, into the room.

She flew to him and embraced him, and as the Dauphin returned her embrace, he saw a look of disgust pass over her face. That was because he was not clean. He felt uneasy.

The men began to ask Madame Royale questions; they concerned herself and her brother. What games had they played when they had been together? Did her brother ever handle her improperly?

Madame Royale did not even know what they meant. She and her brother had always been good friends, she said.

They they began to ask questions about her mother. Madame Royale did not understand exactly what they meant, but she had an inkling and, as she listened to them, a slow flush crept up over her face.

'These are lies,' she said.

'Your brother says they are not lies.'

'They are lies . . . all lies!' cried Madame Royale.

'Take her away,' said Hébert, 'and bring in the aunt.'

❖ ❖ ❖

It was easier to explain to Madame Elisabeth. She listened to the infamous story, first with incredulity then with horror.

'This is preposterous. It is impossible.'

'We have the word of this boy.'

'I cannot believe it.'

Hébert turned to the Dauphin and said: 'Did these things happen between you and your mother?'

'Yes,' said the Dauphin defiantly, 'they did.'

'And was your aunt present, and did she see these things happen?'

'Yes,' said the boy.

'Did you lie between your mother and your aunt, and did they urge you to do these things, and did they laugh together?'

'Yes, they did.'

Madame Elisabeth was so pale that she appeared as though she would faint.

She turned to the boy: 'You . . . you monster!' she cried.

The Dauphin's face crumpled. He began to whimper.

'Take the woman away!' commanded Hébert quickly.

She came before the judges. No one would have recognised her as the gay and lovely young Queen who had danced in the ballroom at Versailles or on the grass of the Trianon. The daylight hurt her eyes and she could not bear to open them wide; she could scarcely walk; she was pale from haemorrhage and her joints were stiff with rheumatism; there were lines of deep sorrow carved on her face.

She stood before these men, knowing that her trial would be farcical; they had determined to find her guilty of all the charges they were bringing against her.

'What is your name?' they demanded.

'Marie Antoinette of Lorraine and Austria, widow of Louis Capet, sometime King of the French.'

'Your age?'

'I am thirty-eight years of age.'

'It was you who taught Louis Capet the art of that profound dissimulation wherewith he deceived the good people of France.'

'It is true that the people have been deceived,' she answered calmly, 'but not by my husband nor by myself.'

'By whom then?'

'By those who had an interest in deceiving the people; but it was not in our interest to deceive them.'

'Who do you suggest deceived the people of France?'

'How should I know? My interest was to enlighten the people, not to deceive them. The happiness of France is what I desire beyond all things.'

'Do you think kings are necessary for the happiness of a people ?'

'That is a matter which no individual can decide.'

'You regret that your son has lost a throne?'

'I regret it not, should his loss be the gain of his country.'

The courtroom was full. All those who had been able to, had crowded into it. In the gallery many women had gathered; some of them were women from the market; they sat knitting, but that they did without looking, for their eyes were on the Queen. They had come, vindictive and angry, to see a woman whom they had long hated brought to justice; and now they looked at her, this woman in the black dress with the shawl about her shoulders; there was a mourning cap on her head, and they were reminded that she was a widow grieving for a husband recently taken from her. It was not so easy to believe all those stories they had heard about her, now that they were in her presence.

The questions went on. They wanted to know how much money had been spent on the Trianon, how much money on jewels; how many times pictures of her had been painted.

'Where did you get the money for Trianon? Who paid for all those fêtes and extravagances?'

'There was a special fund for Trianon.'

'It must have been a very big fund.'

'We became involved in the expenditure by degrees. I have nothing to hide. I hope everything connected with the expenses of Trianon will be made public, for it has been vastly exaggerated.'

Her prosecutor then cried: 'Was it not at Petit Trianon that you first made the acquaintance of a woman named de Lamotte?'

'I never made the acquaintance of such a woman.'

'But she was your scapegoat in the well-known and disgraceful affair of the Diamond Necklace.'

'I do not understand how that could have been, since I have never met her.'

'Do you persist in your denial that you know this woman?'

'I am not persisting in a denial. I persist in saying I have never seen her, because that is the truth, and I shall continue to speak the truth.'

Hébert was then called as a witness.

He folded his hands together and turned his eyes upwards while he made the monstrous charge of incest against the Queen.

Everyone in the court was tense, and the silence which followed Hébert's words was dramatic.

All eyes were on the Queen. She sat stiff and her face was drained of all colour. She did not protest; she did not move.

The women in the gallery had stopped knitting; they were

deeply shocked; angry lights appeared in their eyes, and that anger was directed towards the man who had spoken, for they knew him for a liar. Instinct assured them that he lied. They could accuse the prisoner of extravagance, carelessness, pride – any folly – but not this.

Hébert grew uneasy. He sensed that something was wrong; he had expected shocked cries from the women, and abuse to be hurled at the prisoner. This silence unnerved him.

He stood uncertain for a moment; then he plunged on. 'I . . . I . . . it is not my belief that this criminal conduct was indulged in for its own sake, but because the prisoner wished to weaken her son's health, not only physically but mentally, that she might thus be enabled to dominate him and bend him to her will should he ever gain the throne.'

There was that silence again. The Queen still said nothing. Her expression betrayed nothing. It was uncanny.

One of the jurors said: 'This matter must be clarified. The prisoner has made no comment on the accusation.'

Antoinette now rose to her feet; her hands fell to her side, and many saw that they were clenched tightly. She looked at Hébert with such disdain that he winced and cowered.

Then she spoke, and her words rang throughout the court with a note of innocence which was unmistakable even to the most insensitive: 'If I have made no reply, it is because nature refuses to answer such a charge brought against a mother. I appeal in this matter to all the mothers present in court.'

The women in the gallery were with her. Motherhood had been insulted.

All those who were determined to bring the Queen to the scaffold were furious with Hébert.

It was necessary to bring the proceedings to a close for that day, as the sense of excitement in the court was ready to break into open revolt. The market-women had begun to whisper and shake their heads in shocked disapproval.

It was possible that had the trial continued then they would have demanded the liberation of the Queen, questioning whether, since she had been so basely slandered on one matter, she might have been on others?

The Queen was taken back to her cell.

Robespierre was furious with Hébert.

'The fool! The idiot! To bring such a charge against her. One only has to look at her to know it is false. All those women . . . all those mothers can see in her face . . . can sense in her voice . . . her love for her son; and they know it for a mother's love. Is it not enough that she should be Messalina? Must she also be Agrippina? This is a public triumph for Antoinette. For the love of the Republic bring the trial to an end to-morrow, and let this foolish matter be ignored as though it had never been brought up. Concentrate on her extravagance, the matter of the necklace . . . oh, yes . . . very particularly on the matter of the necklace. Concentrate on her extravagance and her desire to bring civil war to France. And when she next leaves the court let it be as a woman condemned to die.'

And the next day this was done.

When Antoinette returned to the Conciergerie she knew that there were but a few hours left to her.

In her cell she wrote to Elisabeth.

'It is to you, dear sister, that I write for the last time. I have been sentenced to death, but not to shameful death, since this death is only shameful to criminals, whereas I shall rejoin your brother. I hope to be firm as he was in his last moments. My conscience is clear although I feel great grief because I must forsake my children. Through you, I send to them my blessing, in the hope that some day, when they are older, they will be with you once more and able to enjoy your tender care . . .

'I have to speak to you of a matter which is extremely painful. I know how much my little boy has made you suffer. Forgive him, my dear sister; remember how young he is, and how easy it is to make a child say whatever one wants, to put words he does not understand into his mouth . . . I hope a day will come when he will grasp the full value of your kindness and of the affection you have shown to both my children . . . '

She stopped and buried her face in her hands. She could not go on.

But after a while she picked up her pen and resolutely continued to write.

✤ ✤ ✤

Rosalie came into the cell.

She brought a bowl of soup with her.

The Queen was lying fully dressed on her bed.

'It is seven o'clock, Madame,' said the girl. 'Will you not take a little soup?'

'I am not hungry, Rosalie.'

'Madame, you ate nothing yesterday. You will be so weak. To please me . . . '

478

The Queen smiled. 'You have been good to me, Rosalie,' she said. She took the bowl and tried a spoonful; she looked apologetically at the girl, for she could manage no more.

Rosalie turned away because she was crying.

After a while she said: 'Madame, there are orders that you should not wear black.'

'Do they care then what I wear?' She laughed. 'They have always been interested in what I wore. Is this interest to continue then . . . right to the end?'

'You are to wear your white dress, Madame.'

'I will change. I need new linen.'

'Has the haemorrhage been bad, Madame?'

The Queen nodded.

'I have a clean chemise here now. I washed it.'

The gendarme, stationed at the door, advanced into the room as the Queen slipped behind her bed to change.

He stood watching her insolently.

'Cannot I have this little bit of privacy?' asked Antoinette.

Rosalie cried: 'Stand back awhile.'

'My orders are not to let the widow out of my sight,' said the man.

Rosalie stood in front of him and lifted her blazing eyes to his face.

He was a little man, and Rosalie's face was on a level with his. He was abashed by the scorn and contempt he saw there; even as Hébert had been made to feel by the women in the gallery of the court.

He did not attempt to advance, and so the Queen changed her clothes and put on the white dress.

She was praying when, an hour later, her cell was invaded by the judges, the executioner and a priest.

Her sentence was read again; then Henri Samson, the executioner, cut off her hair and tied her hands behind her back.

'Is that necessary?' she asked.

'Those are my orders,' said Samson.

❖ ❖ ❖

The tocsins were ringing. The people were lining the streets. The troops were on guard, and many of the streets were barred to other traffic.

This was the day for which so many had longed. They would stand in safety and see the Queen ride by to her death.

It was a little past eleven o'clock when the tumbril drew up outside the gates of the Conciergerie. The Queen took her place in the rough cart; there was merely a bare board on which to sit, yet she, in her white cap with her ragged hair showing beneath it, sat as though this were the glass coach in which she had made her entry into France.

Samson stood behind her guarding her on her ride through the streets.

It must not be too quick, that ride. All the people of Paris wanted to see her during her last hour on Earth. In the crowd pamphlets were being sold: *La Vie Scandaleuse de Marie Antoinette*. Most of these had been composed by Jeanne de Lamotte.

Many had come out to shout their scorn at her; but it was not easy to do this, for the woman in the tumbril, sitting so erect, her hands tied behind her back, rode as though she were still a Queen.

As the tumbril passed the church of Saint-Roch, someone

cried out: 'Death to the wicked woman who tried to ruin France! Death to the Austrian whore!' But no one took up the cry, and the Queen did not seem to hear it.

The tumbril had crossed the river and was rumbling along the rue Saint-Honoré. There a man raised his sword and shouted: 'There she is, the infamous Antoinette. She's finished at last, my friends.' But no one responded.

⚜ ⚜ ⚜

Into the Place de la Révolution. Here the crowds were thickest. Two objects dominated the grim place; one the statue of the Goddess of Liberty, the Phrygian cap on her head, and the sword of justice in her hand; and the other that grim instrument of death – the guillotine.

Beside this last the tumbril had come to a halt. Antoinette stepped down almost eagerly.

She mounted the steps looking neither to right nor left; she showed no sign of fear. As Louis had done before her, she was ready and, it seemed, fearless.

For a moment she looked at the Tuileries and thought she saw instead the glorious Palace of Versailles, and herself coming there as a young girl to the shy husband who had seemed afraid of her. She thought of Trianon – her own beloved Petit Trianon – and of the days and nights she had spent there with Axel de Fersen. All so unimportant now – of such small significance; for this was the end. The end of sorrow; the end of pain.

The executioner and his men had seized her and forced her into a kneeling position, so that her throat was resting on the lower half of the circular hole; the board was fitted over her neck, imprisoning her.

She closed her eyes. 'Farewell, my love,' she murmured. 'Try to find some happiness in this life, for you have long to live, I trust. Farewell, my little ones, and do not grieve, my dearest, for what you have done . . . I know they made you do it; and when you are old enough to understand, I want you to forget . . .'

'Farewell, life . . . Farewell, France . . . Farewell . . .'

The great knife had descended.

Then the executioner lifted that bloody and once lovely head.

'Long live the Republic!' he cried; and those who had been unable to see because the press of people was so great knew that the moment had come. Marie Antoinette of Austria and Lorraine, widow of Louis, one time King of France, was dead.

❧ Author's Note ❧

Few people maintain an attitude of impartiality towards Marie Antoinette. At the time of her death she was compared with Messalina and Agrippina. Later, on the return of the Monarchy, she became the 'martyred Queen', and was spoken of almost as a saint. Neither extreme is, of course, the true picture.

When I set out to find this, at first it seemed to me that there emerged from my research a not very intelligent woman, concerned chiefly with glorifying her own dainty charms in which she delighted, careless, light-hearted, pleasure-loving, almost stupid in her failure to see the looming shadow of revolution, yet generous and good-hearted – a very ordinary human being.

But the fascination of Marie Antoinette is the sudden emergence of the brave and noble woman who took the place of the frivolous one almost overnight. It is difficult to believe that the butterfly of the Trianon is the same woman who endured so stoically her sufferings in the Temple and the Conciergerie, whose thoughts were mainly for her husband and children, and who was in such deep mental and physical agony as she rode so bravely and so royally in her tumbril to the Place de la Révolution.

It has been an absorbing pleasure to try to understand this woman of dual personality, and I have been greatly helped in this by the following:

M. Guizot. *The History of France*.

G. Lenôtre. Translated by H. Noel Williams. *Paris in the Revolution*.

Thomas Carlyle. *The French Revolution*.

Iain D. B. Pilkington. *Queen of the Trianon*.

Stefan Zweig. *Marie Antoinette*.

Louis Adolphe Thiers. Translated, with notes, by Frederick Shoberl. *The History of the French Revolution*.

Catherine Charlotte, Lady Jackson. *Old Paris, Its Courts and Literary Salons*.

Hilaire Belloc. *Marie Antoinette*.

J. B. Morton. *The Dauphin*.

Nesta H. Webster. *Louis XVI and Marie Antoinette Before the Revolution*.

Frédéric Barbey. *A Friend of Marie Antoinette*.

Nesta H. Webster. *The French Revolution*.

JP.

Louis the Well-Beloved

France eagerly awaits the day the young King, Louis XV, comes of age and breaks free from the rule of his ministers. The country envisions Louis bringing back glory and prosperity to France. However, the young King is too preoccupied with the thrills of hunting and gambling to notice the power struggle going on in his own court. Soon, the King is introduced to the pleasures of mistresses and a succession of lovers follows. From the gentle persuasions of Madame de Mailley to her overtly ambitious sister, Madame Vintimille, France stands by and watches a king ruled by his women . . .

The Road to Compiègne

No longer the well-beloved, Louis is growing ever more unpopular – the war and his mistresses having taken their toll. As the discontent grows, Louis seeks refuge from any unpleasantness in his extravagances and his mistress, the now powerful Marquise de Pompadour. Suspicions, plots and rivalry are rife as Louis's daughters and lovers jostle for his attention and standing at Court. Ignoring the unrest in Paris, Louis continues to indulge in his frivolities but how long will Paris stay silent when the death of the Marquise de Pompadour leads to yet another mistress influencing the King . . .

arrow books

The Plantagenet Prelude

When William X dies, the duchy of Aquitaine is left to his fifteen-year-old daughter, Eleanor. On his deathbed William promised her hand in marriage to the future King of France. Eleanor is determined to rule Aquitaine using her husband's power as King of France and, in the years to follow, she is to become one of history's most scandalous queens.

The Revolt of the Eaglets

Henry Plantagenet bestrode the throne of England like an ageing eagle perching dangerously in the evening of his life. While his sons intrigue against him and each other, Henry's conscience leads him to make foolish political decisions. The old eagle is under constant attack from three of the eaglets he has nurtured, and a fourth waits in the wings for the moment of utter defeat to pluck out his eyes . . .

The Heart of the Lion

At the age of thirty-two, Richard the Lionheart has finally succeeded Henry II to the English throne. Now he must fulfil his vow to his country to win back Jerusalem for the Christian world. Leaving England to begin his crusade, Richard's kingdom is left in the hands of his brother, John, who casts covetous eyes on the crown.

arrow books

Madame Serpent

Broken-hearted, Catherine de' Medici arrives in Marseilles to marry Henry of Orléans, son of the King of France. But amid the glittering banquets of the most immoral court in sixteenth-century Europe, the reluctant bride changes into a passionate but unwanted wife who becomes dangerously occupied by a ruthless ambition destined to make her the most despised woman in France.

The Italian Woman

Jeanne of Navarre once dreamed of marrying Henry of Orléans, but years later she is instead still married to the dashing but politically inept Antoine de Bourbon, whilst the widowed Catherine has become the powerful mother of kings, who will do anything to see her beloved second son, Henry, rule France.

Queen Jezebel

The ageing Catherine de' Medici has arranged the marriage of her beautiful Catholic daughter Margot to the uncouth Huguenot King Henry of Navarre. But even Catherine is unable to anticipate the carnage that this unholy union is to bring about . . .

arrow books

IF YOU LOVE GEORGETTE HEYER'S HISTORICAL NOVELS, LOOK
OUT FOR HER WONDERFUL CONTEMPORARY MYSTERIES

A Blunt Instrument

Ernest Fletcher, a man liked and respected. So when he is found
bludgeoned to death, no one can imagine who would want him
dead. Enter Superintendent Hannasyde, who slowly uncovers the
real Fletcher, anything but a gentleman, and a man with many
enemies. But the case takes a gruesome twist when another
body is found . . .

Behold, Here's Poison

Gregory Matthews, patriarch of the Poplars, is found dead. Imperious
Aunt Harriet blames it on the roast duck he ate, but a post-mortem
determines it's a case of murder by poison. Suspicion falls
immediately on his quarrelsome family, and it is up to Hannasyde to
sift through their secrets and lies before the killer strikes again.

Death in the Stocks

When the body of Andrew Vereker is found locked in the stocks on
the village green, Hannasyde soon realises that this may be his
toughest case yet. Vereker was not a popular man, his corrupt
family are uncooperative, and the suspects are many.

They Found Him Dead

The morning after his sixtieth birthday party, Silas Kane is found
dead at the foot of a cliff. The coroner rules death by misadventure,
but when Kane's nephew and heir is found murdered, a new
and sinister case develops for Hannasyde to investigate.

arrow books